Villains in Training

Julia S. Mandala & Linda L. Donahue

Villains in Training
Julia S. Mandala & Linda L. Donahue
First Edition Copyright © Julia S. Mandala & Linda L.
Donahue, 2017

Published by Yard Dog Press at Create Space

Print Version ISBN 978-1-937105-95-2
Villains in Training
First Edition Copyright © Julia S. Mandala & Linda L.
Donahue, 2017
First Electronic Edition Copyright © Julia S. Mandala & Linda L. Donahue, 2017

Yard Dog Press
710 W. Redbud Lane
Alma, AR 72921-7247

http://www.yarddogpress.com

Edited by Selina Rosen
Copy Editor & Technical Editor Lynn Rosen
Cover art by Brad Foster

First Print Edition April 1, 2017
First EEdition 2017
Printed in the United States of America
0 9 8 7 6 5 4 3 2 1

DEDICATION

To our fathers, who taught us how to be funny. We miss you so much!

ACKNOWLEDGEMENTS

Thanks to our writers group, past and present members, Chris Donahue, Kathy Turski, Frank Summers, Amanda Guzman, Andrew Jones and Shalana Collins. Also, big thanks to Jerry Knowles for his comments and contributions. Thanks to Brad Foster for the terrific cover. And most especially, we thank Selina and Lynn Rosen for all that they do for their writers and artists.

CHAPTER ONE

The blue portal swirling before Mandrake looked like freedom. Thank the Darkness, summer vacation was over and he could get back to the university.

Around Drake, hammers rang against nails as the fortified city of Ludton-upon-the-Grimy-Teague bustled to rebuild. Peasants hauled away rubble and charred, broken timbers. Drake's parents had caused almost as much damage using magic to hold Ludton as "Good" King Marcus's men had with their catapults. But Bane the Black-Hearted and the Dread Witch Tiffany had driven Marcus's troops back across the border. Cities could be rebuilt and repopulated. Recovering lost ground was difficult.

Drake's mother fussed over non-existent lint on his cloak. "You look, like, totally awesome. All the witches at college will freak out when they get a load of you."

Even after living in her husband's dimension for over twenty years, the Dread Witch Tiffany Owens of Beverly Hills hadn't shed the dialect of her home world. Witches felt little pressure to conform. Having heard his mother's strange speech all his life, Drake understood almost half of it.

Tiffany looked skyward for inspiration. "Um, let's see. Don't just follow the herd. And try to get some UVs. You're as pasty as...paste."

Drake nodded. He found it easiest to merely accept the unneeded advice. His mother had repeated this ritual sendoff every year since Drake left for prep school. Only at start of term did Tiffany show the least bit of maternal interest.

She pulled a rectangular box labeled "Trojans" from her purse and thrust it into Drake's hand. "Here. I wasn't worried before, because no witch would be caught dead doing the nasty with an underclassman. I mean, gag me with a spoon! But you're a junior now, and you're, like, pretty rad. The witches will be all over you. So use protection."

Drake frowned in puzzlement. "A protection spell?"

"No, you spaz, *protection*." Tiffany tapped the box in Drake's hand.

He glanced at the drawing on the back. "Is this for my wand?"

Tiffany giggled. "You college dudes are, like, so cute. You

can't even say the word." When Drake continued to look baffled, she added, "The directions are, like, inside the box. Read them when you get to the frat house."

Drake shoved the box into his trunk.

Tiffany glanced at her wrist clock, then slapped her forehead. "Look at me jabbering on. Your father will have a cow that we're wasting portal minutes. The overage charges are killer." She patted Drake's cheek. "Now vamoose before I turn you into a newt and gouge out your eyes for spell components."

She would, too. Drake settled his trunk on his shoulder. "I'll see you at the winter solstice break, mother. Best of luck holding King Marcus's troops at bay."

Tiffany winked. "Oh, we'll do more than hold those douche bags at bay. King Marcus is in for a major bummer of a harvest season. Your dad and I have a bitchin' new plan."

Her last plan had caused great distress in Marcus's kingdom. She'd cast a spell—as long as his men attacked Bane's army, every girl born in Marcus's kingdom would be the sort described as having a "nice personality." Drake wondered what horrors this new plan envisioned.

"Go on, you." Tiffany pushed him toward the swirling blue portal.

Drake stepped through into the vastness of space, then stumbled into the portal chamber housed in the Student Union basement. Dozens of dormant portals hung closed on the wall. Most portal frames were uninspired diamonds and circles, but a few were works of art. Drake had always admired the silver skull frame whose mouth hinged open when the portal activated.

He adjusted his grip on the trunk and climbed up the back stairs to the university commons. Scattered trees provided shade for students wanting to study outside. In open grassy areas, witches worked on their tans. Gated walls surrounding the Colleges of Dark Arts, Arcane Sciences and Olde Wyrd Charms bordered three sides of the commons. The university administration building and Student Union made up the fourth. Behind the Student Union lay the Unenchanting Forest, so-called because of its decaying trees, thorny bramble and vicious, malodorous creatures.

Rather, the forest used to be there. A new cobbled path led between the Student Union and Administration to an archway in a twenty-foot-high white wall. Above that towered a glass-and-steel skyscraper near the golden turrets of a fairytale castle.

Drake blinked hard, but the disturbing image remained. "Apparently, I should have read the summer bulletin."

After dropping off his trunk at the frat house—and reading the summer bulletin—he returned to the commons.

His friend Dex waited under a shady elm.

"Doom is upon us, Dex," Drake said, glaring at the newest addition to the University of Dark Arts and Arcane Sciences. Princes led horses while their vassals hauled wooden trunks, and superheroes carted matching sets of bulletproof luggage toward the new quad—the so-called College of Valor, Honor and Justice for All.

Drake shook his head. "The thought of sharing our campus with holier-than-us do-gooders curdles my stomach. It was bad enough when the Transdimensional Supreme Court ordered the university to admit witches...well, not that I mind having them here. I just don't think the court had the right to threaten our funding if the university didn't admit them. And now *this* outrage."

"Look at those prissy dweebs." Dex sneered, fidgeting with the pocket protector in his lab coat pocket. "I haven't seen that much spandex since the Miss Trailer Park pageant."

"You calling someone a dweeb is like the cauldron calling the kettle black." Drake nudged Dex's ribs hard enough to send him stumbling. "I thought being a dweeb was an admissions requirement for Arcane Sciences."

Dex rubbed his side. "For the hundredth time, you have to be a *geek* or *nerd*."

"I suppose you would know."

"Met your new roomie yet?" Dex asked.

As juniors, Drake and Dex were saddled with mentoring freshman roommates.

"Jeffrey won't arrive until next week," Drake said. "He was injured in a freak encounter with a rabid salamander."

"A room to yourself? You lucky dog."

"Perhaps I'll sneak Hexaba in." A warm tingle rippled across Drake's pale skin. "I haven't seen her since the end of last term. She should be ready for some Mandrake magic."

"I'm sure the clinic has cured her of the previous dose of your magic," Dex said drily.

Drake swallowed the urge to turn Dex into a toad. After all, friends were rare at a university where Cutthroat Tactics was a required sophomore class. "Have you met *your* roommate?"

"Gilbert's unpacking." Dex pushed up his tape-patched horn-rimmed glasses. "He appears a bit slow, but easy to lead. I expect we'll get along fine."

Drake stroked the short beard he had cultivated over the summer, waiting for Dex to notice it. Even a narrow-focused scientist such as Poindexter should see how evil the beard made Drake look. Last year, Drake could only manage a patchy scruff. It had been mortifying to look deranged rather than sinister.

"You've got dirt on your chin, or maybe chocolate—" Dex's

gaze froze on something behind Drake. "Geez, get a load of those two."

Drake turned. Two superhero students trotted down the Student Union steps. The cherub-faced one wore a plain white jumpsuit and boots. The other wore the most magnificent costume Drake had ever seen—not that he would admit it. The superhero's black jumpsuit glistened with a metallic green sheen. His helmet had multifaceted eyes and feelers that swayed as he strutted.

"We should greet them," Drake said.

Dex looked at Drake as though he had grown a third eye.

Drake touched his forehead to be sure he hadn't. "Know your enemy," he said, surprised Dex had forgotten such a fundamental principle.

When Drake and Dex intercepted the superhero duo, the impressive one removed his fly-head helmet. He was a good-looking black man with a flattop haircut clearly designed so his helmet wouldn't smash it. He held out his gloved hand, its palm covered with sticky-looking hairs. Drake took the proffered hand between his index finger and thumb and shook gingerly. The hairy palms may or may not aid in wall climbing, but they certainly held on to donut crumbs.

The black superhero grinned. "Are you dudes the welcoming committee?"

Drake had never been accused of being welcoming. He wasn't sure why the superhero felt the need to insult him right off.

"They call me 'The Buzz,' 'cause the buzz is all about me." The Buzz clapped Drake's shoulder.

As Drake stepped out of touching range, the cherub-faced fledgling added, "Isn't that a spiffy-neato name?" He hopped in excitement. "I'm Mikey. I don't have a superhero identity yet, but once I determine it, I'll design a super-duper costume with super gadgets and—"

"How about 'Chirpy Boy'?" Drake said. "Or 'Cricket'? You're pretty good at hopping."

"'The Flea' seems more like it," Dex said in a stage whisper.

Mikey just chuckled and hopped, damn him. "I can't believe I'm hanging with The Buzz." Hop. "He apprenticed with Captain Perfect, so he's tested out of twenty credit hours. Isn't that the coolest thing you've ever heard?" Hop.

"Chilling," Drake said. Being from techno worlds, superheroes fought mad scientists, so The Buzz could be a problem in Dex's future. Drake cast his friend a sympathetic smile.

"That's quite a costume," Dex said, his gaze fixated on The Buzz's helmet.

"I'm still refining it," The Buzz said. "It takes just the right combination of technological innovations to be super. Of course, it helps being filthy rich so you can buy whatever technological innovations you want."

Drake rolled his eyes at Dex. The mad scientist-in-training ran his fingers over the helmet's multifaceted eyes.

The Buzz jerked away the helmet. "Hey, dude, it ain't cool to touch another cat's equipment."

Dex glowered. "I was merely showing scientific interest in the workings of your helmet."

"Well, keep your scientific interest to yourself." The Buzz drew a deep breath, then let it out. "I never got your names."

"I am Mandrake the Malevolent," Drake said in the deep, scary voice that had earned him top marks. Mikey's eyes widened, but The Buzz grinned.

"Around here, we call him Mandrake the Mediocre," Dex added helpfully. "He's working toward malevolence."

"It's good to have a goal." Hopping in his white boots, Mikey bounced to face Dex. "I see you're wearing white. Are you undeclared too?"

Dex puffed his narrow chest until it looked almost normal sized. "*I* am Poindexter, the student scientist voted most likely to conquer a world without destroying more than half of it. I am *not* undeclared. I earned the League of Evil Geniuses Scholarship based on my SAT scores and psychotic profile."

"And you claim *my* ego is overblown," Drake muttered.

"My word." Mikey hopped back from Dex. "I'm guessing we won't have any classes together then."

"Come along, Mikey." The Buzz's attention had drifted to the sunbathing witches. "Let's introduce ourselves to the ladies."

Witches, lusty wenches who never spoke to a mad scientist except to say "You're standing in my sunlight," or "You're polluting my view," favored the company of evil sorcerers. Witches and sorcerers belonged together as part of the natural order. Since all female students on campus were witches, The Buzz would be disappointed.

Yet, as Drake's gaze followed the strutting Buzz and his hopping sidekick, Mikey, another disturbing sight unfolded. The witches gazed with gooey expressions at the approaching superheroes. Skimpy halter tops barely contained the witches' heaving bosoms. Heroes and superheroes, being virtuous, looked anywhere but at the sighing women's half-naked bodies.

Dex snickered. "Looks like you sorcerers have been replaced."

"The witches are just trying to make us jealous."

"From your green complexion, I'd say it's working."

A horn's blare and clanging cymbals saved Drake from having to formulate a clever retort. Twenty maids in blue gowns danced in time to the "music" along the path from the portal chamber. From baskets draped across their arms, they strewed rose petals. Behind them pranced the cacophony's creator—a minstrel encased in a tangle of instruments hooked together so he could play several at once and quickly shift between others. Behind the minstrel and flower girls strutted King Marcus's son, Prince Valorous. Not a jet-black hair was out of place and his gold-plated armor gleamed. Valorous led a white charger, its braided mane decorated with flowers. Beside the prince, looking a tad embarrassed, walked his vassal, Sir Eloquence, in serviceable steel armor.

Valorous nudged the knight, who halted the maids and minstrel. After handing off his horse's reins, Valorous approached a hunched, stringy-haired drodent who was sweeping the path. The ragged man looked up with vacant brown eyes.

Drake shuddered. "That's Roderick the Rotten."

"Your old mentor?" Dex squinted through his thick glasses. "He's been mind-wiped?"

"Roderick was a lousy mentor, but I didn't realize his grades slipped so badly in his senior year." A chill crept through Drake, though he wasn't surprised Roderick had ended up a soulless husk. Thanks to Roderick's "guidance," Drake had come within a hair of washing out himself as a freshman.

Prince Valorous thrust a scroll at Roderick.

Dex shook his head. "Is that idiot questioning a drodent?"

"Valorous isn't noted for his intelligence," Drake said.

"You know that pretty boy?"

"Unfortunately. He's from my dimension."

After several failed attempts to communicate with the drodent, Prince Valorous and his entourage changed course—straight toward Drake and Dex.

"Are we wearing some sort of goodness homing device?" Dex patted his pockets. All he turned out was a slide rule and a calculator with its buttons so worn the numbers were gone.

Prince Valorous halted before Drake and Dex. Be-ribboned sleeves poked out from the prince's vambraces. Blue suede shoes showed under his elaborately etched greaves. Sir Eloquence wore tastefully plain clothes under his armor. His dark eyes challenged Drake.

"Eloquence, Valorous," Drake said, ignoring etiquette and social rank. "I didn't know the university offered remedial training."

The maids and minstrel gasped in horror.

Valorous raised his chin. "That's *Prince* Valorous and *Sir*

Eloquence."

"Down, prince." Under his breath, Drake added, "Good dog."

Valorous's gaze narrowed. "And who, pray tell, is your aesthetically challenged friend?"

The minstrel played a rim shot on his drum. Prince Valorous preened.

Drake glared until the minstrel cringed. "This is Poindexter from the College of Arcane Sciences."

"Your stallion is a magnificent animal, Your Highness." Dex's gaze traced the horse's form.

"Thank you," Valorous said. "Thank you very much."

"Would you consider, say, loaning him out?" Dex asked.

Why was Dex sucking up to the prissy prince? Leaning close, Drake whispered, "Are you planning to use it in some experiment?"

Dex blinked. "I hadn't thought of that. But we never received the new vehicles we were promised and I might need transportation. Plus, I heard you sorcerers need glue for dark arts and crafts."

Valorous cleared his throat, as if the sunlight glaring off his breastplate wasn't reminder enough of his unwanted presence. "I spoke to yon hapless lad, but he was of no help. I wonder if you could aid a new student."

Drake grinned. "How may I be of assistance?"

Valorous held out a map of the new quad. "I've located the quarters for Sir Eloquence and myself, but I can't find where my maids will be housed."

"Too bad for you, Prince Vanity," Drake said, hardly glancing at the map. "You'll have to send your maids away."

"That's Prince *Valorous*—and why must I send them away?"

"The only women allowed on campus are witches, faculty and university staff," Drake said.

Valorous huffed, but the maids looked relieved.

"You ladies had best head back to the portal," Prince Valorous said, sounding put out.

The maids flung their remaining rose petals in the air, then danced off.

Valorous frowned. "It's hot out here."

Sir Eloquence nodded.

The prince's frown deepened. "I *said* it's hot out here."

The minstrel almost tripped in his haste to reach his liege. Somehow, without bonking Valorous with his instruments, the minstrel produced a handkerchief and mopped the prince's brow.

"So," Drake drawled, pinning the armored nit with his most menacing glare. "Does your presence mean you were run out of your father's kingdom?"

Valorous's scathing gaze flicked across Drake. "Sir Eloquence and I have come to complete our training. Then we shall free our conquered territories from the tyranny of that most foul sorcerer, Bane the Black-Hearted."

The minstrel played ominous-sounding music on his lute.

Sir Eloquence drew a dagger with a gold cross embossed on its hilt. "With this, I'll cut out his evil heart." He gestured symbolically at Drake.

"Good luck with that," Drake said. "Don't get any ichor on your codpiece."

The heroes bristled, then led their stallions away. The minstrel played "Hail the Conquering Hero," as though those two idiots had already destroyed Bane.

From the look of them, Drake's father had nothing to worry about. And if those tin-heads succeeded, Drake would swoop in while their army was exhausted from fighting Bane and take the whole kingdom. Still, a family slight provided a good excuse for vengeance. From his robes, he pulled out a water pistol, a gift from Dex. Squinting, Drake shot a stream of potion at a vine trailing off the administration building. "*Virat!*" he intoned.

The vine snaked and coiled, then shot across the sidewalk. Valorous and Eloquence tumbled in a clatter of armor.

Several witches, along with Mikey and The Buzz, ran to aid the flailing men. The girls cooed and tutted as they helped the heroes up.

Drake glared. "You'd think those idiots had slain a dragon instead of tripped over their feet."

"A *shallow* female might consider them good-looking with their perfect hair and chiseled features," Dex said. "The more intelligent woman prizes a man for his mind and ambitions."

"Keep telling yourself that."

"And what do you tell *your*self?" Dex jerked his chin toward the fawning witches.

Drake growled as more scantily clad witches converged on the "fallen" heroes. "Do those foolish wenches truly believe that the nosy do-gooders won't interfere with their plots?"

"Don't look now," Dex said, an insane grin on his razor-nicked face, "but I think your plans for the week have changed."

Drake blinked hard. Hexaba—*his* Hexaba—led a group of witches carrying baskets covered with frilly cloths, toward the interloping good guys. Her short leather skirt showed her long, tanned legs to advantage. Drake swallowed a string of drool.

"How does it feel to be dumped?" Dex asked, his lip curling.

"You'll never know, since you'd first have to get a *date*." Drake stroked his beard. "Maybe I should cut out one of their hearts and send it to her. My father won my mother by sending her the heart of her other suitor. No, wait! A head on a pike. Nothing says you're serious like a head on a pike."

"Some men send roses," Dex observed.

"How unimaginative."

Dex squinted through his thick lenses. "What's she carrying in that basket?"

Using a freshman-level spell, Drake enhanced his senses. Amid the stink of goodness and honor, he smelled something even more sickly sweet...chocolate chips.

"She baked them cookies!" he fumed.

Dex smirked. "You said she couldn't cook."

"That's what she always claimed."

Hexaba draped herself across The Buzz and ran a hand along his metallic suit.

"Hey!" Dex said indignantly. "He's letting *her* touch his helmet."

"That's it!" Drake huffed in outrage. "These interlopers must go."

"Agreed," Dex said. "It's hard enough for a mad scientist to get a date with you sorcerers around, let alone these pretty boys. Besides, the static electricity from all that spandex is bound to play havoc with my scientific equipment."

CHAPTER TWO

Asmodeus Corleone, Head Dean of the University of Dark Arts and Arcane Sciences, scowled at the flaming letters on the scroll clutched in his fist. "Bad" didn't begin to do this day justice. The board of trustees had summoned him on the first day of this sure-to-be-disastrous school term. That could well mean Asmodeus's untimely end, and not just as university dean.

Asmodeus grabbed his imp-hide briefcase. In his agitated state, iron will alone let him retain human form. He approached the Nexus, the most powerful transdimensional portal in creation, and spoke the empowering words. "Open or I'll smash you to smithereens." Not that he could. No one remembered how the Nexus was created, let alone how to destroy it.

The eye-shaped portal remained closed.

"Pretty please?" Asmodeus coaxed.

The iris grudgingly swelled open. A glowing spiral vortex appeared to point inward, then in a blink, to point outward, like a spiral top illusion. In reality, the Nexus pointed everywhere at once, even to places that had no established portals. That was just one of many features that made it the most powerful and unique portal in existence. And Asmodeus controlled it—well, mostly controlled it...on a good day, which this wasn't.

"Trustees' boardroom," he instructed the Nexus.

Fighting centuries of demon-inbred trepidation, Asmodeus stepped into the light. The Nexus swallowed him whole. In the vast reaches of space, a grotesque creature, like a cross between a rabid yeti and Rodney Dangerfield, snarled at Asmodeus and feinted with a clawed hand. Every year, the Nexus beast grew more powerful, more dangerous and a bit snottier. Asmodeus shifted partly into demon form and belched a noxious green cloud to remind the beast who was boss—for now.

The Nexus coughed up Asmodeus like a hairball into the trustees' boardroom. As the temporary iris closed, the beast muttered, "No respect."

A bronze table filled the dark chamber. Only half the candles on the chandelier were lit. Several board members abhorred light. Two were so allergic that, even in candlelight, they wore hoods and heavy sunblock. Like most board decisions, the semidarkness was a compromise.

"Come forward, Asmodeus," the board chairman said.

Asmodeus strode to the foot of the table. Red, yellow and orange eyes glowed in the dark corners. In the semi-lit areas, humans, devils and demons stared with emotionless expressions.

A familiar voice asked, "How much were you paid?"

An ugly devil leaned into the candlelight. Budding horns covered his acne-scarred face. Recognizing the head of the Innermost Circle of Benefactors, Asmodeus shifted nervously. Whoever said "Better the devil you know" didn't know many devils.

"Bob? I didn't know any benefactors would be here."

Bob's jagged grin didn't improve his looks. "Hey, Asmodeus. I would have warned you, but you know our policy."

"Better to stab a man in the back than risk him running away. Now, what's this about? If it's the skimming—"

"We expect a little skimming," Bob said. "Accounting says you're the most honest university dean ever—which concerned us, but wasn't worth looking into—until now."

Asmodeus made a mental note to skim more.

The board chairman, "He Whose Name Cannot Be Remembered," shook his three-eyed head sadly. Due to a protection-racket spell, no one could finger him because no one could remember who had threatened them. "I've seen many an evil future go bleak, Asmodeus, but none as promising as yours. How could you allow heroes and superheroes into the university?"

Asmodeus's face heated. Blood red colored his vision. Crimson veins snaked across his skin as his complexion darkened to demon green. His eyes swelled into red orbs with glowing yellow pupils. Horns punched through his forehead. The stench of brimstone rolled off him. Blood dripped from his fingertips where claws ripped through the human facade.

The board members were unimpressed.

"What part of *Dark* Arts and *Arcane* Sciences don't you understand, Asmodeus?" a resonant voice asked from the shadowed doorway. Asmodeus squinted, but couldn't see the speaker.

"It was bad enough when we had to let the witches enroll," Bob said. "At least they're borderline evil."

"And they're hot," the chairman added.

The other members murmured their agreement.

Asmodeus literally fumed. "The Transdimensional Supreme Court issued an order of integration—just like with the witches. My hands were tied."

The resonant voice said, "I don't see any rope burns."

The board chairman shot Asmodeus a glare that scorched

the bronze table. "I'll wager the do-gooders also brought loads of cash."

Asmodeus smiled, remembering the delightful clink of coins. Heroes paid in gold. Although the superheroes also had donated generously to the new college's endowment fund, the crinkle of a check was less satisfying. "The funds to build *their* college had to come from somewhere."

"Hmph!" From the shadowed doorway stepped Lucifer, Jr., a cocky devil whose father was a big deal in the transdimensional netherworld. Physically, Junior stood half a head taller than the typical devil or demon. Mentally, he was a pipsqueak. Still, he was the golden boy of the netherworld. Hordes of demons, devils, succubi, incubi and harpies hung on his every word. That didn't explain his presence at this meeting, however. Junior was neither a board member nor a benefactor. He sure as Hell wasn't an alumnus.

"Junior," Asmodeus said. "I should have recognized that voice."

"It's Lucifer, the Two Thousandth."

Asmodeus let out a puff of steam. "Why are you here?"

"Following your downward-spiraling career is my latest hobby. Once I heard what a mess you made at the University of Dark Arts and Arcane Sciences, I couldn't resist the opportunity to discuss your failings as dean—and to offer myself as an alternative."

Asmodeus readied a comeback, but the board chairman raised a gnarled hand and said, "Lucifer has the floor."

Asmodeus bit his tongue. Acidic ichor burned his mouth.

Junior strutted the table's length. With every step his fiery wings unfurled wider. He stopped so close the flame-edged feathers singed hairs on Asmodeus's neck. Junior's polished horns gleamed. His fitted trousers and smoking jacket showed off every muscle. Considering that dandy had no responsibilities, it was no wonder he had time to keep in shape.

"Asmodeus, you've sold out," Junior said.

Remembered the chairman's warning, Asmodeus sputtered, "Permission?"

"When Lucifer is finished."

Asmodeus repeated his calming mantra, *Like Hell I will, like Hell I will....*

Junior sneered. "Why else would you kowtow to a court order? Had I been in charge, I'd have assassinated some justices, then demanded a new ruling. *You* opened the gates and let a bunch of contractors build a college for the forces of good. I'm ashamed to have called you friend."

Asmodeus quirked an eyebrow. They had never been friends.

Until now, he'd never thought enough of Junior to call him an enemy.

At the chairman's nod, Asmodeus said, "Has *anyone* considered that I've only appeared to acquiesce to court demands? Sure, I let them build on campus grounds—extensive libraries and research facilities we could never afford."

"What use are those to evil students?" Junior demanded.

"Asmodeus has the floor," the chairman said in a placating tone. That wasn't good. How many board members and benefactors did Junior have in his pocket?

"The facilities belong to the do-gooders *now*," Asmodeus said. "Do you believe our students from Dark Arts and Arcane Sciences welcome these interlopers? The do-gooders' very presence is already inspiring their twisted young minds to devise ways of eradicating the problem. Meaning *we* won't be responsible. The courts can do nothing and we'll claim the abandoned facilities and expensive equipment."

"What if that doesn't work?" Junior asked. "What are *you* doing to remedy the situation?"

The board members nodded. Lucifer, Jr. had inherited one trait from his infamous father—his intensely persuasive voice. Junior could claim that glowing coals were ice cubes and most listeners would pour tea over them and drink it down.

"If the university graduates do-gooders, where will that leave the universe?" Junior ranted. "Because the universe is an important place."

The board members and trustees nodded as though this statement weren't blindingly obvious.

"Yet you propose we put our"—Junior shuddered—"*faith* in students. *Students!*" he said, elongating the "u," as if this constituted proof positive. Asmodeus had long noted that extreme pronunciation did, indeed, constitute proof positive to roughly seventy-two percent of any population—a rather sad commentary.

Junior continued, "The various planes and dimensions depend on this and other evil institutions to turn out quality villains. Yet the University of Dark Arts and Arcane Sciences has fallen behind. If your students were properly trained, none of them would ever be turned into drodents."

Like Hell I will, like Hell I will.... "Five years ago, *I* instituted the drodent motivational program. The dropout and expulsion rates among sorcerers and scientists are now at zero. If a student's grades drops too far, he's placed on probation and given one semester to raise his GPA to acceptable levels. If he fails, he gets a mind wipe and a permanent job in grounds maintenance."

"You're too soft, Asmodeus." Junior snorted. "One mistake and it's time for a mind wipe. No more coddling students with probation. This isn't kindergarten."

Asmodeus's spine stiffened. "Some of our finest students had a rough start. I stand behind each and every graduate."

Junior smirked. "What about Dr. No-no?"

Asmodeus swallowed a groan. Of all the examples....

"He blabbed his entire plan to that super-spy, then left before assuring the man was dead and the ventilation ducts blocked," Junior said. "To make matters worse, 'Dr. Oh-no-no' posted the blueprints of his secret lair on the Internet. Result: disastrous failure."

That Dr. No-no hadn't put his lair's address on the website hardly seemed a strong defense. The lair had been magnificent. In his pride, Dr. No-no just had to share. Vanity was often a villain's undoing.

"Then there's Horace the Horrible," Junior continued. "If ever an evil sorcerer was aptly named—"

"Anomalies," Asmodeus said. "Most of our graduates spread chaos and evil throughout the dimensions."

"Most? As in 'more than half'? That's the best you can claim?"

Asmodeus resisted the urge to claw the smirk off Junior's face.

"Look, Asmo, old boy," Junior said, "no one is saying that *every* student has what it takes to be an evil mastermind. But you lack vision. That's where I would excel as university dean. Using only half my brain, I can think of two dozen better uses for drodents than as gardeners."

Asmodeus bit his tongue, certain the comment "I didn't know you had even half a brain" wouldn't be as well received by the board members as it might have been a year ago.

"You must admit, Lucifer, the grounds have never looked nicer," Bob said.

Junior whirled to face the devil. "You're missing the big picture, Bob."

The few remaining unsinged hairs stood up on the back of Asmodeus's neck. Junior had no interest in molding young minds. That devil must be out to take over the universe. After all, he *was* at that age.

Wearing a self-satisfied smile, Junior said, "Let me demonstrate how drodents could better serve...us." From his jacket pocket, he produced a cell phone and punched in a three-digit code. An answering beep came from the hallway.

A greasy-haired drodent shuffled in, a matching phone duct-taped to his forehead. The screen showed the white "walk" stick-figure used at crosswalks. "You paged me, master?"

Asmodeus turned a blazing glare on Bob. "Is that one of the drodents I loaned you?"

Bob shrank from the fiery gaze. "I lost them in a game of Texas Hold 'Em. It's not as easy as it looks on TV."

"You lost them to *Junior*?"

"That's Lucifer, the Two Thousandth," Junior said testily. "Useful creatures, these drodents—when someone with *skill* takes charge of them."

Junior punched in a number on his phone, and the one on the student's head played "Funeral March for a Marionette."

"Hell-o," the drodent intoned.

Junior put his phone on speaker. "Check this out."

A tinny female voice said, "If you'd like to add programming, press 1. To delete previous programming press 2. To institute self-destruct mode, press 3. To hear this menu again, press the star key."

Junior punched 1.

"To turn this model into a fierce killing machine, press 1. To have your house cleaned, press 2. To have this model do the chicken dance, press 3. To leave verbal instructions, press the pound key and wait for the tone."

Bob raised an oozing eyebrow. "The chicken dance?"

Junior shrugged. "I like the chicken dance."

The board members, in a rare unanimous vote, agreed the chicken dance was amusing.

That Junior liked any sort of dance was curious, since devils had two left feet and two left hands. That he got such great cell reception in the transdimensional netherworld was astounding. Asmodeus could never get more than one bar. Could it be magic? Probably not. Mixing magic and technology was generally forbidden, as it generated unstable and often destructive results. Asmodeus didn't object to that in theory, but in application the outcome could be uncontrollably disastrous.

He rubbed his chin. With proper programming, drodents would make a powerful army. If Junior wrested away Asmodeus's job, the devil would control both the drodents and the Nexus. That edge could well allow Junior to succeed in his plans for universal conquest where countless devils had failed.

Asmodeus shuddered. Like all devils, Junior believed in ordered evil—an order where *he* ruled. As a demon, the concept of ordered evil made Asmodeus's skin crawl. "Train the little monsters, then spread them to the winds" was his philosophy. The "order versus anarchy" debate between devils and demons had divided the board for centuries.

Junior ordered the drodent to serve a round of fire whiskey. He claimed it only served as a demonstration, but Asmodeus knew a bribe when he saw one. Fire whiskey cost a fortune—and was strong enough to make an elephant forget.

"Alcohol is prohibited at board meetings," Asmodeus said. "Have you forgotten the slaughter at the 1802 vote?"

"So some board members were killed," Junior said with a dismissive wave. "Most were just maimed. Anyway, *we're* far more civilized devils and demons than they were."

When everyone had a fire whiskey in claw, hand, tentacle or whatever, Junior gestured expansively, careful not to slosh his drink. Nitroglycerin was more stable. "Gentlemen, it is time for a change. Our university is stultified—"

"*Our* university?" Asmodeus interrupted.

"Yes, *our* university," Junior said, mimicking Asmodeus—if he'd been a squeaky old lady. "Asmodeus's heart is in the right place, but he lacks the right stuff. Only I possess the power and nerve to drive the do-gooders from our campus. *I* won't let students do a demon or devil's work."

"What you suggest is incredibly dangerous," Asmodeus said. *Not to mention stupid.* "The Transdimensional Supreme Court and the Affiliated Council of Heroes and Superheroes won't take *our* interference lying down."

Junior scoffed. "The university is protected from attacks."

"By *their* laws. If we defy the court order, we lose the benefits of being a public educational institution. Heroes and superheroes would turn our university into their private training ground. We would be attacked weekly. The cost to install defenses and repair damages would be astronomical. Between that and the loss of public funding, we'd be ruined."

"Enough!" the chairman shouted. He and Bob conferred in a whisper. At Bob's nod, the chairman said, "The board and benefactors will consider your arguments. Once we've chosen a course of action, we'll be in contact."

Asmodeus reached into his pocket for the portal return device and pressed the glowing red eye. The temporary portal reopened and he stepped into the spiral light. The Students of Dark Arts and Arcane Sciences had better not let him down.

CHAPTER THREE

Dex stormed away from the display of muscles and fancy equipment, through the iron gates to the College of Arcane Sciences. A stone wall topped by electrified razor wire encircled the quad. Anyone who tried to scale these walls would be sliced into ribbons, then barbecued. Curious birds and triple-dog-dared candidates for Darwinian elimination tested the defenses regularly enough to feed the roving pack of guard dogs.

One bong from the clock tower marked the afternoon time. In the main courtyard, an astrolabe tracked the sun's progress. Dex took the path to the fraternal house of Gamma Ray Delta.

In his room—a coveted tower room on the fourth floor—his roommate Gilbert was hauling a massive iron-and-wood trunk from his footboard to the arched window.

Dex's eyebrows shot up. Those chests, even empty, weighed fifty pounds. Yet Gilbert carried his as easily as Dex would a pillow. For a scientist to have muscles was unnatural!

Dex let out a low whistle.

Gilbert whirled around. "Poindexter. I didn't see you."

Dex nodded at the chest. "How'd you move that so easily? And why? It's a footlocker."

"I thought a window seat would be nice." Gilbert sat on the chest. Like 98.2 percent of students at Arcane Sciences, Gilbert wore dark-rimmed glasses, his only physical resemblance to the other mad scientists. "Natural light is better for reading. And there's fresher air here."

Dex snorted. "*Now* the air's fresh. Wait until the sorcerers start classes. My—our—room is downwind. Some of the odors they produce defy description." He shuddered. Last year, the sorcerer's dragon mascot had developed indigestion from eating a delivery truck and belched diesel fumes for a week.

"How'd you get so strong?" Dex repeated.

Gilbert shrugged. "Working on my parents' farm. Besides, the chest is empty."

That was apparent. Gilbert's clothes lay folded on his bed, along with shiny red and blue, footed jammies.

Dex shook his head. "Underclassmen."

Gilbert's gaze slid toward the childish jammies. Wearing a sheepish grin, he wadded them in a ball then shoved them into the chest. "My mom made them." He grabbed the freshman orientation booklet and waved it. "I've been waiting to register. According to page one—"

"Yeah, yeah. Come on." Dex had preregistered last semester. Gilbert, as a freshman, had to go through the more complicated process—unfortunately, with Dex as his guide.

"I'm surprised the university doesn't have online registration," Gilbert said as they headed down the curving stairs.

"We *did*," Dex said, already out of breath, "until last year when The Jokester demonstrated a 'focused EMP' as his proposed entry for the Spring Project Fair. It wasn't as focused as intended—took out every piece of electronic equipment in the Arcane Sciences quad. Lucky for us that the power plant is outside the university grounds, or we wouldn't even have electricity. We were *supposed* to get new equipment, but the money went to the superboob quad. Dean Corleone said we'd have to 'make do.' So our professors got all the old, non-electronic equipment out of storage. As I'm sure you were told, portal travel fries all electronic equipment—except for the portal in Dean Corleone's office. I think it's the University's way of controlling information flow and communication."

"Why would the University do that?"

Dex rolled his eyes and shook his head. Freshmen.

He led Gilbert down the stairs to the Life Sciences basement. There had been talk of turning the basement into a natatorium, but since mad science majors had no time for extracurricular activities, especially something as useless sports, the plans were dropped.

Instead, they used the Life Sciences basement for registration and the predictable-as-clockwork emergencies. Last year, when an infectious virus project got out of hand, the basement served as an immunization site. The year before, a radiation leak forced the scientists to take shelter in the basement. Dex wondered what this year's emergency would be.

"Wow." Gilbert stared at the maze of tables and lines. "This place would make a great natatorium."

Sighing, Dex pointed to a banner: *Class Registration Forms.* "We start there."

Dex nodded in passing to Dr. J-and-H, one of the instructors assigned to maintain order. That Dr. J-and-H was still in his Jekyll form indicated that no line-jumping or horseplay had provoked a transformation into Professor Hyde.

Under the banner, a Formica table held a shuffled mess of colored paper. A flowchart, complete with decision diamonds and round stop points, diagramed the registration process.

The first diamond asked: *Are you a student at the College of Arcane Sciences?*

Gilbert said, "No."

Dex elbowed him in the ribs, then winced, his funny bone jangling. "Yes, moron, you *are* a student of Arcane Sciences."

"I haven't attended any classes."

"For the sake of argument, let's follow the 'no' option. Are you a student at the College of Dark Arts?"

"No."

"Are you female?"

Gilbert grinned like an idiot. "No."

That answer bypassed the information square stating the student belonged in the College of Olde Wyrd Charms. It warned that "she" should make a speedy exit before any registering nerds noticed her. The "no" arrow proceeded to the square reading: *Leave the campus at once. You do not belong here,* followed by a round stop symbol. Dex sighed. If that were still true, there would be no interloping do-gooders.

Gilbert scratched his head. "How am I supposed to register?"

Dex pointed to the first question diamond. "The answer is 'yes.'" For a grueling half-hour, he explained the registration process to a dazed-looking Gilbert.

"Because this is Monday," Dex recapped, "you need *ten* cyan-colored papers."

He walked Gilbert through the first of ten identical forms, which required Gilbert's name, fraternity, mentor's name, allergies to medications and blood type. Every instructor kept emergency information on hand. According to statistics, for every bathroom injury, there were two worse classroom incidents and five even worse lab incidents. Lifesaving and "spare part" information could prove crucial.

Certain even Gilbert could handle repetitive forms, Dex started filling out the mentorship form—all fifteen pages.

Question 1: *What is your roommate's favorite color?*

Question 2: *On a scale of 1 to 10, how would you rate your roommate's personality?*

The form was supposed to ensure Dex actually had met his roommate—and not disposed of him yet—but it read like a dating questionnaire.

Question 78: *If your roommate committed suicide, what method would he use?* Dex resisted the urge to write *whatever method he chose, I'd be happy to help.*

"Finished," Gilbert said.

Dex scribbled an answer to the last question. *Dumb as a box of rocks.* He scratched that out and wrote: *A box of rocks is smarter.* "I'm finished too."

At the front of a long line, Gilbert handed over his stack of papers to a man sitting at a table.

"Name?" the administrator asked without looking up.

"Gilbert."

"Just the top page." Through Coke-bottle lenses, the administrator scanned the information. He handed Gilbert a printed card, then waved him toward the next line.

"We should rename the school 'The College of *Archaic* Sciences,'" Gilbert said.

"Just fill out the card."

Gilbert moved his glasses down his nose and squinted. "It wants to know if anyone in my family who likes me has political clout or works in public relations."

"Well, do they?" In Dex's freshman year, the question had been more blunt: *Does anyone important care if you live or die*?

Gilbert checked "no."

"Too bad," Dex said. "That was your chance to test out of Using Public Relations to Your Advantage. No matter—it's an easy class." Given Gilbert's brain deficiencies, he could use some easy grades.

At the front of the next line, the administrator fingerprinted Gilbert, thrust a thick book into his hand, and congratulated him on completing his first course registration.

Gilbert handed the next administrator just the top page and announced his name, proving the farm boy *could* be taught. Maybe.

The administrator peered over pince-nez glasses. "You misspelled your name."

Hastily, Gilbert erased his name and rewrote it.

Dex sighed. He would earn a better grade mentoring a retarded monkey.

The administrator handed Gilbert a course card.

Gilbert read, "Zen and the Path to World Domination. Who's Zen—the instructor?"

"Just fill out the card."

Three hours and fourteen lines later, Gilbert had collected and turned in seven more cards. At last, Gilbert was enrolled in nine classes, adding Domination for Mankind's Good, Maniacal Laughter, Mannerisms for Madness, Justifying the Psychotic World View, Introductory Alchemy, Moral Corruption 101 and Autopsy for Beginners.

From behind a scalp-high stack of books, Gilbert asked, "Are we done yet?"

"You need a lab."

"Gee, Dex, I must be taking a hundred hours."

"It's only twenty-seven, twenty-nine counting the lab. You freshmen have it easy."

Thirty minutes later, Gilbert was enrolled in Cultivating

Hazardous Plant Life.

"Come along, Gilbert. We're almost finished."

Gilbert's eyes bulged behind his glasses. "You said I just needed a lab. I won't have enough study time as it is."

"Quit whining. This is for your I.D. and stuff."

In the next line, Dr. Moreau, a wizened instructor in a white lab coat, gave Gilbert a dozen shots—two more than Dex received his first year. But times changed. Or maybe Dr. Moreau was experimenting on freshmen again.

"Why so many shots?" Gilbert asked.

"In case of a virulent outbreak." At Gilbert's shocked stare, Dex added, "Hey, *e. coli* happens."

Next, Gilbert had his photo laminated onto a cafeteria card, which no one ever used—-twice.

"This'll be handy." Gilbert tucked it into his wallet.

"No, it won't," Dex said. "Trust me." The Arcane Sciences cafeteria was the cheapest way to dispose of failed experiments without getting caught dumping hazardous materials. The common joke after a disappointment at the Life Sciences Lab was, *Oh, well. Deep fry it, cover it with gravy and nobody will know.*

By the time Gilbert was processed, he possessed: a university I.D.; a useless parking permit, as the College of Arcane Sciences had no parking lots; a medical card—also useless, since the only university medical staff was a bogus witch doctor; and a box containing tools of the trade—a slide rule with a spiffy $E=MC^2$ logo, a formula chart with measurement conversions, a basic calculator, test tubes, a magnifying glass (mostly used for burning ants), pliers, wire-cutters, a dozen leaky black pens, two mechanical pencils, a pocket protector, templates for making electrical diagrams and flowcharts, and tape to repair broken eyeglasses.

Gilbert carted everything in a single load to their room. He collapsed on the bed and stared woefully at the heap. "I'd hoped college would be more fun than high school."

Dex grinned. "Want to have some fun?"

"Sure, Poindexter. What do you have in mind?"

"How about a little prank?"

"Are we going to pull a prank on the evil sorcerers?" Gilbert rubbed his hands. "Tee hee hee."

Dex shuddered. Thankfully, Maniacal Laughter was a first-year course, so Dex wouldn't have to put up with girly giggles for long. "No, Gilbert, we're *not* playing pranks on the sorcerers. We're going to give the superheroes a first class welcome."

Gilbert frowned. "A prank isn't a the best way to welcome newcomers."

"Isn't that too bad!"

"You know, Poindexter, the world would be a nicer place if we all got along."

"A *nicer* place?" What could matter less? Dex considered signing Gilbert up for the Arkham Law seminar, *Yes, You ARE the Center of the Universe*. Instead, Dex drew a long breath and stepped proudly onto his personal soapbox.

"Do you think *they'll* leave us alone once we graduate? That *they'll* step aside and let us carry out our plans for world domination? No! While you and I try to bring order to worlds and regulate people's lives—for their own good—*they'll* try to stop us, as though *they* know what's best. Why? Because *they* think 'free will' is a desirable thing. Some even claim it's everyone's right. *It's a privilege*. Most people can't handle it, Gilbert. Deep down, most people don't want it. So it's up to us to alleviate them of that burden and make their world a simpler place, one their pea brains can comprehend."

"I was just saying," Gilbert said.

"Shut up and follow me."

A curving staircase led to the fraternity basement housing a practice lab. Under few bulbs dangling from wires sat tables littered with overdue library books with passages blacked out and more accurate information scrawled above. A mad scientist student stood before a chalkboard.

"Still trying to build a robot?" Dex asked.

Isaac, a sixth-year senior, wiped away part of his drawing. "Not just a robot—my dream woman."

"Yeah, right. Come on, Gilbert." Dex parked Gilbert before an abandoned chalkboard covered with gibberish, equations and bad drawings. Someone had been designing a cold fusion force field, apparently intending to generate a tsunami and submerge an island. Overall, the design wasn't bad. Dex memorized the key components then wiped the board clean.

Disgustingly cheery hunks of pastel chalk sat in the tray. Dex grabbed a nub, grumbling, "I hate pink." He shook the chalk at Gilbert. "After the EMP, Dean Corleone promised to provide new computers with Autocad. Instead, those funds—funds which were rightfully ours—have been wasted on building *those rich playboys* a new quad. No doubt, their facilities are state-of-the-art, while we're stuck using antiquated boards. The least the administration could do is buy us some dry-erase boards." Dex counted to ten. "But never mind that. We're here to design the perfect prank."

The perfect prank required the perfect patsy. Who better than The Buzz? He was more annoying than a blob of gum on the sole of a shoe—

Eureka! Like a fiend, Dex sketched an enormous pink shoe suspended by yellow laces from a lavender tree. Underneath, a stick-figure superhero stared up in terror.

"I like your use of pastels," Gilbert said. "If you flunk out of Arcane Sciences, you could become an artist."

"I'm *not* flunking out. No one flunks out." Dex would lie, cheat, steal and murder before washing out and becoming a mind-wiped drodent. Actually, lying, cheating, stealing and murder were part of his future plans anyway. "I'll have you know I'm ranked first in Arcane Sciences' junior class."

Once Dex had however much attention a farm boy with mush for brains could muster, he detailed each stage of his plan.

"Won't The Buzz see a giant shoe?" Gilbert asked.

"It'll be hidden in the branches."

"If it's as big as you've drawn, won't it snag in the tree?"

"Then I'll hang it from the lower branches."

"Where will you find such a big shoe?"

Dex had seen a giant shoe in the Acme Summer Catalog, along with rocket backpacks and meteor magnets. Unfortunately, he was on a tight budget. Maybe Drake could help. Any evil sorcerer worth his black blood could conjure a giant or troll and steal his shoes. Still, Dex hated asking Drake. The sorcerer never let anything go. The only way Dex had stopped Mandrake from gloating over his last semester's higher GPA was to buy him that stupid water pistol. Given all that, Dex said, "I'll make the shoe."

"Do you know how much leather you'll need? But it's just a prank, so it doesn't matter if the shoe is heavy enough to *hurt*. Besides, given the size of the shoe and using a rough calculation for its weight, you'd need a hundred-foot tree for a decent impact."

"Fine!" Dex erased the drawing. "We'll think of something else." Squinting, he turned on Gilbert. "How did you figure all that in your head?"

Gilbert shrugged. "It's like hoisting a bale of hay into the loft. Except backwards."

A fly zig-zagged through the chamber, as though The Buzz were nettling Dex via the pesky insect. It circled Gilbert's head. To Dex's astonishment, Gilbert smashed the fly into mush.

"That's it!" Dex furiously sketched a catapult armed with a giant flyswatter. As luck would have it, the scientists had a catapult left over from last year's Spring Games.

Gilbert opened his mouth.

"Don't say it," Dex warned.

A week later, the catapult-swatter was in position.

Dex and Drake lay in wait on the edge of Champion's Field in the new quad.

Too bad Gilbert had to miss the fun. He had detention for failing a basic lab experiment—"fridge critter." Gilbert couldn't leave his mold culture alone, so instead of a nasty, mottled green life form, he produced cherry yogurt. At this rate, Gilbert would be a drodent by finals—not that a mind wipe would change much.

Champion Field was hedged in by the glass-and-steel skyscraper, the castle with its prissy gold spires, and the wall surrounding the quad. Beyond the wall, the second story windows of the Student Union overlooked the field.

Fledgling superheroes in "undeclared" white jumpsuits flocked to the field like ugly ducklings for a flying lesson. Gooney birds had more grace. Yet Dex admired their try-or-die attitude. Too bad they wasted their lives on pointless crusades to aid the hopelessly helpless.

The first-years launched. Ten feet off the ground, one flailed and grabbed another's ankle. They tumbled into a third, then a fourth. Soon a jumble of white spandex and protruding limbs rolled across the sky.

Drake snickered. "Look at the silly goons."

"I am," Dex said.

"No, at the Student Union—oh, I forgot you can't enhance your sight."

Drake described a sea of faces pressed against the plate glass of the two-story building. As Dr. Jekyll taught, human nature was predictable and thus easily manipulated. People were like moths, drawn to the flames of disaster, though their own wings might get singed. In this instance, though, the gawking students had nothing to fear. The plate glass had been made and tempered in Hell. It was damn good glass.

The fledgling superheroes disentangled themselves. For a second, they flew straight—straight into the Student Union, like bugs hitting a windshield, then slid to the ground. Sadly, no one broke anything bigger than a nose.

Dex grinned. "I'm not sure we need to do anything to discourage these bozos."

"Indeed," Drake agreed. "These beau-zoos, as you call them, have the intelligence of a village idiot."

"It's bozos—as in clowns, or court jesters. Bozo was a famous clown...oh, never mind."

More experienced superheroes-in-training, denoted by their individual costumes, stepped up to the launch line.

"That armadillo getup must be the dumbest costume ever," Dex said, "though I admire the craftsmanship."

"Quite. He almost looks like a real—what did you call it?"

"Armadillo. Except for the red-white-and-blue boxer shorts and the cowboy boots, the costume's fairly accurate."

The armadillo flapped what little of his arms extended beyond his costume. The articulated shell moved with him. Still, the outfit looked hot and cumbersome. Doorways had to give him trouble. And restrooms.

"What's he saying?" Dex asked.

Drake muttered some gobbledy-gook. Suddenly, the armadillo's rants sounded as though he stood whining right beside Dex and Drake.

"Cool spell," Dex said.

"It's better than repeating everything to you."

"Armadillos don't fly," the would-be superhero said in a Texas twang. Drake's spell worked so well, Dex even heard the pop of the beer cap, which the armadillo opened with his claws. The would-be hero chugged the beer.

The instructor snatched away the empty bottle. "You know the rules regarding alcoholic beverages."

"Bring enough to share?" the armadillo guessed.

"*Never* during class," the instructor corrected. "Alcoholic beverages may be consumed only with the evening meal or at appropriate commemorative events or celebrations."

"In Texas, pretty much anytime is 'Miller Time,'" the armadillo said.

"This isn't Texas."

"That explains a lot about superheroes." Dex clapped a hand over his mouth. Whispering through his fingers, he asked, "That spell doesn't work both ways, does it?"

"Of course not," Drake snapped. "I'm not an imbecile."

The instructor said, "Listen, Armadilloman, all superheroes fly by *some* means."

The armadillo superhero spun around. "Do you see wings on my danged back? Armadillos don't fly. Armadillos jump."

"Then jump really high and stay up a long time."

"Okay, but that's how armadillos get killed on the highway," Armadilloman said.

"Then that," the instructor said, "will be your mandatory superhero weakness. Now jump."

Armadilloman shrugged, his round-backed shell riding up around his face. He set down his shotgun, then launched himself. For an armored rat, he jumped pretty well. Happily, he jumped while under a tree. A branch cracked as it clocked him. He slammed against the ground and curled into a ball. The curled-up superhero resembled every other armadillo Dex had ever seen. Unfortunately, this one got back up.

Dex let out a low whistle. That bulky costume was more flexible than it appeared.

Armadilloman shook his head sharply. "Good thing my head's

as hard as a rock."

That, Dex had always assumed, was a prerequisite for all good guys. Armadilloman had hit the branch hard enough to split his skull. Ergo, the helmet, which resembled an armadillo's pointy head, must be made of sturdy stuff.

The Buzz strutted into the open, well clear of the tree. "Watch how it's done."

A viridescent veil spread from under The Buzz's armpits, making him look like a deranged flying marsupial. He launched in perfect T form. The instructor lavished praise on the stuck-up superhero wannabe as The Buzz circled the adoring crowd. His little "wings" produced an annoying buzzing whine.

"He's not coming this way," Drake said.

"We need bait." Dex looked around. What lured flies? Honey. Didn't have any. Shiny objects? No, that was crows.

Drake raised his hands and his sleeves fell back, revealing bony wrists. He uttered more mumbo-jumbo. A shimmering image of Hexaba sunbathing appeared beneath the pale shade of the bramble-covered flyswatter.

The Buzz flew toward the shimmering illusion. Dex mentally calculated The Buzz's speed. To verify the results, he slid the bars of his slide rule. The device should have been a solar-operated scientific calculator and would have been, had the money not been reallocated to the do-gooders.

Dex pulled the lever. Bits of bramble broke off as the swatter whistled through the air.

The Buzz zipped outside the swatter's range, and it whacked the ground. He cocked his bug-eyed, helmeted head and gave a buzzing tsk. Since the illusion of Hexaba had vanished, The Buzz flew off in serpentine zigs and zags.

Drake howled with laughter. "I knew that contraption would fail. I've seen better engineering from drunken beavers."

Dex huffed. "There's nothing wrong with my design. Your illusion threw off my timing."

"Any fault lay with your poor planning. *My* spells worked perfectly."

"So did *my* catapult-swatter."

"Except that it missed."

"Well, if you think you can do better," Dex snipped.

"I could do better with a broken wand shoved up my nose."

"I'd like to see you try."

"Wait and see what *I* have planned for them."

Somehow, Dex suspected Drake's plan wouldn't involve a wand up his nose. Shame really. He'd have paid to see that.

CHAPTER FOUR

Other than Dex's amusing failure against The Buzz, Drake's week had been infuriating. Hexaba's sorority sisters at Hex Omega Tau thwarted his every attempt to see her. Worse, Drake had to abandon his head-on-a-pike plan for garnering Hexaba's favor. New university rules (which the do-gooders had foisted upon them) forbade killing other students—even a rival.

He settled on sending a raven with a missive forgiving Hexaba's lapse of judgment in flirting with The Buzz and asking to see her. He half expected the returning raven to sneer, "Nevermore." Instead, the bird said, "Meet me at *The Lusty Wench* in Bramblethorp at noon. Be on time—or else."

Either Hexaba still desired Drake or she had some use for him. He harbored no illusions about a witch's ability to love deeply. His own mother never loved without a web of strings attached. Drake respected that.

Bramblethorp village reminded him of home—not surprising, since most of the populace had emigrated from Drake's dimension. Thatched cottages and shops of rough-hewn stone lined the rutted streets. Drake wove around ox-drawn wagons, sidestepping the smelly byproducts of said oxen. When he opened the creaky door to *The Lusty Wench* tavern, the scent of sour ale and smoke engulfed him. Although it was mid-afternoon, a crowd of locals huddled around tables shoved in a corner. Today must be another holiday the commoners had invented to shirk their duties.

Drake ordered an ale, then carried it to a booth in the dark corner farthest from the cheery townsfolk.

When the tavern door creaked open, Drake's chest tightened. He strained for a glimpse of Hexaba's glorious body.

The glare of sunlight off armor blinded him. Wiping his tearing eyes, Drake shrank into the shadows as Sir Eloquence clomped into the room. Prince Valorous was nowhere to be seen.

Seeing Eloquence head toward the villagers, Drake muttered the eavesdropping spell.

"Thank you for coming, Sir Eloquence," said a man with a jagged scar across his cheek.

"It's good of Prince Valorous to send his vassal," added a plump man in a flour-dusted apron.

Drake stroked his short beard. What were the prissy prince

and his tin-plated toady up to?

"Your missive intrigued Prince Valorous and myself," Sir Eloquence said. "It appears we have mutual goals."

"If you mean ridding ourselves of those evil sorcerers, mad scientists and witches, you're right." The scarred man lifted his shoulder. "Well, maybe not the witches."

That was gratitude. Many villagers had come here to escape the burdensome taxes Valorous's father and grandfather had levied to support their frivolous lifestyles. How short was a peasant's memory!

The plump man wiped sweat from his brow. He glanced around as though fearing an evil sorcerer might be listening, then plunked down a clinking pouch. "The guilds took up a collection to support your cause. This dimension won't be a decent place to live until those evildoers are gone."

Drake huffed. The denizens of Bramblethorp arrived long after the university was established. They were like people who built beside a charnel house, only to complain about the stench.Sir Eloquence looked a bit embarrassed as he tied the pouch to his belt. "Prince Valorous and I want only to root out evil wherever it takes refuge."

Sanctimonious hypocrite. Valorous's father, King Marcus, was a greater plague on the common folk than Bane the Black-Hearted had ever been. Marcus just had better PR. As Dex said, good PR was essential to success.

Not long after Eloquence left, Hexaba swished in. A sudden wind (which she created) whipped her skimpy skirt, almost...almost revealing more than decency allowed. Drake's thoughts evaporated as the blood departed his brain for points south.

No, no! Her amazing body would not distract him. His mother, during one of her farewell advice rants, taught him about witches' wiles. Drake wouldn't succumb to such tricks. He wanted an alliance with Hexaba, but on even terms—or as close to even terms as possible. Hexaba's skill at witchcraft matched Drake's at sorcery. Together, they could conquer whatever kingdom they set their sights on. But only if Drake kept his wits, only if he guided their enterprise. Without firm male guidance, witches seldom sought such lofty goals as conquering kingdoms, satisfying themselves with conquering individual men.

As soon as a safe path cleared, the villagers raced for the exit. Hexaba cast them a wicked smile, then headed straight to Drake. Her hair, dyed ruby red, meant she wanted to attract attention—or that she wanted to go shopping, Drake couldn't recall which.

She slid onto the seat across from him. Her full breasts

strained her halter top nearly to its breaking point. Drake knew how the poor garment felt. Even now, the pressure of her beauty strained his willpower. What had his mother told him? Something critical. Ah, yes. *Don't look at the breasts. Never look at the breasts.*

Drake dragged his gaze to meet hers. Hexaba's eyes were a vivid green. Who knew?

"Thanks for meeting me." Drake winced at his meek tone. Hells, *she* had wronged *him*.

"After your last missive," Hexaba said, her tone cold enough to frost his ale, "I almost decided never to speak to you again. *You* forgive *my* indiscretions?"

"I wasn't the one draped over The Buzz like a cloak."

"Do you even know why I'm mad at you?" Hexaba asked, literal sparks in her eyes. Dramatic Evil was her favorite class.

Drake searched his memory. At the end of last term, they shared a hot and sweaty goodbye, but Hexaba ended matters before they reached any satisfaction. Surely she wasn't angry that he didn't take her against her will. They hadn't seen each other all summer. He couldn't have angered her when he wasn't even around.

She snorted. "You *don't* know. That's typical."

"Why don't you tell me?"

"Figure it out for yourself." A dangerous glint filled Hexaba's eyes. Drake was starting to think looking at the breasts was safer. With an unconvincing pout, she continued, "Suffice to say, if you want my favor, you must earn it back."

Witches never granted simple forgiveness. Half the time, Drake knew he was in the right and they should be earning back *his* favor. Around witches, though, he couldn't think of a clever retort—no doubt due to a lack of blood in the brain.

"What do you want me to do?" Drake asked in resignation.

"Get rid of Prince Valorous and the other meddling heroes," Hexaba said.

"That's it? I planned to do that already. Do you want his head on a pike?"

Hexaba raised her eyebrows. "Intriguing, but no. Your becoming a drodent would put a damper on our relationship."

"What relationship is that?" Drake gave her a melting look and reached for her hand.

She slapped his hand away with a stinging smack. "That depends on your success."

"Ridding the campus of those annoyances could take awhile. Can't you give me a little encouragement?" Drake asked in his most seductive tone.

Heat entered Hexaba's eyes. She leaned across the table until her mouth was a feather's width from his. Her warm breath tickled Drake's lips, but kissing her first would only earn him another slap.

Her tongue traced his lips, then slid inside his mouth. The single point of contact sent shuddering, heated delight though Drake's body. He leaned into the kiss, deepening it.

Hexaba broke contact. Her green eyes went icy. "Get rid of the good guys. Then we'll talk."

Drake stalked through the cobweb-festooned corridors of the Fraternal Order of the Black Sash, the most prestigious fraternity for evil sorcerers throughout the known universe. Portraits of evil alumni lined the walls, their eyes tracking him. Eerie cold zones surrounded several portraits, making the nearby rooms popular hangouts during hot days.

Things with Hexaba had gone better than anticipated. Drake had expected her to inflict serious humiliation. Once, when he forgot to open a door for her, she'd sent him on a quest for the rare one-eyed toad. After days of searching, Drake grew desperate and tried to pass off a regular toad with one eye poked out. He paid dearly for that bit of poor judgment.

On reaching his chamber door, Drake tensed. Today his new roommate arrived. Drake hoped Jeffrey wasn't a moron like Gilbert. Anything would be better than that—or so Drake thought until he opened his chamber door.

The room was sparkling clean, not a cobweb or dust mote in sight. Someone had rearranged the furniture so that Drake's things filled half of the room, instead of three quarters. The black curtains were tied back, and the open window let in glaring sunlight and a fresh breeze. He could even see the floor—it was wood. Drake had always imagined it was slate.

"What in the name of all darkness is this?" Drake roared.

From behind a half-dead, rat-eating plant emerged a young man. The brown hair falling across his forehead looked as though it hadn't been combed in weeks. His green eyes glared through wire-rimmed spectacles. "If you're referring to the fact that I cleaned away the filth and cobwebs, you're welcome. It's your turn next week."

If it wouldn't have ruined Drake's mentoring grade, he would have throttled the little snot. "I assume you're Jeffrey?"

Jeffrey rolled his eyes. "Brilliant deduction."

"Dust and cobwebs, Jeffrey, set the mood for evil study. As does darkness." Drake shut the casement windows and whipped the drapes closed. "I can't concentrate with that infernal sunshine and cheer. Anyway, nothing says evil like large spider webs."

"All it says to me is that you're too lazy to clean."

"Being surly is *not* the same as being evil," Drake said

between gritted teeth.

Jeffrey's lip curled. "Oh, yeah?"

"I'm your mentor. You must trust my guidance."

"Why should I? You're evil."

Drake shrugged. "So are you—or you're supposed to be. Dean Corleone understands the evil mind. That's why mentors are graded on their protege's academic performance. If you fail, I fail."

An opportunistic gleam filled Jeffrey's eyes. "So you need me."

"If you fail, I fail one course. *You* end up as a soulless husk of a drodent. And believe me, I will put you through whatever torment it takes to earn my A."

Jeffrey paled. Putting on an unconcerned expression, he flopped onto his bed. "Very well. Tell me about being evil."

What sort of parents must this boy have? Even Drake's father, who previously had spoken no more than five words to him in his entire life, spent ten minutes explaining what Drake must accomplish at college. It didn't do for an evil sorcerer-lord's son— even the unimportant third son—to perform poorly.

"First, you must *think* evil," Drake said. After all, it was his burden to teach his assigned freshman the ropes, even if Drake's first inclination was to *hang* Jeffrey with the ropes. "Visualize your goals. Anyone in your way is your enemy and must be removed."

"If you say so."

"Is it so different in the techno-magic world?" Drake asked.

"Don't you know? Your mother came from there."

Drake blinked in surprise. That Jeffrey had studied up on him showed promise—and a possible threat.

The Dread Witch Tiffany seldom talked about her home dimension. Drake only knew what everyone at the university knew: the techno-magic world was a demonic experiment to see how the two forces coexisted. While demons found the experiment amusing—from a safe distance—the results had been disastrous. Sorcerers and witches were forced to hide their powers from hysterical technos, who tended to stone them or burn them at the stake. Even white wizards weren't safe from fear-driven purges. And while blending magic and technology on a small scale sometimes proved useful, attempts at larger-scale combinations had resulted in the explosive destruction of several large countries.

Pathetic mewling drew Drake's gaze downward. A fuzzy white kitten scrabbled from under Drake's bed. It stared up with huge blue eyes. It was the most repulsive thing Drake had ever seen. Trilling, it bounced over and rubbed against Drake's legs. He shuddered. An affectionate cat—how vile.

"What...is...that?"

"It's my familiar, Spike," Jeffrey said.

"A *white* familiar?" The kitten was now clawing his black comforter. Drake's eyes narrowed. "Bad cat!"

The kitten continued sharpening its claws on Drake's bedspread. Thank the one-eyed Dark Lord, House-Training Your Familiar was a first semester freshman course. Drake lifted the kitten by its scruff and tossed it onto Jeffrey's bed. His own familiar, Malice, a properly surly black cat, lay sulking in a corner. Drake flashed him a wink. <<Fear not, Malice. We'll whip these two into shape.>>

Malice stretched. <<Will it involve real whips?>>

<<Doubtful.>>

<<Pity.>> The cat opened its mouth in a gaping yawn. <<I want tuna.>>

<<You always want tuna.>>

<<Your point being?>>

Drake broke the telepathic contact. Jeffrey half-heartedly scattered dirt from the window box across the floor.

"Stop that," Drake said. "The dust will accumulate naturally. Keep the window and curtains closed, put the furniture back the way it was and we'll call it good."

Jeffrey scowled. "Don't you mean evil?"

"That's the spirit." Drake strolled to a glassed-in case holding class notes and a half-dozen spell books, all he could afford. His father had clothed Drake in fine robes and provided a transportation pass for the portal, but the rest he left to Drake. His hard-won scholarship covered tuition, room and board, and the barest number of books. While it burned Drake's soul that his father had paid fully for his two older brothers' schooling, keeping a scholarship forced Drake to greater heights than he might otherwise have attained.

While cleaning, Jeffrey had arranged Drake's books alphabetically. That bit of obsessive neatness might be useful.

Drake pulled out a spell book entitled *Animation: Livening Up Everyday Objects with Potions, Wands and Enchanted Staffs.* Too bad he had squandered his plant animation potion on tripping Valorous and Eloquence. Well, maybe it hadn't been a *waste*, as watching Valorous and Eloquence tumble had been vastly amusing. But Drake lacked funds for the ingredients to brew another batch. He could try stealing them from the lab, but no one had cracked the new security spells, and Drake didn't relish the thought of being transfigured into pus. He glanced at his stock of ingredients.

Jeffrey had arranged the bottles by shape and color, as

though they were knickknacks instead of spell components. Drake had Eye of Newt and a vintage bottle of '97 fungus spores he won cheating at cards, but he lacked the fairy wings needed to animate plants. He wished he could travel to his home dimension to collect some. Drake loved pulling the wings off fairies. Grounding the pesky buggers until their wings regrew served them right. They always flitted around using their magic to blunt the effects of evil sorcery. Unfortunately, the university only allowed off-dimension portal travel around designated holidays.

After reorganizing his ingredients, Drake flipped through the animation spell book. There must be a potion he could make with the ingredients at hand to use against those hose-wearing princes and their tin-plated knights. The superheroes didn't worry Drake. Most were just gender-ambiguous dressers with meager, gadget-enhanced powers. Plus, superheroes mainly contented themselves with interfering in the plots of mad scientists. Princes, despite their frilly outfits, wielded political clout in the magic dimensions and had a golden shininess that made idiot peasants flock to their banners.

"Have you seen the new quad?" Jeffrey asked.

Drake growled at the interruption. "Disgusting, isn't it?"

"I thought it looked impressive and...shiny."

Idiot peasant.

"The heroes have this huge field for lance and sword practice." In his excitement, Jeffrey forgot to be surly. "They built a life-sized target dragon of cloth, wood and sand, but it's painted to look like the real thing."

"That quad represents a major slash in funding for the College of Dark Arts," Drake said. "Thanks to that dragon dummy, you freshmen must practice transformations on each other instead of rats. Pray you get a competent partner. Thanks to that dragon, you will sit at splintery, rickety desks instead of the new ones we were promised before the Invasion of the Tin Men. Thanks to *that dragon—*"

Drake glanced again at his stock of ingredients, then grinned. That dragon of cloth, sand and wood. Perfect.

"One single day, Dex," Drake crowed. "That's all it took to brew my potion—unlike the seven interminable days it took to make that ridiculous failure of a fly smasher."

"Fly swatter," Dex muttered. "And you've yet to prove your potion will yield positive results."

"Animation is my major field of study. Watch and learn—that's your scientific method, is it not?"

"Absolutely. The most effective way to study phenomena is

to observe cause and effect—"

"Did you bring what I asked?" Drake asked, hoping to distract Dex from a long-winded explanation.

"Of course." From a canvas bag, Dex pulled a plastic rifle with a big reservoir at the top. "Though it's called a *Super-Soaker*. A howitzer is a completely different weapon."

"It's hard to keep the names straight," Drake said. "Your world has so many types of projectile-hurling devices."

Solemnly, Dex handed Drake the Super-Soaker. "Be careful. It's even more expensive than the water pistol I gave you."

Drake could only imagine the cost of turning out such a rare and unnatural substance as plastic. From a wine skin, he poured magic fluid into the Super-Soaker and plugged the reservoir. He paused to admire the strange rune on the plastic rifle, a triangle formed by three curved arrows, with the number 2 inside it and the letters "HDPE" inscribed below. The same rune and letters adorned his water pistol. The symbol possessed great power, Drake was certain of it. HDPE must be the first letters of words in an incantation. Though Drake had tried to puzzle through it, he hadn't yet figured out the spell.

"According to the course schedule Jeffrey procured, the 'heroes' should arrive for lance practice at any moment," Drake said. "Let's give them a real lesson." He pointed the water rifle at the dummy dragon. As tall as three men, it loomed over the field, its painted scales and claws looking too real for Drake's comfort. His few close encounters with Blackie, the College of Dark Arts' dragon mascot, had been harrowing.

Dex laid a hand on Drake's arm. "Aim a little above where you want to hit. The water will arc and—"

Drake jerked free. "I made high marks in archery and siege engines. I understand trajectory." Mad scientists acted like all others were idiots.

Drake squeezed the trigger. The potion shot through the air and smacked against the dragon's feet. Perfect aim. Then the potion stream died out.

"I didn't break it," Drake said.

"You have to pump it to keep up pressure. I don't suppose you studied *that* in your siege engines course."

After Dex demonstrated how to pump the Super-Soaker, Drake saturated the dragon's feet and legs. He needed only the spell words to bring the sand dragon to life.

The clip-clop of hooves announced the heroes' arrival, their instructor in the lead. He trotted his horse to the dummy dragon then wheeled the animal around. Pulling off his golden helm, he shook out the raven black hair framing his sculpted features.

"Prince John of the Moors." Despite himself, Drake felt a bit awed.

"Who's he?" Dex asked.

"The most successful hero ever. No one has slain more dragons, rescued more maidens or deposed more evil sorcerers."

"Do you collect his trading cards or something?"

"Know your enemy." Drake had lost an uncle and cousin to Prince John's skills.

The student heroes arrayed their horses in an arc before their instructor. They removed their helms so they could hear— and no doubt to show off their pretty-boy faces and hair that remained perfect despite having been crammed into boxy helmets.

Drake grinned. "All lined up for the slaughter."

"Let's see it, then," Dex said, a challenge in his spectacle-blurred eyes.

"*Virat!*" Drake intoned.

Behind Prince John, an evil purple glow spread across the dragon's sandbag feet. The glow oozed up its wooden legs. Several student heroes shifted on their mounts, but were too polite to interrupt their instructor.

"The key to slaying dragons is location, location, location," Prince John said. "Where you stick your lance is far more important than how many times or how deep."

Though Drake and Dex snickered, none of the heroes did. Those goody two-boots were too virtuous and dim-witted to think in double entendres.

The purple glow engulfed the sand dragon. The creature's mouth opened in a silent roar. It wrenched at the frame holding it in place. Wood splintered with a resounding crack.

Undeterred from his lesson plan, Prince John spoke louder. "Your lance is your sole defense. Polish it daily...."

Drake muffled a snort. Dex didn't quite manage. Prince John's gaze flicked their way. They ducked behind a bush. The prince returned his attention to his students.

The dragon lumbered like a giant shifting meal sack straight for Prince John. One more step and the legendary hero would be squashed like a rotted gourd. Then Drake would be the legend.

A hero raised his hand. As the dragon lifted its front leg over Prince John's head, the instructor recognized the student hero, who pointed upward. Prince John nudged his mount forward and the dragon's foot smashed against the ground.

"So close," Dex jeered. "Like all those times with Hexaba."

"It's not finished yet," Drake said through clenched teeth.

The dragon spewed a stream of sand. The student heroes choked on the swirling, gritty cloud. Their mounts shied and squealed. Several tin-plated twits crashed to the ground. Drake felt the glow of triumph.

At Prince John's shouted instruction, the heroes regained control of their mounts. Those on foot drew their swords. In an annoyingly organized formation, they approached the sand dragon. The dragon spewed more sand, halting the advance.

Dex snickered. "Genius. Every time it does that, it loses mass."

Drake furrowed his brow.

"It gets smaller, you pea-brained charlatan," Dex explained.

Sure enough, the dragon's size deflated with each spewing cloud. The heroes poked the animated sandbag with lances and swords. Sand poured from the wounds, reducing the dragon to a mound of rags and sand piles. The grit-covered heroes cheered.

"That didn't take long," Dex said, smirking. "And not a hero was harmed in the making of your dragon."

"You slimy little wart," Drake growled. "*Your* prank didn't so much as inconvenience anyone."

"Ooh, I didn't realize we were aiming for inconvenience—"

The branches overhead parted. Prince John of the Moors loomed over them, sand dusting his hair. He pointed a lance perilously close to Drake's eye. "You there. Did you animate that target dummy?"

Drake floundered. Perhaps he could pin this on a class rival, claim he'd come to warn—

"He sure did." Dex clapped Drake on the back. At Drake's shocked stare, Dex added, "Always take the credit due you—before someone else does."

Drake glared venom at his supposed friend. That skinny toad would pay—

Prince John laughed. "My thanks. I couldn't have asked for a better training class. Could you return next week and do it again? It will take that long to sew our dummy back together."

Laughing and clutching his sides, Dex rolled on the ground.

"I fear I lack the funds for such an undertaking," Drake said, forcing out the words.

"We have plenty of gold to pay for the potion," Prince John said. "Think it over."

"I shall." *Not.* Drake stomped off.

Dex rushed to catch up, his narrow chest heaving. "Hey, slow down."

"Why, so you can stick another dagger in my back?"

"Did you learn nothing from Using Public Relations to Your Advantage class?"

Drake stopped dead. Dex stumbled a few steps then halted.

"What if Prince John *wasn't* amused?" Drake demanded.

"What if he went to Dean Corleone and the dean revoked my scholarship? I'd be turned into a drodent before you could say abracadabra."

"Oh, Drake, don't be ridiculous," Dex said. "I'd never say abracadabra. Anyway, we're going about this the wrong way."

"How is that, O Mighty Brain?"

"Don't *you* know?" Dex sneered.

"You're the mad genius. You tell me."

Dex gave a conspiratorial smile. "It's simple. We need to team up."

CHAPTER FIVE

Tex propped his cowboy boots on the coffee table. Six open pizza boxes lay scattered around the living area of his dorm room. Several other superheroes were sprawled on the conversation-pit sofa.

The Buzz, in full costume, sauntered in.

Tex gave a backhanded wave toward kegs stacked along the wall. "Help y'all's self to a beer."

The Buzz grinned. "What's the occasion?" With his head in his fly helmet, his voice came out a high-pitched whine.

While The Buzz poured a frothy mugful, Tex called for everyone's attention. "Boys, it appears we-all have been invited to join in a fraternity tradition."

Tex's half-brother and roommate, Mikey, stared wide-eyed. "Hazing?"

Wombat Willie, a lanky Aussie, tossed his hat with dangling corks onto the coat rack. "Who's doing this hazing, mate?"

"Son, hazing's against university rules," Tex said. "I'm talking about the good ol' boys club. You know, where we play a few pranks on each other? Just good, clean fun."

Willie's mouth split into a grin. "Oi, are you talking about those science geeks and their cross-dressing, wand-waving mates? If so, I'm in."

"I danged sure am." Tex finished his fourth beer, then grabbed a slice of pizza. He should cut back. Scuttling in armadillo form was hard enough without hauling around a spare tire of blubber.

The Buzz hummed. "I don't call nearly being swatted 'good, clean fun.'"

Tex slapped his knee. "Them boys was just messing with you. That flimsy pancake slapper wouldn't have bent your antennae."

"I've been hit harder by a drunken 'roo," Willie said. "You gadget heroes are wimps."

The Buzz removed his helmet and his high-pitched voice dropped five octaves. "Automatic potato-peelers are gadgets. My high-tech helmet has receivers, amplifiers, video equipment and an extendible drinking straw."

Tex snickered. "If it's so high-fallutin', how come you didn't test out of costume design class?"

"I have a few kinks to work out." The Buzz squeezed his

gloved hand into a fist. The tiny gripping hairs—like super velcro—interlocked. Though he struggled and shook his hand, the fist stayed locked. He squirmed free of the glove and picked at the hairs to open it back up. "Kinks like that. But the helmet is a masterpiece."

"I guess every superhero has some kinks to work out," Wombat Willie said. "'Cept for Tex and me—but we come with bonafide superpowers."

Jealousy tinging his street-cool voice, The Buzz said, "This is the first time I've seen you out of costume, Armadilloman. No offense, my man, but you lack style."

"When I lounge, I like to be comfy." An old pair of jeans and a western shirt made him feel almost at home. The friendly pranks, although a surprise, had also made Tex feel welcome.

Back when Tex was a Texas Ranger, he and his buddies pulled lots of pranks, like the time he and Clayton hid the beer and told Clint that they'd drunk it. They'd been in a dry county, and Tex thought ol' Clint would pass out at the thought of going a whole night without beer. The Texas Rangers were a lot like a fraternity. Except with guns and badges.

"What do you guys say?" Tex asked. "Do we ignore their pranks or play back and rattle their cages? After all, it's part of the college experience."

"Beats the heck out of doing nothing," The Buzz said.

"Then let's eat some pizza, knock back a few beers and plan some danged retaliation." Tex dragged his feet off the table, remembering what his mamma told him. A good host never put his feet on the table first.

"We could steal their mascot," The Buzz suggested, picking a mushroom off his pizza.

Kachina-Man set aside his massive, carved headdress, revealing a spiky, blonde Mohawk and Anglo-blue eyes. "First, stealing is a crime. Second, where would we hide a dragon or a semi-evolved chimp?"

"Okee dokee...what about this?" the Avenging Ninja said, his voice already slurred, "We paint the Gamma Ray Delta house...we paint it...pink!" He looked around and grinned like an idiot. "Huh? Huh?"

"Do you have that much pink paint?" The Buzz asked.

"Uhhhh...no."

"Do you have any paint?"

"Uhhhh...no."

"Okay, then," The Buzz said. "Besides, painting their frat house sounds more like work than a prank."

The Whatchamacallit, a superhero who defied description, said, "Maybe we could talk them into doing the painting for us."

"Nobody falls for the Tom Sawyer bit anymore." The Buzz shook his head. "Does anyone have a *good* idea—something we could actually do?"

The superheroes-in-training snarfed more pizza and beer. Several surfed the Internet on their phones and tablets for prank ideas. Dean Corleone had charged a fortune to bring the electronics through his portal. Fortunately, the superheroes could afford it.

"What if we...naw, that wouldn't work," Mr. Gizmo said, swiping to another page.

"We could...no, it says here Peyote's real unpredictable," Kachina-Man said.

"Guys! Hey, guys!" the Avenging Ninja said, stumbling over an empty pizza box. He waved a video playing on his tablet, so no one could actually see the images. "Get this! We get the witches to...dress like chickens."

"No wait," the Flying Mole said, tripping over the Avenging Ninja. "*We* dress like chickens. No, that's not right." He chugged another beer. "We dress up a chicken...."

"Let's call it a night," Tex said. "We're out of beer and pizza, and we've long been out of ideas. Y'all think about it, and we'll hash it out when we get back together."

"I second that," The Buzz said.

Cat-Man-Do raised a clawed glove and in a slurred, purring voice said, "How about this? We sneak into Arcane Sciences and swap out the geeks' black pens for blue."

The superheroes snickered. Several fell off the sofa like dominoes.

Willie guffawed. "Oi, that's brilliant, mate!"

Tex raised his mug. "Sounds like a plan."

The oval mirror of Hexaba's vanity framed her face as though she were the fairest in the land—which she was. She maintained that spell religiously. From a rack of bespelled combs, she selected a teak-colored one. The imbued magic came from the scales of different colored dragons. As Hexaba pulled the comb through her hair, her ruby tresses turned auburn.

"Eeek! I'm as big as a cow!" Phoebe screamed from across the room.

Startled, Hexaba dropped the comb. She reined in the urge to give Phoebe a wart on her too-perky nose. Roommates had to make allowances for each other.

"I've gained five pounds!" Phoebe cried. "How could that have happened?" She jumped off the scales and shoved the weights to the lower end.

Prudence, Phoebe's twin sister, looked up from reading

Vogue. "Two words—chocolate cheesecake."

Phoebe, her gaze wistful, licked her glossy pink lips. "Oh, yeah. That was great."

Hexaba traded the teak comb for a honey-colored one. She combed small shanks of hair, adding blonde highlights to the auburn. "If you ask me, it all went to your butt."

Phoebe twisted at the waist and tugged on her cutoff shorts. "You're right." She traipsed to Prudence's bed and flopped beside her sister. "May I borrow that magazine?"

Prudence flipped to a middle page. "What about her?"

"Definitely her." Phoebe spread the magazine on the frilly purple bedspread and sat on the picture. In a singsong voice, she incanted, "Across time and space, through every dimension, let my spell pass without intervention. With she who is thin and poor of health, allow me now to share the wealth. A sacrifice of flesh and fat is sent without a tit-for-tat. From myself I give five pounds, to settle on her where none abounds."

From across time and space, Hexaba faintly heard the scream of a supermodel discovering five new pounds on her rump.

Phoebe checked out her smaller, tighter derriere.

Prudence giggled. "Ooh, let's look for someone I can trade hair with. My ends are split something terrible."

Her own hair finished, Hexaba swivelled on the vanity stool. "Do that later. We have scheming to do." She swung her hair from side to side. "The highlights ought to throw the boys. They won't know what mood I'm in."

Prudence sighed. "Your hair always looks great. I wish my mother had thought to have ten dragons slain to make me a set of combs."

Hexaba grinned. Naturally, her mother had dumped the knight once he completed the task, and without keeping her promise to sleep with him. Anyone stupid enough to deliver the dragon corpses *before* receiving payment deserved to be stiffed.

Prudence flipped through *Vogue.* "So I presume your plot involves Mandrake?"

Phoebe dug through her clothes, tossing aside skimpier and skimpier tops until finding a halter that barely qualified as clothing. She peeled off her clingy tank top. "I thought you'd dump Drake after what happened last summer."

"I *will* dump him—but not until he's convinced he can have me. I want him so smitten that the news will crush his spirit." Hexaba squeezed her fist. When she finished, Drake would be a husk of his former egotistical, thoughtless self.

"I get it," Phoebe said. "A lesson in humility."

"I'm just doing his next girlfriend a favor," Hexaba said. "A man is only as good as his training."

"You're so thoughtful," Prudence said.

"I'm like a missionary for all women, out to teach men their place."

"I'd like to teach that Prince Valorous a lesson." Prudence purred. "He's yummy."

"Hands off," Hexaba warned. "He's my next project."

"But I saw him first," Prudence said, "while you were oohing over that giant fly-boy."

"You mean The Buzz?" Hexaba shrugged. "I'd hoped he'd be a challenge. Now, I'm just giving his name to our freshman witches, for practice."

"Then you admit I saw Valorous first."

"Forget it, Pru," Hexaba said. "I've already put my plan into motion. After meeting Drake in Bramblethorp, I 'happened' to run into Valorous. If both boys do as I asked—which they will— we'll have live entertainment all year."

Phoebe bounced, nearly jiggling her pert breasts out of the tiny triangles. "Don't keep us in suspense."

Hexaba gave her roomies an evil smile. "I've challenged the boys to get rid of each other."

"You asked them to *murder* each other?" Phoebe whispered, her brown eyes alight with excitement.

"I didn't specify. Giving slack to their leashes adds interest to the game."

"You are so wicked," Prudence said. "I'm jealous."

Hexaba motioned toward her vanity stool. "Come on, Pru, let's see what I can do with your hair. I think you'd look drop-dead gorgeous with raven black curls."

Prudence settled onto the stool. "Don't make me too drop-dead. I don't want the men dying before I'm through with them. Zombies make such boring dates."

CHAPTER SIX

Greasy smears where superheroes had splattered into the Student Union streaked the plate glass. Eventually, the drodent cleaning crew would get around to washing the tall windows. Drodents shirked their duties as they once shirked their studies. Nasty-tempered imps prodded them to work—usually with an electric cattle prod.

Gilbert tagged alongside Dex, chattering about the fine weather, how interesting his classes were, and on and on. When his roomie gave high praise to Dr. J & H, Dex smirked. Obviously, Gilbert had only met the Jekyll half of J & H's "split" personality. Dex found Professor Hyde to be the more motivating instructor.

On the Student Union's lower floor, signs for an Environmental Conquest picket lay against a wall. One sign proclaimed: "It's our world! We can pollute it if we want to!" A banner read: "If (insert the higher being of your choice) liked trees, man wouldn't have axes and chainsaws."

The second floor housed a relaxation and snack area. Big screen televisions with Direct-to-Earth-and-Beyond satellite occupied every corner. Overstuffed leather couches and beanbags lay in an arc before the massive screens.

One TV showed Mexican soap operas, a campus cult favorite. On weekends, when there were no *telenovelas*, fans reenacted episodes in bad Spanish.

A thud and rattle shook the chamber. Another white-clad superboob bounced off the plate glass. No wonder the imps hadn't bothered making the drodents wash the windows. Until those spandex-wearing goody-goodies learned to navigate *around* large objects, cleaning was pointless.

In the far corner, carts offered foods from the known dimensions, and a few unknown ones. A beefy superhero in black tights and a tank top bought enough to feed ten normal-sized people.

A scantily clad witch clung to his elbow. "Are all your appetites so healthy?"

Dex grimaced. The only polite thing a witch ever asked a scientist was, "Have you finished my physics homework?"

Sexy witches lounged everywhere. None noted Dex's passing. His spine stiffened, along with other parts. Someday, when he became a world dictator, he would have ten such luscious babes clinging to him and hanging on *his* every word.

Dex and Gilbert passed a group of black-robed student sorcerers, shouting and shaking their fists. On the TV, a broom rider zipped by and made a goal. Half the sorcerers cheered while the other half called "foul." Dex rolled his eyes. Sports were for the brain-numb.

"All right!" Gilbert said. "I love a good match. Who's playing? And, uh, *what* are they playing?"

"Who cares?"

"Dex!" Drake waved from a table with a prime view of the colliding superheroes. As Dex and Gilbert approached, Drake said, "I thought you'd enjoy *this* sport."

A sign lay on the table. Beneath an upward-pointing arrow, Drake had printed: "Safe Landing Through Here." He adhered the sign to the glass with chewing gum, then waved his arms and muttered nonsense. The sign swelled until the most dim-sighted superfreak could see it from the new quad.

"I love it," Dex said.

Drake pushed a chair toward Dex then dragged his own closer. "Why trust to random chance when one can guide it?"

"Aren't we sitting in the aisle?" Dex asked, watching the student traffic from the food lines to the tables.

"They can go around. We're not invisible," Drake said.

Jeffrey zipped past Drake. "Hello, Gilbert."

"You know each other?" Drake asked.

Gilbert nodded. "We sit together in Zen and the Path to World Domination and in Moral Corruption 101."

Drake stroked the scruffy beard he was so proud of. "I forgot about the freshman core classes."

"You 'forgot' because I earned a higher grade than you in Moral Corruption," Dex said.

"By half a point," Drake retorted.

"You should see the girls in our classes," Jeffrey said. "They're gorgeous."

"Enjoy it while you can," Drake said. "After freshman year, you'll never see another *witch* in your class. Word to the wise, don't call them 'girls' to their faces."

"Don't say that behind their backs either," Dex added, not wanting to be outdone in mentoring. "Witches have ways of finding things out."

Gilbert and Jeffrey settled in. Their heads close, they whispered and snickered worse than teenage girls.

"Jeffrey is a different person around Gilbert," Drake said. "Your roommate is a good influence on him."

"Sorry," Dex said. "I'll tell Gilbert to knock it off."

"Thanks. Now, about our plan. I have a few ideas as to where we each went wrong."

"I've given it some thought as well."

"The problem is—" Drake pressed his finger to his moustache-obscured lip and nodded toward an approaching hero.

The prince pranced with two witches in tow. The gentlemanly boob balanced all three of their trays.

"Watch this." Drake stuck out his pointed bootie.

The hero walked right into the freshman-level trap. He stumbled. Trays flew straight up. The witches' salads tossed in midair. The hero's cheesy potatoes and gravy-soaked meatloaf splattered over Dex and Drake. Stumbling and weaving, the hero caught the tray and plates. The plastic cups, however, pelted Dex and Drake before clattering to the floor.

Dex scooped seafood gumbo from his lap and plopped it onto the table. "If I'd wanted something to eat, I'd have gone through the line."

Drake brushed meatloaf from his shoulder. Cheesy potatoes clung to his goatee and corn speckled his hair.

"A thousand pardons." The prince set down the trays and whipped out a lacy handkerchief. He wiped gravy from Dex's glasses. "It was an accident."

"I'm sure." Dex glared at Drake through greasy streaks.

Drake waved off the prince's fussing. Not a golden curl on the prince's head was out of place. Not a speck of gravy stained his shirt. The witches' clothing—what there was of it (and where they weren't clothed was glorious)—likewise remained spotless.

After the prince and his entourage headed back toward the serving lines, Drake leaned forward. "That, Dex, illustrates our problem. I believe the witches are helping the heroes. Witches keep a protection spell around themselves at all times—ever since Salem. The spell prevents all manner of inconveniences."

"Like hangings and burnings?"

"Like passing carriages splashing water. Or flying food."

"Why would the witches' spells protect heroes?"

"They *wouldn't*—unless the witches cast protection spells on the heroes as well."

"The witches weren't anywhere around when our pranks failed. You're looking for excuses."

Drake stared hard at several tights-clad princes. "Perhaps you're right. I sense no magic auras around those ne'er-do-bads."

"We just need better planning," Dex said.

"What do you have in mind?"

Reluctantly, Dex admitted, "I'm working on it."

From behind, Gilbert oohed and whispered, "Cool. Do you think they'd let me audit the class?"

"You can't," Jeffrey said. "It conflicts with Cultivating Hazardous Plant Life."

Gilbert sighed. "You're right." A moment later, he was oohing some more.

Drake snatched a booklet from Jeffrey's hand, flipped to the front and read aloud, "College of Valor, Honor, and Justice for All—Curriculum Catalog." He flapped the pages at Jeffrey. "I told you to dispose of that."

"You always say, 'Know your enemy.'" Jeffrey kicked at the floor with his slipper.

Curiosity, the main trait of a good mad scientist, needled Dex. He sidled around the table. "Let's have a look." At Drake's disgusted expression, Dex added, "It might give us a laugh—or an idea."

The catalog was divided into two degree programs: Hero and Superhero. "Harumph, " Drake said. "If we don't eradicate this plague from our campus, they'll soon each demand their own college."

Dex skimmed the superhero courses. Freshman classes included *Flying without Airplanes*. Dex smirked. Most of the students he'd observed were failing that one. *Fighting Atop Moving Objects*; *Property Damages and Your Legal Responsibilities*; *On Becoming a Multi-Millionaire (at the least)*. Dex's eyebrows rose; maybe some cross-curricular education wasn't a bad idea.

A course title snagged his imagination: *Costume Design for the Sewing Impaired*. With a little sleight-of-hand swapping, those spandex-wearing pansies could be so humiliated they'd never show their faces on campus again.

"Do you see what I see?" Dex asked.

Drake nodded enthusiastically.

"Costume Design," Dex said, as Drake said, "Battlefield Horsemanship."

"What?" they said simultaneously.

"No, what you said," they said in chorus.

"I said," they began in unison, then finished, their voices overlapping, "Costume Design," and "Battlefield Horsemanship."

"My idea is better," they said together.

"Mine is." They glared at each another.

Dex waved his hands. "We're supposed to be collaborating."

"Very well," Drake said drily, "tell me your idea."

"If you're going to ask in that tone, I'll do it without your help."

"I would rather work without your undermining efforts as well." Mandrake's gaze narrowed. For an instant, he almost looked malevolent, but Dex wasn't about to compliment him.

Dex folded his arms. As his mind raced through permutations

of his idea, it dawned on him that he could use Drake's unique talents. Sleight-of-hand swapping lacked the efficiency of a spell. Moreover, by sneaking into the classroom, Dex stood a greater chance of being caught.

Drake's expression also changed from stubborn to malleable. Speaking together, they said, "But we did agree to collaborate."

"To increase our odds of success," Dex added.

"Not that we couldn't succeed on our own," Drake said, "but, as Professor Malfeasant says, 'Luck favors conspiracy.'"

"Wasn't he burned at the stake last year?" Dex asked.

"Several times. But he has tenure."

University tenure was a powerful thing.

Dex thrust out his hand. "Partners?"

Drake sniffed down his nose, but gripped Dex's hand with his forefinger and thumb.

"All I'll need from you is a swap spell," Dex said. "Assuming you can handle it."

Drake sneered. "Easily. I need something more complex from you—assuming your simple mind is capable."

"Try me."

"I need a mix of hormones and vitamins suitable for bringing mares into season."

Dex affected a superior air he hoped exceeded Drake's earlier one. "No problem. I'll slip into the chem lab for the ingredients."

Drake bowed his head. "Until I hear from you then."

Dex called over his shoulder, "Come along, Gilbert."

"What about my catalog?" Jeffrey asked.

From the corner of his eye, Dex glimpsed Drake rolling the catalogue and thumping Jeffrey's head.

Wondering what would most embarrass a superhero, Dex scurried across the tiled floor. Gilbert jogged behind him.

Two witches approached, their lithe hips swaying. Flashes of belly buttons mesmerized Dex. Sweat beaded on his forehead. He shook off the urge to crawl at their feet and beg to serve them.

One day, *they* would serve *him*. Dex wiped away drool. What a glorious day that would be. It would rank only second to the day he conquered a world. No, wait. Strike that—reverse it.

A week later, Dex and Drake met in a sunny, tree-lined glade behind Champion Field. There, Drake had hidden two dozen mares, wild horses summoned from the distant plains. Originally, Drake had stashed fifty mares in the sorcerer's quad, but Blackie, their dragon mascot, escaped from his dungeon and ate half before Drake could lure him away.

The scientists' mascot, Professor Chimp, caused far less

trouble, and at times even aided the college. Several times, Professor Chimp had substituted for absent instructors. On some topics, such as genetics and evolution, he had a fresher and more personal take. Professor Chimp began as Dr. Moreau's experiment to debunk Darwin's Theory. In the end, even Dr. Moreau wasn't sure what he had proven.

"What's that?" Drake pointed at the playbills Dex carried.

"When you see the costumes I've made for those prancing super-dolts, you'll understand. For now, can you magically post these around their quad?"

"With a wave of my hand."

Dex waited expectantly.

"Actually, it will take several waves." Drake grabbed the handbills. "While I do that, you can administer your concoction to my mares. I trust you brought it."

"It's in my backpack. Out of curiosity, couldn't you have *brewed* something? I never thought you'd rely on science."

Drake mumbled, "I flunked monster husbandry." Louder, he snapped, "Who cares about turning cows' milk sour and making calves two-headed?"

From a scientific standpoint, Dex thought it sounded interesting.

Drake ambled up the gravel path, handbills tucked under his arm. Dex injected mares with the supercharged hormone and vitamin mixture. The mares raised their tails and pranced about in an agitated manner.

By the time Dex finished, Drake had returned from posting the phoney playbills. They herded the mares toward Champion Field. Where the dummy dragon once stood, wide chalk lines marked boundaries on the field.

Two sides, princes versus knights, were mounted and ready for a mock battle. Golden tabards covered the princes' armor while knights wore silver. Prince John of the Moors rode between the lines, carrying a lance with a green flag tied to its grip.

Prince John shouted, "Make ready, gentlemen." He pitched the lance in the air. It flew in a large arc, then drove into the dirt. The green flag fluttered from its quivering grip.

Both sides charged.

Shouting and waving their arms, Dex and Drake rushed the mares. The mares raced into the fray.

The charging stallions raised their noses, battling tugs on their reins. Hooves pounding, they veered toward the mares. Stallions bit at other stallions, vying to get ahead. Some bucked their riders, unseating princes and knights.

Dex raised his palm, expecting a high five. When Drake stared in confusion, Dex said, "I'll explain the practice later."

Princes wobbled atop their mounts, which attempted to mount the mares. Unseated knights chased stallions chasing mares. Others, too embarrassed to meet Prince John's gaze, milled about inspecting their armor. Not a sword or lance clashed in the scheduled mock battle.

Guffawing, Dex and Drake fell to their knees. A flash of gold momentarily blinded Dex. Above them, Prince John of the Moors sat astride a calm horse. Sunlight glinted off his golden armor. His gaze pierced them. "You two again?"

This time, he sounded less congenial.

"How can your horse ignore this—" Dex asked.

"This equine orgy?" Prince John smiled. "We older and wiser princes know the value of a well-trained gelding. Now come with me to Dean Corleone's office."

"What, no thanks for our hard work?" Dex asked.

"Don't misunderstand, boys"—that last irked Dex and he glared while Prince John continued—"I laud your efforts to welcome us, but this time, your intentions, however noble, could have injured students and cost us several horses. Fortunately, this is an advanced class. I'd hate to imagine what would have befallen less experienced horsemen."

Drake's expression shifted from confusion to frustration. Dr. J & H couldn't have changed faster.

Prince John marched them to Dean Corleone's office. Having never been there, Dex was curious—though just morbidly so. Rumors claimed the dean had an appetite for living flesh. Standing outside the office door, Dex wondered how literal a "chewing out" they might receive. Drake looked close to exploding from tension.

Prince John rapped on the door then pushed it open. "Asmodeus, do you have a moment?"

The dean growled, "Always for you, John."

The prince recounted Dex's and Drake's transgressions. Dean Corleone listened, only his dull-eyed stare betraying his boredom.

Dex's gaze locked on an eye-shaped portal frame of a multi-hued metal. Colors shifted and flowed across the frame's golden surface. Dex longed to examine the metal more closely, but the dean's stern gaze held him in place.

Once Prince John finished, the dean said, "I'll take care of the matter, John."

Dean Corleone rose. His human complexion darkened to green. His eyes bulged and glowed a fiery yellow. Horns tore through his forehead. Blood wept from the wounds. The stench of brimstone rolled off him in a hazy cloud.

"Do you two realize the trouble you caused? I should rip out your esophagi and make suspenders with them."

Smiling, Prince John nodded then slipped from the chamber.

Once the door closed, the dean's stench retreated. His horns shrank to nubs and his bulging eyes assumed the look of man with high blood pressure. Dean Corleone winked. "Nice job. Next time, try not to get caught. If anyone asks, you've been given detention and put on probation."

Drake paled, an impressive feat given his pasty complexion. Not that Dex's skin was familiar with direct sunlight.

"It won't affect our class rank, will it?" Drake asked.

The dean grinned, his fangs gleaming. "Only in the best way. Rid me of these *noble* pests and your GPAs will experience a sudden jump."

"I don't suppose we could get that in writing?" Dex asked.

The dean's complexion darkened. The horn nubs grew. Drake grabbed Dex's arm and dragged him from the office. As he closed the door, he called, "We understand. Thank you, sir."

In the outer hallway, Drake rattled Dex's narrow frame. "Are you mad?"

"Of course."

"Even so. You never make an agreement with a demon *in writing*," Drake said. "Do they teach you nothing in Arcane Sciences?"

Dex snorted. "They teach us demons don't exist, that it's all smoke and mirrors."

"There's certainly a lot of smoke," Drake conceded. "Anyway, how do you explain Dean Corleone?"

"He's an anomaly." Dex wiggled his eyebrows. "Did you get a look at that portal frame? I've never seen metal like it before. I'd swear it was...liquid."

"An immense power that chilled my soul emanated from inside the portal," Drake said. "But with the dean breathing down my neck, I couldn't sense its nature. Next time I'm in the Dark Arts library, I'll research portals and see what I can learn."

"Let me know if you find anything," Dex said.

In the lobby, a drodent pushed a broom across the floor, leaving a semi-clean wake. Another rubbed a window with a dry rag, smearing dirt around. Three more napped under a potted shrub.

Loudly, Dex said, "Do you hear that, Drake?"

He nodded. "Sounds like a cattle prod being charged."

The drodents lurched back to work.

"Since we have the dean's approval," Dex said, "it's time you lived up to your end of our bargain."

Behind a dense bush, Dex had hidden a cardboard box containing the results of his sewing efforts. They carried the box stuffed with pink satin, tulle and feather plumes to the new quad. Not a student was in sight. Heroic-types never skipped class.

Dex and Drake crossed a grand courtyard. In the center stood a three-story, pyramid fountain. Water spilled down its sides into a square pool. Statues of kings and angels stared from the corners. Beyond this waste of concrete rose the superheroes' skyscraper frat house and the heroes' castle with a hundred pennants snapping in the wind.

Harsh-sounding steam whistles assaulted Dex's eardrums. "Is that a calliope?"

Drake pointed between two flowering trees. "The noise is coming from that monstrosity."

Dex sputtered. "A-a carousel! I don't believe it."

"Perhaps that's where the dumber-than-usual princes learn to ride." Practically salivating, Drake pointed at the castle. "Solid gold turrets. What a waste of precious spell components."

"I'm sure it's paint."

"I'm sure it's *not* paint."

Between class buildings, Dex's phony playbills ran along the stone walls in those annoying lines where the same poster repeated endlessly. Dex grinned. "I like it."

"I thought you might," Drake said.

They slid between bushes and a classroom building. What few glimpses Dex snatched through the windows left him queasy with envy. The superheroes had state-of-the-art computers and lab equipment. It wasn't fair.

They peeked over a window sill.

"This is the class," Dex said.

Inside, twenty superheroes were pulling on the gaudiest display of colors Dex had seen outside of a prom.

Drake cast a spell and the classroom babble could be heard outside—or maybe in their heads. Dex didn't know.

"I wish *I'd* thought of turquoise and purple," a superhero said. "The contrast emphasizes your biceps."

"I wish I hadn't used a lightning bolt," another said. "Does anyone else think it's been overdone?"

A dozen hands raised.

Drake poked Dex. "Open the box. We should do this while the instructor is out of the room."

Dex cut the masking tape sealing the box.

"Those garments are hideous," Drake said.

"Thanks." Dex pulled out a pink ballerina tutu, tights and fluffy epaulets. "I got the idea from 'Swan Lake'—except I call my production Flamingo Pond." He chuckled. "You think they'll like the costumes?"

"Let's find out." Drake flapped his arms like a goose and

muttered some gibberish. The ballerina costumes vanished. An instant later, they reappeared on the superheroes and their own costumes materialized in the cardboard box.

Dex rifled through bullet-proof tights, metallic capes, gaudy gauntlets, and ridiculous cowls and helmets.

"What are you looking for?" Drake asked.

"Armadilloman's costume." With its flexible, yet hard material and articulated ridges across the back, the suit promised to be an incredible feat of engineering. On reaching the bottom, with the last helmet in hand, Dex gave up. Then he realized he held The Buzz's fly helmet. *All right!*

From the classroom, dismayed superheroes cried, "Hey! What happened?"

And, "This is not my beautiful cape."

And, "These are not my spandex tights."

And, "Hey, this tutu won't come off!"

Drake chuckled. "That's a bonus spell. The tutus *will* come off...eventually."

One superhero squealed in delight. "Ooh! This is *way* better than my original design."

"Great, Balletboy likes the outfit," Dex muttered.

"So? The rest look *suit*ably miserable," Drake said.

Dex groaned. "No puns, okay?" Before he thought too hard, he pulled on The Buzz's helmet. The stench of sauerkraut and jalapeño sausages assaulted Dex's nose. He gagged and tears welled. No wonder The Buzz could fly. He was full of gas.

"We should make good our escape," Drake said.

"Relax. We have time to play—er, study. Besides, I want to see their instructor's reaction."

"Yes, because having the instructor around has proven so *beneficial*," Drake sneered.

Inside the helmet, buzzing filled Dex's ears. A green light flickered on. The enormous, bulbous, insect eyes held a dozen small screens, divided into dozens of smaller pictures. Each screen segment displayed varying angles and degrees of detail. In one, Dex saw all of Champion Field, in another, a single knothole on a distant tree.

Cool! I want one. But Dex knew better. "Never get caught holding the evidence" was a corollary of the university motto, "*Nulla Corpus, Non Crimen*"—"No Body, No Crime."

Drake snatched off the helmet. "Play dress-up later."

The costuming instructor, a matronly woman, entered the classroom. She glared through wire-rimmed spectacles at her students. Almost every superhero stood with arms wide and shook his head.

One pirouetted, arms arched overhead. "Call me Tutu

Tornado, a devastating force of dance."

"How do you explain this?" the instructor demanded. "Plagiarism—or more specifically being *caught* plagiarizing—is taken seriously at this university."

Being *caught* plagiarizing was grounds for being turned into a drodent or thrown into a fiery pit of Hell—depending on Dean Corleone's mood. Too bad those provisions of the admissions contract didn't apply to the superbozos. The stupid court had decided those punishments were too "onerous" and "subject to abuse."

Dex smirked at Drake. "Do you think they'll get expelled?"

"It would be a good start," Drake said.

CHAPTER SEVEN

Drake strolled from the Student Union into the noontime glare. Sunlight grated on his nerves. Before the heroes came, the university dimension had far more gloomy days. No doubt those lousy do-gooders were to blame for the disgusting cheer.

A cool hand touched Drake's neck. He whirled as Hexaba jumped away, laughing. Her honey blonde hair, a tricky indicator, could mean she didn't care to be studious, or that she felt like luring in her prey, then destroying it. Or it could just be Tuesday.

"How is your plot progressing?" she asked sweetly.

Definitely the "lure and destroy" mood.

"Those pranks should have worked," Drake snapped. "The second one technically did."

Hexaba's eyes taunted him. "The time-honored lament of the failed villain. I thought you capable of better. Certainly, *I'm* worth better."

Ah, ha! Drake knew the proper response to this one. "You deserve the best—which is why you'll give me another chance."

"You? You can't even manage to *not get caught.*"

Drake had no answer to that. "I have class, Hexaba."

"That remains to be seen."

"I *mean* I have Advanced Summoning class," Drake said. "You can grind my spirit to dust later."

"Am I grinding you to dust?" She ran a hand down Drake's back, then cupped his buttocks. "You feel pretty solid to me."

When Drake recovered his scattered thoughts, he said, "So you may treat me as a toy while I must keep my hands to myself?"

"At last, a man who understands the rules." Hexaba patted Drake's cheek. "If you want me, prove your worth. Rid the campus of those virtuous prigs." She gave Drake a gentle shove. "Hurry or you'll be late."

Drake glanced at the clock on the Student Union tower. *Four minutes!* He raced to the Dark Arts quad.

Drake hauled open the class building's oak door. As he stepped on the flagstone floor, the building shimmered and shook, then teleported. The hourly "Campus Rearrangement Program" discouraged tardiness—and loitering on the grounds. According to rumor, reappearing buildings squashed a dozen students each year.

A basilisk hall monitor slithered through the corridors, yet another tardiness deterrent. Six student sorcerers, petrified while running, decorated the halls.

Drake ran to Advanced Summoning. He slid into a seat at the back as the bell tolled its last note.

Amid demons' skulls and black candles, informative posters decorated the room:

Demons are not your friends. Keep them inside the summoning circle and yourself outside. Make friends elsewhere. Or better yet, don't bother.

Don't dress demons in funny outfits. This only enrages them.

Professor Manfred the Malfeasant burst through the door and stalked to the podium. His robes billowed like an impending storm, and his age-lined face was scarlet. He tossed a rolled parchment on his desk. All in all, Professor Malfeasant seemed in good humor. Then he huffed a fiery stream onto the scroll. The magic page remained impervious to destruction. "We suffer outrage upon outrage from those weak-willed do-gooders and now this!" he roared.

Drake felt a tremor of unease.

"My young sorcerers, I bring bad news." Professor Malfeasant grabbed the scroll and crushed it as though it were a hero's windpipe. "The addition of the College of Valor, Honor, and Justice for All"—the professor spat the name with another gout of fire, singeing the facial hair of a front-row student—"has enraged the Innermost Circle of Benefactors. Some even threatened to withdraw their endowments. At their request, the Board of Trustees is sending auditors to investigate possible misuses of funds and the effectiveness of the core colleges under Dean Corleone's guidance."

Drake raised his hand. "Professor, did Damian the Depraved threaten to withdraw his endowment?"

Damian's generosity came with dodgy strings, but his money had built a wing of the library, not to mention a splendid new torture chamber. His endowment also funded Drake's scholarship.

"Yes," Malfeasant said. "Damian the Depraved, Sorian the Supercilious—even Barbie the Barbarian. All claim the terms of the endowments have been violated. It's a potential fiscal disaster."

"Will this be on the test?" Nestor the Nervous asked. Professor Malfeasant glared. Undeterred, Nestor's hand hovered in the air. "Why do we need endowments?"

Steam rose from Professor Malfeasant's neck. "Endowments fund the grounds keepers, who keep the strangling vines, black mold and those cursed daisies at bay; the funds pay for housekeeping staff and cafeterias—"

Scardos the Scary muttered, "We could lose the cafeteria."

"—your scholarships, classroom spell components, laboratory paraphernalia, such as cauldrons, mortars, pestles, sacrificial animals, treats for Blackie and so on."

"Then what's my tuition pay for?" Nestor persisted.

"Silence! If the auditors make a bad report, our college could be forced to sharply reduce enrollments, or even close."

"So we'd have to transfer?" Nestor asked.

"No." Malfeasant's flat tone sent a chill through Drake. "Those students who don't make the cut will wash out."

Horror tightened Drake's chest until he could hardly breathe. He couldn't, *wouldn't* become a drodent—not after all his hard work.

Malfeasant drew a deep breath. The singed student cringed, but no fiery breath was forthcoming. "All is not bleak. If the auditors discover nothing improper, that is, if we use the endowment funds only for the evil activities for which they are intended and if you students demonstrate competence, perhaps the benefactors ruffled feathers can be smoothed."

Drake relaxed a notch. He couldn't imagine Dean Corleone allowing the auditors to see something they shouldn't.

"While the auditors are here, I expect everyone to be on their top behavior." Malfeasant pointed a gnarled finger at Nestor. "I expect *you* to remain in your dorm room."

Professor Malfeasant thunked a spell book onto the podium. "Today, I will demonstrate major demon summoning. While a goat suffices for most demon summoning, to command a major demon, a human 'goat' works best." Malfeasant pulled the grade book from his desk drawer. The book stuck out its leathery bookmark tongue at the class. "Who has the lowest class average?"

The book smirked. "Torrence the Terrible."

"Rat fink," Torrence mumbled.

"Come forward, Torrence."

"Uh, I hurt my leg in Escaping From Angry Mobs class," Torrence said.

"Excellent. I don't need you to *move*." Malfeasant waved his wand. Torrence disappeared, then reappeared inside a silver pentagram surrounded by an ebony circle.

"A-are you s-sure th-this is s-safe?" Torrence stammered.

"Certainly—oh, for you?" Malfeasant said. "Of course not."

Torrence scrambled up, but a wave of the professor's wand knocked him back down. "No, no, Torrence, don't strain your injured leg. Now, this double-walled pentagram is suitable for containing demons smaller than an elephant."

Torrence squeaked.

"An African elephant or an Indian?" Nestor asked.

"Arcturian. Now, class, which demons are best summoned when the blood candle is on the sigil of Gormosh?" The professor pointed to Ungmar the Unimaginative, whose GPA was .03 above being in the pentagram himself.

"Demons of blood corruption, howling insanity, flayed flesh, ur, and something nasty, but I forget what." Ungmar ducked down.

Professor Malfeasant smiled. "Yes, perhaps one of those will be appropriate for our *next* summoning."

Ungmar gulped.

Malfeasant drew a jagged-edged dagger. "First we draw blood from the sacrifice to gain the demon's attention."

"B-blood?" Torrence's eyes bulged.

"You won't even feel it. Hold still."

The professor levitated the dagger. It drifted into the pentagram. Torrence cringed and yelped as the dagger cut a shallow slice down his arm. Malfeasant lit candles at each point of the pentagram, then stepped back.

"I summon Zemiah, Demon of Disastrous Dates."

The class gasped in horror.

Sickly green mist filled the pentagram. A sulfurous stench flooded the room. Torrence scooted to the edge of the encircled star. Sweat streamed down his face. When a bulky, ram-horned shape solidified in the mist, Torrence's sweat puddled at his feet—at least, Drake hoped it was sweat.

"Pr-professor?" Torrence's voice wavered.

Drake was glad he had sat in the back. This way, he could beat everyone back to the fraternity and have first pick of Torrence's possessions.

Laughter rumbled from the demon. "I am Zemiah, Demon of Disastrous Dates. Fear me, mortals, for I can prevent you from ever getting laid."

Every sorcerer shuddered. A fate worse than death.

The demon's bulbous yellow eyes locked on Torrence and it sniffed. "Ah, delicious virgin blood."

Torrence stiffened. "Am not."

"Are too," the demon jeered.

Zemiah stepped toward Torrence, who curled up like a pill bug. A clawed hand reached out and grazed Torrence's robe. Torrence's body dissolved, then reappeared in his seat. He collapsed in a quivering mass onto his desk.

Roaring, the demon turned on Professor Malfeasant. "How dare you summon me, then cheat me out of my sacrifice! Once I break your puny wards, I'll assure that certain of your body parts never function again."

"You think that's a threat at my age?" Malfeasant chuckled. "Begone!"

The demon disappeared with a pop and a whiff of brimstone. Malfeasant tutted at a still-shaking Torrence. "Perhaps now you'll devote more attention to your studies. Any other year, I would have sacrificed you as an example to others. But those blasted heroes had student sacrifices banned. I don't know how I can be expected to teach under these conditions."

That was one change that Drake favored.

Having met with Professor Malfeasant after class, Drake trudged back to the Fraternal Order of the Black Sash. The professor had made it painfully clear that, as the Dark Arts' top student, Drake was responsible for impressing the auditors. Actually, Malfeasant made it clear failure would *be* painful.

As if Drake's day weren't bad enough, his chamber remained dust-free. He suspected Jeffrey secretly cleaned just to annoy him.

Malice raised his furry black head from where he lay curled atop the wardrobe, then twitched his tail.

"What a day, Malice." Drake threw himself onto his bed. The auditors were trouble—his own personal trouble. "What a black foul day." He glared at the cat. "And I mean that in the worst possible way."

Malice jumped onto Drake's bed and rubbed against him.

<<Pretending to comfort me won't get you tuna,>> Drake said. <<I have more important concerns than your stomach.>>

<<Drat.>> The cat stalked off.

To impress the auditors and to stay first in his class, Drake needed a magnificent project for the Spring Project Fair. Sadly, great projects required money.

Scardos's parents pampered him with a large allowance. No such luck with Bane the Black-Hearted. When Drake's younger brother had been taken hostage, Bane refused to pay his ransom. King Marcus was stuck with the pest until the king paid *Bane* to take his son back. No, Drake's father wasn't the solution to his financial woes. If only there were a spell for making money.

Thinking of spells tickled the back of his mind. Leafing through his animation spell book, Drake scanned until finding "Weather Animation." The perfect project. It required a magic staff, which he didn't have, several gem stones, which he didn't have, and powdered spell components, which he didn't have. All required money, which he didn't have. Perhaps he could sell his precious plastic water pistol. Surely Dex would understand.

Drake decided to see Dingo. The fence's motto was: "If I don't have it and it can be stolen, you'll have it within a week—or it's half price."

Drake crept through the alley between brick buildings. He hated techno towns. Nuevo Pittsburgh was little better than a hive of filth and petty thievery.

At the alley's dead end, a bulky form swathed in hooded cape leaned against the wall. The glowing ember of a cigar reflected in his red eyes.

"There was a farmer had a dog, and Dingo was his name-o," Drake said, giving the code phrase.

"Who's looking for him?" a voice rasped.

"Mandrake the Malevolent," Drake said in his ominous voice.

"Oooh, alliteration. Scary." Two furry arms below the one holding the cigar pushed aside the hood.

Drake drew back at the sight of Dingo's furry face. His long snout curled into a smile, baring yellowed fangs. A tangled mane of snakes writhed atop Dingo's neck. As they swayed from side to side, their beady eyes tracked Drake's movements.

Some students whispered that Dingo was a demon. Others claimed he was an escaped experiment from Arcane Sciences. Whatever his origins, Dingo was the best fence in the university dimension. He was the only fence in the university dimension.

"I need to sell something," Drake said.

"Then I'm your creature." Dingo drew deeply on his cigar, then spewed a cloud of smoke. "Let's see the goods."

Keeping an eye on the snakes keeping an eye on him, Drake produced his water pistol. "What will you give me for this?"

The snakes arched back. Dingo choked and spat out his cigar. He stuck one of his right paws into his cloak pocket. "Yep, I have a quarter."

"A quarter!" Drake fumed. "This is genuine *plastic*."

The snakes hissed in laughter.

"I was being generous," Dingo said. "I can get one new for a dollar."

Drake shoved the pistol back in his pocket. He would turn Dex into a maggot for this humiliation. How many times had Dex made Drake feel indebted for this gift? It was contemptible. It was despicable. It was...brilliant.

Dingo waggled his forked tongue. "You want the quarter or not, kid?"

"No, thanks. It won't make a dent in the amount I need." Drake sagged in defeat.

"Hey, kid, do you need money?"

"Does Dean Corleone have horns?"

"Sometimes. Look, I need a few items myself," Dingo said. "You scratch my back, I'll scratch yours."

"You want me to scratch your back?" This was beginning to sound dodgier than the terms of his scholarship from Damian the Depraved.

Dingo rolled his red eyes. "I thought you college kids were smart. I need some things from the Dark Arts campus. In return, I'll get you those project supplies."

"How did you know—"

"Don't ask questions, kid. Just go with it."

A slow smile spread across Drake's face. Cheating and stealing were university traditions. "What do you need?"

CHAPTER EIGHT

Valorous held Sir Eloquence's gaze. The instant his vassal's eyes shifted, Valorous swung his long sword. It clashed against Sir Eloquence's blade, then Eloquence parried. The maneuver completed, they stepped back for their critique. Valorous expected the sort of praise lavished on him since birth.

"Technically adequate, Valorous," Prince Raymond said. "But you lack style."

Valorous scowled. Prince Raymond wouldn't know style if it bit him in his tights-clad buttocks.

"Keep practicing," Prince Raymond said then turned to assess Prince de la Realm's lunges and thrusts.

With the instructor's attention diverted, Valorous rested his sword point on the floor of the cavernous practice chamber. "Tonight, Eloquence, I shall woo the fair Hexaba."

Sir Eloquence pressed his lips together. "Are you sure that's a good idea? She's a witch."

"Precisely." Valorous studied his palms. *Damn! Callouses. How lower class.* "Why do you think Mandrake's father is so hard to eradicate?"

Sir Eloquence shrugged. "He's a powerful sorcerer. He commands a huge army of faithful minions. Plus, he invested well, so he's rich."

"No." Valorous made a slashing gesture. "Father has driven off sorcerers with more skill, money and men than Bane the Black-Hearted. It's his wife, the Dread Witch Tiffany Owens of Beverly Hills. Her power bolsters his, making them almost unbeatable."

"True, a good husband and wife team is hard to beat, but Hexaba *is a witch*," Sir Eloquence repeated as though Valorous were slow. People always talked to Valorous that way. They all underestimated his brilliance. Yet *he* would be the one to drive Bane—and Mandrake as well—from his family's land.

"Yes, Hexaba is a witch, meaning I'd rather have her by my side than Mandrake's," Valorous said.

"That won't be easy," Eloquence said. "She met with Mandrake in Bramblethorp. I fear I spied on them."

"I know all about that," Valorous said. "Hexaba said she was breaking up with him."

"I'm sure that's why she had her tongue in his mouth."

"You will not speak of my lady that way! I will win her heart and Mandrake will suffer."

Eloquence smirked. "So this is about sticking it to Mandrake."

"It's about who has the power!" Valorous stomped his booted foot. The sound echoed off the high ceiling, drawing Prince Raymond's attention. Valorous whipped his sword up to middle guard, and Prince Raymond turned away. Valorous lowered his blade. "King Jonas of Bremia accomplished much good with his witchly wife—drove out the ogres and dragons, not to mention overpriced solicitors."

"You forget—King Jonas got his witchly wife to drink a love potion that turned her into a good witch."

Valorous stroked his downy beard. "You have a point."

Without magical assistance, the narcissistic witches never performed a good deed unless they benefitted. Valorous needed a potion.

"So you'll drop your plan to woo Hexaba?" Sir Eloquence asked, raising his blade to a high attack.

Valorous assumed Prince Raymond was looking and raised his sword to a defensive stance. "Of course not. First, I'll woo her with a serenade. Then, I'll ask her to accompany me to the Winterball. There I will slip her the potion."

"But the Winterball isn't for months."

"It may take that long to find a white wizard to brew the potion." Hexaba was worth it. She was hot, smart, powerful and hot, which must be why Mandrake sought her above all other witches. Valorous sighed. Hexaba was really, *really* hot.

Sappy instrumental music wafted through Hexaba's window. What moron dared to annoy her? If he didn't know witches liked their beauty rest undisturbed, he soon would.

"Who's making that racket?" Prudence asked. With a word, she lit a candle on her night stand.

Still wearing a satin sleep mask, Phoebe sat up. "Hey! Some of us are trying to sleep."

"It's probably for you, Hexaba," Prudence said. "That wretched noise sounds like Valorous's minstrel."

"Valorous's minstrel is courting you?" Phoebe asked.

Hexaba sighed. "No. That idiot prince just can't go anywhere without his sycophant audience." She pulled on her fluff-trimmed slippers, then drew on her sheer negligee's matching transparent robe. "Light all the candles. I want to give the prince an eyeful."

In a silky, golden tenor, Prince Valorous sang some horrid love song about muskrats.

Phoebe giggled while Prudence lit every candle in the chamber. The twins crept up behind Hexaba.

"Don't block my light," Hexaba said. With so many candles behind her, her sheer gown hid nothing. To start, Hexaba leaned coyly out the window, revealing only her head and shoulders.

"Prince Valorous," she cooed. "Is that you?"

Mercifully, he stopped singing. After a wave of Valorous's lacy cuff, the minstrel, too, ceased making a racket. "Fair Hexaba, the sight of you makes me swell with love."

Hexaba resisted the urge to ask exactly what swelled. No doubt the prince would say something effeminate like his heart.

"Dear Valorous, it's late. Though your song moves me—"

"I wrote it for you," Valorous said.

That impertinent twit interrupted her! No matter. In time, she'd crush him all the flatter. Pretending he hadn't irked her, Hexaba called, "For me? Truly?"

"A man in love is incapable of subterfuge."

Hah! Men in love were notorious liars, if only to avoid offending their hearts' desires.

"Dear Valorous, climb the trellis. For your sweet serenade, I want to reward you with a kiss."

"Your wish is my command."

If only.

Valorous dismissed his minstrel. He smoothed his black locks, adjusted his lace collar, flung back his cape with a flourish, then started up. When he was one-and-a-half stories above ground, Hexaba pushed forward so the window framed her entire torso under the sheer-as-glass gown.

Valorous's gaze stayed fixed on the trellis as he made slow progress upward.

Hexaba huffed, then called, "Valorous?"

He looked up; men were so easy. She shifted her shoulders so her breasts rubbed against the negligee, then gyrated her hips. Valorous's eyes popped wide open. He gasped, then his hands slipped off the trellis. He landed on his back with a glorious and satisfying thud.

Hexaba leaned farther out the window and shrieked with false concern. "Are you all right?"

Valorous stared skyward, his gaze unfocused. In a squeaky voice, he said, "I'm fine."

"Won't you try again?" Hexaba purred. Behind her, the twins giggled.

"Not tonight, beloved. I need to ice my back—or maybe take a cold bath." Valorous hobbled into the darkness.

Hexaba closed the window. "That should give him something to dream about between now and the Winterball."

"So you plan to make him suffer while you're there with Mandrake?" Prudence asked.

"Oh, no. Drake will suffer while I'm there with Valorous. Valorous can dream of what he *thinks* he'll get after the dance."

"So you've accepted Valorous?" Prudence eyed the two dozen red roses and gold-embossed invitation to the Winterball.

"He needs to grovel first."

"I'd let him have some, if it were me," Prudence said.

"You'd let anyone 'have some,'" Hexaba said.

"But he's cute."

Hexaba shrugged. "True, he's easy on the eye. If he begs, maybe I'll make it a night to remember. Assuming he's well-enough endowed to make it worth my while."

"I hear he's very rich," Phoebe said.

"Not that kind of endowed," Hexaba said.

"Oh." Phoebe's hazel eyes turned thoughtful and sad. "A lot of good-guys are *under*-compensated, if you know what I mean."

"Why do you think they spend all their time trying to prove themselves?" Hexaba said.

"There *is* a spell to enhance their shortcomings," Prudence said. "But take it from me, The Buzz doesn't need it. Neither does Tex."

"Prudence!" Phoebe said, hands on her hips. "How many superheroes have you slept with?"

"Just fifteen."

"And you didn't invite me?"

The twins faced off. Recognizing trouble brewing, Hexaba jumped between them. "Beauty sleep now. Fight later. You can settle your differences tomorrow during your Dueling exam."

"Perfect," they chorused. Prudence added, "I'll turn you into an envy-green toad."

"I'd like to see you try."

Grabbing pillows, they lunged at each other.

Asmodeus paced around his office. Thus far, Mandrake and Poindexter had failed him. Mandrake's botched animation spell had, of all horrors, *helped* the do-gooders. At the last faculty meeting, Prince John of the Moors suggested more cross-curricular courses and intercollegiate cooperation. Word of this was all Junior needed to gain more support on the board.

To compound matters, the cooks in the Student Union cafeteria demanded a pay raise. They complained it took longer to prepare meals for the do-gooders, with their demands that the cooks wash the food *and* their hands—as if that weren't redundant. Those finicky, pampered musclemen only ate fruits and vegetables from this epoch—like a little mold ever hurt anybody.

His pet desk rumbled. The lines in the wood moved,

animating the normally sleeping face. One of the benefits of a pet desk was the amount of time it spent sleeping—even more than cats. The desk's knothole eyes opened, exposing dark voids that served as irises. Woodgrain formed into a mouth. The desk spat out an envelope.

The seal smoldered and dripped bloody wax. The fresh parchment retained a demonic scent—a bad sign. Only the worst news was delivered on skin flayed off a demon's back.

Asmodeus's demon ridges popped out, punching holes in his Armani suit. He snapped the seal, eliciting a groan from the parchment. The board chairman's scrawled handwriting read: *Auditors selected. Sending them and a supervisor to review your finances and effectiveness. Expect their arrival now.*

The Nexus glowed, waiting on word from Amadeus. If he didn't admit the auditors, he would only annoy them by forcing them to take a more circuitous route to the university dimension.

Reluctantly, he said, "Admit them."

From the oscillating spiral poured a stream of cowled wraiths and stodgy scientists, many of the latter alumni. Lucifer, Jr. exited last.

Asmodeus ground his sharpening teeth into a smile. "Welcome to the University of Dark Arts and Arcane Sciences."

Junior plucked a document from his paisley brocade vest. "This explains everything."

Asmodeus reached for the pages, but Junior yanked them back.

"Allow me." Junior cleared his throat. Self-carboning pages in several colors fluttered in his grasp. "The Board of Trustees, Alumni Association, and Innermost Circle of Benefactors hereby call for an audit of the University of Dark Arts and Arcane Sciences. Asmodeus Corleone, head dean, shall consider said notification the first step in the process to remove said dean from said office, should the findings of this"—waving the multi-page document, Junior indicated himself and the tattered wraiths and decrepit scientists—"delegation prove unsatisfactory."

Lucifer, Jr. plopped the document on the desk's corner, away from its woodgrain mouth. "If you'll be so good as to sign here, Asmodeus." He tapped a line marked by crossbones.

Asmodeus jabbed his finger and signed in blood, as was standard for all demonic contracts and formal documents. It was also considered classy for party invitations and graduation notices.

"Excellent." Lucifer, Jr. flipped to another page marked with several crossbones. "Here. And here. Here, too. Don't forget here. And lastly, here."

Asmodeus sighed.

"Oops!" Junior smiled from horn to horn. "You missed one."

Asmodeus squeezed more blood and signed. Junior added his own bloody, acidic signature as witness. Before Junior's signature burned through the copies, he yanked out the canary yellow pages and handed them to Asmodeus. He waved to cool the smoking documents, then tossed the packet onto the desk mouth. "Board of Trustees."

The desk swallowed the document.

"How long can I expect the auditors under cloven hoof?" Asmodeus asked.

"Until they find what they're looking for."

"You mean, until they find something on me." Asmodeus renewed his vow to keep Junior from getting his hot claws on the university and the Nexus, whatever the cost. The universe was screwed up enough.

Junior swept a hand toward the wraiths. "You know the board's Infernal Affairs Department." He then waved toward the old scientists. "And the Accounting Department. First, the auditors will survey the campuses of Dark Arts and Arcane Sciences, then they'll interrogate students."

"What about the College of Olde Wyrd Charms?" Asmodeus asked.

"This isn't a witch hunt. The board only interested in the university's primary colleges."

Asmodeus snorted. The board members just feared Selena, dean of the College of Old Wyrd Charms. The last board member who looked sideways at her was now a leech. "I'll show our guests around. Shall I open the Nexus for your exit?"

"I'm not going anywhere, Asmodeus," Junior said. "I'm here to review your personal books." He rubbed his palms together.

"Rubbing your palms is a bit hokey, don't you think?"

"My hands are cold. This place is like an ice cavern."

"Sorry," Asmodeus lied. "While you're here, you'll have to make do without Hellish temperatures. Our students aren't damned—not yet anyway."

"You coddle them, Asmodeus. The students owe us—er, the university—everything. Without the knowledge we impart, their pathetic lives would amount to no more than a stint in jail or an early death. We give them the tools to conquer worlds."

"True, but turn up the furnace and those students will be crispy-fried husks. At that point, their knowledge is academic."

"When I'm in charge—I mean, should I be placed in charge—there'll be changes. Education won't be free."

"We charge tuition."

Junior waved a hand in dismissal. "I'm not talking about paltry tuition fees. I'm talking about service—blood, sweat and useful labor. Naturally, scholarship students will serve longer terms. It's only fair."

"What sort of terms are you talking about?" Asmodeus asked.

Junior plopped into Asmodeus's chair and propped his hooves on the desk. The knothole eyes glared at him. "Five to ten years compulsory labor toward achieving the board's goals."

"You mean, they'll be in someone's private army." *Your private army.*

"Every army needs intelligent and talented leaders."

Asmodeus snorted. "Not in my experience."

"Is this so hard to grasp, Asmodeus?"

"Oh, I understand. You and the board intend to use the students then toss them aside. Five to ten years isn't a 'tour of duty,' but rather, how long you estimate they'll survive."

With a university-trained, conscripted army and the Nexus to take it anywhere, the consequences would be catastrophic. Using the Nexus to spy, the army could arrive at the most opportune time. While a brilliant and evil plan, it went beyond reason. Orchestrated, controlled evil was, well, wrong. And boring. Evil was best served through chaotic devices. Chaos was good. Chaos worked. Chaos made the universe a more interesting playground.

Junior's plan would destroy the university. Not that he cared that no new students would come here after he implemented his plan. The student sorcerers and scientists attending now were bound by blood oath—no transfers or dropouts. Once Junior had them in his army, once he controlled the Nexus, he wouldn't need the university anymore.

Smoke tickled Asmodeus's neck. His temperature rose until his skin blistered. He would be damned all over again if he'd let Lucifer, Jr. destroy everything Asmodeus had spent centuries building.

CHAPTER NINE

Normally Dex took copious notes in class. Today, however, he doodled in his notebook. A cluster of balloons turned into a mushroom cloud. Too bad all the cool bombs had been created. A colossal explosion would make an impressive entry for the Project Fair.

Currently, the Jekyll personality of Dr. J & H lectured beside an overhead projector. Images of color-coded molecules and chemical equations shone on a water-spotted screen.

Thick glasses made Dr. J's big eyes even bigger. Curly black hair stood out as though charged by static electricity. A perfectly pressed lab coat draped his scrawny frame. He was a nerd's nerd.

His voice barely above a whisper, Dr. Jekyll said, "...thus the rules governing valence *can* be broken, given sufficient expenditure of energy. Bonding therefore occurs beyond the molecular level, as shown here in green...."

Dex copied the molecule on the screen. Long ago he started carrying colored pencils, since Dr. J & H's lecture notes made little sense without the appropriate color references.

"...by fusing these blue electrons with the red...."

Isaac leaned close and whispered, "You get purple."

"*If* red and blue are pigments," Dex countered.

"Good point." Isaac slipped Dex a folded note.

Dex arched an eyebrow. Note-passing was forbidden—and so third grade. He opened it anyway. Isaac always printed with a number 2 graphite pencil, and wrote in tiny, perfect italics. *I've worked out my motor problems. This year, I'll have my female robot. What's your project? I.*

Though Dex knew he would regret it, he flipped over the note and wrote: *A male robot would be far more marketable. People expect men to perform manual labor. You don't think you can replace women, do you?*

Isaac wadded up the note.

Dr. Jekyll's head snapped around at the noise. He squinted, shrugged, then put up a new transparency showing a more complex formula. "We begin with three oxygens...."

Isaac quietly tore off another scrap, then scribbled furiously. In perfect italics, the note read: *At least I'll have a date for the Winterball.*

The last student in Arcane Sciences to have a date was Egbert. It made him a legend, even though his date, a girl from Nuevo Pittsburgh, was knock-kneed, with a huge hump, and hadn't bathed in a year due to a soap and water allergy. She was also nearsighted—which explained why she accepted the date.

Considering the facts, Dex almost scribbled, *Make one for me too*. But the time spent working out the parameters of his ideal woman would be better spent developing his own project.

Yet a robot woman would be as beautiful on the inside as on the outside—lovely whirring motors and miles of colored wiring. Her organs would be motherboards, her life pulsing through IC chips and diodes. And her brain—a computer with AI programming. Or better still, pseudo-AI. Dex felt suddenly uncomfortable. *Curse you, Isaac.* This wasn't where Dex wanted his thoughts.

Isaac smirked and mouthed, "Jealous?"

Dex huffed, then scooted down one seat. Fortunately, Elton, the seat's assigned occupant, was absent.

Dr. Jekyll squinted at Dex. "Elton? When did you get here? You're late!" The professor's tones grew dangerously harsh.

"Dr. J, it's me, Poindexter. I dropped my pencil"—Dex raised his blue pencil—"and it rolled away. When I picked it up, I must have scooted down a seat."

Dr. Jekyll nodded, disturbing his crop of wild hair. "Fine, Poindexter. Please take your assigned seat."

As Dex complied, he shot Isaac another glare and mouthed, *No more notes.*

"And no talking, Poindexter," the professor said.

Dex glared harder at Isaac.

Isaac grinned and resumed writing in his notebook. Dex couldn't resist a peek. Isaac was making a list entitled, *Robotic Laws*: *1. All robots will love Isaac. 2. All robots will honor Isaac. 3. All robots will obey only Isaac.*

Dex returned to doodling mushroom clouds. In his head, he heard a thunderous explosion. He even felt its rattle. A foul smell shook him from his reverie.

At the front of the classroom, a stinking cloud the color of yuck enveloped Dr. Jekyll. He waved his hands, saying, "...results in a failed valence."

Whatever had been mixed—Dex would borrow someone's notes later—left a greenish-brown film on the professor's face and his glasses. Dr. J cleaned the lenses while pacing along the front row.

"What"—the professor drew out the word, an indication that he planned to spring a question on an unsuspecting student—"should I have used"—he shoved on his glasses—"to facilitate the bonding mechanism"—he whirled and pointed—"Pryce?"

Pryce, a chubby nerd, quivered. Dex didn't know why Pryce sat on the front row, since he rarely had the answer.

Pryce blubbered, "M-magnesium?"

Dr. Jekyll shook his head, his big eyes sympathetic. "Think, young Pryce. Think back to seven minutes ago...du...dutro...."

Pryce scratched his head. He sweated so badly, Dex could smell him. "Du...du...," he repeated uselessly.

The classroom door cracked open. A wild-haired, hunched geezer with inch-thick glasses poked his head inside. At once, Dex felt the chill of a bean-counter's presence.

Dr. Jekyll glanced toward the auditor in the doorway. Dr. J swallowed, visibly uncomfortable, then leaned over Pryce.

Pryce shut his notebook so quickly everyone knew he was guilty of something. Dr. Jekyll snatched Pryce's notes. The longer he stared at whatever Pryce had written, the harsher he breathed. He peeked back at the auditor, who took notes on a worn-edged clipboard.

Dr. Jekyll's words came out slowly and with emphasis. "Pryce, are you working on another assignment?"

Pryce looked around, wild-eyed.

Nonchalantly, Dex turned the page of his own notebook, hiding the doodles.

"I repeat, is this an assignment for someone else's class?"

"Sorry, doc, I—"

The auditor grunted in disgust. *Great,* Dex thought. *Pryce is ruining our report.*

Dr. Jekyll's unruly curls frizzed into something akin to a writhing Afro. His newly bloodshot eyes bulged. Purple veins throbbed at his temples. Hair sprouted over his chin—not quite a beard, but more than a five-o'clock shadow. Warts popped up on his nose and forehead. His hands swelled to the size of sledgehammers.

His now-misaligned teeth made him spit. "How dare you sit in my classroom and do an assignment from another professor!"

The auditor nodded in approval. Dex sighed in relief. Good ol' Dr. Hyde. He had impressive people skills.

Dr. Hyde threw a blue marker at Pryce—a rather calm reaction from this side of the professor's personality.

Pryce scrunched down, as though trying to hide in his own blubber. "The assignment was late. Dr. Marvin said if I didn't have it by this afternoon, he'd disintegrate me."

With one meaty hand, Dr. Hyde grabbed Pryce's collar and hauled him from his seat.

"Yiiiiii!" Pryce flew across the room like a dirigible with a broken steering mechanism. He crashed against the screen. For an instant, the colorful molecule shone across him. Pryce struck the floor, then lay whimpering in a lardy puddle.

Knuckles dragging the floor, Dr. Hyde shambled toward Pryce.

The auditor slipped out and the door swung shut. Luckily for Pryce, the bell rang.

Dr. Hyde straightened and ran a hand through his hair, realigning the frizzy shock to calmer, more distinct curls. His features lost their primitive squareness and returned to the familiar wild-man look of placid Dr. Jekyll.

Everyone bolted from their seats.

"One last thing," the professor called.

Everyone froze.

"In dealing with the auditors, remember: Never volunteer facts which may prove detrimental to the university." No one moved until Dr. J said, "Class dismissed."

Dex bustled through the packed halls, intent on spending the afternoon in the library. The doodled mushroom cloud danced before his eyes. He needed a bomb that had never been done. Bigger than fission, more impressive than fusion. It had to be—

"Dex! Wait up!" Gilbert's cries drove the thoughts from Dex's mind.

He groaned. "I almost had it." Remembering his mentoring grade, he asked, "What bit of trivia has stumped you this time?"

From Gilbert's horrified expression, this emergency might be genuine—unlike the one from this morning, when he'd been frantic about having a number 2.5 pencil instead of a number 2.

Gilbert bounced from foot to foot, then grabbed Dex's shoulders. "I went to the Student Union supply store, but they don't carry any. Said I had to get my own. Said everyone does."

"Get what?"

"A cadaver for Dr. Frankenstein's class." Gilbert practically foamed at the mouth.

Dex snorted. "Is that all?"

"I need a *human* cadaver, Dex."

"What other kind is there?"

"Well—where do I get one?"

Dex didn't remember being that stupid even in grade school. "You could kill someone."

Gilbert choked as though he'd swallowed his tongue. "I could never commit murder."

"It's not murder if you hire out and kill a person whom someone else wants dead. Then it's a contract. Plus, you make some extra spending cash."

Gilbert paled. "You're saying I should *assassinate* somebody?

That's so wrong."

Dex threw up his hands. "You'd rather autopsy the guy while he's alive? Because—"

"No. I'd never. That's...madness."

"No, it's vivisection and that's a sophomore class."

Gilbert looked ready to swoon. "I just can't kill anyone."

"You mean," Dex corrected, "'I can't kill just anyone.' Word placement can convict or clear you—but you'll learn that in Corrupt Politics."

"I believe I said it right *my* way."

"Sissy." Dex considered letting Gilbert figure this one out for himself. But Gilbert looked so pathetic that Dex relented. "When do you need the cadaver?"

"Thursday."

"You're bothering me *now*? We've plenty of time." Before Gilbert could start another tantrum—or worse, faint—Dex said, "Tonight we'll go to the cemetery and look for a corpse. Okay?"

"That'll be great, Dex. You're a lifesaver. I mean it."

"Don't gush. It's unbecoming a mad scientist. In the meantime, if you want to expedite matters, look at last week's obituaries. Or, if you wise up, check out your classmates' GPAs." At Gilbert's confused look, Dex explained, "It's the easiest way to move up in class rank." At Gilbert's horrified expression, Dex shrugged. "Whatever. It's your grade."

"Are obituaries posted on the bulletin board?"

"No, you nitwit. You'll need a newspaper from either Nuevo Pittsburgh or Bramblethorp. They have the closest cemeteries."

Dex grinned maliciously at a sudden thought. He could demonstrate his bomb on one of the local towns or villages. Real devastation always impressed more than modeled devastation.

CHAPTER TEN

"Your behavior is unacceptable," Dean Malodorous ranted. News of Drake's failed dragon-dummy prank finally had filtered up to the dean of Dark Arts. "I expect better from a student of your caliber. Prince John of the Moors came to *my* office." Dean Malodorous's voice dropped to a growl. "That snarky do-gooder *commended* me for training such courteous and helpful sorcerers. I still haven't eradicated the stench of his virtue."

Drake found the dean's office ripe, but not from Prince John's virtue. The dean wasn't called Malodorous for nothing.

"Do you know what Prince John wanted?" The dean's voice squeaked. "Thanks to your *philanthropy*, he proposed that a student sorcerer animate their target dummy every week. 'It will be good for both our colleges,'" Malodorous mimicked. "'My students can train against a moving target while yours practice magic.' Dean Corleone actually agreed, probably to shut him up."

Malodorous leaned in close. Drake gagged on the dean's fetid breath. "You appear contrite. But we sorcerers are not in the business of training heroes to cut our throats. Select your punishment from the Cauldron of Shame."

Dread filled Drake as he trudged to the cauldron filled with tiny scrolls. Positioning his body to block the dean's view, Drake pocketed a fist-sized crystal ball, one of the items Dingo wanted, from a nearby table. Reaching blindly, Drake grabbed a scroll from the cauldron.

He unrolled the parchment. His flesh turned cold. "Brush Blackie's teeth? May I choose again?"

"Get on with it," Dean Malodorous snapped. "I suggest in the future you put your energies into a more appropriate outlet. You're fortunate the auditors haven't learned of your escapade."

He was also fortunate Dean Malodorous hadn't heard about the mock battle fiasco. Drake trudged into the relative clean air of the vaulted corridor. He clomped down several flights of stairs into the administration keep's dungeon. It was Dex's fault Drake had to face this punishment. *Dex's* laughter had attracted Prince John's notice. *Dex* told Prince John that Drake animated the dragon dummy.

Drake opened the round-topped dungeon door. The brimstone smell confirmed Blackie's presence. Evil sorcery always came with noxious fumes. They played hell with the sinuses.

A growl echoed through the dungeon corridors. Drake's heart pounded. More than one student sorcerer had lost a hand tending Blackie. He didn't fancy becoming "Lefty the Fourteenth."

He passed through the stone archway into the dragon's lair. The college treasury glittered in tempting gold piles. Even with his need, however, Drake wouldn't touch the coins. If anyone but Dean Corleone took a single ducat, Blackie would devour the thief.

Cake and cookie crumbs covered a table. Blackie had a ferocious sweet tooth. Drake grabbed a bucket of sulfur-and-mint flavored paste and a scrub brush. "Blackie? Here, boy!" He tried to whistle, but fear kept his lips from puckering.

A growl emanated from a shadowy alcove. Splendid. The dragon was in a playful mood. Blackie loved playing "crouching student, hidden dragon." After that, he usually played "bury the bone," never mind whether it was covered in flesh.

Standing within leaping distance of the exit, Drake said, "Come here, Blackie. I see you in that alcove."

Blackie's indignant roar shook the chamber. Drake swallowed his heart as it tried to leap out his throat. He should have remembered—dragons loathed being spotted while lurking.

"I *meant*...I heard your fierce growling. Come out, Blackie. It's time to brush your teeth. Let's clean those"—Drake gulped—"razor sharp fangs, shall we?"

He cringed at his groveling tone, but as Practical Fawning class taught, a wise sorcerer knew when he was outmatched.

The black dragon lumbered into the torchlight. Blackie stood as tall as three men. His cavernous mouth dripped with drool and his yellow eyes regarded Drake with suspicion.

Drake raised the bucket and scrub brush. "It's sulfur-mint, your favorite."

The dragon cocked its head. On a sweeter animal, such as a rabid Doberman, the pose would have been endearing.

"Think how shiny your teeth will be."

Blackie strutted over, each step shaking the stone floor. Dragons' vanity matched that of witches. The same sort of inane flattery worked on both. Until recently, anyway.

Blackie lowered his head and displayed an imposing array of foot-long, viciously sharp teeth. A gust of rot breath blew across Drake. He breathed through his mouth, then gagged. Now he tasted, as well as smelled, cow-and-cake dragon breath.

Fighting every survival instinct, Drake leaned into Blackie's cavernous mouth to scrub the dragon's back teeth.

"My, those are frightening," Drake said, trying to maintain

Blackie's good cheer. A dragon's mood could turn without notice. "Female dragons must battle for your company."

Blackie arched his neck with pride. The sudden shift nearly impaled Drake's chest on a fang. His heart pounded so hard he thought it would burst. Yet he *had* to do at least a cursory job. Resolutely, Drake resumed scrubbing.

"BRAAAP!" A belch burst from Blackie's gullet, engulfing Drake in the foulest stench he had ever suffered.

Drake gagged again. "Damnation, dragon, have you been eating your own dung?"

Fool! As he jumped free of the dragon's snapping jaws, Blackie's razor teeth scored Drake's hand. Drake threw the brush and bucket toward the corner, hoping to distract Blackie with a game of fetch. The ploy failed. Drake ran through the archway and down the hall. Suddenly, Escaping From Angry Mobs class seemed tame.

Drake jerked open the dungeon door and glanced over his shoulder. A cloud of fire billowed toward him. He slammed the door and jumped back. Tongues of flame licked past the cracks around the door.

Gasping, he doubled over, his hands resting on his thighs for support. His right hand throbbed, and blood trickled from the scrape. He could go see the campus witch doctor, Mumbojumbo, but Drake could shake a rattle and throw bones in the air, for all the good it did.

Straightening, Drake glimpsed himself in a mirrored sconce. His face was as pale as death, and a band of white streaked his black hair. Drake's heart still pounded. *Dex should be the one scared witless—*

Chuckling, Drake pulled an empty vial from his robe pocket and collected the fear-enriched blood dripping from his wound. He knew the perfect way to even the score with Dex.

Drake hid behind a non-man-eating shrub. Ahead, two wraith auditors dragged a screaming, struggling townsman between them. They floated toward an underfed patch of strangling vines and tossed the bedraggled peasant into the writhing, black-leafed tendrils. His screams died quickly.

"I told you this plant was starving," one wraith said in rasping tones. "Any healthy strangling vine would have toyed with him for an hour."

"Pitiful," the other wraith agreed.

Taking advantage of the distraction, Drake sprinted across the quad. Didn't wraiths ever sleep? Then again, they were dead, so probably not.

To achieve his planned revenge, Drake had to break into the

Arcane Sciences quad. Thorny wire, infused with the power of lightning, topped the stone wall surrounding the quad. No one could pass that way. At this late hour, the main gate to the quad was barred. In any event, Drake wasn't on the list of those approved to pass. Fortunately, he knew a secret way in.

The top fraternities had secret "after-hour" entrances—at least those in the original colleges had them. Drake doubted any fraternity in the College of Virtue needed such an entrance, as those pablum-eating do-gooders never broke the rules.

Drake knew the way into Gamma Ray Delta because one night in their first year, Dex got falling down drunk. Freshman curfew had passed, so Drake half-carried Dex back to his room via the secret entrance.

Remembering Dex's instructions, Drake started at the gate and walked clockwise, counting mounted carriage lights. At the thirteenth one, he stopped.

The secret entrance's security system had a retina scanner that admitted only members of Gamma Ray Delta. But Dex had blathered about a "back door." The nerds harbored the absurd fantasy that someday a witch would seek admittance to their pathetic fraternity. Not wanting to miss such a rare—and improbable—opportunity, they had programmed the scanner to admit anyone with a female figure.

Drake's injured hand throbbed as he cinched his robe to give the impression of curviness. He zapped away his facial hair, hoping it would grow back—he would hate to lose the evil aura it added to his presence. His long hair would help create the needed impression. From a bag, he took two balled wool socks and strapped them to his chest with a strip of cloth. Unsure of the scanner's sensitivity, Drake pulled out a tube of lipstick and applied it to his lips, then smeared more across his cheeks.

If anyone caught him in this getup, he would summon his own hole to jump into. He had memorized the spell, just in case.

The opening sequence to the secret door had to be done just so or an alarm would sound. Drake stepped onto the flat rock with his right foot, then raised his left knee as high as he could. He was amazed any mad scientist could open the entrance, with their bad coordination. Teetering, he laid his left index finger against his nose and reached for the knob atop the carriage light with his bandaged right hand. Three times to the left, four to the right, one left. How the idiot scientists thought a witch would figure out how to open the entrance mystified Drake.

The panel covering the scanner slid open. Drake bent one knee, puckered his lips and put his hand behind his head in what he hoped was a sexy pose. Green light swept across his body.

Drake held his breath. The door creaked inward. Clearly, the geeks had no standard of beauty programmed into their "back door." Drake slipped inside, shut the secret door and enchanted his boots to make no sound. A short tunnel led to the fraternity house.

To keep from landing official suspicion on himself for this prank, Drake thought it best to bespell all the geeks instead of just Dex. Besides, it would be more entertaining. He sneaked from room to room, collecting hair from every scientist's brush—or, in the case of those who didn't groom themselves, from sink drains. The snoring from many deviated septums covered any noise he made.

As Drake crept back toward the tunnel, a groggy nerd stumbled from his room. He settled thick-lensed glasses onto his nose. His gaze locked on Drake. "It's a miracle!"

Drake froze.

"Do not fear, my delicate flower," the nerd called in a fake nasal accent, starting toward Drake.

He'll wake the entire fraternity and I'll be humiliated. Worse, with the scientists' bad eyesight, Drake could be the victim of a pathetic gang wooing. He ran, praying he reached the exit before the geek roused the house.

"Ah, *la belle femme* witch *fatale*, she wants ze chase, yes?" the nerd gasped, his feet thudding in a galloping rhythm. Drake heard the hiss of an inhaler, then more galloping. "It will make ze passion for each other grow."

"Leave me alone, you pathetic geek," Drake said in a falsetto voice.

"Ah, she is shy," the nerd said, still galloping.

I'll show you shy, Drake thought, tempted to turn and pummel the amorous twig senseless.

"I will begin with ze wooing," the nerd said.

"I'm not that kind of girl!" As Drake ran, he spotted the tunnel. He skidded, turned and sprinted for the exit.

"Come back, *cherie,*" the nerd called. "Ah, *c'est l'amour.*"

On the way to the Black Sash Fraternity, Drake dodged two wraiths taking a whiny bridge troll's statement. The troll claimed he had been stereotyped and that not all trolls liked damp working conditions. He had applied to be a councilor.

Back in his room, Drake clunked his cauldron over the fire. Jeffrey stirred and rubbed his eyes. Without the glasses, Jeffrey's features were almost as disgustingly perfect as those of the chiseled pretty-boy heroes—except Jeffrey's unruly hair hung almost into his eyes. That boy needed a scar to make him look more evil.

"It's almost dawn," Jeffrey said. "What are you doing?"

"Repaying Dex for drawing Prince John's attention to me."

"You mean for getting you in trouble with Dean Malodorous." Jeffrey snickered. "How is Blackie?"

"Never you mind," Drake growled.

Jeffrey squinted, then grabbed his glasses. "Why are you dressed like a woman? Is that lipstick?"

Drake started. He had been so focused on his revenge, he had forgotten about his disguise. His face went hot. He pulled out the balled socks and threw them at Jeffrey, who ducked.

"Is there anything you want to tell me?" Jeffrey asked.

"No." Drake scrubbed off the lipstick and "rouge" with a handkerchief.

He filled the cauldron with premixed Spell Stock (Chicken Flavored) and dropped in the clumps of scientists' hair. He added a chunk of hair from his new white streak, then poured in the vial of fear-enriched blood. "Essence of terror, bound by my blood, send this fate to mine enemies' hood."

"That doesn't rhyme," Jeffrey said.

"It does on paper," Drake snapped.

The liquid in the cauldron bubbled. Fingers of green cloud drifted up. The streaky clouds floated out the window toward the Arcane Sciences quad.

"That should occupy them for a while," Drake said.

"Don't you mean Dex?"

"I thought I'd include all the lads at Gamma Ray Delta."

"Suppose they retaliate?" Jeffrey asked.

Drake's lip curled. "What can a bunch of second-rate tinkers do against magic?"

CHAPTER ELEVEN

A shriek yanked Dex from sleep. "Wha—?" he slurred. Why was someone screaming? Midterms were weeks away.

Gilbert shrieked again. "White! It's white!" He ran around the room, pausing to stare at any reflective surface. Clutching handfuls of hair, he slid across the floor in his socks and white sleep shirt and stopped before Dex's bed. "My hair's turned white!"

Dex blinked. So it had.

Gilbert screeched and pointed. "Yours is white too!"

"Calm down, Gilbert." Dex dragged himself from bed. Gilbert's panic had made him delusional.

"See for yourself." Gilbert pushed Dex toward the washstand with a sink and mirror.

The fraternity shared a single communal bathroom. Since no geek liked showering gym-style, the residents of Gamma Ray Delta had adopted a complex shower schedule to ensure privacy. This week, Dex had the shower on Monday, Wednesday and Thursday at midnight, two p.m., and eleven a.m. respectively.

"Look!" Gilbert said, then resumed stomping around like a madman.

"It's a shame your professors can't see you, Gilbert. You've finally got a good tirade going." Dex wiped his gummy eyes and settled his black horn-rims on his nose. His reflection had hair as white as his sheets were supposed to be. Lousy drodents. It wouldn't kill them to add bleach to the wash.

He grabbed a handful of wiry hair and tugged. It hurt. Not a wig, then. "Hmm. Our hair turned white overnight." Reality struck and Dex screamed, "Our hair has turned white!"

Tears streamed down Gilbert's cheeks. "I miss my soft brown hair."

"It was the color of dirty bath water," Dex grumbled.

"That's better than white. Worse, it's as stiff as wire."

Dex tried to run a comb through his own hair, but it snagged and tangled. He had to admit, it worked well for the look he wanted when he conquered his first world.

"Have we aged prematurely?" Gilbert asked. "I don't feel older. But my hair...." He sobbed and patted his hair as though that would make it better.

Amazingly, Gilbert raised a reasonable concern. Dex felt no

older. He did a deep knee squat. His knees popped and creaked. He fell over while trying to stand. That was normal at least.

"I think we're fine," Dex said.

"But what happened, Dex?"

It should have been obvious to anyone, but Gilbert, being Gilbert, had no clue. "The sorcerers did this."

"Or the witches."

Dex shook his head. Gilbert had much to learn about women. "Such a prank would require they acknowledge our existence. Ergo"—Dex liked that word; it made his conclusions sound more scientific, and it reminded him of breakfast waffles—"they're innocent."

Dex pulled on his bathrobe and led Gilbert into the hall. "I daresay," Dex said, "we're the first ones up. Which reminds me, why are you up so early?" He glanced at the clock. "Nine! In the morning?"

Gilbert shrugged his beefy shoulders. "I woke up hungry. I was going to sneak down for a sandwich, but I've lost my appetite."

Dex started pounding on doors. Mumbles and curses arose from behind each. Shuffling, stumbling and cursing preceded the opening of several doors.

"Is there a fire? Because there'd better be," someone said, poking his white-haired head through a door.

That was one.

"Who's the joker getting us up so early?" another asked, rubbing his statically charged white hair. He made two.

Members of Gamma Ray Delta rarely rose before eleven a.m. No important classes were scheduled before noon.

The first of many screams erupted. White-haired morning zombies staggered into the hall, bumping into doorframes and each other.

A thorough job. Dex might even congratulate Mandrake. It had to be him; only Drake knew how to sneak into Gamma Ray Delta and get close enough to cast a spell like this.

I wonder if he stood on one foot and touched his nose. Dex smirked. Even drunk, he'd made up some bullshit to mess with Drake's mind. But how did Drake get past the retina scan? That sneaky spell caster probably conjured a doppleganger of Dex.

Citing "tit for tat," whatever that meant—Dex was lousy at Latin—he had guilted Drake into showing him how to sneak into the Fraternal Order of the Black Sash. That knowledge soon would be very useful.

"Who did this?" someone shouted.

Gilbert piped up, "The evil sorcerers."

"What do they have against us?" Pryce asked, his many chins

quivering.

"They wanted to steal the plans for my girl robot," Isaac said. The white hair gave him a sort of crazed, reclusive author look.

"Don't be paranoid, Isaac," Dex said. "They want to make us look bad before the auditors."

"Yes," Lexington agreed. His GPA was a mere .00001 percentage point below Dex's. "No doubt they hope to make it look like some failed experiment."

"That's just evil," Gilbert said.

Everyone stared at him.

"Well, duh," Pryce said. That was low, to be duhed by a dullard such as Pryce.

"If we're the only ones who get a bad report," Dex said, "we may be the only college sanctioned or closed."

Lexington's expression grew determined. "Well, gentlemen, we can't allow that to happen. If we *both* receive a bad report, they can't close both founding colleges."

While Lexington's logic held some flaw, his cultured voice made everything sound, well, logical.

"Shall we leave a welcoming message for their auditors?" Lexington asked, grinning maliciously.

"You want to pass them a note?" Pryce asked. Apparently his lucid moment had passed.

A wicked glint shone in Isaac's blue eyes. "I think I know where you're going with this, Lexington."

"Going is the right word." Lexington motioned for everyone to follow. "Dr. Marvin's laser gun should do the job."

Nested Faraday cages covering the astronomy dome— formerly a source of great ridicule from students and faculty— had shielded the electronic equipment below from the Jokester's mini EMP. For once, Dr. Marvin's paranoia had paid off.

Dressed in lab coats over pajamas, the scientists of Gamma Ray Delta sneaked into the tidy astronomy lab. Dr. Marvin was meticulous about everything. Students had to angle their notebooks just so. Lefties learned to write with their other hand or be downgraded for being "inferior specimens." Although Dr. Marvin often threatened to disintegrate someone, no one had witnessed such an event, which just meant there was no evidence.

"What should we write?" Isaac asked.

Dex rubbed his chin. Gilbert did likewise, having taken to copying Dex's every mannerism. While an annoying habit, mimicry was the sincerest form of flattery. No, wait—it was just annoying. Dex slapped Gilbert's hand away from his chin.

"I'm trying to learn," Gilbert whined.

"I have an idea." Isaac switched on the laser. A warm, fuzzy hum filled the domed chamber. The power coursing through the massive machinery sent chills through Dex and raised goose bumps on his arms.

"I love lasers," Lexington said.

"Yeah," Dex said. "The awesome power of destruction is a thing of beauty." *Someday, I'll have an even bigger laser.*

A red beam shot out. Isaac swivelled the gun toward the evil sorcerer's quad. The beam raked the ground, leaving a smoldering furrow. He steered the beam upward. It melted stone and mortar, creating an *M* in chiseled, metamorphic italics. If this prank upset anyone important, the handwriting would implicate Isaac.

An hour later, the message on the sorcerers' wall declared: *Mad Scientists Rule; Evil Sorcerers Drool.*

Dex chortled. "They can't call it libel when it's true."

Everyone shook Isaac's hand. Pryce suggested putting the slogan on a T-shirt for the Spring Games. An unofficial contest for designing background art arose.

Lexington folded his arms. "Interesting slogan, old man, but you've given us away."

"I can fix that," Isaac said. A half hour later, he had added a parenthetical: *(Or So We've Heard).* "Now they'll think someone else wrote it."

"Doubtful," Lexington said, "but it creates plausible deniability."

As they tiptoed out of the astronomy lab, the quad clock tower bonged eleven times. Dex stopped, remembering the shower schedule. "Hey, this is Thursday, isn't it?"

Isaac nodded. "One day until our project proposals are due."

"Don't remind me," Dex grumbled. Knowing what he wanted and knowing how to go about it were two different matters. But the shower room was his and he was awake, so he may as well shower.

"Oh my gosh!" Gilbert wailed. "It's Thursday, Dex. And you forgot!"

Whatever it was, Gilbert had forgotten until now as well. "Forgot what?" Dex asked.

"My cadaver! I've got to have one *today.*"

"When's your class?"

"Four o'clock."

Dex rolled his eyes. Underclassmen—always panicking when there was plenty of time. "Fine. We'll go to the graveyard after I shower. But I wish you'd reminded me last night."

"I wish I had too." Gilbert wrinkled his forehead. "Why do *you* wish I had?"

"Dr. Frankenstein's first rule: Grave-robbing is more fun at night."

Dex drove the rickety mule cart into the cemetery. "We *would* be driving a truck, but those lousy heroes complained that trucks would spook their precious horses. Then the superheroes said our vehicles didn't meet California emissions standards. I ask you, are we *in* California?"

"I'm not really sure *where* we are."

"It sure ain't Kansas, Dorothy," Dex said.

"I know. I'm familiar with Kansas." Gilbert jumped off the driver's seat and patted the mule. "So what if we don't have a truck? It's not like we go that many places."

Dex climbed down. His lab coat pocket snagged on a protruding nailhead and tore. Then his foot slid on a mossy rock, twisting his ankle.

Dex clenched his teeth to keep from screaming. They were at a cemetery, and one never knew if anything might awaken.

Instead, Dex let out a tirade. "What's wrong with a little pollution? Do you realize how boring and unromantic a sunset would be without pollution? Does anyone think to compliment the various gases and dust particles in the air while gazing wide-eyed at a pink and orange sky? Well? Do they?"

"Dex," Gilbert said gently. "Next time I look at a sunset, I promise I'll praise the crap in the air. But for now, can we look for a cadaver?"

"*Look*?" Dex swept his arms wide. "They're everywhere. Pick a spot and we'll start digging."

He grabbed a shovel from the cart. Gilbert, looking a bit green, took the other. Dex glanced back, saying, "Don't forget the crowbar."

As they walked along the gravel path, Dex asked, "Did you read the obituaries?"

"You were serious?"

Dex swallowed a string of oaths. "Fine, we'll do this the hard way. Look for freshly turned soil."

"Huh?"

"You want a *fresh* corpse. Dr. Frankenstein always gives the 'Techniques of the Successful Graverobber' lecture in the first week of Autopsy for Beginners. Weren't you paying attention?"

"The first week kinda overwhelmed me. I'm not used to having so much information thrown at me."

Dex wondered what the brain-matter-to-cottage-cheese ratio was in Gilbert's head. "Follow me. And steer clear of any grave with a sorcerer's mark."

"Why?"

"Because you never know *what* they've buried, much less

whether or not it's dead. It's certain that if you disturb one of their marks, *something* will come looking for you."

"Ah. Good tip." A moment later. "Uh, Dex, what does a sorcerer's mark look like?"

Dex rolled his eyes.

They prowled the graveyard, heading for the freshest mounds. The first one looked promising—the death occurred a week ago.

"Lilian May," Dex read. "Looks like you're heading back to school, Miss May." Judging by her tall tombstone with an angel statue, she'd been wealthy. Meaning, she might have been buried with jewels. Dex salivated, imagining the wealth encircling her neck, wrists, and fingers. Suddenly, a *really* big bomb project seemed in his grasp.

Gilbert shook his head. "Digging her up wouldn't be gentlemanly. Besides, the body's gonna be naked for lab and I couldn't look at a naked dead woman."

Dex groaned. "Fine."

The next prime choice had been a minister and Gilbert didn't want to incur God's wrath. By Dex's reckoning, God must not have cared, since the minister died at age thirty-two from choking on a chicken bone. Of all things the man might be remembered for, someone included that tidbit on the tombstone. Ergo, having his parts reanimated might well be the most exciting thing to happen to the man. Yet Gilbert wouldn't see reason.

"Not him either," Gilbert said at the next fresh mound. When Dex gave a questioning look—although he always regretted knowing the reason—Gilbert said, "Dex, he has *my* name. I can't cut open a Gilbert."

At this point, Dex could have opened up the Gilbert standing beside him. "How about that one?" Dex asked, pointing.

Gilbert stared at Dex's fingers. "I thought you bathed."

"I did."

"You didn't clean under your fingernails."

This time, Dex did scream. "Like it matters? *If* you ever find a suitable cadaver, I'm pretty sure my fingernails will get dirty."

Gilbert wandered where Dex had pointed, to a grave under a sickly tree with more parasitic growths than leaves. According to the splintery slab of wood serving as a tombstone, the interred man had been hanged for murder.

"He'll do," Gilbert said.

Dex stabbed the soft earth with the shovel. He hauled out five shovelfuls before noticing Gilbert stood watching. "Aren't you going to help?"

"Oh, yeah." Gilbert gouged earth and flung it wildly. Most ended up on Dex.

"On second thought, this might go faster without your help,"

Dex said.

"If you say so." Gilbert lounged on the diseased tree's exposed root. "I've been thinking. Maybe we shouldn't have written that message on the sorcerers' wall."

Dex paused. "Excuse me?" He grabbed a handful of what had been clean hair—until now. "*They* started it."

"We have no real proof—"

Dex glowered. "Deductive reasoning is proof enough. Do you know how slow science would progress if we waited for solid proof before proceeding? Really, Gilbert. Sometimes you worry me."

"I must admit, the white hair suits you. Your rants are much more frightening now."

Maybe the sorcerers had done them a favor. Not that Dex would admit it to Drake—wait, yes he would. That would bug Drake even more. The longer Dex thought about it, the more he liked the idea of making it seem this prank was the greatest thing ever. Between helping the heroes train against dragons and making the scientists look even madder, Drake was well on his way to blowing his GPA.

"Dex? I have to be back by four."

"If you'd taken the first stiff, we'd be done—"

The shovel struck something hard. Dex scraped away dirt. Gilbert climbed down, then dragged out the box. He dug in the tip of the crowbar and pried the lid off the cheap pine coffin.

Stink rushed out, worming into Dex's sinuses. It raked at his eyeballs until Dex was sure they were bleeding. Gagging, his lungs threatening to collapse, Dex staggered toward the leaning wooden marker and clung to it. He wiped his eyes until they cleared enough to read the message carved into the wood. "Oh, hell. He's been dead a month. I'll wager Doc Frankenstein assigns you a corner all to yourself."

Gilbert shrugged. "We don't have time to dig up another. Do you think this'll affect my grade?"

Dex blinked. "Hell, yes! You'll be lucky to get a C-."

Gilbert's expression brightened. "Whoo-hoo! That's passing. For a moment, I was worried."

As Gilbert reached for the putrid body, Dex stopped him. Despite his senses pleading with him to back away, Dex examined the body. The definitely not-recently-deceased wore a ring and a fat gold chain. "All right. Loot!"

He snatched the jewelry off the decaying body. As they passed Lilian May's grave, Dex paused and bowed. Under his breath, he said, "I'll be back to check on you later."

Unlike Gilbert, Dex had memorized Dr. Frankenstein's ten traits of the successful graverobber. As Rule #3 stated, "The Dead

Can't Take It With Them, So They Shouldn't Have Tried."

CHAPTER TWELVE

A train screeched past.

"Whoo whee!" Tex exclaimed. "She must be barreling at a hundred miles an hour."

The Buzz's antennae tracked the train. "My fly senses read it at a hundred and thirty miles per hour." Thanks to his helmet, his voice sounded like he'd sucked helium then spoken through a walkie-talkie.

Cricket hopped up alongside them. Since developing his superhero identity, he no longer answered to "Mikey." Gadgets on his simulated-chitin costume made a chirping racket. "Actually," he said, checking his radar unit, "the train is moving at one hundred and twenty-nine point two miles per hour."

This week's guest instructor for Fighting Atop Moving Objects class, the famed Cloaked Crusader, called for attention. "Today, my stalwart students, we'll train atop that very train."

The train came around again on the oval track, then slowed to a brake-squealing halt.

A rope ladder unfurled from atop a boxcar. Already on the train roof stood the Cloaked Crusader's sidekick, Zap, wearing the most painfully bright yellow outfit Tex had ever seen. The Cloaked Crusader scrambled up. "Now, my law-abiding students, form an orderly line."

Tex and The Buzz climbed up first. Heat waves rose from the gleaming metal. Tex's armadillo persona loved how his armored shell warmed. The rest of him just felt sweaty.

"I've got to redesign my boots to withstand greater heat," The Buzz said. "My feet are blistering."

Tex tapped the toes of his huge cowboy boots. "Had these special made, to fit my feet and take the heat." The boots, the red-white-and-blue shorts patterned after the Texas flag, and the cowboy hat were all the "clothes" he wore in armadillo form.

From the ground, Cricket hopped and landed atop the boxcar. Several undeclared superheroes muttered, "Line jumper."

"*I* could have flown up," The Buzz said.

"We know," Tex said, glaring at his half-brother. "But you don't gotta show off for us."

Kachina-Man pulled himself onto the train roof, then hopped up and down, yelping, "Moccasins not thick enough!"

"They could have recommended insulated footwear in the

syllabus," The Buzz commiserated.

The Cloaked Crusader gathered the superheroes into a circle. "Watch and learn. Zap, assist me."

Zap and the Cloaked Crusader faced off. Arms out, they circled like wrestlers.

Then the Cloaked Crusader straightened. "Pair off and practice the basic circling maneuver. Four men per car."

"You and I can partner, Cricket," Tex said. After all, they were kin. "This'll be a piece of cake."

"Like our pranks?" The Buzz muttered.

Hairs on Tex's armadillo ridge raised and the plates shifted defensively. "It ain't my fault them geeks have their noses stuck so far into a book that they never noticed."

"The sorcerers didn't notice the prank we played on them either," The Buzz said, pairing up with Kachina-Man.

The Cloaked Crusader shouted, "Start her moving."

The train lurched forward. Tex wobbled and Cricket toppled over. His antennae whipped around while he flopped like a fish on a boat deck. Since hitting a man when he was down—even your little brother—was bad form, Tex waited until Cricket scrambled up. And promptly fell back over. And again.

In the meantime, Tex noticed paramedics waiting beside folded gurneys and medical cases. "I get the feeling we should have read that class waiver a little closer."

Giving whoops of pain as they hopped, The Buzz and Kachina-Man looked more like they were doing a rain dance than circling the enemy.

The train sped up. Grit pelted their faces. The wind whipped at Tex's shorts, then his hat blew off and rolled across the dirt. He swore. That was an expensive Stetson, custom made to fit his pointy armadillo head.

As the train accelerated, the wind grew more fierce. Though Tex's round back was aerodynamic, his flat underside caught the wind like a sail. It drove him toward the break between cars. He hunched, curling partway into a ball, lessening the wind drag.

Kachina-Man let out a string of Hopi curse words. Dangling feathers ripped free of his costume and blew away. When he looked up, the wind slammed into his huge mask, knocking him onto his back.

The train banked into a curve.

A thud made Tex glance back. An undeclared superhero had fallen off. Two paramedics stubbed out their cigarettes and ambled over to help. As the curve deepened, the Flying Mole tumbled off. Cat-Man-Do followed, his claws screeching against the metal. Then Mr. Gizmo hit the dirt.

By the time the train reached its starting point, Tex and

Cricket somehow had managed one uneventful circle around.

Shaken (not stirred) like martinis, the few superheroes remaining on the train wobbled toward the ladder. Only Wombat Willie seemed unaffected, scrambling down the rope rungs.

"Oi! That's more fun than wrestling crocs on a rolling log," Willie exclaimed. "Who's up for another go 'round?"

The Buzz wavered, then said, "To heck with climbing." He launched into the air, then spiraled down like a World War I aircraft shot down by the enemy. He crashed into a bush.

Paramedics wandered over to help.

"Maybe you oughta climb down instead of jumping," Tex said to Cricket.

Cricket clutched his stomach. "You read my mind."

The Cloaked Crusader scribbled class performance notes, then said, "Not bad for your first time. Next week, Jackie Chan's stunt choreographer will be your guest instructor. You'll be swinging from cranes onto a moving train a split second before it enters a tunnel. Good times, good times."

The Buzz hobbled up. "Tell me I heard that wrong."

"We're going to need more danged paramedics," Tex said.

Drake swallowed a lump of nervousness and headed toward Hexaba sunbathing on the commons. Her skimpy shorts showed off her shapely rear, and her halter top was untied to avoid tan lines. Drake salivated at the thought of pulling away the scrap of fabric to reveal her pert breasts in their bewitching glory. But that act would assure he finished the semester as a newt.

At least Hexaba was alone. Working up the nerve to ask a witch out was hard enough. Asking her in front of her giggling, witchy little friends was impossible.

Drake's shadow fell across Hexaba's glorious body.

"You're blocking my sunlight, you creep—Oh, Drake. It's just you."

Just? Drake winced inside. "May I sit?"

She propped herself on her forearms, holding the halter top on, then tossed her chestnut hair. "As long as you don't block my light, I don't care what you do."

Drake gave her a wicked grin as he sat. "So, if I don't block your sunlight, I can do *anything* I want?"

She groaned. "Don't try to be glib. It's just sad. What do you want?"

Brown hair must indicate a bitchy mood. Drake swallowed another lump. "I was wondering...that is, I was hoping...." He took a calming breath. "Would you do me the honor of allowing me to escort you to the Winterball?"

Hexaba gave him a mock-touched look. "That's the second-sweetest invitation I've received. Too bad you didn't ask sooner. Valorous's invitation came ages ago—and with gifts—so I accepted."

Drake managed not to smack his forehead. How could he have forgotten gifts? That explained why she was pretending she had a date with Valorous. No way would Hexaba go to a dance with a do-gooder prince who wore more lace than she did—although Hexaba was more of a skintight leather kind of witch.

"Come on, Hexaba." Drake touched her cheek—as much contact as he dared without permission. "It'll be fun. We can turn the other girls' dresses vomit green like we did last year, or maybe—"

Hexaba jerked away. "I *told* you. I'm going with Valorous."

"You were serious?"

"I can't be seen with a pathetic loser like you."

"Loser!" Drake huffed. "Have you seen the mad scientists' hair? That was *my* work of genius."

Hexaba cast him a disdainful look. "I didn't ask you to play childish pranks on inconsequential dweebs. I asked you to rid the university of the heroes."

"So your solution is to *date* one?" Drake snorted. "Then again, an hour or two of being jerked around by you should make the prissy prince flee screaming from this dimension."

Hexaba's expression darkened like a thundercloud. "I ought to turn you into a...." Her eyes fixed on something in the distance, and her expression changed from rage to delight.

Drake followed her gaze. Carved into the outer wall of the Black Sash fraternity house in perfect italic print was *Mad Scientists Rule; Evil Sorcerers Drool (Or So We've Heard)*.

"Those wretched little weasels," Drake grumbled. "'Or So We've Heard.' Who do they think they're fooling?"

"The geeks have a point," Hexaba said. "You *do* drool."

Drake lurched up. "Have fun on your *date*. I'm sure a virtuous stick-impaled prince will make an amusing escort."

Drake sat on his bed, fuming and fiddling with his robes. Those wretched scientists. Thanks to them, the entire Black Sash fraternity, including Drake, had to waste an afternoon trying to remove the scientists' juvenile message from the fraternity wall.

Something slithered around Drake's ankle. An acid sting seeped into his flesh. A red tendril coiled up his calf. After a jolt from Drake's wand, the blob monster flopped, stunned, onto the floor. Drake growled. Jeffrey should pay more attention to his assignments or he would fail Monster Husbandry 101. Drake poured the stunned blob monster into its glass and metal tank, then slammed the lid.

Carrying the tank, Drake headed to where the Black Sash brotherhood tried vainly to remove the melted-in taunt. A wraith auditor in a tattered cloak floated nearby. Its hood opening turned toward the defaced wall as it scribbled notes.

Grinding his teeth, Drake thrust the glass and metal tank into Jeffrey's arms. "You're supposed to keep your creature with you at all times," Drake admonished.

"I forgot." Jeffrey scowled at the unconscious blob, then glanced uneasily at the wraith.

"Evil creatures guard the lair while you perform spells," Drake lectured. "If you don't take care of them, they will not take care of you. This poor creature is half starved. It was so desperate, it tried to devour *me*."

"Sorry." Jeffrey grimaced. "It's just...well, it eats living creatures."

"So?"

"Live food either bites when I grab it, or costs too much."

Drake glanced sidelong at the wraith, hoping it noted his mentoring efforts. "If your blob monster dies, you'll fail the class. That reflects poorly on me—which I won't have."

"Then you feed him."

"Leave his feeding to me, and you'll find yourself on a platter." The wraith hummed approvingly, then drifted over the wall.

"You must admit," Scardos said, staring at the mocking words, "it's a clever slogan."

"Yeah, but who wrote it?" Torrence asked.

Drake stared incredulously. "Mad scientists, idiot."

"But it says 'So *We've* Heard,'" Torrence persisted. "Do you think they heard it with super hearing? Maybe a superhero carved this message with x-ray vision."

Heaving a long-suffering sigh, Drake thumped Torrence's head hard enough to knock him down.

"We should have a slogan." Jeffrey tapped his chin. "'Evil sorcerers do it with big wands'?"

"That's a terrible slogan," Drake said. "Everyone knows we use wands. Besides, the size of the wand doesn't matter."

Jeffrey snickered, then said, "I'll think on it. What I can't figure out is how they did this without magic."

"I expect they used their 'taser ray gun,'" Glaring at Torrence, Drake added, "And *not* x-ray vision." On occasion, listening to Dex's inane babble produced valuable information.

"What's a taser?" Scardos asked, as several other sorcerers moved closer to hear Drake's wisdom.

Since the auditor had left, Drake felt free to explain. "It's a light beam, amplified by bouncing it off mirrors. For such a homely lot, they create many devices requiring mirrors."

"Too bad their mirrors weren't dirty." Jeffrey sighed. "Now we have to spend all afternoon—"

"Not dirty—bespelled." Drake draped an arm around Jeffrey's shoulders. "Perhaps you have the makings of an evil sorcerer after all. Come, let's do some research."

"Why shouldn't you two have to help with the wall?" Scardos demanded.

"Because I know how to exact our revenge," Drake said.

"Though it pains me to admit it," Dolomar the Dreadful said, "Drake is our best chance at avenging our honor." The others shrugged and nodded.

Leaving his fraternal brothers to bungle through removing the scientists' message, Drake led Jeffrey, still toting the half-starved blob monster, toward the college library.

Except for the auditor wraiths' presence, it was a typical day on campus. Several students stood locked in the stocks. Sorcerers from Abracadabra Fraternity tried to zap flies with their wands, which resulted in a lot of singed and angry shrubbery. A foursome played hacky-sack using someone's freshman roommate transformed into a toad.

The obsidian library glinted in the afternoon sunlight. Jeffrey stared in awe. "What's it like inside?"

"You've never gone in?"

"I almost did. I had my hand on the door handle"—Jeffrey shuddered—"but it was so...dank and creepy. Then I remembered the Student Union had a sale on ginger spice muffins."

"I don't understand your prejudice against dank places." Drake grabbed the human thigh-bone door handle. "It's really quite homey. In any event, you'd best get used to it. Most places in the Dark Arts quad are 'dank and creepy.'"

Drake opened the creaking iron door. The pleasant aroma of mildew wafted out. Gargoyles leered from the shadowed ceiling.

The librarian, Gladys, sat behind a mahogany counter carved with spiders, bats and snakes that, when viewed from the corner of one's eye, appeared to crawl, fly and slither. Gladys looked like the typical librarian, grey hair pulled into a bun, reading glasses on her nose, and a severe black dress with a white lace collar. On her desk lay stacked books, an inkwell and feather quill, a skull paperweight and, of course, a double-edged axe. Her gaze was fixed on a racing form. Drake took three strides toward the counter, stopped, retraced his steps, grabbed Jeffrey's wrist and dragged him in tow.

"Knock it off," Jeffrey grumbled, wrenching free.

"Good day, Madam Gladys," Drake said in his best fawning-without-being-sycophantic voice. "I was hoping you could direct

Jeffrey and myself to the books on mirror spells."

Gladys looked up. "Mandrake. Nice to see you. Mirror spells are in the south tower. Don't make a ruckus, or I'll chop you off at the kneecaps." She smiled sweetly and patted the axe.

"No, madam," Drake said.

As they strode off, Jeffrey gave Drake a sidelong look. "I can't believe you were so polite. It's not very evil."

"It never pays to anger Madam Gladys." Drake shuddered. He had made that mistake once. Luckily, he lived to regret it, and Professor Licentious had regrown Drake's fingers.

They entered the study area. Student sorcerers, manacled to long tables, hunched over books and scribbled notes. The lucky students had chairs. Drodents lumbered about, fetching and returning books. Imps used hot pokers to keep bleary-eyed students awake and focused. The smell of coffee and burned flesh drifted on the air.

"That's horrible," Jeffrey said.

"It's Dean Malodorous's idea of remedial study hall. That's where you'll soon be if your marks don't improve."

"They can't do that—can they?"

Drake rubbed his wrist, the feel of raw skin under metal seared into his memory. "Of course they can. Didn't you read the superfine print in your admissions contract?"

Drake wished *he* had read it. The drodent clause had come as a shock. He later learned university graduates were bespelled so they couldn't warn others about the admissions contract's terms. "Did you at least read the pamphlet in your orientation packet—'Graduate or Else'?"

Jeffrey scowled. "No."

The temperature dropped to iciness. A wraith drifted from the stacks and hovered over a chained student. "You," it said in a chilling whisper, a bony index finger pointing.

The student turned ashen. "Y-y-yes?"

"I will ask questions," the wraith said, "and you *will* answer truthfully."

Drake grabbed Jeffrey's arm and they hurried to an archway.

"I didn't know they were questioning students," Jeffrey gasped, his green eyes wide behind his spectacles.

Drake felt a stir of unease. If Jeffrey told an auditor about the pranks, Drake, and possibly the entire College of Dark Arts, would be in serious trouble.

"Stay away from them, Jeffrey," Drake said. "Keep alert at all times."

"You don't have to tell *me* twice."

A narrow staircase wound upward. Burning candles atop wall-mounted skulls provided the only light.

"Hey, Mandrake, good to see you," a skull said, its teeth clacking as it spoke.

Jeffrey jumped, clutching his blob tank to his chest.

"Who's your skittish friend?" the skull asked.

"Hello, Saul. This is my roommate, Jeffrey."

"Jeffrey, I could tell you a thing or two about your roommate. I knew him when I was in the flesh, so to speak."

"What happened?" Jeffrey asked.

"Aw, I got on the dean's list," Saul said. "Word to the wise: never cheat at bowling with a demon."

"Sage advice," Drake said, leading Jeffrey up the stairs.

"So how did you know him?" Jeffrey asked.

"He was my sage my freshman year."

"Was his advice any good?"

"He's a skull on a wall. What do you think?"

Skulls along the way greeted Mandrake with varying degrees of cordiality, or lack thereof. Some were inexplicably bitter about their current position. Some were glad to have a job. Others chatted about the weather or fashion.

"You must spend a lot of time in the library." Jeffrey gave a crooked grin. "Do you do anything besides talk to skulls? They all seem to know you."

Drake glared the grin off of Jeffrey's face. "There are reasons to talk to the skulls. They've each made a mistake *you* don't want to repeat."

"It's amazing anyone graduates from here," Jeffrey said, "between the punishments, penalties and fines."

"Why do you think a degree from *this* university is so coveted?" Drake said. "We have the highest standards." When they reached the first landing, he spoke to another skull. "I seek a book on mirror spells."

"Ooh, Mandrake you little devil," a woman's voice cooed from the skull. "Who's your handsome friend? Is he available?"

If Lola had had eyelashes, no doubt she would be batting them. Jeffrey blushed and ducked his head.

"Lola, the books?" Drake prompted. The spell holding her soul to the skull compelled her to answer all questions about book location and contents. Unfortunately, the spell didn't specify *when.*

"You promised me a ruby-red lipstick," Lola reminded him.

Drake fumbled in various robe pockets until he found the purloined tube in an inner pocket.

Jeffrey's lip curled. "You're still carrying that? Though the way you were dressed last night, I shouldn't be surprised."

"Quiet. I promised it to Lola in exchange for a favor."

"Please, *don't* tell me the sordid details of your private life."

"Scardos and I needed the same book for a research project," Drake said between clenched teeth. "Lola was kind enough to stall him so that I reached the book first." He opened the tube and gave it a twist. "Is this right?"

"Perfect. Put some on me, sweetie. Draw nice bow-shaped lips. Why you're an artiste." Lola sighed. "I feel so...feminine. If you ever need another favor, say the word."

"I need to know the location of the Mirror Spell books." Drake tried not to stare at his bizarre handiwork.

"They're on the third floor." The skull leered with her painted "lips."

Drake started up the stairs, Jeffrey on his heels.

"Come back and see me, sweet cheeks!" the skull called.

"Your first college girlfriend," Drake said drily.

"It makes her look like a tart," Jeffrey whispered to Drake.

"What do you think she was before?"

The blob monster, recovered from being stunned and having grown bored and hungry in an empty tank, banged its tentacles against the metal lid. The sound echoed off the walls.

"Quiet that thing," Drake ordered, looking around in panic.

"What are you afraid of?"

"Do it!"

"Okay, okay." Jeffrey pulled out his wand and tapped the metal lid. His body jerked and he collapsed into a heap.

"Idiot." Drake leaned over his stunned roommate. "Didn't anyone tell you metal conducts magic?" At least the blob monster had been stunned too.

Drake considered leaving Jeffrey unconscious on the stairs as a lesson, but Jeffrey's humiliation in such a public place would reflect poorly on Drake. After pulling out his own wand, Drake muttered some spell words. Ammonia fumes drifted from the wand tip. He held it to Jeffrey's nose. The boy coughed and shook his head.

"What happened?" Jeffrey asked, his eyes bleary.

"You stunned yourself."

Jeffrey smacked his forehead. "Metal-framed tank."

Quoting Dean Malodorous, Drake said, "Surviving sorcery is all in the details."

Jeffrey grabbed the tank and stomped after Drake to the third floor. When they entered the low-ceilinged stacks, Drake addressed another skull sconce.

"Mirror spells?"

"Dude, is that any way to treat your Uncle Blaine?"

Drake shuddered. He wasn't surprised that someone from his mother's family had ended up with his skull nailed to a wall. "Don't tell me. You cheated at bowling against Dean Corleone?"

"No way! I tried to eyeball those witch betties grooving naked under the full moon. I got my first gander, then everything went black. When I came to, here I was. Total bummer." He sighed dreamily. "But it was totally worth it."

"I'll be sure to tell mother," Drake said.

"Righteous," Blaine said. "You always were a good little dude."

Jeffrey raised an eyebrow. "Oh, really?"

"I was a perfectly evil child," Drake growled.

"Any chance you could get me out of this jam?" Blaine asked.

"Mirror spells, Uncle Blaine."

"Third row, you little prick."

Drake and Jeffrey sidled past closely packed shelves to the third row.

"Which book are we looking for?" Jeffrey asked.

"One containing the Vanity Mirror Spell." Drake had heard about the spell in his "Appeasing Royalty Until You Can Dethrone Them" seminar.

Drake handed Jeffrey a book. "Start looking."

The cover snapped at Jeffrey's hand, then slammed shut. Jeffrey dropped it on the floor.

"Careful," Drake said. "Damage a book and Madam Gladys will nail your skull beside Lola's."

"It tried to bite me."

Drake glanced at the title. "Oh, my mistake. Only upperclassmen are allowed to look at that one."

"You did that on purpose!"

Drake gave a malicious grin and handed Jeffrey another book. "This one should be more on your level."

Jeffrey eyed the book dubiously. In a rush, he threw open the cover. When the book lay calmly in the crook of his arm, Jeffrey leafed through the pages.

Drake shelved the snapping book, entitled *Mirror Spells with Bite*. He doubted the Vanity Mirror spell lay within, but watching the book attack Jeffrey had been amusing.

"How about this one?" Jeffrey said. "*You're Okay, I'm a Mirror: The Self-Esteem Boosting Mirror Spell.*"

Drake smacked the back of Jeffrey's head. "The last thing we want is for those spindly worms to realize looks aren't as important as attitude. They have enough attitude as it is."

"Ooh, ooh, here's one: *My Reflection Looks Good On You.*"

Sighing in exasperation, Drake pulled out a promising book entitled *Spells to Please an Evil Queen*. Evil queens loved Vanity Mirror spells.

"How about *The Inspirational Quote-A-Day Mirror?*" Jeffrey asked. "That sounds obnoxious."

"Now you're catching on." Drake tapped a page in his book.

"But here's the spell I want."

"If finding it was so simple, what did you need me for?"

"Be glad I got you out of repairing the wall. Now we need to find *The Book of Portals*."

"What does that have to do with cleaning the wall or getting even with the scientists?" Jeffrey asked.

"Nothing." Drake grabbed Jeffrey's arm and dragged him toward the landing and Uncle Blaine. "Just satisfying my curiosity on a certain matter." The chilling sense of power from Dean Corleone's portal haunted Drake's thoughts.

With Uncle Blaine's surly help, they found *The Book of Portals*. They trotted downstairs, Drake ignoring the calls and catcalls from various skulls, Jeffrey stammering answers before rushing after Drake.

The auditor wraith was nowhere in sight as Drake and Jeffrey hurried to the checkout counter. Drake smiled at Gladys. "I've found the books. The skulls were most helpful."

"How nice for you. Sign the check-out agreement in blood and scurry on your way." Gladys held out a sheet of paper with superfine print, and a needle to prick his finger.

Drake had read the fine print before, but glanced over it to assure no one had sneaked in any changes. Then he pricked his finger and squeezed to raise a bubble of blood. As he scratched a signature, the blob monster awoke and banged against the metal lid. The noise echoed off the high ceiling.

Drake's mouth went dry. Red flames ignited in Gladys's bulging eyes. Fangs pushed past her cracking lips. "Young man, cease that racket, RIGHT NOW!"

"Er, sorry, uh, yes, ma'am," Jeffrey stammered while standing frozen in the fury of Gladys's literally blazing gaze.

Drake whipped out his wand and zapped the tank. Jeffrey's body spasmed and collapsed. Inside the tank, the blob monster fell still.

Drake turned to the fuming librarian. "Sorry."

Gladys shrank back into a sweet little old lady. "You should teach him better, Mandrake."

"I will, madam. I promise." Drake would succeed—or Jeffrey would die trying.

Once Drake revived Jeffrey and they went outside, Jeffrey leaned close and whispered, "Was that a dead body behind the counter?"

"No, Gladys is just your average demon librarian."

"Not her. On the floor."

Drake shrugged. "Could be. The late fines will kill you."

The Student Union was quiet on Sunday morning, when heroes and superheroes exercised or worshiped the deities of their choice and witches caught up on beauty sleep after late-night carousing beneath the full moon. Sorcerers and scientists rarely rose this early on any day. Drake spotted Dex approaching from the stairs. Seeing Dex's wiry white hair, Drake fought a grin.

"Thanks for meeting me," he said when Dex slouched into the chair beside his.

"Thank *you*, by the way, for your little prank," Dex said. "Now I look madder than ever."

Drake scowled. Dex couldn't like looking that way. Then again, the white hair did give an impression of madness. "We have bigger issues than pranks. I've uncovered information about the portal in Dean Corleone's office."

Dex's eyes brightened. "What did you find?"

"According to the Mythology chapter of *The Book of Portals*, the power I felt resembles the Nexus portal. White wizards created it millennia ago, then a demon relieved them of it. The portal in the drawing was in a different frame, but it's the closest thing in the book."

"What makes this Nexus portal special?"

"It's a hub, a direct link to any and all other portals, and even to places without portals," Drake said. "I've never sensed anything so powerful."

Dex gave a crooked grin. "There's one way to find out if this portal is the Nexus."

"You're not thinking—"

"Yep. Tuesday is Dean Corleone's bowling night and he'll be off-dimension," Dex said. "It's the perfect time to break into his office and have a look."

"There's never a perfect time to break into the dean's office." Drake sighed. "Still, there's more happening at the university than our professors admit."

"And if there's an object of vast power around, you can bet it's at the heart of the trouble." Dex pounded a fist into his palm. "We have a right to know what we face."

Drake nodded reluctantly. "Then we go in Tuesday night."

Drake's ward-breaking and unlocking spells worked perfectly. Although he would never admit his surprise, he had expected better of Dean Corleone. While Dex set up his portable chemistry kit, Drake approached the portal. If this was the legendary Nexus, what powers might it hold? And how could Drake use it to get girls?

"I'll examine the frame," Dex said, "while you explore that weird power you felt."

Drake reached with his magic senses toward the heart of the

portal's energy, while Dex angled a lighted microscope to view the frame. They both jumped away.

"It's alive!" they exclaimed.

Drake furrowed his brow. "How did you know there's a living creature inside the Nexus?"

"There's a creature inside?" Dex said. "I was talking about the frame. If you look at it under the microscope, you can see actual cellular mitosis going on."

Drake stared blankly at Dex.

"The *metal* is alive," Dex explained.

Drake shrugged. "It must be hellion. That's the only living metal I've heard of. This *must* be the Nexus. Dean Corleone, or someone, changed the frame so the Nexus could grow. I'll bet it has capabilities its creators never envisioned."

"Like what?"

"How should I know?" Uneasiness washed over Drake. "We should leave now...before the dean returns."

Dex chuckled. "I'd kind of like to wait around, in hiding of course. I'd love to see the dean in his bowling outfit."

The Nexus's iris dilated. Fascinated, Dex and Drake moved closer. A cloudy haze resolved into a bowling alley. The dean, in human form, wore a striped bowling shirt and a pair of khakis. The shirt back read "Meanie Greenies" and had a picture of an elongated alien face, its slanted eyes squinched in rage. Dean Corleone lifted his blue and green swirled ball, which looked like a miniature planet, then rolled it onto the lane. Bowling pins cracked. He pumped his fists. "Strike!"

From a nearby bench, a bunch of little green men squealed. They ran to Dean Corleone and hugged his legs.

"Well. That's disturbing," Dex said, shaking his head.

Drake blinked hard. "Do you realize what this means?"

"The dean's ready for the pro circuit?"

"No!" Drake huffed. "The Nexus is also a spying device. No wonder the dean knows so much."

Dex rubbed his hands together. "So who should we spy on?"

"We should leave," Drake said. "Now."

"Oh, come on," Dex said. "How can you have a spying device right in front of you and not use it?"

"Hmm. Not using it *would* be a wasted opportunity." Drake stroked the frame. "We could spy on the auditors."

"Genius!" Dex said. "Yours or ours?"

"Spying on wraiths is risky."

"Ours then." Dex cleared his throat and said, "Show me the auditors from Arcane Sciences."

The portal clouded, then solidified into a sterile room reminiscent of a hospital ward, with a row of adjustable beds and wheeled tray tables. Crazed-looking old men in white lab coats lay in their beds, while a huge red devil paced before them.

"You've proven *nothing* yet?" the devil thundered.

"Patience, O Great Lucifer, Jr.," an auditor said in a creaky voice. "We've just started interrogating the students. It's difficult. Most of their free periods are at night and we fall asleep around seven."

Steam hissed off the devil's red flesh. "I need proof that funds are being misused and the students poorly trained! Only then can I convince the Board to hand the university and control of the Nexus over to me."

"Ah, the Nexus," another auditor mused. "It defies scientific explanation."

"Never mind the Nexus," Lucifer, Jr. said. "Once you make your inevitably bad report, the board will name me university dean. From the underperforming students, I'll create an army of drodents. Under the new admissions contract that all students will have to sign, graduates of the colleges of Dark Arts and Arcane Sciences will have a duty of service. *They* will lead my drodent army. With the power of the Nexus, I can transport them instantly to anywhere and turn any world into a living Hell." Lucifer, Jr. rubbed his hands together. "I will be unstoppable. I'll be a god. Finally, my dad will love me."

"Geez, this guy spills his guts worse than a Bond villain," Dex sneered in a whisper. "Clearly, he never attended Dean Evil's lecture on "Loose Lips Sink the Best Laid Schemes."

A geezer coughed to gain the devil's attention. "O Great Lucifer, Jr., every attempt to make sorcerers and mad scientists work together has failed utterly. The sorcerers and scientists argued endlessly over whether to use destructive magic or destructive gadgets. And each one thought *he* should be in command."

"Those armies weren't led by *me*...." A truly evil smile spread across Lucifer, Jr.'s face. "No, wait! I have a brilliant idea. Only one college will have a term of service. As for the other—"

The view went hazy and an inward-outward spiral materialized in the vast space.

"Someone's coming!" Drake shouted. "Grab your things and let's go!"

Dex scooped his chemistry set into the kit and they ran out the door.

CHAPTER THIRTEEN

Stars twinkled through the sliver-sized opening in the astronomy dome. Midnight was the best time for class. Sunlight's buzzing quality disturbed Dex's thoughts. Indeed, if the world were forever cloaked in silent darkness, he could accomplish so much more.

Perhaps his bomb should obliterate the sun. Unfortunately, late changes to a project description carried an automatic penalty. Maybe next year.

Dr. Marvin cranked the dome opening wider. According to his calculations, Martians from the Alternate-Earth 60's Dimension were preparing an assault on that instance of Earth. During their last attack, Martians carried off every natural blonde woman. The popular bet had redheads as the next target.

Dr. Marvin's tennis shoes squeaked as he paced, stiff-legged and slightly stooped. Hands clasped behind his back, he lectured to the floor. In all, he was one of the least peculiar instructors at Arcane Sciences.

He was also easy to hear. Dr. Marvin's nasal voice echoed off the metal ceiling. "The insignificant Earthlings in the Alternate 60's Universe will soon learn their planetary neighbors are eons ahead, evolutionarily speaking. We are most fortunate to witness the launching of the A-60's Mars attack fleet. Note the ion streams charging their atmosphere."

Dr. Marvin stooped before the telescope. "Hmm. This isn't right." Without peering into the eyepiece, he cranked the massive mirrored telescope a fraction from where it had been.

Dex tensed. Had one of them bumped the telescope last week when they "borrowed" the laser gun? Oh, well. Until someone got caught, no wrong had been committed.

Dr. Marvin spun around. What remained of his hair stood up like a static-charged Mohawk. "Oh, it makes me very angry when someone messes with my settings."

Dex looked at Isaac, who sat with his hands folded, playing innocent. Other white-haired classmates looked at the domed ceiling, at the floor or their notebooks. One idiot whistled tunelessly.

"Oh, never mind." Dr. Marvin made another adjustment. "I have corrected the problem. Now everyone form a neat queue. Anyone caught queue-jumping will be disintegrated."

Same old threat. Still, no one ever cut in line.

Dex stood first in line, with Isaac right behind.

Dr. Marvin stepped down from the dais and motioned for Dex to approach. As Dex peered into the eyepiece, he glimpsed a reflection of his eye.

The mirror clouded. When it cleared, it reflected an inhuman eye with a turquoise iris and sideways-slitted pupil.

Dex jumped back. "Dr. Marvin! There's an eye in the telescope."

"It's a reflection of your own, imbecile."

Dex bristled and muttered, "I know my own eye." Louder, he said, "Have a look...please."

Dr. Marvin scuttled over. "Oh, my. That is most unusual."

Someone shrieked, "Is it a Martian? Are they spying on us?"

"Calm down, Wells," Isaac said.

"Oh, dear," Dr. Marvin said. "This is most disturbing. Everyone, return to your seats." He whipped out a ratchet screwdriver and opened the telescope's casing. Its inner workings included several magnifying, parabolic mirrors.

For an instant, the mirrors reflected Dr. Marvin. Then they clouded and cleared, revealing peculiar, green-skinned faces with slanted turquoise eyes.

Wells shrieked, his eyes as big as saucers behind his thick lenses. "Green-faced Martians!"

Dr. Marvin rubbed his chin. "Those aren't Martians. Martians are much better looking."

"Greetings," the longest face said from the largest mirror. Smaller faces chimed in, "Greetings, scientist-lings."

"I do hope," the long-faced creature said, "you won't ask, 'Who is the fairest of them all?' I hate delivering bad news."

Dex had a sinking suspicion the faces were sorcerous conjurations. He searched his brain for anything Drake might have said regarding spelled mirrors. Something about the phrase, *the fairest of them all*, struck a chord.

"Get out of my telescope," Dr. Marvin said, his voice rising to new levels of shrillness.

"Hey," a less repulsive green face said, "we would if we could. Flat dimensions aren't all they're cracked up to be."

The mirror faces laughed.

"My, but you 3-D's are fussy," the long spokesface said.

The fairest of them all. Drake had cast a Vanity Mirror spell. He said many sorcerers raised capital by selling such mirrors to vain nobles.

If Dex remembered right, the mirrors were waiting for a question. "We're not interested in physical beauty. So I ask, magic mirror: Who's the *smartest* of them all?"

"What foolishness is this, Poindexter?" Dr. Marvin demanded.

"If I'm right, after they answer a question, they'll leave."

The green spokesface smiled eerily. "The answer is clear. He with the greatest brains and then some, is the rich and brilliant Dr. Arcanum."

Not a surprising answer. "Thank you," Dex said. "You've fulfilled your purpose."

"I think not, scientist-lings," a squeaky-voiced face said. "Surely you wish to know more."

"Indeed," the long spokesface said. "There is *smart* and there is *clever*."

"And ingenious," another added.

"And pure genius," another said. The faces chimed in like a thesaurus—intelligent, witty, cagey, and astute, cunning, wily, quick-witted and acute.

"Which am I?" Pryce shouted, bouncing in his seat.

The mirrors chorused, "As your body is fat, so is your brain; to call you a scientist is truly inane."

A deep voice added, "As far as being an astronomer goes, Dr. Marvin is the one who knows. His knowledge of stars beyond mortal sight, leads to the conclusion he is the most bright."

Dr. Marvin clapped at the barrage of compliments. "How very keen these mirror faces are. Indeed, they have recognized a great intellect. Tell me, magic mirror, how does my intelligence measure up to Dean Evil's?"

"For wild schemes none bests Dean Evil, though he boasts the I.Q. of a meager boll weevil."

Entranced, the entire classroom chanted, "Me next, me next."

Dex smacked his forehead with his palm. *I'm an idiot.* Drake had warned that vanity was contagious and consumed the afflicted like a disease.

Dex scooted down the row, shaking fellow students by their dirt-ringed collars. "Don't listen. It's a spell—a dangerous spell." That grabbed the professor's attention. Dex explained, finishing with, "A person could waste away listening to their empty flattery."

Considering how skinny Dr. Marvin was, that wouldn't take long.

"What are you?" Dr. Marvin asked the largest mirror face.

"We're like oracles," the spokesface answered.

"Only not so farsighted," another added.

"That's right, 3-D's," a cherubic face squeaked. "We bring order to the world, sorting you by intelligence, charm, looks, and other attributes. Ask us, and we provide guidance to choose the right leaders and teachers."

"Such as your professor here," another added.

"Follow cultured Dr. Arcanum for style and grace," the mirror faces intoned, "but for astronomical standards, Dr. Marvin sets the pace."

Dr. Marvin listened intently, swaying on his squeaking sneakers. Half the class was glassy-eyed and nodding.

"Can your knowledge help us get women?" Isaac asked.

Now that would be helpful advice. Knowledge was power. Dex sank back into his seat. "Maybe a witch hottie?"

"You'll be our finest project," the faces promised.

Project. This sideshow was distracting Dex from his project. He cupped his hands over his ears. "La la la," he shouted, a trick he'd learned from Gilbert. Amazingly, the spell's hold loosened.

"Ignore them!" Hands covering his ears, Dex ran between the rows. "Their words are lies. Empty promises. Shut them out."

That rattled the class. They shouted, mostly dismayed that the faces couldn't help them get women. Soon, the spell was broken—the faces remained, but stayed silent.

Dr. Marvin paced, his scuttling growing faster and faster. "Oh, this makes me very angry. Those puny sorcerers have ruined my view of A-60's Mars." He looked at the class and raised a finger. "Of course, you realize, this means war!"

The astronomy professor shuffled to the door, muttering, "Wait until the next faculty meeting. I'll have my revenge. The cost to replace those mirrors alone...."

His voice faded down the corridor.

Lexington, who had the enviable ability to remain calm under any circumstances, said, "Gentlemen, we must organize. If we wait for our instructors to handle matters, the College of Arcane Sciences will be a footnote in the yearbook. We must teach those sorcerers a lesson they won't forget."

"This prank demands retribution," Dex said.

"I see they got you too."

Dex's head snapped around at the familiar voice. What was Gilbert doing here? Apparently, he didn't know this wing was off-limits to freshmen.

Gilbert ambled inside. "From what I've seen, every mirror in the college has been affected. We were in the middle of a refraction experiment when ours changed."

Dex wrinkled his forehead. The physics lab was way across campus. How did the doofus get here so fast? They must have been enthralled longer than he realized.

"How did you break free of the spell?" Lexington asked.

Gilbert blushed and looked down. "I, uh, accidentally dropped my mirror."

"As I was saying," Dex said, "we must plot our revenge."

"We could kidnap their mascot," Gilbert suggested. "We

always did that in high school before the homecoming game."
Gilbert giggled; clearly, Maniacal Laughter was not going well for
him. "It really made the other team mad."

"What sort of mascots do they have back home?" Dex asked,
waiting to see if Gilbert remembered anything unusual about
the sorcerers' mascot.

"Goats, pigs, crows. One school's mascot was a sheep. Oh,
yeah, and the cow was real tricky. A cow is easy to tip, but they
won't walk downstairs. Had to get a crane—"

"Enough!" Dex felt a groan rise. "The sorcerers' mascot is a
black *dragon*. A *dragon* is not a farm animal. *Dragons* don't take
kindly to being kidnaped." He figured if he stressed the word
"dragon" enough, Gilbert might get the message.

"What do *dragons* like? That's how you lure them."

Or maybe not. "Geez, Gilbert, *dragons* like to eat. You try to
kidnap a dragon and it'll most likely eat *you*—because they're
not picky." Dex ran a hand through his hair, feeling the wiry
strands—if this white-haired spell didn't wear off or grow out,
Drake would regret it big time. *Maybe I'll shave his head.* Drake
was rather vain about his hair.

"It's not like I was thinking of sneaking in and throwing a
sack over it," Gilbert said.

Dex stopped himself from asking, "Why not?", certain the
answer would be, "Because I don't have a big enough sack."

Instead, Isaac asked, "You think you could do it?"

"No," Dex said, "he can't. No one in their right mind would
kidnap a dragon." Though maybe that wasn't the best argument
when it came to Gilbert—or any mad scientist.

"Isn't that the point? They'll never expect it." Isaac paused.
"Or maybe they would. The plan is mad enough—they might
anticipate it. Then again—"

"Is everyone here confusing madness with stupidity?" Dex
shouted. Isaac would get that dumb kid killed. If Dex didn't
watch Gilbert twenty-four/seven, that farm boy would be dragon
chow, then fertilizer—

Dex laughed. "Gilbert has given me an excellent idea.
Gentlemen, we'll make the sorcerers *wish* we had kidnaped
Blackie." He rubbed his hands together while dredging up a
deep, mad laugh. If Gilbert had any sense, he would pay
attention.

"Don't keep it to yourself, Dex, old man," Lexington said.

Dex glared. "First let me finish my laugh." A moment later,
he elaborated, "The best part of my plan is this prank won't look
like a prank. It'll seem like the sorcerers failed to care for their
mascot, a black mark on *their* record with the auditors. My plot
involves Blackie and a lot of beans—or whatever slop is cooking

in our cafeteria tonight."

Saturday night, for the first time ever, the residents of Gamma Ray Delta in their entirety appeared at the fraternity mess—so named because it was an actual, bona fide mess. When the cooks weren't preparing food, they were literally slinging hash. Considering the cooks came from ape stock, it was an evolutionary step up.

Gilbert pushed his tray down the line behind Dex. Like everyone else, Dex asked for his food "to go."

"Aren't we eating here?" Gilbert asked.

Dex blinked hard. Nodding back toward Gilbert, Dex said, "His is 'to go' too."

"What's wrong with eating here?" The chimp waved a ladle, splashing something green and lumpy on the wall. Judging by its decayed smell, it might have once been guacamole, or maybe cake.

"We have a big exam," Dex lied. "We're all eating in our rooms."

The chimp cook picked a flea off his coworker. Hair nets only covered so much. Flicking the flea into the stew, the chimp said, "Did you know we had so many students?"

"Maybe it's rush week," the groomed chimp said.

"I'll have some of that." Gilbert pointed to something vaguely orangish. "I love mashed sweet potatoes."

Dex quirked an eyebrow. "Uh, that's fish."

"Oh, well. Fish is brain food." Gilbert nodded for the cook to continue pouring the "fish" into the Styrofoam container. When the cook started to drizzle on the accompanying sauce, Gilbert stopped him. "No, thanks. I'm watching my weight."

"Not that it matters," Dex said, adding under his breath, "since we *aren't eating* any of this, but with that fish, the sauce is crucial. Without it to counteract the fish's natural poisons, it would literally be your last supper."

Gilbert's mouth formed a silent, "Oh." He smiled at the chimp. "I'll have loads of sauce, thanks."

Dex hurried down the line. Gilbert took a sample of everything until his Styrofoam container would barely close. Grinning, Gilbert asked, "Is this enough for a dragon?"

"Is that why you got some of everything?" Dex asked.

"You think I'd eat this slop?"

"I'd *hope* not." Thus far, however, Gilbert hadn't shown much of a survival instinct.

Under the clock tower, the scientists dumped the noxious slop into a stock pot. The concoction bubbled and writhed. Someone murmured, "It's alive!"

"Well, good luck, Dex, old man," Lexington said.

Dex blinked. "How's that?"

"It's your idea," Lexington said.

"Only you know the secret way into the Black Sash fraternity and thus into the sorcerers' quad," Isaac said.

Dex never should have mentioned that. "I can show the way."

Everyone except Gilbert wished Dex luck and made a hasty retreat, leaving Dex and Gilbert alone with the frothing pot of "stew."

"I'll go with you," Gilbert offered.

He would just get himself eaten—and that would reflect poorly on Dex—so he sent Gilbert to their room.

Alone—discounting whatever life form was being "birthed" in the pot—Dex staggered across university grounds. The pot strained his shoulders and noodle-thin biceps. If he wasn't careful, these pranks would ruin his classic nerdy looks. Then he might never get a job at one of those high-powered, secret labs lacking proper security.

Staying to the shadows, he crept around the wall enclosing the sorcerer's quad until he stood behind the Fraternal Order of the Black Sash. At the hidden entrance, Dex dropped the pot. Thankfully, the plastic wrap and lid held tight. He could only imagine what that concoction would do to grass. Dex wouldn't have cared, except this land was the university commons and Dean Corleone was particular about them.

Dex's arms twitched. Water oozed from every pore. He was dehydrating. At this rate, he'd soon be a desiccated husk, a shriveled, mummified specimen. The sorcerers must have added a protection spell to their defenses!

Dex panted and wiped the stream from his forehead. He tasted salt. *Wait,* his calm, inner voice told him. That same voice regularly stoked his ego, promising a great future. As such, Dex listened to it.

Sweat. That drippy stuff was sweat. So this was what it felt like. Nasty, sticky and wet. Yuck.

Above the secret entrance, a dragon-gargoyle perched atop a stone platform. Its arched neck angled the head downward. *For a kiss.* Grimacing, Dex kissed the dragon-gargoyle's scaly lips. The gargoyle's eyes popped open. It unfurled its wings and grabbed Dex in an embrace.

Dex struggled in the gargoyle's grasp. It nuzzled him and licked his face with a grainy tongue. Then it planted a kiss on Dex's mouth. It tasted like making out with cement.

When the gargoyle released him, Dex spat small pebbles and wiped off wet mortar. The stone dragon gazed at him with adoring eyes.

Dex said, *"Nulla Corpus, Non Crimen."* How original—using the university motto as their password.

The gargoyle pressed a stone. A portion of wall pivoted open, revealing a narrow entrance. Time to feed the dragon.

CHAPTER FOURTEEN

Valorous's hand rested on his sword pommel as he walked through Nuevo Pittsburgh. Cars zipped past like charging dragons. Noise roared in his ears and noxious fumes choked him. The techno town was much like a dragon's lair—except instead of caches of gold, there were vast amounts of litter.

Across the street, a sputtering neon sign proclaimed, "Wu's Chinese Laundry." Beneath it, a cardboard sign added: "Your clothes clean and pressed inside an hour or you have our most humble and sincere apology." As Valorous opened the filthy glass door, a bell rang. Spicy incense hazed the air.

The place looked nothing like a laundry—not that Valorous had ever been near one, but he had expected a dozen washerwomen. Instead, cushions surrounded a low table. Bottles and jars filled shelves on every wall. A curtain in the back wall moved aside and a hunched old man wearing a satin beanie entered.

"Welcome," the man said, bowing. "I'm the Wizard Mortie."

Valorous raised his eyebrows at the man's peculiar accent. "I am Prince Valorous."

"What a joy it is to have you in my shop, Your Highness." The Wizard Mortie gestured toward the cushions. "Sit, sit."

Valorous sank onto a satin cushion. His velvet tunic slid along the slick fabric. He gripped the table. "I was surprised to find a white wizard in the University Dimension, especially in a techno town."

"We're always expanding into new areas," Mortie said. "Right now, we're taking advantage of the New Age craze."

"I thought demons didn't allow magic in the techno worlds," Valorous said. "Except for charlatan magic." Eyeing the so-called wizard, he added, "You're not a charlatan, are you?"

"I'm the finest white wizard ever to be bar-mitzvahed." Mortie gave a secretive smile. "Demonic interference is why I disguised my shop as a Chinese Laundry. That, and I make a little extra on the side business."

"So you do laundry here?" Valorous needed a good laundry service. University laundry drodents had burned holes into Valorous's best tunic and stretched out two pairs of tights.

"Oh, no. I run a *mah-jong* den in back." Mortie nodded toward the curtain. "Care to play? There's free rice."

"No, thank you."

Mortie opened his arms wide. "What brings such an august personage to my humble shop?"

Valorous shifted on the slick cushion, then forced out the words. "I...need a love potion."

"*Oy*, a fine-looking boy such as you? I wouldn't think you'd need a love potion to win a girl."

"She's a witch."

Mortie threw up his hands. "Are you *meshugana*? What would you want with trouble like that?"

"Suffice it to say I want her to love me."

"You're right. It's none of my business. I'm sure you know best. So what do you want this love potion to do?"

"I want it to turn her into a good witch."

"Don't you want her to be a good wife too?" Mortie asked.

"The basic love potion doesn't cover that?"

"Of course not," Mortie said. "You can love someone, yet be a terror to live with."

"Okay, so I want her to be a good wife," Valorous said.

"That'll be fifty gold for the basic potion and an extra fifty for the good wife additive."

"I'll take it." Valorous dug out two fifty-gold pieces.

"Don't you care if she's faithful?"

"Isn't that part of being a good wife?"

"Aren't you a funny one?" Mortie leaned across and patted Valorous's hand. "A woman can make her husband comfortable and still get a bit on the side. Amazing creatures, women."

"Fine, then. How much for fidelity?"

"Fifty."

"Are all additives fifty gold?"

The Wizard Mortie shrugged. "It's a nice, round number."

Valorous shoved another fifty-gold piece over to Mortie.

"What about potion insurance?" Mortie asked.

"*Insurance!*"

"In case of misfire," Mortie said.

"You should take care of that anyway."

"What, a poor schmo like me should have to bear the risk of dabbling in magic when it's you rich boys who want the spells? Magic is unpredictable. Ingredients vary in quality with no visible indication. I guarantee to make the best possible potion. I can't guarantee outcomes."

Sighing, Valorous slid over another fifty-gold piece.

"So, would you like her to do this?" Mortie leaned forward and whispered the most lewd and improbable sexual act Valorous had ever heard.

"Oh, my, yes. I definitely want that." Valorous shoved over

another fifty-gold piece.

"*That* additive is a hundred," Mortie said.

And well worth it.

By the time they finished with other sexual additives, Mortie had quite a stack of gold before him and Valorous had spent six months' allowance.

"The potion will be ready in a week," Mortie said. "There's two doses, so you have two tries to give it to her."

"I'll only need one." Valorous rose from the cushion.

"That's what they all say," Mortie muttered.

Hexaba waved the one wand witches considered magic, the Housecleaning Wand. Fingerprints vanished, clothes were put away, bed covers smoothed, and dust bunnies hopped out the door, seeking residence beneath someone else's furniture.

Prudence entered carrying a cauldron, an ancient family tome of magic recipes and a grocery sack of fresh ingredients. Phoebe carried a hand mirror.

"Who are you expecting?" Phoebe asked as the twins set down their supplies.

"Gilbert," Hexaba said, "the boy that Drake's puny friend Poindexter is mentoring."

"It's called *de*mentoring on their quad," Phoebe said.

"Why Gilbert?" Prudence asked, hanging the cauldron over the fireplace. "He's a freshman *and* a useless scientist."

"They're not entirely useless," Phoebe said. "I wouldn't have passed intercurricular physics or whatever it was if Lexington hadn't done my homework. The instructor thinks I'm a genius. He sends flowers and cards asking me to be his TA."

"That's not the T and A he's interested in," Prudence said.

"Gross," Phoebe said. "Dr. Jekyll is such a nerd." A wicked gleam dotted her eyes. "But Professor Hyde isn't bad."

"Animal lover," Prudence said.

"What did you call me?" Phoebe snapped.

"If the leather pants fit—"

A knock interrupted. "Have I come at a bad time?" Gilbert asked from the open doorway.

"Of course not," Hexaba said. "My roommates were just playing around."

"So you girls really have pillow fights? That's so cool. Wait until I tell the guys at the frat house."

"Come on, Pru," Phoebe said. "We can do homework later."

"I think big Tex has this period off," Prudence said.

"You mean Armadilloman?" Phoebe said. "He's kind of scrawny, if you ask me."

"You'll see what I mean," Prudence said. The twins sashayed

their tight buttocks out of the room.

Grinning, Gilbert watched them walk down the hall.

Hexaba cleared her throat. "Quit ogling. It's unbecoming a gentleman." When Gilbert's gaze flicked back to the hallway, she snapped, "Come on, I have no time for dawdling."

Gilbert scooted inside. "Yes, ma'am."

Hexaba's back bristled. "Don't call me ma'am." The main reason she became a witch was to never be called ma'am. Once she mastered the soul swap spell, she could always have the body of a twenty-year-old...any twenty-year-old she pleased.

"I don't see how I can help with your homework," Gilbert said. "I haven't had any anthropology classes."

"Phrenology is the study of the skull to reveal your personality."

Gilbert knocked on his head. "My skull's as hard as a rock, my dad says. And Dex claims I have no personality."

"Sit down," Hexaba ordered, then quickly rephrased, "I mean, won't you please have a seat?"

"Yes, ma'—" Gilbert swallowed hard. "Yes, miss?"

"That's a marginal improvement." Maybe scientists could be taught. Or maybe Gilbert's farm-boy rearing made him easy to handle. The dumber the man, the easier he was to wrap around her finger. Gilbert had come pre-curled, a one-size-fits-all human pinkie ring.

Gilbert sat on the stool while Hexaba circled him. He had nice shoulders for a scientist, and his bulging biceps strained the sleeves of his lab coat. Through his glasses, he watched her with blue, puppy-dog eyes. She half-expected his tongue to loll out of his mouth.

Hexaba ran her fingers through Gilbert's hair. His thick hair felt silky soft, except for the wiry white ends left from Drake's spell. She took a moment to enjoy the texture and feel.

Gilbert's body sagged as though turning to mush. "That feels nice. I like phrenology."

"Quiet. I need to concentrate." Hexaba pressed her fingers against his skull and stroked in all directions. His head was as smooth as a hard-boiled egg—which explained why geeks were called egg-heads.

She studied him through a squint. The boy was a blank page!

"Well?" Gilbert asked. "What did you learn?"

"That you're exactly what you seem."

"What's that exactly?" he asked, determined to be insulted.

Hexaba didn't care for kids or innocents, but she didn't enjoy hurting them—unless they annoyed her. And Gilbert was starting to annoy her, even if he had pretty blue eyes hiding behind his glasses.

She debated whether to be diplomatic, or be brutally honest and watch him crumble. The latter promised to be more entertaining, so Hexaba began, "Poindexter is astute when it comes to his fellow man."

"Dex? Nah, if he had any interest in people, he wouldn't be trying to build a bomb."

Hexaba changed strategies. This information could prove useful. "Tell me more."

Gilbert blushed. "For his junior project, Dex is making a bomb. I don't know the details, but it'll kill lots of people and could ruin the environment. Dex doesn't think in small terms. I wish he was more ecologically-minded, like Mandrake."

Hexaba choked on a laugh. "Are we talking about Mandrake, son of Bane the Black-Hearted?"

"I guess so. I don't know his father."

"Why do you call Drake ecologically-minded?" Hexaba asked.

Gilbert's face animated with excitement. "Jeffrey told me about Mandrake's project. It's so cool. It could end famine and stop hurricanes."

Though she doubted that was Drake's plan, she asked, "What *is* Drake's project?"

"A weather animation staff."

Hexaba smiled. Gilbert's brain *was* as dull-witted as his smooth skull indicated, but within its vacuous confines, interesting information bounced about. Hexaba grudgingly had to admit—only to herself—that, Drake had the most talent of all the Dark Arts students. His project would likely represent their college at the Project Fair next spring. At the very least, knowing more about his staff would show the witches what they had to beat.

"Gilbert, would you and your big muscles like a massage?"

"For me? Why?"

"For helping me with my phrenology assignment, silly boy. Come now. Let me reward you."

"Is there chocolate cake?"

"If you want." Hexaba linked her arm through Gilbert's muscled one. "Tell me about Drake's weather staff."

CHAPTER FIFTEEN

The mahogany staff Dingo had procured rested on the worktable. Beside it, precious powdered elements lay in neat piles on paper squares. Drake carved the rune for storms—a frowning cloud—then sprinkled crushed amethyst into the grooves. He spoke an incantation. The rune glowed purple, sealing the spell. As he started carving the rune for tornados—a tin house on wheels swirling in a funnel cloud—Jeffrey stomped into the room.

"It stinks in here," Jeffrey said. "Why are you always closing the window?"

Before Drake realized his roommate's intent, Jeffrey threw open the window. A foul stench blew inside. Drake's papers went flying, scattering precious powdered elements. As the powders struck the wall, crevices glowed orange, purple, green and red.

"Damnation," Drake shouted, then gagged on the noisome wind. "Do you—urk—know how much—gak—those elements cost?"

Jeffrey gagged and, for the first time in Drake's recollection, swore. For a freshman, he knew some impressive curse words. Jeffrey slammed the window shut.

Drake would worry about replacing his supplies and throttling Jeffrey later. The stench took precedence. Those weren't the usual foul odors that emanated from dark sorcery, but a gagging reek even the wind could not dilute.

"What's causing that stink?" Jeffrey asked.

Drake said the words he expected to regret. "Let's go see."

Drake and Jeffrey ran out to the sorcerer's quad. The stench grew even more unbearable. They covered their noses with their sleeves and followed the rushing crowd. Outside the administration keep, imps chortled, doing back flips as though the foul smell was a spring breeze. Professors, luscious but deadly succubi on the administration staff, and students with sleeves or handkerchiefs covering their noses stared at the keep.

"What's going on?" Drake asked Scardos and Torrence.

"Someone slipped Blackie a mysterious indigestible glop," Scardos said, a pocket cloth muffling his voice.

Torrence wiped his tearing eyes. "He's got explosive diarrhea. Dean Malodorous sent someone to fetch Mumbojumbo."

The witchdoctor soon appeared in all his dubious glory.

Seemingly undisturbed by the stench, he staggered toward the administration keep. *He's probably too drunk to smell.*

Dr. Mumbojumbo wore a kilt of colors even Hell wouldn't put into plaid. Bones decorated his bushy red hair and beard, and another bone pierced his nose. Bangles jingled at his wrists, and gold chains hung around his neck. Seeing the man's hairy legs was bad enough. But the witchdoctor's bared chest was unnecessary cruelty. The auburn fur covering his chest and back had been shaved in spots to make room for tattoos from bars he frequented, sort of permanent club stamps.

He stumbled, bandy-legged, into the keep. Ten minutes later, he emerged looking a tad green. "I shook the rattle a wee bit and did m'dance, but it didna help."

Drake snorted.

Mumbojumbo glared. "I'm a witch doctor, not a miracle worker. So I'll be needing a case of twelve-year-old scotch."

Professor Malfeasant gasped. "Are you sure giving alcohol to a *fire-breathing* dragon is a good idea?"

"The scotch is for me, ye stupid git," the witch doctor growled. "For the dragon, I'll need six cases of Pepto-Bismol." Mumbojumbo let out an impressive belch. Rubbing his stomach, he said, "Ye'd best be adding a bottle for meself."

A wraith drifted by, scribbling and muttering, "Dragon neglect costing university funds...."

"Who would do this?" Jeffrey asked through his sleeve.

Once the wraith drifted out of earshot, Drake said, "The mad scientists did this. The do-gooders would wet their tights if they found themselves in the same building as Blackie."

"My thinking precisely, Mandrake."

Feeling Dean Maldodorous's glare boring into him, Drake clenched his entire body. For the first time, Drake hadn't smelled the dean coming.

"If the rest of you will excuse us"—the dean glanced at the distant wraith—"I wish to speak to Mandrake. Alone."

Drake's gut knotted. "Good day, Professor."

"Unctuousness is not required under the circumstances, Mandrake." Dean Malodorous led Drake into a classroom building upwind of the stench. Due to the dean's presence, the smell improved only moderately. "I understand you and your scientist friend have instigated a war between our two colleges."

"Uh, er," Drake said wittily.

"I hope your tongue is more glib come finals."

Drake wondered how the dean knew he and Dex were friends. How closely did the faculty watch students?

"No matter who started this little war, Mandrake, I plan to finish it—and you shall help."

"What do you want me to do?"

"I understand you infiltrated the Gamma Ray Delta fraternity house a few nights ago."

Now Drake felt *really* uncomfortable. "Uh, er."

"Having trouble communicating, Mandrake? Fear not. There will be no repercussions—this time," Dean Malodorous said, "so long as you assist your college in obtaining vengeance."

Drake's muscles unknotted. "Of course."

"I need you to sneak into Arcane Sciences this afternoon."

"Their gate security is pretty lax during the day," Drake said. "But I'll need to dress like a mad scientist." In case Dean Malodorous didn't know the *precise* details of Drake's last incursion, he saw no reason to mention he had donned women's apparel.

"Ahead of you, as always." The dean handed Drake a cloth bag. "Inside, you will find the absurd garb those skinny tinkers wear. By the way, the Black Sash fraternity should consider changing the security on its secret entrance. I suspect that's how the scientists obtained entrance to our quad."

"Uh, er." The dean knew about their after-hours entrance? Drake wondered if Dex actually kissed the gargoyle.

"Say 'uh, er' one more time, Mandrake, and you'll be mucking out Blackie's den for a month. Anyway, we old fogies aren't so unaware as you might think," the dean said. "Never forget—the walls have ears and the ceilings have eyes. By the way, Mandrake, you make a fetching female."

Drake thought he said, "Urk."

"Returning to the matter at hand," the dean said, "the professors and I plan a twofold attack. You will implement phase one. My sources tell me the scientists are endeavoring to create an army of living corpses."

Drake furrowed his brow. "It takes magic to raise zombies."

"Not zombies—corpses stitched together from select body parts to create stronger-than-normal fighting men. The scientists plan to harness lightning's power to give them life."

Lightning really *did* have a thousand and one uses.

"We cannot allow them to succeed." Dean Malodorous leaned close for emphasis. Drake choked on the dean's breath, then coughed to cover. The dean added, "Should the auditors catch wind of our actions, you know who will be the sacrificial goat. I won't have *my* funding cut because of a bad report."

Drake gulped.

"Slip into the Anatomy Laboratory and animate the corpses before the scientists infuse them with life." The dean gave a malicious chuckle that filled Drake with envy. "Instead of a resurrected army of slaves—or 'meat machines,' as Professor

Polydouris called them at the last faculty mixer—the mad scientists will have a ravenous mob of zombies."

"Someone might get hurt," Drake said, grinning.

"Precisely, Mandrake."

From his robes, Malodorous dug out a jeweled amulet. A thumbnail-sized ruby winked in the middle. Drake salivated as the dean handed it to him.

"If you fail to return this promptly, I shall transfigure you permanently into a female—and a homely one at that."

The amulet felt weighty and cool in Drake's palm. His finger stroked the ruby. "What does it do?"

"It's a Power Amulet of Animation. The potion-and-power-word method is too slow for this task."

Drake stared in awe at the amulet. Students only studied power amulets in graduate school—or by self-study, which often proved fatal.

The dean instructed Drake on the amulet's use, then cautioned, "Slip in, cast the spell, then get out. Don't dally."

"Why not?"

"Because you will regret it. Now, go. You have one hour."

Drake rushed to his chamber to change. The bag held a white shirt and lab coat, tape-patched glasses, a pocket protector with an $E=MC^2$ logo and several leaky black pens.

The strange garb was bloody uncomfortable. The binding pants and too-short sleeves explained why scientists were so fidgety. Hurriedly, Drake transformed his hair into a short white buzz with dark roots. Then he zapped away his new growth of facial hair.

Drake ran to the scientists' quad. The iron gates stood open. Although two scientist students sat in the gatehouse, they were too engrossed in slide rule calculation races to pay Drake any heed.

Hunched old men with wild white hair and thick glasses roamed the quad. Judging by their lab coats and clipboards, Drake deduced they must be the Arcane Sciences' auditors.

To avoid contact with a passing auditor, Drake hunched over a directory. Many such directories dotted the quad. Apparently, mad scientists were too absent-minded to find their classrooms unaided. Considering *their* buildings remained stationary, Drake found that rather pathetic.

Inside the Life Sciences labs, more signs directed Drake toward the second-floor Anatomy Lab. Before he reached the stairwell, however, a clipboard-carrying geezer cornered him. For an old man—and a scientist—he sure moved fast.

"I have some questions," the auditor creaked.

Drake winced. Dean Malodorous had warned Drake to hurry

and the dean never gave warnings lightly. Drake considered giving foolish answers to make the mad scientists look bad. A negative report, however, bolstered Lucifer, Jr.'s position and could have devastating effects on the entire university—and thus on Drake. So, he decided to answer as Dex might.

"Answer this, student. Given a supercollider with an impact element of, say, the atomic weight of helium—"

Panic welled inside of Drake. He blurted "I have to pee!" then ran down the hall. From around a corner, he watched until the auditor left, then raced upstairs to the Anatomy Lab.

Drake peered through the glass window in the lab door. On stainless steel tables lay two dozen corpses in various states of decay. One was positively rotting, the flesh bloated and maggoty. A woozy-looking Gilbert tottered beside it.

At the room's front, the professor gesticulated, using a gleaming scalpel for emphasis. His kinky auburn curls stuck out to each side, as though lightning had struck him. According to Dex, it had—several times.

"Your cadavers have cured over the weekend," the professor said. "Now, my little gods, we'll carve out the choicest pieces. Look for organs and limbs with the least decay and most perfect development. We're building titans here! Our creations will be better than before death—better, stronger, faster!"

You'll build nothing today. Drake pulled the amulet from his lab coat pocket and gripped it in his fist.

"Using markers, divide the body according to this wall chart." The professor pulled a dangling string. The unfurled chart depicted a naked man, dotted lines segmenting the body into labeled parts.

The freshmen scientists measured, then drew dotted lines on the corpses, labeling various segments "heart," "lung," "kidney," or in Gilbert's case, "squishy part." Gilbert's marker kept poking through his cadaver's putrid skin. Where it did mark, the lines were hard to see against the blackened skin.

"Now pick up your scalpels," the professor said. "And cut!"

Drake waited until the scientists poised their scalpels, then spoke the words, "*Virat hominus á la Georgus Romerus!*"

Two dozen dead eyes opened. Corpses jerked on the slabs. Student scientists screamed and ran into each other, then screamed again. Zombies sat up, their bodies stiff and jerky. They glared at their naked, marked-up bodies. Angry grunts and groans rumbled in their rusty vocal chords.

"Brains," one groaned.

"Brains, brains." The others took up the chorus.

"Liver!" a zombie groaned. There was one in every crowd.

Students and professor stared in confused horror as the

zombies stood on wobbly legs. A couple toppled over. The legs from Gilbert's decayed zombie plopped to the floor. Gilbert fainted, landing with a heavy thud beside them.

"Everyone evacuate," the professor said, nerves in his voice. "Move in an orderly fashion—"

A zombie grabbed a student. The lad screamed and tore free. Students ran for the door, climbing over each other. Drake jumped aside a second before the door slammed open. Screaming students burst out, followed by their professor. As he ran, the professor shouted in a hysterical falsetto, "Remain calm! Move quickly and safely to the nearest exit! Should you be unable to open the exit doors, ask someone larger or stronger for help."

When the first decaying corpse reached the doorway, Drake jogged after the scientists, adding the occasional girlish scream to blend in. Zombies weren't the least bit dangerous to him, since he could stun them with his wand—

Realizing that would draw unwanted attention, Drake picked up his pace. A foul-smelling canvas bag magically appeared in a doorway. Recognizing the nauseating aroma of dragon dung, Drake ran full speed. Seven more bags appeared in doorways. No wonder Dean Malodorous warned that Drake would regret lingering.

Students streamed from classrooms. Several passed out instantly from fumes. Wheezing and the hiss of inhalers replaced the screams.

The bags smoldered then explosions rocked the floor. Liquified feces pelted the walls and ceilings. They oozed down in greenish-brown streaks and plopped like lumpy rain to the floor.

Dragon dung was naturally self-igniting. Well-formed lumps— called fire paddies—were handy for starting campfires. Until broken, the paddies were quite safe. The stinking fire also drove off insects. Explosive, mushy dragon dung, however, was extremely volatile. Drake's father had once used it when besieging a stubborn walled city and accidentally burned it to cinders.

On the ground floor, flaming dung set fire to everything, even things that shouldn't burn. Professors and students passed sloshing pails from hand to hand. Every bucket of water fed the burgeoning fire as though they were dumping lamp oil on it.

"You, there," a professor called. "Come help!"

Drake grinned and shook his head. Gagging on a putrid breath, he forged on. Three steps from the door and freedom, someone jolted him. Drake stopped cold and Dex did too. As they stared at each other, Drake felt a twinge of guilt that he didn't like.

Dex shrugged. Drake did likewise. Their silent stares

screamed an unspoken revelation. This really was war. Neither of them could stop it now that the faculties were involved. Dex and Drake shook hands.

Dex hacked on the disgusting air, then squeezed a puff from his inhaler. "May the best college win," he wheezed.

"That will be mine," Drake said. "Evil cunning defeats madness every time."

"Only in theory."

Gagging and coughing, they scurried outside. Students, professors and smoke poured from every building.

"By the by"—Drake's sleeve, still covering his mouth and nose, muffled his words—"watch out for zombies." He turned and ran.

Dex's exclamation echoed behind him. "Somfleas? What the heck are somfleas?"

CHAPTER SIXTEEN

"Dex," Gilbert whined, his voice doubly annoying through the gas mask. "It's not my fault."

"No," Dex snapped, his mask making his own voice more nasal. "It's mine. I never should have listened to you."

"I said we should *kidnap* their mascot, not feed it." Gilbert sat on his footlocker. A stupid smiley face sticker decorated Gilbert's mask like some happy hazard sign.

Dex scooped his clothing into a pillowcase. "Yes, it was my idea to give ol' Blackie the runs, and now we're paying for it."

Though the flaming dragon poop had burned out, the stink lingered. The count on the once-burning bags was incomplete. Dex had put his money on two-hundred seventy-three, taking into account the number of bags which had appeared in the upper floor of the Life Sciences building then extrapolating based on the hall's length versus those of all the other halls in all the buildings in the quad. Then, he added seven to the tally—because it was his lucky number and because all great equations had a seemingly insignificant constant added to them.

Gilbert had chosen a gazillion—because it sounded "cool."

"Come on," Dex grumbled.

Gilbert slung his footlocker across his back. "Can I carry something for you?"

"No, thanks." Under his breath, Dex muttered, "Farm boy. All muscle and no brain." *A gazillion—really.*

Batting aside hanging pine tree-shaped air fresheners and sidestepping charred bags oozing stink in green waves, Dex led Gilbert through the halls of Gamma Ray Delta.

In the courtyard, they removed their gas masks. Beneath the giant astrolabe, the students and faculty of Arcane Sciences had gathered, ready to eat, sleep, and conduct classes outside until the buildings aired out. Auditors, shaking their heads and scribbling, tallied the damage.

Dex pulled Gilbert aside. "Avoid the auditors. They're questioning students now. Some poor guy got so scared he had to run off and pee."

"They're not so bad. The only thing one asked me was if I'd seen any misuse of university funds or equipment."

Dex felt faint. "What did you say?"

"That we used Dr. Marvin's laser—stuff like that."

When Dean Evil caught wind of this....Dex shuddered.

"Dex, you okay? You look green."

"Never mind. I'm sure you'll enjoy grounds maintenance." If drodents enjoyed things.

Fragments of zombies littered the grounds. The stench of rotting flesh was perfume compared to Blackie's explosive diarrhea. An arm lay by the walkway. A foot stuck out of a bush like a five-toed flower. From atop a short wall, the dead eyes of a disembodied head tracked them.

Dex set down his sack. The pillowcase flopped open and a fresh wave of stench rolled out. He gagged. "Great. I think we'll have to burn *all* our clothes."

Gilbert shrugged. "Fine by me. Mine never did fit."

"That's because you're too tall and wide. Try slouching and eating less—then you'll develop a respectable, scientific appearance. Wait here. I want to check something."

Dex started toward the low wall. Sure enough, the eyes followed him.

Gilbert's footlocker thunked against pavement, then his footsteps clomped after Dex.

"That head's still animated," Dex said, pointing.

"Poor man. He must be in misery."

Dex grunted. "I'm more concerned that his eyes are spying for the sorcerers."

Dex grabbed the head by a hank of long hair. The head swung like a pendulum. On the third pass, its teeth bit deep into Dex's forearm. Dex wailed. He released the hair, then shook his arm. The head clung like a hairy leech. Crushing pain radiated up Dex's arm.

"Get it off me!" Dex jumped around, flapping his arms. He batted at the head, but it bit down harder, sending a new jolt up Dex's forearm. Its bloated tongue licked the wound. As Dex's blood trickled out the head's severed neck, Dex thought he would be sick—or faint like a little girl.

Gilbert, arms stretched before him, chased the head. "I can't grab it unless you stand still."

"*You* try standing still with a zombie latched to your arm!"

Gilbert thrust out his foot. Dex tripped and his forehead collided with the short wall. Moaning, he fell onto his back. Another head atop the wall—this one dead, then reanimated, then killed again—landed on Dex's chest and stared with vacant eyes.

Dex screamed.

Gilbert kicked the dead head away with enough power to make a forty-yard field goal, then straddled Dex. "This may sting."

Gripping the animated head still clamped onto Dex's arm,

Gilbert yanked and twisted. The head ripped free and flew over some bushes. A chunk of Dex's arm went with it—but he was, admittedly, free of the zombie. Blood gushed from a jagged hole. Teeth protruded from Dex's flesh. His stomach queasy, Dex plucked them from his bleeding arm.

Gilbert struggled out of his too-tight lab coat, tore a strip from the hem, then wrapped Dex's forearm neatly.

Dex stared in awe. "Where'd you learn that?"

"Someone's always getting injured on a farm."

"Nice job. You'll do well in the Basic Mummy Wrapping segment of Egyptology 101."

Gilbert gave a half-cocked grin. "I could use a passing grade."

Sighing, Dex patted his coat pocket. He always carried broad spectrum antibiotics—a habit he'd developed as a freshman after contracting a nasty transdimensional bacterial infection. After all, he didn't know who else that zombie had bitten. He dug out a small, brown tablet from the pill box. As he closed the case, a red and orange pill fell out and rolled away.

When Gilbert started after it, Dex said, "It's past date." Besides, what were the odds Dex would contract extraterrestrial venereal disease, even had he possessed that third part?

Dex staggered toward the bushes where the head had flown.

Gilbert followed. "Where are you going?"

"The head is still animated. Someone has to kill it."

"Wait." Gilbert headed back to the walkway, then returned carting his footlocker.

"No one will steal your stuff," Dex said.

"I know."

They crept toward the head. It was hooking grass tufts with its tongue and dragging itself along the ground.

Gilbert dropped his footlocker on the head, then ground it around. "That ought to do it."

Dex gagged. "It certainly should."

Gilbert lifted his footlocker, looked at the splattered brain, blood, and bone, and turned a faint shade of green.

"*I'll* clean it off later." Dex rolled his bandaged arm, where a patch of blood was soaking through. It needed cleaning and stitches, but the bleeding had slowed. "Call it my thanks."

Dex retrieved his pillowcase. Its contents were ruined, but it was all he owned. Gilbert carried his trunk, topside against his back. Gore dripped in his wake.

Well beyond the stench, Isaac and Lexington huddled before a small fire, roasting marshmallows for s'mores.

"Reanimating autopsy corpses was bad enough," Lexington groused, "but the flaming feces were in bad taste."

"Will I have to get another corpse?" Gilbert asked.

"Quiet, Gilbert," Dex said. To his peers, he said, "That was *two* strikes to our one. We must retaliate big."

"Because I can't afford to fail another class," Gilbert said. "And if I do need another corpse—"

"Quiet, Gilbert." Dex shook his finger. "This is much more important than homework."

"But Dex, I'm talking about *grades*!"

Isaac grabbed Gilbert's arm. "Normally, kid, we'd be with you—but this is personal."

Gilbert rested his chin on his knees and pouted. "It's not fair. Now the sorcerers have the only reanimated army."

Lexington's head jerked. "What's that, old man?"

"They aren't grave-robbing, are they?" Dex asked.

"Oh, no," Gilbert said. "They're creating their undead army out of clay. What did Jeffrey call them? Golems."

"Gilbert, if the *bodies* are made of clay, even once animated, they won't be undead," Dex explained. "To be *un*dead, a body had to first be *dead*. To be dead, it had to die. To die, it had to live. Do you understand the difference?"

Gilbert nodded. "So...they're creating a live army."

Dex sighed. "Not exactly."

"Animate means to give life to, not to make alive," Lexington said. "It's a fine distinction and therefore difficult for the uneducated mind to grasp. These clay golems will have a semblance of life, without possessing true life. For that, one needs a soul."

"Just as my robots," Isaac added, "will move and think and react like living persons. However, they, too, shall lack souls. Thus, they won't be alive."

"Then they'll be unalive," Gilbert said, "which is dead."

Dex shook his head; he would never receive high marks for mentoring this one. Isaac threw up his hands. Even Lexington rolled his eyes.

"No, Gilbert. They'll be neither dead nor alive." Dex sketched illustrative stick figures in the dirt.

"Isn't that what undead means?"

Dex groaned. Lexington looked on with sympathy. Isaac screamed and jumped up.

Before Isaac could stalk away, Dex grabbed the hem of his stinking lab coat with his good arm and pulled him back to the ground. "Gilbert," Dex said, "They're animate—that's it, plain and simple. Not undead. Not non-dead either." He added that last on anticipation.

"Think about it, gentlemen," Lexington said. "The sorcerers created an army of clay golems. Then they turned our corpses into zombies, knowing we'd have to destroy them." He nodded decisively. "We must retaliate. Dex can get us inside."

"To do what?" Dex wasn't sure where Lexington was heading, but he already liked the idea. Too bad he'd have to sabotage Lexington's project later to ensure his own was selected for the Spring Fair. But he'd engineer that bridge when he came to it.

Lexington pursed his lips. "It may cost me my project"—Dex liked the plan even better—"but I know how to ruin their golems." He smiled like a true madman—a product of extra credit work. "Let's go to my lab."

Lexington, Isaac, Gilbert and Dex crossed the quad under the light of a full moon, which in the university dimension occurred three times a week. Dex suspected Dean Corleone used the Nexus to spy on the witches while they danced naked, and thus created the frequent full moons.

Eerie music drifted over the hill from the witches' quad. Gilbert strayed toward the violin and flute strains. Dex grabbed his shirt. Though Dex tugged, sweat beading on his face from the pain shooting up his arm, he couldn't halt Gilbert.

"You can't go there," Dex said. "That's the College of Olde Wyrd Charms."

"So?"

"It's only for witches."

"I just want to listen to the music."

Pointing at the full moon, Dex said, "Don't you know what that means?"

Gilbert thought hard for a full minute. "There'll be plenty of light to see the concert?"

"They're witches, not an all-girl orchestra. It's a full moon. They'll be dancing under it, *naked*." Dex suppressed a delicious shudder.

Gilbert grinned like an idiot. "Even better. They're hot."

"Let him learn for himself," Lexington said.

"Yeah," Isaac said. "We don't need him."

"Easy for you two to say," Dex said. "You aren't mentoring him."

Gilbert wrenched free. "If you don't need me—"

"If the witches catch you," Dex said, "you'll finish out the semester as a newt or a frog."

"I was a newt," Isaac said with a wistful smile.

Gilbert stared, wide-eyed. "They'd turn me into a newt?"

"In a heartbeat. Now come on." Dex walked away. It was Gilbert's responsibility to make the wise decision. At that thought, Dex whirled around, readying another argument. Surprisingly, Gilbert had forsaken the music to follow Dex.

They reached the Genetic Engineering building, which also housed private labs for the upper classmen. Lexington unlocked his lab and returned with a crate. Amid hay packing lay several test tubes filled with glowing algae-like mush.

"That's it?" Dex said. "Algae?"

"It's more than that, old man." Lexington grinned. "This 'algae' grows super-fast. If it didn't also contain a mind-controlling agent, it would end world hunger. As it is, it'll end world hunger *and* supply me with a world of yes-men."

"Cool project," Dex said. Shame it was being used here. It might have earned Lexington the coveted right to represent the College of Arcane Sciences at the Spring Project Fair. Hmm, no, it *wasn't* a shame.

"Let's see how they like having Chia golems," Lexington said. "Ones that obey *my* commands."

CHAPTER SEVENTEEN

Teetering on the window sill, Drake grabbed a thick tree branch. Below, golems rampaged through the Dark Arts quad. Judging by their directed behavior, a mad scientist controlled them via the strange vines sprouting like curly green hair from their scalps. Despite this, Escaping From Angry Mobs class continued. Professor Leo the Licentious merely incorporated the golems into the lesson.

Lounging against a tree, Professor Licentious shouted at a fleeing student, "If you can't evade simple creatures, the first demon you lose control of will devour your soul."

Drake swung a leg over the tree branch, snagging his robe on the bark. Clouds of gnats surrounding the golems' green "hair" now homed in on fresh prey. Like a buzzing miasma, gnats bit Drake's face and swarmed up his nose. He swatted wildly, then slipped sideways, barely grabbing the branch and avoiding a leg-shattering twenty-foot drop.

After Drake's heart slowed from a pound to a gallop, he shinnied to the ground, shredding the hem of his robe. He hated Escaping From Angry Mobs class, but considered it his most important course. An angry mob had nabbed Drake's oldest brother, referred to in his epitaph as Sladen the Slow. Drake's family never found more than one tattooed body part.

More gnats swarmed Drake from behind. He threw himself to the ground and rolled. A crazed golem lumbered by. Professor Malfeasant poked his head from behind a tree, pointed his wand and spoke an incantation. Purple light engulfed the golem and it crumbled. The green foliage, however, slithered toward Drake.

From his pocket, he pulled a wrapped package holding one of Blackie's fire patties and whisked it at the spreading plant life. The patty exploded *too* well. Fire whooshed toward Drake. He whipped his bell sleeve over his face. Flames blazed across his arm. Drake rolled in the dirt, quenching the fire on his sleeve.

Someone applauded. Standing beside Drake, Professor Licentious said, "Impressive, Mandrake—right up to the part where you almost roasted yourself."

"But I didn't." Drake grinned as he rose.

"Yes, yes. I suppose only the results matter."

Evil sorcery was very results-oriented.

Professors and students soon reduced the golems to dust.

The stench of burning dragon dung filled the air as the mind-control vines burned.

A cold, rasping voice intoned, "Well done."

Drake's every muscle froze, yet he forced himself to face the auditor wraith. How could he have been so careless as to let one slip up on him? Then again, he had been a tad distracted.

Drake kept his gaze on the wraith's clipboard. Lucky men dropped dead from terror after seeing a wraith's face. Unlucky ones turned into gibbering madmen.

"I will ask questions," the wraith rasped. "You will answer truthfully."

Not if I can help it.

"I understand certain Dark Arts funds have been allocated for animating target dummies for the heroes to practice slaying. How did such a ghastly waste of funds occur?"

Drake opened his mouth to deny all knowledge regarding the subject, but to his horror, he said, "The deal was the unintended result of a prank where I sabotaged the heroes' target practice."

"Ah, yes. The...pranks."

Gak! The wraith had cast a truth spell. Drake prayed the creature didn't ask him any more inconvenient questions.

"Tell me about the sophomoric prank war between the Colleges of Dark Arts and Arcane Sciences."

Damn! I knew prayer didn't work. Compelled by the wraith's powers, Drake spilled out the sordid details, his confession filling nine pages. When Drake had nothing left to divulge, he stood shaking while the wraith glided away.

Its muttering drifted back. "These idiots are distracting themselves from driving out the *real* enemy—while wasting valuable resources."

Cold with sweat, Drake had to agree—though he had a different opinion about who was the enemy. As long as Dark Arts and Arcane Sciences warred with each other, they were playing into Lucifer, Jr.'s claws. If the pranks didn't stop soon, they would all end up indentured slaves in Lucifer, Jr's army— or worse, as drodents in his army. Even so, Drake's blood burned for revenge for the scientists' sabotage of the golems. How could both sides fight their evil instincts and work together to defeat their common enemy? Then again, what was the point of being evil if you had to control your impulses?

Two months passed. Drake suffered no repercussions from his forced confession. The auditors had left a week ago to meet with the Board of Trustees and the Innermost Circle of Benefactors. Drake prayed the auditors kept their sources confidential.

Recalling that prayer didn't work, Drake just had to hope.

Winter was upon the campus, dusting turrets and roofs with snow, and crowning the distant mountains in white. Winter was Drake's favorite time of year. Jeffrey left their chamber window blissfully closed. Most days were cloudy, and on those rare sunny days, the weak winter sunlight couldn't penetrate the black drapes. It set the perfect mood for study and plotting.

After paying Dingo for new supplies—Jeffrey somehow found the money to replace the powdered spell elements he had ruined— Drake spent all his free time working on the weather animation staff. He had finished the runic carvings and had inlaid jewels, each possessing a special power, along the handle. Drake even found a use for the miraculous mood-sensing stone pried from a ring Dex had given him during last year's solstice festival. After a week of incantations, magic energy hummed around the staff. He longed to unleash its destructive powers.

Whistling a lighthearted tune, Jeffrey bustled into their chamber. Spotting Drake, he pasted on a scowl. "Oh, you're here. As usual."

"It's my room," Drake said.

"It's *our* room, and I never get a moment to myself. You're always here muttering and raising a stink with your spells."

"I finished the staff." Drake leaned back in his chair. "Not even your pouting can spoil my mood."

Jeffrey glared. "I'm not pouting; I'm being evil."

"For the hundredth time, being surly isn't the same as being evil." Drake raised his fingers and ticked off, "Neither is moody, cranky, sulky, whiny—"

"Okay, I get it." Jeffrey sprawled on his bed. "Since you finished your project, are you going to the Winterball?"

Drake growled and ran a finger across the gems. The color of Dex's mood-sensing stone read Drake's mood as "vicious."

"What, you don't have a date?" Jeffrey said.

It was Drake's turn to glare. "No, I do not."

"I'm taking Samantha, a Hex Omega Tau pledge. She sort of cornered me into it. I don't even know how to dance."

"Oh, that's perfect." Drake's surly roommate had a date he didn't want, while Drake—an excellent dancer—had none. Having a quirky, out-of-character interest, such as dancing, made an evil sorcerer appear well-rounded. It also fulfilled a liberal arts requirement. Torrence pressed flowers, and Garius's fine needlework paid for his tuition.

"I hear the band is good," Jeffrey said. "The Gratefully Undead. Gilbert says they do a mean Bob Marley cover."

"Maybe I'll go to listen—hold on, you're still speaking to Gilbert?"

"I have to," Jeffrey said. "We have a project together in World Domination. Besides, we're friends."

Friends. Drake had to admit—only to himself—that he missed Dex's company. *Friendly* rivalry was hard to come by. Drake ranked at the top of his class and the other sorcerers would have to topple him to advance. Already he had fended off several sabotage attempts against his staff.

"Is Dex going to the ball?" Drake asked.

Jeffrey shrugged. "One of his frat brothers is debuting his girl robot, so most of the scientists will be there."

"A girl robot?" Drake chuckled. "There's a new low. It sounds amusing."

"Great. We can air out this stuffy chamber while we're gone, and maybe you'll even have some fun."

Fun seemed a bit much to hope for. But perhaps Drake could assure Hexaba and Prince Vanity had a miserable time.

Drake paused outside the Student Union ballroom. This was the first dance he had attended without a date. Now he knew how Dex felt.

Drake had dressed with extra care, donning his finest black velvet robe embroidered with silver moons and stars. His hair, restored to a decent shoulder length, looked particularly menacing with the new white streak. When Hexaba saw him, she couldn't help but realize her mistake in choosing Valorous. After she groveled a bit, he would take her back.

Who was he fooling? If she wanted Drake, she would have him. His future plans depended on having a powerful witch by his side. It didn't hurt if she was also a hot wench.

Drake slipped into the dim ballroom. Fly paper hung in scalloped rows along the ceiling. A hundred pine tree-shaped air-fresheners hung from sticky, fly-coated festoons. Scented candles lined the stage and decorated every table. Despite that, the smell of rotting flesh permeated the air. The student body shouldn't have left the entertainment to the freshmen, who hadn't yet learned how to extort—er, raise—funds.

A reggae version of "I Fall To Pieces" blared from the stage. The lead zombie of The Gratefully Undead opened his jaw wide for a sustained note. His bloated tongue waggled amid broken yellow teeth. When the note warbled on long past its time to end, the zombie smacked his jaw to loosen it.

The three dozen sorcerers in attendance were alone. No surprise there. Since the semester's start, Drake had heard nothing but grousing, whining and empty threats from his fellow jilted sorcerers. What did surprise him was that neither the witches nor the do-gooders had arrived.

As usual, the mad scientists were dateless—except for one. A hawk-nosed geek in horn-rimmed glasses danced with what looked like two tin cans stacked on a tripod of wheeled, metal legs. Two metal arms ending in clamping "hands" clasped the nerd. Bulbous eyes stared from the top can, which had a speaker where a mouth should be and two more grates where ears should be.

"Oh, Isaac," the can cooed in a metallic female voice. "You're the best dancer."

The geek blushed at the preprogramed complement. Drake rolled his eyes.

"Unbelievable, isn't it?" Dex said.

Shaking off discomfort, Drake turned. "I'm surprised you didn't have him make *you* a robot girlfriend."

Dex squirmed. "The thought never entered my mind."

When the song finished, everyone applauded. It didn't pay to enrage a zombie band—unless you wanted to spend the evening fleeing from flesh-eating undead. Drake felt certain the scientists had done that enough already. After the bass player reattached his thumb, the band launched into "I've Got You Under My Skin."

"Nothing under *their* skin is a mystery," Dex said, grinning.

Isaac and his robot girl swept by. With casters for feet, she was particularly good with spins.

"Ooh, Isaac, you're so smart," she said. "Explain the theory of relativity again. I love a man who can talk science."

"Pathetic," Drake said.

"Speaking of pathetic." Dex swept a bandaged arm, winced, then lowered it. "Where are the witches? I mean, we expect to come stag, yet a scientist is the only one here with a date."

"The planets are out of alignment," Drake agreed.

The double doors opened. A gaggle of heroes and superheroes strutted in, witches draped across their arms and pressing their supple bodies against spandex and armor.

Drake's face heated as he spotted Hexaba molded against Valorous, who looked like a lacy tin can with legs. A bewitching and bewitched gown of shimmering black clung to Hexaba's curvy frame. The low neckline revealed the swell of her breasts, and hip-high slits accentuated her long legs. Remembering how Hexaba felt molded against *him*, Drake shifted uncomfortably.

He pushed aside the thought. Attachments only weakened an evil sorcerer anyway.

"Don't look now, but they're coming over," Dex said.

Drake dragged his gaze from Hexaba's body. Prince Valorous's smug look showed he knew Drake and Hexaba had once been an item.

Hexaba's fiery red hair indicated she was in a sexy mood—or hungry for Thai. Probably sexy. Drake's blood pounded. Surely she wouldn't go all the way with that—that *good boy* when she never had with Drake.

Valorous's smile grew insufferable. "Ah, Mandrake. Alone, I see. Whereas I am with the loveliest lady on campus."

Hexaba stroked Valorous's cheek. "Isn't he sweet?"

"Hello, Hexaba," Drake said, ignoring the interloper.

Hexaba's gaze flicked across his hair. "Really, Drake, the streaked look is *so* last year. You look like a skunk."

Drake's insides withered. A skunk? Well, a skunk was threatening, just not in a way Drake cared to be.

"I see why they're called witches," Dex whispered to Drake.

"Did you just ask to be turned into a bat?" Hexaba demanded, eyes flashing.

"Leave him alone, Hexaba," Drake said.

She smiled wickedly and ran her hand through Prince Valorous's black hair. "See, Val? Drake has a date after all."

The Gratefully Undead struck up their version of "Every Breath You Take." "Ooh," Hexaba said. "I love this song. It can be *our* song, Valorous."

"It's about a stalker," Dex noted.

Hexaba nodded. "*That's* true love."

Valorous looked somewhat disturbed as Hexaba led him toward the dance floor. Drake glared at their backs.

Dex nudged Drake. "Actually, I wouldn't mind being a bat for a while."

"Are you mad?" Drake shook his head. "Of course you are. But why would you want to be a bat?"

"To study their sonar capabilities first hand."

"That's taking dedication a bit far."

Dex launched into a rant on the single-mindedness needed to be a genius. Drake pretended to listen, as a good friend should.

A superhero in black spandex and a chitin-like breastplate hopped up, springs on his boots making an annoying chirping noise. "Mandrake the Malevolent!" he exclaimed. "And Poindexter the Psychotic. It's great to see you guys." Hop. "How's everything been going?" Hop. The superhero's costume chirped like a cricket in heat.

Drake ducked to avoid two swinging antennae. "Mikey?"

"You're not supposed to recognize me in my superhero outfit," Mikey said, lifting a black mask from around his eyes.

"Sorry," Drake said.

"Who are you supposed to be?" Dex asked. "Roach boy?"

"Don't be silly." Mikey sprang high enough that fly paper stuck to his black hood. As he landed, he pulled down a line of sticky "crepe" scallops. Tugging at the mess, he added, "My advisor said Cricket was the perfect identity. I never would have thought of it without Mandrake's help."

"Nice going, Mandrake," Dex said, nudging Drake's ribs.

Drake's face heated again. As Mikey hopped off, trailing a sticky, fly-covered streamer, Drake pointed a whirling mass of pink tulle. "I believe *you* created *that* superhero."

"Make way for Tutu Tornado." The whirl headed for the dance floor. At least he drove Hexaba and Valorous to their seats.

Dex rubbed the bridge of his nose. "This is humiliating. If anyone ever finds out we spawned their superhero identities, you and I will be the laughingstocks of the campus."

"That costume is holding up well," Drake said. "You should have become a seamstress."

"He ruined it," Dex said, shaking his head. "Who ever heard of a blue sash on a flamingo? Doesn't he understand the use of color schemes in themed costumes?"

"Are we really having this conversation?" Drake asked.

"Yes!" Dex's thin chest heaved in indignation.

Apparently Dex was stooping to a new level of madness. "Very well," Drake said. "I suppose my comment would be who ever heard of a flamingo in a tutu?"

"You have no imagination." Dex rubbed his forearm.

Nodding at the bandage, Drake asked, "Lab accident?"

"Zombie bite."

Drake winced. "So, Dex, have your eating habits changed? Do you crave any unusual forms of meat?"

"No. Why do you ask?"

"No reason—"

"I'll get you some punch, fair Hexaba," Prince Valorous announced to the entire room.

Drake tracked Valorous's progress to the refreshment table. "I'll just be a moment, Dex."

Valorous kept his gaze on the two sloshing cups of red punch as he shuffled toward the table where Hexaba waited. Drake charted a course to intersect with the prince. At the last moment, Drake put an extra push in his step and collided hard with Valorous. Red punch spilled all over Valorous's flesh-colored tights. The little that splattered onto Drake's black robe didn't even show. Perfect.

Red-faced, Valorous sputtered. "You...you did that on purpose! Do you realize how much you just cost me?"

"Punch is free," Drake noted.

Valorous started, glanced at Hexaba, then stammered, "Uh, um, the cleaning bill. That's what I meant. Do you know how much it costs to get red punch out of flesh-tone tights?"

"I have no idea," Drake said. "And no interest."

"Gack! Those miserable drodents will probably just dye them pink," Valorous whined.

"Perhaps, if you ask nicely, Hexaba will wash them. Although, having recently become a fashion critic, I'd say pink is your color."

"You think so?"

"You're definitely the pink type."

"I *mean* do you think Hexaba would wash them?"

"Ask her." Drake strolled back to Dex, while Valorous returned to the punch bowl. The embarrassing placement of the red stains brought a smile to Drake's lips.

Dex nudged Drake, then nodded toward a cluster of sorcerers. "Looks like your buddies are getting huffy."

Scardos stood whispering at the center of the huddled group. The other sorcerers responded with "Here, here!" and "Quite so!" Soon, Scardos had them worked into a lather.

"Think they'll start a fight with the heroes?" Dex asked.

"That could be amusing," Drake said. "However, if anyone starts casting spells, take cover. You don't want to get caught in the fallout."

The enraged sorcerers took up the cry, "To the village!" and charged from the ballroom.

"Why are they going to the village?" Dex asked.

Drake frowned in bemusement. "I have no idea—"

"Fine? *Fine?*" The robot's mechanical voice rose to an ear-piercing screech. "What do you mean I look fine? My subtext translator reads that to mean you think I'm fat. Admit it. My cannister butt's too big and I have thunder thighs. Well, it's your fault. *You* built me."

"Now, pumpkin—" Isaac began.

"Pumpkin? *Pumpkin?*"

Drake winced as her voice jabbed his ears. The band fell quiet.

"You think I'm shaped like a pumpkin?"

"No, no. You're shaped just right—"

"I saw you leering at those witches!"

"Uh, er, no, my sweet Rosie. I only have eyes for you."

"Now you're calling me a liar? You think my sensors can't track the direction of your gaze and feel the increased body temperature and blood flow in your groin area?"

"Oh, crap," Isaac groaned, his face blood red.

The witches snickered. The heroes and superheroes looked like they wished they were miles away.

Rosie the robot grabbed Isaac in a crushing grip. Legs telescoping out, she lifted him from the dance floor. She whirled, swinging Isaac like a rag doll.

"Crush, kill, destroy!" she cried.

"You're not supposed to run that subroutine until the Project Fair selection demonstration!" Isaac wailed.

Rosie flung Isaac against the wall. Drake was certain he heard bones snap.

"Speaking of finding cover," Dex said, gripping Drake's wrist. They ducked behind a table and peered over the top. Foolhardy displays of bravery were for heroes and superheroes.

The robot's round, illuminated eyes scanned the room.

The superheroes looked at one another indecisively.

"We can't all rush in at once," The Buzz said. "We'll get in each others' way."

"I can't believe I left my danged shotgun at the frat house," Armadilloman said. "I'd use a beer bottle, but that useless security guard confiscated it."

"How do we decide who fights her first?" Tutu Tornado asked.

"Rock, paper, scissors, lizard, Spock?" Mikey suggested.

Prince Valorous set down fresh punch glasses, placing one near Hexaba's hand, then raised a fistful of drinking straws. "We could draw straws, but they're all the same length."

An undeclared superhero suggested, "We could guess the number of jellybeans in a jar—if we had a jar of jellybeans."

"While you guys dither, I shall stop that runaway robot!" Tutu Tornado declared.

As he whirled in pastel pink fury, another prince said, "One, two, three, four. I declare a thumb war."

Rosie clotheslined the spinning superhero with her steel-reenforced arm. Tutu Tornado spun out of control and crashed into a corner, where he lay in a fluffy heap of pink tulle. Dex would be happy. The blue sash had torn off in the crash.

"I predicted this outcome," Dex said. "Judging from the literature, giving a robot human traits makes it far more likely to go on a murderous rampage."

Watching Hexaba cling in undoubtedly fake terror to Prince Valorous, Drake felt like going on a murderous rampage himself.

Prince Valorous pressed Hexaba's cup into her hand. "Drink some punch, dearest. It will calm your nerves."

Hexaba set down the cup and grabbed Valorous. "I'm afraid."

Drake's eyes narrowed. What was she up to?

"Fear not, fair Hexaba." Prince Valorous drew his sword. "I shall protect you."

As if Hexaba needed it. Witches, with their protection spells, were the only safe ones in the room. Drake wondered what Valorous thought a sword would do against a metal robot.

Rosie reduced her leg size, lowering her center of gravity, and planted her wheeled feet like a bull ready to charge. Her clamp hand hinged open and a six-foot spiked lance telescoped out in a whir of motors.

Valorous charged. Rosie pawed the ground once, snorted, then whizzed toward the prince. A lance being longer than a sword—something Valorous should have realized—Rosie's spiked arm extension slammed into the prince's breastplate before he got off a swing.

He flew backward and landed on his table. It collapsed, shattering the cups and sending red punch and glass shards flying. Daggers of glass missed the witches and their dates, but drew blood from every scientist in the room, except Dex, who ducked behind the table. Valorous shrieked in rage.

"I never imagined a school dance could be so entertaining," Drake said.

Dex laughed. "They should sell popcorn."

Hexaba leaned over Valorous, her breasts nearly bursting from her low cleavage. She stroked his hair and told the idiot how brave he was.

Sadly, Rosie's lance had only dented Valorous's breastplate.

"That's good armor," Dex said. "Isaac used titanium on all weapon attachments. It should have pierced steel."

"A white wizard probably enchanted Valorous's breastplate." Drake gritted his teeth. "His father grants him such luxuries."

The superheroes organized a new offensive. While Mikey and Armadilloman hopped around to distract the robot, The Buzz launched, then flew behind Rosie.

The robot jabbed at Cricket, but he was too fast. Drake shook his head in disgust. He *had* helped the little twerp find his superhero identity.

Armadilloman shouted and Rosie's head swivelled toward him. Hovering, The Buzz unreeled a cable from his utility belt. He attached a grappling hook, whirled it around, then slung it toward the raging robot. The cable spiraled around Rosie, binding her arms to her sides.

The Buzz landed gracefully. "You see, my dears? Nothing to worry about—"

A compartment in Rosie's chest slid open. A buzz saw emerged. Its whining, spinning blades sliced into the cables. Sparks flew, then the bindings burst. Bits of flying cable cut into the scientists' flesh. The robot grabbed The Buzz and tossed him into the fly paper festoons. The Buzz thrashed, but couldn't break free. Items fell from his utility belt, pelting several scientists' heads.

"Help me!" The Buzz cried in a squeaky voice.

A bald-headed mad scientist threw up his bleeding hands and strode toward the robot. "Deactivate."

The robot drooped and fell still.

Drake sighed. "Things were just getting good."

"Lexington must have thought our boys were taking too much damage," Dex said.

Given the mad scientists' multiple lacerations, Drake saw his point. Dr. Mumbojumbo would have to lay in a new supply of bandages and chicken hearts after this mess.

"Why didn't you stop her before now?" The Buzz demanded as Mikey hopped up and pulled him free.

Lexington shrugged. "I assumed Isaac was performing a field test and didn't want to corrupt his data. Once he collapsed into a whimpering pile, though, I thought I should step in."

The zombie band reattached various appendages and launched into an upbeat rendition of "She Blinded Me With Science."

"I guess the fun's over," Dex said.

The double doors burst open. Scardos and his band of disgruntled sorcerers dragged screaming, crying girls into the ballroom. The girls' rat's nest hair and missing teeth marked them as being from nearby Bramblethorp.

"Help!" one cried. "They're going to sacrifice us."

"We just invited you to a dance," Scardos said.

"Knocking on our doors, then dragging us from our homes is not an invitation," another girl wailed.

"Hey, we *knocked* first," Torrence said defensively.

The witches' attention fixated on the sorcerers and their unwilling dates. For an instant, Drake thought that somehow the scraggly, knock-kneed village girls had made their former girlfriends jealous. The witches huddled, then rushed to the crying girls.

"Oh, my dear, we must do something about that hair," Hexaba said, touching a girl's tangled, dirty locks.

Drake scowled. "I've had about all the fun I can stand. How about you?"

"I'd best help get Isaac and the others to Dr. Mumbojumbo," Dex said reluctantly.

The doors to the Student Union Ballroom slammed open again. Dean Corleone, in full demon form, stormed inside. The dean rarely went near merriment except to squash it. Apparently that hadn't changed.

Dean Corleone shooed Drake and Dex back with the rest of their classmates, then mounted the stage. He knocked aside the lead singer, who, on impact, lost three limbs. Grabbing the microphone in his claws, the dean growled, "The auditors have made an unfavorable report. The Board of Trustees has put the Colleges of Dark Arts and Arcane Sciences on probation and slashed our funding."

Icy cold fear washed over Drake. If Dean Corleone couldn't control the auditors, he couldn't hope to defeat Lucifer, Jr.

"In addition," Dean Corleone continued, "many of our benefactors have officially withdrawn their endowments, claiming the admission of heroes and superheroes to the university violated the endowment terms. The board plans to close either the College of Dark Arts or Arcane Sciences at year's end."

Mad scientists and sorcerers gave a collective gasp that seemed to suck the air from the room. Under the admissions contract, the students of the closed college would be turned into drodents.

And it was worse than the other students realized. If Lucifer, Jr. became dean, the surviving college's students would become indentured slaves upon graduation. It was a lose-lose situation.

"This must be Lucifer, Jr.'s new plan," Dex whispered. "*He's* behind this. There's no way this benefits the university—just him."

Drake stared at Dex, who stared back with the same revelation. *Only one of us can survive. It's you or me.*

The dean huffed out a stream of fire. "The remaining college will receive the funding previously budgeted for both, in hopes of graduating a higher caliber student."

"Hey, what's so bad about us?" Nestor the Nervous asked.

Dean Corleone simply stared.

Nestor flushed. "Oh. Yeah."

"How come only our colleges face the threat of closure?" a mad scientist demanded.

"The Colleges of Virtue and Olde Wyrd Charms are exempt under the terms of their integration orders," the dean said. "The college that wins the annual Spring Games & Project Fair will be the one to survive."

"What if neither of our colleges win?" Scardos asked.

"That would be most regrettable."

"You mean the board would close *both* colleges?" Drake asked in horror.

"That's precisely what I mean. The funding budgeted for Dark Arts and Arcane Sciences would be awarded to the winning college. The board wants to assure all participants are motivated to win. Your college deans are scrambling to rewrite the budget so our doors will remain open for this year." Dean Corleone's gaze homed in on Dex and Drake again. "Considering what's at stake, I suggest all pranking end now."

The dean swept out of the room.

Prince Valorous's chuckle broke the quiet. "He certainly knows how to put a damper on a festive occasion."

Naturally, Valorous wasn't worried. *His* future was in no danger.

As for the "no more pranks" edict...well, Drake could think of no better way to distract a bunch of pencil-necked geeks from producing a project worthy of recognition. Clearly, the College of Arcane Sciences was the Dark Arts' chief competition. They both had the most to lose.

"Gee, Drake, I'm sorry to hear you'll be turned into a drodent," Dex said, a hint of sincerity in his voice. "I'll check on you now and then to make sure vermin don't infest that beard you're trying to grow."

Drake fidgeted with his robe. "What makes you so sure a college of tinkers can win the Spring Games and Project Fair?"

"Because *I'm* in it. What makes you think *you'll* win?"

"Because *you're* in it," Drake said drily.

"That's cold, Drake," Dex said. "Even for you."

"Thanks."

Upon returning to his chamber, Drake canceled the wards around the trunk holding his project, retrieved the staff and headed for the secret—well, not so secret—after-hours exit. Once outside, he trudged through a dusting of snow to a high hilltop. Moonlight washed the world in silver.

Drake's breath puffed in the cold air. He held out the staff. "By wailing of wind and roaring of rain, by deepest darkness and devastating destruction, I bring thee to life." Alliteration fueled most staff incantations.

The staff's carved runes glowed in jewel tones. Above the valley, a rotating black cloud formed, then a funnel extended from it. It worked! Drake would surely win the Spring Project Fair and save his college—and his life. Now if he could just figure out how to foil the vile devil's scheme and prevent his own enslavement.

The only way to avoid that terrible fate was to assure that Dean Corleone remained university dean.

Drake willed the tornado to split. Twin funnels wound side by side, then moved closer, like Hexaba and Valorous on the dance floor. Growling, Drake collapsed them. The cloud dissipated.

"Wow."

Drake whirled to find Jeffrey behind him. "What are you doing here?"

"I saw you leaving with the staff," Jeffrey said. "I wanted to see it work."

"I thought you had a date."

"She's probably having a better time without me. Last I saw, she was dancing with Armadilloman."

"That's witches for you."

"Yeah. Well, your staff is amazing."

The praise improved Drake's mood.

"But what if you lose control?" Jeffrey's brow puckered. "Tornados cause massive destruction and loss of life."

Drake gave a nasty smile. "People should worry more if I *maintain* control—especially a certain interloping prince."

"Why do you want revenge on Valorous?" Jeffrey asked. "You don't really love Hexaba."

"It's the principle of the matter."

"You don't have principles. You're evil."

Drake chuckled. "Good point. I think you're getting the hang of this, Jeffrey."

CHAPTER EIGHTEEN

Valorous wiped his sweaty forehead and stared at the test paper. Who knew jousting had written exams?

A knight on a charger leaves Bramblethorp at a trot. Another knight, galloping from Champion Field, heads straight for the first. How soon will they cross lances?

Geez, college was hard. In prep school, vassals had taken Valorous's exams. Here, the faculty expected everyone to know their own answers. That didn't seem fair. What good was being a prince if you couldn't make others perform the hard tasks?

The bell rang. Valorous scribbled a hasty answer, then handed in his paper. With Sir Eloquence at his side, he headed toward the Order of Virtue Hall.

"What answer did you put for that last question, Highness?" Sir Eloquence asked.

"I chose B."

"B, Your Highness?"

Valorous nodded sagely. "I've heard that if you're not sure of the answer, you should always choose B or C."

"Only on multiple choice tests," Eloquence said.

Drat! Valorous never could remember the small details.

They clumped upstairs to their chamber. Valorous's prince-sized bed draped with gold satin curtains filled one wall. A velvet comforter covered the down-filled mattress. Three wardrobes were stuffed with Valorous's clothes. Across the chamber rested Sir Eloquence's cot and footlocker.

"Did you slip Hexaba the potion last night?"

Valorous glared at his vassal. "I did not. I'm certain that damnable Mandrake bumped me on purpose to spill the first cup of dosed punch. I want to know how he found out I had a love potion. Did you blab?"

Sir Eloquence looked wounded. "I would never betray your confidence."

"I know." Valorous kicked a wardrobe in frustration.

"What about the second dose?" Sir Eloquence asked.

"That wretched robot knocked me into the table and the cup broke." Valorous curled a fist to strike the wardrobe, then thought better of it. "Mandrake probably arranged that too. Now I'm out of potion."

"I suppose Your Highness plans another foray into Nuevo

Pittsburgh."

Valorous sighed and retrieved his money coffer. Inside, two fifty-gold pieces clinked together in loneliness. Valorous's father would send no more money until end of term. King Marcus claimed wastefulness injured the peasants who must pay for such waste. This incited them to unrest and made them susceptible to evil usurpers such as Mandrake's father, Bane. King Marcus wasn't going to downgrade *his* lifestyle, so he expected his children to live within their budgets. Valorous only had enough gold to buy the basic love potion and one additive.

So did he want Hexaba to be faithful or a good wife? *Who cares about that?* a dark voice whispered. *Go for a lewd sex act.* But that would take the entire hundred gold and wouldn't turn Hexaba into a good witch. Valorous tried to push aside the thought, but he was a nineteen-year-old male. Everything paled next to lewd sex acts.

A second coffer caught Valorous's eye. He stroked the lid.

Sir Eloquence cleared his throat. "The villagers of Bramblethorp gave us that gold to rid them of evildoers."

"My marriage to Hexaba—as a good witch—is a major step toward that end," Valorous said. "I would be woefully remiss in my duties as a future liege if I don't take some of the donated funds to buy a proper potion."

Sir Eloquence shook his head, but remained silent. Valorous outranked his vassal's conscience.

Valorous pulled out a few coins, shrugged, then dumped them all into his pouch. He hated math.

Junior hovered, occasionally peering over Asmodeus's shoulder. Every whiff of brimstone stoked Asmodeus's urge to throttle the red-skinned devil. Until Junior's arrival, the university's conference room had seemed spacious. Now it felt unbearably crowded.

The college deans sat around the wooden coffin serving as a table. Under the university bylaws, its founder *had* to attend all faculty meetings. Fortunately, the founder seldom spoke.

Deans Malodorous and Evil occupied one side. For once, having Malodorous nearby wasn't so bad; Asmodeus preferred the sorcerer's body odor to Lucifer, Jr.'s sulfurous stench. Opposite those deans sat Prince Raymond, representing the heroes, and Dean Mediaman, representing the superheroes. That their college warranted two deans and two curriculums was just one bone of contention among the other deans. Dean Selena, of the College of Olde Wyrd Charms, sat at the coffin's end, opposite Asmodeus. Her ample cleavage presented a scenic view.

Junior leaned in once more.

Asmodeus hunched over reports containing complaints about the recent rash of pranks. "What do you want?"

"Is Dean Selena seeing anyone?" Junior whispered.

"*That's* why you're pestering me?"

"Does she like chocolate-coated hearts?"

"Only if they're still beating." A shudder ripped through Asmodeus as his demon side tried to sprout. He reined in the impulse. For faculty meetings, he avoided turning demonic. Dean Evil always snickered and said green wasn't Asmodeus's color, and the do-gooders whined even louder than usual.

"If you want to know about Dean Selena, ask her," Asmodeus said. "I don't pry into my deans' private lives." That last bit was a bald-faced lie. He kept fat files on all employees. Asmodeus could have answered any question, from Selena's favorite coffee to her bra cup size—a delicious double D.

Junior slouched in a corner chair and stared goggle-eyed at Selena. Considering her appetites, it would serve Junior right if Asmodeus broke the ice between them.

"I realize these pranks are a major distraction," Mediaman said. "I've reprimanded the ringleader from our college—"

"Who would that be?" Junior interrupted.

"Armadilloman. He's just a big kid at heart," Mediaman said, "and he's learned his lesson. He promised the superheroes will stop playing pranks."

Dean Evil puckered his lips. "Odd. I've received no complaints about *them*." He gave Malodorous the evil eye—a look the man had surely trademarked.

"*My* students didn't start it!" Malodorous roared.

"Did too, you liar," Evil said.

"Did not."

Asmodeus rose, his knuckles resting on the coffin. "Back to the original issue, Dean Mediaman, what pranks did Armadilloman instigate?"

Malodorous frowned. "I don't recall any of *their* pranks."

Dean Mediaman appeared at a loss for words. That alone made this waste-of-time meeting worthwhile. Asmodeus grinned, feeling the prick of teeth sharpening into fangs.

Mediaman twiddled his green-gloved thumbs. "They shorted the sheets in the Gamma Ray Delta house, and replaced the laundry soap in the Black Sash fraternity with itching powder."

"*That's* what softened our robes," Malodorous said.

"You idiots call that pranking?" Dean Selena snorted and tossed her sleek blond hair.

Junior sighed wistfully.

"I see no harm in a little fun and games," Asmodeus said. In truth, he had hoped for a lot of harm, but Mandrake and

Poindexter had failed him.

"That's what Armadilloman said," Mediaman interjected.

After glowering at the dean of superheroes, Asmodeus said, "*However*, under the current circumstances, it would be best if our students found better uses for their time and energy."

"Our students could work together on community service projects," Prince Raymond suggested. "They could clean up litter or assemble food baskets for the poor. Many street youths in the techno towns would benefit from an outreach program, someone to teach them right from wrong."

Dean Evil chortled. "Suppose we'd rather teach them wrong from right?"

"You see?" Raymond said. "We're already working together."

Dean Selena slammed her hand against the coffin. Two coffin screws thudded to the carpet.

From inside, a craggy voice bellowed, "Desist! It's bad enough I've awoken to this boring twaddle. Must you rattle my old bones? They're barely hanging together as it is."

"Sorry, old man." Selena stood. "Not that this hasn't been fun, but seeing as my ladies haven't done anything, I'm off."

Junior scurried back to Asmodeus. "She can't leave."

"Why not? No one has a grievance with the witches. And the witches have no grievances with any of us."

"We have no grievances either," Mediaman said. "No one has been hurt. We just want our students to focus on their goals."

"Whether your students choose to learn is *your* concern," Asmodeus said.

Dean Mediaman and Prince Raymond nodded, then rose. Mediaman said, "Since our students' pranks raise no concerns—"

"They haven't even been noticed." Asmodeus had known about them, but he knew almost everything that happened on campus. He also knew many things that went on in other dimensions. After the Nexus ate Asmodeus's secretary, it had taken the initiative to show him current events of potential importance. Asmodeus considered it a fair trade, especially since neither Junior nor the board knew about the portal hub's new trick.

"Since we're finished, we'll take our leave." Mediaman sketched a stiff bow that barely ruffled his money-green cape. He smoothed the Mighty Dollar Sign on his chest then waved.

Raymond bowed with a flourish. "Do consider my words."

The chamber had emptied to the most important deans— and Junior. Asmodeus studied his unwanted guest, then jumped up and threw an arm around Junior's shoulder.

"Lucifer, old pal, would you do me a small favor?"

Junior's face screwed into a look of distrust. "Why?"

"Aren't you more interested in what it is? Or with *whom*?"

"All right. I'll bite."

No doubt Junior meant that literally. Still smiling, Asmodeus said, "I forgot to have Dean Selena sign some paperwork. She put in a request—"

"I'll do it."

"Don't you care what she requested?"

"Not in the least. The Board isn't out to replace *her*."

"You'll find the paperwork in my desk. Do you know how to get it out?"

Junior rolled his eyes. "I've wrestled with living desks."

"Careful. Sometimes it gets in the mood to shred."

"Worried I'll lose a hand?"

"I just don't want to fill out all that paperwork again."

After Junior skipped out of the chamber—his light, happy gait could hardly be termed anything else—Asmodeus turned back to Evil and Malodorous. "We have a problem."

"What did he mean by they aren't looking to replace *her*?" Dean Evil asked. "Are our positions at risk?"

"Clearly the board will fire the dean of whichever college it closes." Asmodeus would have replaced that buffoon Dean Evil long ago, but tenure was a power even he couldn't defeat. Asmodeus didn't add that whoever remained would likely be working for Junior. Knowledge was power and Asmodeus parsed it out only when needed. If he informed everyone of Junior's nefarious plot, Junior might find allies among the faculty. As long as Deans Malodorous and Evil believed their jobs were on the line, Asmodeus would have their staunch loyalty. Mediaman and Raymond considered Asmodeus the lesser evil. And Dean Selena, of course, never let him down.

CHAPTER NINETEEN

Gilbert lay on his bed. The pillow over his face muffled his whining. "I can't believe I'm failing Maniacal Laughter."

"There's still finals," Dex said. "If you fail, just retake the exam after summer review." Gilbert would be on probation, which meant his grades *had* to improve next semester or he would wash out. However, giving him that lecture when he was hysterical would waste time.

Gilbert pulled the pillow from his tear-streaked face. "Will you help me prepare?"

"Sure. Give me your best laugh." Dex folded his arms. The one the zombie head had bitten had healed, but Dr. Mumbojumbo's work burned, itched and ached.

It was Drake's fault. *He* turned the corpses into zombies. An inadequate warning did not diminish his responsibilities. At least Dex hadn't contracted zombie-ism.

Gilbert looked at Dex's scarred arm. "It healed nicely."

"Nicely!" Dr. Mumbojumbo had filled in the missing flesh with dirt and ashes. Then he sewed on a sliver of sheep's bladder and covered the ugly bump with discolored flesh Dex wasn't sure had ever been human. "If my name was Igor and I had a hump on my back, it might look okay." Returning to Gilbert's dilemma, Dex said, "Now, dredge up madness from deep in your gut. Let it build, then release it in a crescendo of insane cackles."

Gilbert drew a deep breath and let out a deep, "Ho, Ho, Ho." His shoulders sagged from the effort. A silly grin stretched across his face. "Wow. That was my best yet."

Dex stared in numbed shock. "*That's* your mad laugh? Tell me, *Santa*, have I been a good boy? Will I get a pony for Christmas?"

Gilbert knitted his eyebrows. "Not maniacal?"

"Not even for Santa if the elves went on strike."

Gilbert threw back his head and wailed, "I'm going to fail!"

"No, you won't," Dex said, already regretting his promise. "Now, for the sake of all dark matter in the universe, try to emulate me." Dex paced, and shook his arms to loosen the tension. He stared at the floor, drawing on his darkest and most secret desires. Then, Dex let out a long, deep, "Muwah ha ha haaaaa."

Gilbert whistled. "That was awesome, Dex."

"Picture your worst enemy ensnared in a trap and then imagine his expression as he realizes he's at your mercy—such as it is. Go with that feeling." Dex longed to have someone in his clutches, just to gloat and spill his plan to the one person who *could* have stopped him, had he not been captured and helpless.

Gilbert paced, then shook—like a dog drying off. "Tee hee hee hee."

Dex held his head.

"Should I try again?"

"Later. Listen, Gilbert, your project counts for a lot more than any one class—"

"But I'm failing more than one class."

Dex sighed. "Just tell me about your project."

An underclassman's project couldn't contend to represent Arcane Sciences in the Spring Project Fair. With Isaac's rampaging robot and Lexington's mind-control algae project used up, Dex had that honor in the bag.

Gilbert rubbed his hands gleefully. He must have been flunking all his mad scientist mannerism courses. No two ways about it, Gilbert was drodent material. But his failure would bring down Dex's mentoring grade, lowering his GPA. Employing A=B=C logic, Dex encouraged Gilbert to continue.

"I'm working on a microorganism," Gilbert said. "It has a voracious appetite for oil and gas—for any petroleum product."

"Impressive," Dex said. Gilbert's ingenuity surprised him. Gilbert could name his price to the oil companies to keep from introducing the microbes into refinery tanks or oil fields. "How many microbes does it take to devour a barrel of oil?"

"One dropful of microbes will devour an ocean of oil."

Perhaps Dex had underestimated Gilbert. The quiet ones always bore watching—that applied to the living as well as the dead. "It's that powerful?"

Gilbert nodded. "As the microorganisms feed, they reproduce *ad infinitum* until they run out of petroleum. Inside of an hour, they'll clean up the worst oil tanker spill then die."

Dex nearly swallowed his tongue. "*What?*"

"The microorganisms clean up environmental disasters—"

Dex waved off Gilbert's nonsense. "You've been here a whole semester and still don't get it. I wouldn't do this for just anyone, but you need guidance. Come see *my* project."

Dex's private lab in the Genetic Engineering Building lay between Isaac's and Lexington's. Lights shone from under their closed doors. From Lexington's lab came the soft whirring of gears. Apparently, he wasn't out of the project competition. Had it been anyone else, Dex wouldn't have worried.

He unlocked his door and ushered Gilbert inside. Plans were

tacked to the walls. Parts of Dex's bomb, connected by braided colored wire, lay on tables. The coolest parts glowed.

"Wow," Gilbert said.

"Yeah. When my project is selected, and it *will* be"—the selection committee would have to be morons not to see Dex's brilliance—"the College of Arcane Sciences will triumph in the Project Fair. This year, we even have a chance in the Spring Games, since we have you, Muscle Boy. Between my brains and your brawn, we can't lose."

"The College of Virtue will be tough competition."

Gilbert had a valid point—his first this year. "If my project garners the maximum three-hundred points," Dex said, "which it should, it'll offset any losses in the games."

In painstaking detail, Dex explained his bomb's workings and the massive amounts of glorious destruction it would reap. He illustrated the damage radius on a map and drew a picture of the expected tri-fold mushroom cloud on the chalkboard. Gilbert's jaw dropped in appropriate awe.

While Gilbert stammered, Dex added to the equations, then scribbled on the cloud drawing. At the final stage, the tri-bloom cloud would spell D-E-X as it dissipated. All great artists signed their work.

"Dex." Gilbert paused thoughtfully. "I'm not sure mankind is ready to handle such power."

Dex ushered Gilbert into the hallway, then slammed and locked his lab door. Dex took a step down the corridor, then whirled around. The tirade building inside erupted with a force equaling the planned capability of his bomb.

"Evolution doesn't wait! If it did, man would still be swinging from the trees, throwing dung at each other. We've progressed *despite* not being ready. We learned to throw stones. Then we sharpened them and made spears and arrows. We made projectile weapons smaller and propelled bullets via gaseous explosions through gun barrels. Were we ready for that power back then? No! We're not ready for it now. But it hasn't stopped us from creating even more powerful and devastating weapons. Why? Because mankind, as a whole, is a bunch of suit-wearing apes. But a few select members of humanity have evolved to a higher state. We're called scientists."

"I thought we were called *mad* scientists."

"We're labeled that because ordinary men don't understand our genius. They're incapable of it! They—"

"Dex?" Two voices spoke at once.

Isaac and Lexington stood in the doorways of their labs. Isaac said, "I thought I heard your voice."

"I recognized your rhetoric," Lexington said, jealousy lacing his words.

Dex trembled until the urge to shove his personal doctrines down Gilbert's throat subsided. Dex had many personal doctrines, something that made his resume stand out. Where others listed useless hobbies, Dex aired his views. Surprisingly, his applications had yet to yield a summer job offer.

His resume *had* garnered him a scholarship at the College of Arcane Sciences—and a free vacation at a criminal psychology conference. Oddly, he was never asked to speak, but was, for lack of a better word, put on display.

"What are you working on?" Dex leaned, trying to peek into Lexington's lab.

"Care to have a look?" Lexington asked.

Dex nearly choked as he stumbled toward the door.

Lexington's arm blocked his way. "Sorry, but we're in competition. You'll have to wait, like everyone else."

Dex fumed.

Gilbert, who stood a head taller than Dex, stood on his toes. "Wow," Gilbert said, the word oozing out on a long breath, "cool metal hats. Are they radio hats? Can you load them with beer cans?" At Dex and Lexington's blank stares, Gilbert added, "For wearing at ball games."

"Metal hats." Dex hummed.

"In pairs, connected by a curly wire," Gilbert said. "Oh, it's a sort of his-n-hers ball cap. Great idea for dates. You'll make a fortune. Gimmicky things sell like hot cakes. Remember the Hula-Hoop?"

"Connected by wiring," Dex mused.

Lexington grunted. "If you must know, it's a personality exchange device."

"Have you tested it?" Dex thought about volunteering Gilbert to be half of the exchange test dummy. The problem would be finding a suitable second half—though there *were* some large melons in the garden.

"Sadly no," Lexington said. "I must know the subjects well enough to ensure their personalities have truly swapped."

"You could try it on extreme opposites," Isaac said. "An idiot and a genius. A man and a woman."

Dex grinned. "Or an evil sorcerer and his familiar."

"I like it." Lexington rubbed his hands in an appropriately mad manner.

Dex pointed at Lexington. "See, Gilbert? Like that."

Trying to copy the move, Gilbert looked like a hamster grooming itself.

"Is your project ready to test?" Dex asked.

"Yes," Lexington said.

"Then what are we waiting for?" Dex stifled the urge to laugh maniacally. Then, remembering Gilbert's struggles with the course, he let it out.

"Wow," Gilbert said. "I'll bet you got an A."

"Why is it," Lexington asked, "we always seem to use *my* projects for *your* pranks?"

"*Our* pranks," Dex said. "Besides, your project is more practical to test against those future drodents."

"You make a valid point," Lexington conceded.

Gilbert coughed pointedly. "Uh, Dex, we're not supposed to play any more pranks."

"How better to distract the sorcerers from developing projects superior to mi—any of ours?" Dex hoped Lexington hadn't caught his near slip.

"I don't know," Gilbert said. "The dean looked pretty mad."

"Think of this as a last hurrah," Dex said. "No...Eureka! It's not a prank. That'll be our defense. It's a valid test of a school-required project."

Gilbert shuffled his feet. "It won't hurt them, will it?"

"*How* did you get into this university?" Lexington sighed. "Most likely, it'll just leave a bad taste in their mouths."

Isaac grinned. "A fuzzy taste, I'd say."

Dex clapped Gilbert's shoulder. "I know you're friends with Jeffrey—I'm friends with Drake—but only one college will survive and I intend it to be ours."

Lexington let them into his laboratory. He was one of those rare, neat scientists who labeled everything. Sticky notes colored the room—stuck to the walls, chalkboard, electronic gear, tool boxes, drawers—and one on the stack of sticky notes, labeled "sticky notes." On Lexington's lab coat pocket, a note read, "Armadilloman must die."

"I need a portable generator," Lexington said. "Would you carry that, Gilbert? It's rather heavy."

Gilbert lifted the bulky case with one hand.

Dex reached for the conical, wire-connected caps, but Lexington jumped in front. "I'll handle those, Dex."

"Just offering to help."

"You can carry the clips," Lexington said. "And towels. For some reason, there's a lot of sweating."

"Is that a problem?" Dex asked, grabbing the box.

"Not really. Well, sort of. Worst case it *might* electrocute them, but I doubt the generator would produce enough juice to fry more than an organ or two."

"Acceptable risk," Dex said.

Gilbert giggled. "Man, I wish I could be a fly on their fraternity walls."

"Perhaps there's a way." Isaac ran into his lab and returned with a tiny camera. "We can view the experiment via this robotic eye. We'll install it in a ceiling corner, where we should have a grand view of everything that happens."

CHAPTER TWENTY

Drake dragged his foggy mind from sleep. His tongue felt rough and dry. Exhaustion left him limp. As he stretched, his spine arched farther than expected—farther than humanly possible.

Something was wrong. His body was wrong.

Drake's eyes flew open. Malice's fuzzy black paws extended before him. Glancing down, Drake saw a furry black belly. Swiveling his head, he watched a black tail twitching with a mind of its own.

His scream came out a screeching yowl. Feeling like a loose spring with legs, Drake flopped onto his stomach. Without moving another muscle—except for the self-activating tail—Drake surveyed his surroundings. He lay atop the dresser. Through the faint light, for which he could find no source, he saw his human body huddled in a corner. It shook as though with convulsions.

This was Dex's doing, or that of his mad cronies. Those rotten scientists had broken Dean Corleone's edict against pranks! Never mind that Drake had planned to do the same. Great minds *did* think alike. Of course, this required retaliation—once his mind was restored to his body.

<<Malice?>> Drake thought to his familiar.

<<Blind! I'm blind!>>

<<What?>>

<<I can't see anything.>>

<<Human eyes don't see in the dark.>>

Malice wailed. Drake cringed at the sight of himself in such a pathetic state.

<<What's wrong now?>> Drake asked.

<<My eyes are leaking!>>

<<Then quit crying.>>

Jeffrey's cat Spike stalked by, his white fur fluffed. He grabbed the tattered black curtain in his teeth and pulled it open. <<This is worse than when I was transformed into a rat.>>

Drake was surprised to hear his roommate's thoughts. <<Jeffrey?>>

<<I see those pencil-necked geeks got you too.>> Jeffrey thought. <<You should choose a better class of friends.>>

<<Do you think Gilbert wasn't involved?>>

Jeffrey-in-Spike's-body gave an audible sigh. <<I see your point about the hazards of friendship.>>

Malice-in-Drake's-body rubbed his eyes, then his head jerked upward. His gaze locked on a shiny can. <<Tuna, tuna, tuna.>>

As steady as a drunk at closing time, Drake's body rose, then stumbled into the wall. Leaning on it for support, Malice reached for a tuna can. With his fingers curled, he swatted at the can, knocking it to the floor with a clunk.

He nosed it around, then batted at the can. <<How do I make the tuna come out?>>

Drake ignored his familiar.

<<Do you think we can hear each other because our familiars communicate with telepathy?>> Jeffrey thought.

Drake's claws extended. <<They probably talk about us behind our backs.>>

<<Who in the bloody hell cares? Are we stuck like this?>> In a cat's body, Jeffrey's surliness seemed more natural.

<<Let me try a transference spell.>> Drake opened his mouth to speak the incantation, but with his sandpaper tongue and strange vocal chords and mouth shape, he could only yowl. <<Malice's mouth can't form the words, and it isn't enough to just think them.>>

<<Can you get Malice to speak them with your mouth?>>

<<If he knew how to talk.>> Drake glanced at his body, now trying to gnaw the can open. He hoped the idiot cat didn't break his teeth.

Malice stopped gnawing, set the can down and wiggled his thumbs. A glint flashed in his eyes as he snatched the can and stumbled toward the counter. <<Can opener, can opener.>>

Drake caught himself licking his paw. <<When we mind-link with our familiars, we hear a translation of cat thoughts. I could teach him to speak, but that would take months.>> Malice had figured out thumbs—sort of—but speech was far more complex. Mispronunciations in spells led to disaster. <<We must reach Professor Rasputin. No one knows transference spells better.>>

<<My body is huddled in the corner,>> Jeffrey thought. <<Spike kept falling over. I think he cracked my ribs. He's certainly given me some deep bruises.>>

Jeffrey's body crouched, glaring at them from a corner. Without his glasses, Jeffrey's green eyes looked doubly bright.

<<How bad is your eyesight?>> Drake asked.

<<Terrible.>>

<<That's probably it. Tell Spike to put on your glasses.>> Drake flicked his paw toward the night stand where Jeffrey's wire-rimmed glasses lay folded.

Jeffrey leapt onto the night stand and took the glasses in his teeth. He padded to where Spike sat huddled and shaking. Jeffrey butted his cat head against his human body. <<Put these on, Spike, and you'll see better.>> After much coaxing and coaching, Jeffrey got the glasses on Spike.

<<You're handling the cat body well.>> Drake felt a tad envious.

<<I told you I was a rat for a while.>>

<<You're still a rat, Jeffrey.>>

<<This from someone who licks his own butt.>>

Drake was about to retort when he discovered he *was* licking his butt. He jerked his head away and scraped his raspy tongue across his teeth. Drake wished he could sanitize his mouth with grain alcohol.

<<Animals have strong instincts,>> Jeffrey said. <<You have to focus hard to counteract them.>>

Now he tells me. Hoping to prevent more disgusting instinctive acts, Drake sat up rigid and still—and too close to the dresser's edge. He slid and fell in a writhing ball of fur and claws. Miraculously, he landed on his feet.

<<Tuna, tuna.>> Malice batted the can opener. Jeffrey had bespelled it to work without lightning power. Combining technology and magic violated university rules, but since it was a useful violation, Drake hadn't reported it.

At a whirring sound, Drake's ears perked up. His feet were already running toward the can opener when he remembered he had *four* legs. He stumbled, rolled, then scrabbled to his feet.

<<Malice, stop that. We have a big problem.>>

Malice pressed on the can opener and watched the cutter spin. With a gleeful expression, he set the can against the turning blade. The can flew from his grasp. Growling, Malice dropped to all fours and picked up the can.

<<Malice, now is not the time—>>

<<Tuna time, tuna time,>> Malice thought back. <<*I* have the opposable thumbs now, sorcerer boy. So go chase your tail.>>

The idea of chasing his swishing tail held an inexplicable appeal. Malice whirred the can opener again. Drake found himself salivating. Again, Malice pushed the can against the blade. Again it spun from his grasp.

Drake sighed. <<If I tell you how to open the tuna, will you do what I ask for the rest of the day?>>

Malice glared with a malevolent look Drake hadn't known his face capable of. He felt a deep pang of envy. He could have used that expression during freshman finals.

<<Very well,>> Malice conceded with a huff.

Drake talked Malice through opening the can. After several abortive attempts and a cut on Drake's hand that would no doubt leave a wicked scar—the only plus so far—Malice pried up the half-open lid. Using his fingers, he dug tuna from the can and stuffed it into his mouth. He paused, then licked the blood trickling from the cut.

<<Stop that,>> Drake growled. <<The cut will fester.>>

<<That's because *your* mouth is filthy,>> Malice retorted.

<<This from a creature who licks his own butt.>>

Jeffrey nudged Drake's furry shoulder. <<Copycat.>>

As Malice resumed gobbling tuna, Spike-in-Jeffrey's-body perked up. "Mwow," he said, crawling toward Drake's body.

<<Great, Spike wants tuna or *he* won't cooperate,>> Jeffrey thought.

<<All right, but *he* operates the can opener. I'm not losing a hand over this.>>

It took forever to get their familiars moving. Now Drake truly understood the difficulty of herding cats. Gorged on tuna and sporting several new cuts, Malice and Spike crawled on hands and knees. Walking was out of the question.

Drake took a step, then stumbled. <<Damnation. Jeffrey, do cats' feet move same side together or in opposition?>>

Jeffrey shook his furry white head. <<Top of your class and you don't know how your familiar walks?>>

<<It never mattered until now.>>

<<Watch and learn.>> Jeffrey stalked toward the closed door. His left legs moved forward, then his right.

Drake lifted his right paws, edged them forward, then shifted his weight.

<<Speed it up or we'll never get changed back,>> Jeffrey thought.

Drake tried to scowl, but his cat lips refused to move from that ridiculous smirk Malice always wore. <<Why don't you work on opening the door instead of badgering me?>>

<<Fine. I'll see if Spike can manage a door lever.>>

After a few swipes at the latch, the door swung open. In the hall, Black Sash members clung to walls or crawled on the floor while their familiars staggered and stumbled like drunkards.

Dex is better than I credited him, to pull off this prank on the entire fraternity—

A growl vibrated in Drake's throat. <<Did you forget to set the wards on our chamber last night or did they fail?>>

<<Neither. You told me to ward against enemies. Dex is your friend. Next time be more specific.>>

<<That's it!>> Drake gathered his haunches beneath him and sprang at his roommate.

Jeffrey sidestepped. Drake's head banged into the stone wall. He dropped to the floor, then shook away the black spots.

<<I'm disappointed, Drake. Didn't you tell me striking out in anger and without planning is a fool's tactic?>>

Drake tried to stalk away in a huff, but only wobbled on, careening off the wall. Once he was restored, he would test Jeffrey's animal adaptability as a toad—or perhaps a worm.

They crawled down the hall at a snail's pace. Familiars in their masters' bodies stumbled around. A sudden jolt shot up Drake's spine. He screeched and jumped straight up. Tail throbbing, he bit the offender's calf until he tasted blood. Amid the yowling, Drake wobbled on.

<<Scardos will have a limp when he's restored,>> Jeffrey thought with a mental chuckle.

I can't believe I'm crawling—literally—to beg a professor for aid. This was more humiliating than the time Drake's wand had gone droopy in transformation class.

Professor Rasputin's office lay two buildings over. An hour later, Drake, Jeffrey, Spike and Malice reached the chamber.

Impressive spider webs adorned Rasputin's office. Snakes crawled on the shelves. Drake's back arched and he spat at the slithering reptiles.

From the corner, two eyes glowed in the dim lamplight. "How dare you stumble into my office in a drunken stupor!"

"Mwrow," said Malice-in-Drake's-body.

Professor Rasputin's intense gaze pierced Drake's body, then shifted to Drake in the cat body. Drake shivered. Even the faculty members feared Rasputin. He had survived several apparently successful assassinations. "I see the mad scientists have been at work. Your wards must have failed. It would serve you right if I left you this way."

Drake hissed at Jeffrey, who turned and licked his paw.

Rasputin furrowed his unibrow. "But letting them win would cost me my job. Sit your bodies down while I brew a potion and scrounge up a sack."

A sack?

Rasputin rubbed Drake's fuzzy head. "We must drown you for the spell to work. Fortunately, cats have nine lives."

<<What about us?>> Drake demanded.

To Drake's surprise, Rasputin heard his thoughts. "How else do you propose I get a soul *out* of a body?" His voice took on a hypnotic quality as he intoned, "Drown a cat and poison a lad...you recall the adage."

Drake had a horrible suspicion about the potion Professor Rasputin planned on brewing.

Jeffrey butted his fluffy white head against Drake's ribs.

<<What adage is he talking about?>>

<<You know—'when good succeeds over bad, drown a cat and poison a lad.'>>

<<Won't we die of poisoning when we reenter our bodies?>>

"Oh, I'll have an antidote ready to administer," Rasputin said. "It *should* revive you."

<<And if it doesn't?>> Jeffrey persisted.

"You can't make an omelet without breaking a few eggs," Rasputin muttered, rummaging through his wardrobe.

<<That's just splendid.>>

For once, Drake agreed with his roommate. Perhaps they should have crawled to Dex and asked him to reverse whatever-it-was he did.

No, I'd rather die. Well, that sentiment was about to be tested.

<<What about our familiars?>> Jeffrey asked.

"Both your cats have several lives remaining." Rasputin held a cloth sack open on the floor. "Here, kitty, kitty."

CHAPTER TWENTY-ONE

Dex hung a computer-generated poster over his bed. "How's it look?"

Gilbert lay curled in laughter on his bed. The laugh was a deep, tickled chortle, but it was the best he had. "Mandrake should be a model."

Dex grinned at the poster of Malice in Drake's body grooming himself with his tongue. "It's a work of art."

"Too bad Lexington's project burned out on that last transference," Gilbert said.

That comment raised another grin.

"You know, you could sell copies," Gilbert said.

"That, Gilbert, is brilliant. I'd make a fortune." The money could finance Dex's first coup.

He flicked off the lights and crawled into bed. The poster cost eighty cents to print. If he sold it for three dollars—no five— that left a four dollar and twenty cent profit.

Dex drifted to sleep, dreaming of becoming a poster mogul. He founded a factory, then an empire of wall art. Every poster contained subliminal messages. As his posters covered walls from libraries to teenagers' bedrooms, Dex built an army of subjugated, angry youths.

Hexaba, his personal secretary, sat on his lap. She couldn't type or take dictation, nor would she make coffee. No matter. Any temp could do menial tasks. Hexaba only had to be Hexaba, and she was highly qualified for that.

The AC blasted freezing air. Snow flurries danced around his office. Hexaba's nipples hardened under her skimpy halter. That almost made the cold tolerable. Then Dex's glasses iced over and he couldn't enjoy the view. He fell out of the chair...and fell and fell—

A heavy thump knocked him from his dream. Cold air blew under the covers. Dex huddled into a ball, his eyes closed tight. "Enough with the fresh air, Gilbert. Close the window."

"I did," came Gilbert's muffled reply.

Dex opened one eye. "I see stars. Close the window and turn off your reading light."

"Uh, Dex, I see stars too. And that's the moon, not my reading light."

Dex bolted upright. Instead of cinder block walls, trees and shrubs surrounded them. In the distance stood shadowed classroom buildings and the astrolabe. Razor wire atop the perimeter wall glinted in the moonlight.

"What the heck happened?" Dex asked.

Beds lay sprawled across a dirt indentation shaped like the missing fraternity house. Through chattering teeth, Dex's fraternity brothers called out curses and confused questions. Next came the obvious blame. Only a sorcerer—several sorcerers—could have managed such a feat. That they cooperated was even more surprising than the fact they'd made the Gamma Ray Delta frat house vanish.

Dex grinned. "The sorcerers know they're beaten."

"From where I'm sitting—*which is outside and in the cold*—I'd say they're winning hands down." Gilbert wrapped his blanket around his massive shoulders.

Dex shook his head. "They've realized our chosen project would defeat theirs. After all, science is innately superior to magic. But"—Dex raised his index finger defiantly—"they don't realize our projects *aren't* here."

"Don't you mean *weren't* here?" Gilbert asked.

"Immaterial, my dear Gilbert."

Blanket-wrapped students dragged themselves into a huddle.

"Someone must inform Dean Evil," Lexington said. "We're talking grand theft here."

Everyone looked at everyone else. No one liked to bother the Dean of Arcane Sciences with bad news. Dean Evil might throw the bearer into a shark tank, cut him in two with a laser beam, or devise some other torturous death, whatever spy movie he'd last watched providing the inspiration.

Before the members of Gamma Ray Delta worked out the rules for selecting their emissary, the entire faculty of Arcane Sciences, dressed in doctoral robes and flat-topped, tasseled hats, swept across the lawn. The stream of men was a blur of brilliant minds, not a one hindered by a pesky conscience. They were legends. Role models. Inspirations.

Dean Evil led the group. Dr. J & H, in mid-transformation, became more Hyde than Jekyll with each step. Soon his knuckles dragged the ground.

Dr. Frankenstein and Dr. Arcanum walked with heads together in discussion. On passing, Dr. Arcanum glanced up and nodded. Dex nodded back. Most likely, the mad doctor was nodding to them all. No matter, Dex would swear on his deathbed that Dr. Arcanum had made eye contact, thus acknowledging and honoring Dex alone.

One robe floated by, seemingly unoccupied. Dex waved. "Good to see you, Dr. Iman."

Dr. Iman had been Dex's favorite instructor last year. No one could sneak up on cheaters better than an invisible professor. It bothered Dex that the man was naked when conducting class, but it explained the thermostat's high setting.

The "empty" robe floated toward Dex. As the robe flapped, bright red longjohns flashed beneath. "Poindexter, my best student. We've had a breach of security."

"Can you get our fraternity house back?" Dex asked.

"Certainly." Dr. Iman's flat hat cocked. "I'm not sure....We hope so."

"Excuse me, doctor," Lexington said. "What are we to do in the meanwhile?"

"I'm freezing," Pryce whined.

Pryce was such a baby—"Oh, Professor J & H, there goes my patella"—but he was right about the cold. Dex couldn't feel his toes. He nodded and shrugged, unsure how far to back Pryce.

"Do we have to stay in the Life Sciences' basement *again*?" Isaac complained.

"No," Dr. Iman said. "It's flooded. A pipe broke."

The ranting faculty passed through the open gates in a V-formation. Unsure what to do, the student scientists stayed in a close group. Dex's extremities numbed one by one until, at last, the faculty returned.

With help from two instructors, Dean Evil climbed onto a marble bench. "Students, we have a crisis."

"There's an understatement," Isaac muttered. His friends—the ones with higher GPAs—shushed him. They didn't want Isaac dragged off for "punitive measures."

"We met with the faculty of Dark Arts," the dean said, "and have agreed upon a resolution."

"Then why am I still freezing my butt off?" Pryce yelled.

Dex took three casual steps away from Pryce.

Dean Evil squinted and pursed his lips. He flicked a finger toward Pryce and mouthed something. Dr. Hyde and Dr. Moreau grabbed Pryce by the upper arms and then dragged him off, wailing and kicking.

"Think we'll ever see Pryce again?" Isaac whispered.

Dex and Lexington shrugged. It was only Pryce.

"As I was saying," Dean Evil said, "some of you and the sorcerers have ignored the truce Dean Corleone imposed. Dean Malodorous has agreed that if no pranks occur in the next two weeks, the sorcerers will return our property. With luck, Dean Corleone will never be the wiser."

"Yeah," Lexington whispered. "He'll never notice a missing building."

In a puff of fire and smoke, Dean Corleone appeared, with

horns, hooves, tail and green skin. Sulfurous fumes rolled off him. Dex heard the distant wailing of the damned, or maybe it just seemed that way—Dean Corleone was *that* impressive.

Dean Corleone rolled his eyes at Dean Evil. "Get down from that bench, doctor. You look ridiculous."

After Dean Corleone turned away, Dean Evil stuck out his tongue. Nonetheless, he climbed off the bench.

Dean Corleone swept his arms wide, striking Dean Evil in the chest. Everyone swallowed their laughter. Dex's own chortle nearly choked him and escaped as a small cough. Even Gilbert had the sense not to laugh. He still stared, horrified, in the direction where Pryce had been dragged off.

"Although you've brought this disaster on yourselves"—Dean Corleone's forked tail twitched—"I've arranged for you to stay at the Alpha Omega House and the Order of Virtue Hall."

Dex's eyebrows rose, as did his respect for the university dean. Alpha Omega was the super-pansies' fraternity, and the Order of Virtue Hall was where those prissy princes and their tin-plated dog-boys lived.

"I trust you'll repay your hosts' kindness...as is appropriate." Dean Corleone flashed jagged, yellow fangs. "Drs. Arcanum and Frankenstein will divide you into groups."

Dean Corleone's glowing gaze met Dex's own before he vanished in a puff of fire and fumes.

Twice, Dex had been singled out from the crowd. Ergo, it wasn't paranoia that the quack psychiatrists claimed he had. Dean Corleone had charged Dex with striking at the good guys. Perhaps, if in a desperate act of honesty, Dex confessed to breaking into the dean's office and discovering the Nexus's power, Dean Corleone would take Dex into his confidence and enlist his aid in defeating Lucifer, Jr.'s plot.

Professors Arcanum and Frankenstein took turns dividing the students, as though picking teams for dodge ball. Dex shuddered at the childhood memory and prayed he wasn't chosen last.

When Dex and Gilbert's names were called—not last, thankfully—they joined the group around Dr. Arcanum. The professor was GQ among the scientist set—perfectly shaven and his hair fashionably rakish. Only designer silk shirts and pants touched his skin—which, rumor had it, was highly sensitive and allergic, a condition oddly common with mad scientists.

Once inside the new quad's gates, Dr. Frankenstein led his charges toward the Order of Virtue Hall. Because it resembled a famous amusement park castle, the scientists and sorcerers called its members Cinderella boys, preferably to their faces.

Dr. Arcanum waved to his charges. "You'll be sleeping at the

Alpha Omega fraternity."

Dex grinned at Lexington and Isaac. They had hit the jackpot. "I have an idea," Dex whispered.

Lexington patted the pockets of his velour robe. "You realize I'm not carrying any projects with me."

Dex motioned for them to draw closer. "Imagine the gadgets we might *accidentally* find. It'd serve the super dopes right to lose some of their ill-gotten gains."

"Yes," Lexington mused. "Gadgets *our* funds purchased."

From behind, Gilbert said, "Dean Corleone might consider theft a form of prank."

Isaac sneered. "Listen to the farm boy."

"First, stealing isn't a prank," Dex said. "B, a bunch of do-gooders wouldn't tattle on us anyway. And ð, what Dean Corleone doesn't know won't hurt us."

"You're only trying to justify your plan," Gilbert said. "You know what he *meant*."

"I *know* what he said." At Dex's earlier meeting with Dean Corleone, his words were much clearer. Take out the "good guys," get a few extra grade points. Surely the dean's meaningful look tonight reiterated that statement. In any event, Dean Corleone's edict didn't forbid *sabotage*. Dex pulled his trio of companions aside. "I have my reasons, okay?"

"We're supposed to be under a truce," Gilbert whined.

"Our truce is with the sorcerers," Lexington said.

"Do you think Pryce will be all right?" Gilbert asked.

"Who?" Dex blinked. Gilbert's mind took the oddest jumps. "Oh, Pryce. Nah. He's a washout."

Gilbert paled, and pointed at two drodents huddled against a hedge, waiting for morning and new orders. "Y-you mean he'll be one of...*them?*"

"If it helps, Pryce got what he deserved," Dex said.

"It doesn't help at all, Dex."

For a mad scientist, Gilbert had a weak stomach. Despite himself, though, Dex shuddered as he watched the shivering, filthy, soulless drodents.

Dr. Arcanum stopped before two-story double doors displaying an etched Á on the left and Ù on the right. Wrought iron twisted around across the glass, incorporating dozens of logos worn by famous super-snoops. The obviously phallic symbols, such as shooting stars and rocket ships, no doubt compensated for physical inadequacies. The gleaming glass and metal walls rose more stories than Dex could see.

The double doors swung open. A man with silver hair, but a youthful, ruddy face, stood in the vaulted opening. He flung back his green cape. Gold tights covered his legs. On his chest was a dollar sign with a plumed pen across it.

The man flashed million-dollar teeth. "I'm Dean Mediaman." He perched his fists on his hips in the clichéd "superhero arms akimbo" stance, his head turned in profile—no doubt to show off his better side. "We of the College of Valor, Honor, and Justice for All have heard of your plight. You have our sympathy and our aid. No thanks are necessary—it's our calling. Welcome to the Super Quad." As Dex and the others filed past, Dean Mediaman said, "While here, you're expected to abide by our rules."

"We can't upset the media, can we?" Lexington murmured.

"Excellent," the dean said. "Cooperation is always best."

Inside the skyscraper, Dex found it hard to concentrate on Mediaman, flamboyant though he was. Bizarre, twisted sculptures captured Dex's gaze. They resembled some of the culinary "delights" the Gamma Ray Delta cooks prepared.

"Ah, admiring our sculptures," Mediaman said.

Dex half-shrugged, half-nodded, trying to be polite, since "admire" wasn't the right word by far.

Mediaman strolled toward a piece with two humanoid shapes contorted in ways the human body wasn't meant to twist. Dex had never seen such positions, even on the last pages of his well-worn copy of *The Kama Sutra*.

"It's called *Man's Indecision*. It was commissioned after a difficult voting year, when there was an actual tie." Mediaman flashed his perfect teeth. "Fortunately, within hours, my fellow members of the media convinced everyone to settle the tie in the way most compatible with our political views."

"Swell," Dex said, not caring. All politicians were bad. All politicians pretended they weren't; the least dishonest ones pretended they weren't *as* bad as their opponents. In the end, all politicians employed mad scientists. Some had even been mad scientists before turning to politics. Had they been great mad scientists, they wouldn't have needed politics to rule the world.

Dex cocked his head, curiosity overcoming judgement. "May I ask how much these sculptures cost?"

"About four billion dollars."

"For all this"—Dex sputtered, stifling the word *garbage*—"this...stuff?"

"Oh, no. Apiece. The works weren't that expensive, but shipping and handling to the university dimension is obscene." Mediaman bowed. "I leave you in my students' capable hands." In a flurry of gold and green, he swept from the atrium.

Dex couldn't stop himself from counting the sculptures in the lobby. *Twelve!* He felt faint a nanosecond later when he had calculated their worth, plus shipping and handling. Dex staggered into Gilbert.

"Is that a mural?" Isaac asked.

"It's an authentic, ancient Grecian frieze," Lexington said. "But check out the original Van Gogh...between the Rembrandt and the Picasso."

Gilbert nodded toward a list posted by the elevator. "Come on, Dex. We're staying on the seventeenth floor."

According to the gold plaque by the elevator, the Alpha Omega house had thirty-nine floors. Dex groaned from the impending headache likely to come from banging his head against a platinum wall. It wasn't fair.

The elevator doors slid opened. Out blared the din of Muzak. That the College of Yada, Yada, and Blah-Blah for All tormented its students with Muzak provided a small consolation.

Gilbert held the elevator door for everyone. Sticking his fingers in his ears to blunt the Muzak assault, Dex trudged onto the spacious elevator car. It rose at an excruciatingly slow rate. The elevator stopped on each floor, depositing two scientists, then continued upward.

Finally, Dex and Gilbert exited on the seventeenth floor.

"See you later, Dex," Isaac said.

"Enjoy the 'music,'" Dex said.

"I think it's *Stairway to Heaven*," Isaac said, "or maybe the theme from *Gilligan's Island*. I can never tell those two apart."

Dex and Gilbert stood facing a single door. Dex shook his head. Why would anyone put in a door just to section off the elevator from the dorm rooms? Maybe it was a *feng shui* thing.

Dex grabbed the handle. It twisted on its own and the door opened. A grey-haired man in his mid-fifties bowed. "Welcome to the seventeenth floor, gentlemen. I'm Alfred, the butler."

"Batman's butler?" Dex asked.

"No, sir. I'm from the Alfred Butler Agency, the ABA. All their butlers are Alfred. My birth name was Ferdinand. But that, of course, has been legally changed."

"Of course," Dex said. "Does everyone here have a butler?"

"Of course, sir."

More money wasted.

"Won't you come in, sirs?" Alfred moved aside.

Dex and Gilbert stepped into an enormous suite.

Cricket hopped into the sitting room. "Hey, guys!"

A skinny, red-haired man, about ten years older than most undergrads, sprawled on the conversation-pit sofa. He raised a long-neck beer. "Make y'all selves at home. There's Lone Star beer in the danged fridge and we've got nachos in the microwave."

"Do I know you?" Dex asked.

The unsuperhero-like fellow grinned. "Shoot, you probably know me as Armadilloman. Call me Tex."

"If it's all the same," Dex said, "I'd rather not get on too friendly of terms."

"Suit yourself. Won't stop me from being a good host."

On opposite sides of the huge living area stood two desks, each loaded with a high-powered computer and a three screen setup. Dex ground his teeth. It was so unfair. "Is *all* this yours?"

"Oh, no," Cricket said. "We just get this one floor."

"The *whole* floor?"

Cricket nodded, his suit making annoying chirping sounds, while Armadilloman said, "Whole danged thing."

"Are all the floors like this?"

Cricket gave a noisy nod while Armadilloman shrugged and said, "More or less. The Buzz has him a rock-climbing wall and Tutu Tornado put in a blasted dance floor, if y'all can believe it, but yeah, they're pretty much the same."

"Ooh, and the Flying Mole has tunnels," Cricket added. "But Mr. Gizmo has the coolest place."

Armadilloman rolled his eyes. "Cricket—he don't like being called Mikey no more—is real into gadgets."

Cricket chirped as he hopped up. Stealth would never be his strong suit. "I'm sorry to say we only have one bathroom and one bedroom. You two have to sleep on the sofa-sleeper and the daybed."

"Oh, the hardship," Dex said. At least they didn't have to share with The Buzz.

Suddenly Dex remembered Armadilloman's intriguing suit. Pasting on a smile, he strolled to the conversation pit sofa. "Since you're willing to be a good host, I suppose I can try the good guest thing."

"Glad to hear it." Armadilloman raised his beer in salute.

"So," Dex drawled, "I was hoping to get a closer look at your outfit. Why did you pick an armadillo?"

"It picked me." A ding went off in the kitchen. Armadilloman soon returned with a tray of bubbling hot nachos, loaded with jalapeños.

Dex declined the snack. Jalapeños gave him heartburn. "About your costume...?"

"It ain't a costume." Armadilloman wiped cheese off his chin. "As part of my superpowers, I *become* the armadillo. A few years back, when I was a Texas Ranger, I had a warrant for this Indian medicine man. I tracked him alone, figuring I could wrangle one Indian geezer to the hoosegow. When I found him, he was summoning an animal guide, and, well, I guess it took a shine to me. Since then, I've been imbued with armadillo powers."

"That's interesting," Dex lied. "But where's the suit?"

"There ain't no suit. It's just there when I need it."

"Can I see it?" *Up close, this time.*

Armadilloman, in man form, thunked his bottle on the coffee table and kicked off his boots. He stood, wiped his cheesy hands on his jeans and closed his eyes. "First, I gotta meditate."

Armadilloman's skin turned yellow-grey. He shuddered as tiny bumps rose on his skin. His nose stretched. A hump rose on his back, then armored plates formed, grew larger, overlapped then thickened. His fingers bent and sprouted long, sharp claws. Within moments, Armadilloman stood before them in full armadillo glory, minus the boots, hat and colorful shorts. The transformation was the most fascinating and repulsive thing Dex had ever witnessed. He wondered how he could meet an "animal guide"—though something cooler than an armadillo.

"Where are your clothes?" Dex asked.

"Dunno. Don't care, so long I don't gotta get naked to change or turn up naked when I change back. I figure it's a superpower thing. Or do you mean my boots and stuff?"

"I meant the first, but since you've brought it up—"

"They're in the closet." Armadilloman fetched the articles that completed his superhero identity. He slipped on the three-color shorts, stuffed his big, flat armadillo feet into a wide pair of boots, then settled a custom-made cowboy hat on his head. Grabbing his beer, he said, "That's all there is to it."

Armadilloman shifted back into his country bumpkin self. The shorts fell around his ankles, and Dex, too, felt glad that Armadilloman didn't change back naked.

"You seem like a nice enough fellow," Armadilloman said. "What made you turn evil?"

"Free will," Dex answered smugly, "something you 'good guys' lack." No doubt, Armadilloman had expected some heart-wrenching story of a horrible childhood.

"We defend free will," Armadilloman argued.

"Not from my perspective. I'll explain this as simply as I can." Normally Dex wouldn't have gone to such lengths, but Gilbert could stand to hear this in terms his dim brain could process. "Good and evil are merely terms to designate opposing sides."

"Yeah, right from wrong."

Dex sighed. "That's a matter of perspective—not that I'd expect you to say differently or even to understand. Who's to say good is better than evil?"

"We do."

"And I say evil is better. Evil allows for absolute free will. You'll never hear someone evil say, 'Oh, you can't do that,' unless it's physically impossible. In any situation, evil has far greater options. You 'good guys' do everything the hard way. Say someone is spreading vile rumors about you. You'd file a lawsuit for slander. Now there's a waste of time. We'd kill the guy and stop the rumors. Fast, easy and direct. If you examined our propaganda, you'd see evil is the logical choice."

"I still say you're wrong, but I admire your conviction."

"Then you concede my point?" Dex asked, amazed.

"No, I just see that I can't change your mind."

Smart man. Armadilloman could prove a future threat—assuming Dex *had* a future. The looming danger brought a heavy wave of fatigue. He yawned. "If you don't mind, it's been a long night."

Dex never slept better in his life and awoke feeling great. When he realized the reason, he felt worse than ever. Before he conquered some world, he might have to take over Alpha Omega. It would be good practice. He might even get extra credit for it.

CHAPTER TWENTY-TWO

Tex wormed through the crowd in the Alpha Omega basement. The room, though large, wasn't designed to host a meeting of every superhero member. Cricket, his suit still stuck in that danged chirping mode, hopped behind Tex.

Someone cursed in Japanese. "Crickets are supposed to bring good fortune, not pain to bunions."

Cricket turned in mid-hop. "I thought ninjas were fast."

Standing atop an overturned crate, Dean Mediaman waved the many printed pages of what the scientists had stolen.

"What are you going to do about this?" Kachina-Man demanded. "My spirit grows weary of white man stealing my property."

"You ain't no Indian, Marty," Tex said.

"Fine, so I empathize with the underdog," Kachina-Man said, his Brooklyn accent slipping out.

"Ooh, Underdog. He's cool," Cricket said.

"Everybody hush," Mediaman said. "I've reviewed the list and I must say I'm dismayed."

"Them fellas ain't nothing but thieves, mate!" Wombat Willie shouted from the back.

"Lexington stole my chemistry set!" Cat-Man-Do complained.

"Isaac stole a set of probes and my collection of IC chips, resistors, and capacitors," Mr. Gizmo said.

The Flying Mole raised a clawed fist. "One of those geeks took my best Bunsen burner."

"Someone drank all my milk," the Whatchamacallit added, "then put the empty carton back in the fridge."

"Consider how unfortunate they must be, how underfunded and ill-equipped their labs must be for them to stoop to stealing test tubes and Bunsen burners." Mediaman shook the twenty page printout. "It's pathetic, really."

"But I can't finish my project," an undeclared superhero said. "No place in the university dimension carries high-enough quality equipment, and Dean Corleone refuses to open his portal until the next travel day, which is after the projects are due."

"And I'm out of milk," the Whatchamacallit whined.

"Yes, well, that *is* a problem," Mediaman admitted. "We'll have to retrieve our stolen property—not the milk, of course."

"Back in the 'hood, cops lined up the usual suspects and

spread 'em for a search," The Buzz said.

"I suggest a full-cavity body search," Kachina-Man said, "not that I'm volunteering to perform it."

"I appreciate your suggestions," Mediaman said, frowning, "but we'd be violating their rights."

"Drat," Cat-Man-Do said. "He's right. Without a search warrant, we'd be no better than they are."

"What if we got a search warrant?" The Buzz asked.

The Flying Mole shook his head. "By the time we got it, they'll be gone—assuming we could find a judge in this dimension who would issue such a warrant."

"We could tap the phones and see who they call," Mr. Gizmo suggested. "I bet they call a fence."

"Again," the Flying Mole said, "we'd need a court order."

Tex snapped his fingers. "What about metal detectors?"

"And surveillance cameras," The Buzz added.

Mediaman rubbed his smooth chin. "That's a workable solution—though we'll have to post signs warning that the area is under surveillance. And it'll cost."

In unison, the superheroes said, "We can afford it."

"Fraternity dues will have to be raised by, say, three hundred dollars."

"Three hundred a week!" Kachina-Man raised his arms to the sky. "That's white man robbery!"

"A month," Mediaman said.

Kachina-Man let his arms drop. "Oh, that's fine, then."

"I'll have to dip into my emergency fund," Tex said, "but I figure it's worth it."

"Oi, bugger it all," Willie said. "I say we shake 'em down and see what falls out."

"You heard the dean, my man," The Buzz said. "We're the good guys. We gotta do things by the book."

Willie sighed. "A bloke can't help but wonder how them princy boys are getting along with their guests. I'll wager they don't have a problem ordering a strip search."

Asmodeus patted his desk. "Phone."

The woodgrain stayed as still as...woodgrain.

"Are you sulking because I sent Junior to get a document?"

Lines of woodgrain wavered and a grumble shook the desk.

"I had my reasons. Now, give me the phone. And don't chew on the cord. It was cute when you were an end table, but you're a full-sized office desk now."

The woodgrain mouth puckered shut. Knothole eyes opened in angry slits. Asmodeus exploded into full demonic form in an instant. The sudden transformation produced a noxious yellow cloud. Waves of heat, the by-product of a sudden burst of energy, rolled off him. The puckered woodgrain opened.

Maintaining his stern stare, Asmodeus grabbed the telephone—from who knew where, since the inside of the desk existed in its own dimension.

"Good desk." Perhaps Asmodeus would give it a bottle of lemon polish to drink. He set the phone on the edge, far from the mouth, and called the nearest florist.

"I'd like to send a bouquet to Dean Selena at the College of Olde Wyrd Charms," Asmodeus said. "What? No, this is no joke. I want a bouquet of feverfew, hemlock, hellebore, wormwood, devil's claw, adder's tongue, St. John's wort—on second thought, forget the St. John's wort. Add some sprigs of nightshade, and tuck in a witch hazel branch....You don't have those? What do you have?...Fine, poppies and roses will do....No, not thornless. The bigger and sharper the thorns the better. I want the card to say: Thanks for all you've done for the university. I can always rely on you. Sign it, Asmodeus."

A bouquet was the least he could do. Junior had slept for two days after his date with Selena, giving Asmodeus two days of headache-free planning. He had moved stocks around and transferred funds—just in case—and arranged to buy a few more votes on the Board of Trustees.

Junior poked his ugly mug past the door. "You were thinking about me. Tell the truth." He strolled in.

You don't run the place yet. Not feeling up to smiling, Asmodeus bared his teeth. Another few votes, though, would bring out a million dollar grin. Considering what he'd spent so far on bribes, it could well end up a billion dollar grin.

Junior's eyes glazed. "Selena is some woman. I'd take her to meet Dad, but he'd just steal her. Dad gets all the babes."

"Your father has already had Selena. Didn't she tell you?"

Junior's sunburn red complexion darkened to a bloody crimson. "You're lying!"

Asmodeus rolled his eyes. "You think she existed in a vacuum before meeting you?"

"She is *here*."

"But she wasn't always here and she still visits abroad."

Junior's color dropped back to scarlet. "When I'm running things, she'll see the wisdom in devoting herself to me."

"I wouldn't count on it."

"Selena's all about a man of power."

Asmodeus snorted. "That's no secret. What I meant was I wouldn't bet on your running the university."

"Bet?" Junior's eyes turned vacant. An idiotic smile tugged at his drooling lips.

An even bigger smile tried to escape Asmodeus. He had just learned from his sources that Junior had a compulsive gambling disorder. Several times, Junior's daddy had bailed his son out after he made bad bets. Feeling as though his luck had changed, and hoping Junior's luck hadn't, Asmodeus draped an arm across Junior's back, avoiding his excitedly stiff wings.

"You seem confident," Asmodeus said.

"I am, despite the few votes you've managed to buy. Don't look so surprised. I have ears everywhere."

"Would you be willing to make a wager?"

Junior's irises burned like liquid fire. "What wager?"

"For control of the university and the Nexus."

Junior chuckled. "As things stand, I'll get that anyway. What would I gain?."

"I hold a certain sway over Selena. And you can't be sure I won't win the board vote. I'm close to a tie. Besides, where's the fun, the challenge and the risk without a wager?"

"Not good enough, Asmodeus."

Asmodeus had feared as much. Gritting his teeth, he made Junior an offer he couldn't refuse. "*If* I lose, I'll serve you for five years."

"Twenty," Junior countered.

"Twelve."

"Ten."

Asmodeus smirked. "Done."

"I can't wait until I have you pinned under my hoof," Junior said. "Gambling does make life worth living. What should we base the wager on?"

"The outcome of the Spring Games and Project Fair?"

Junior scoffed. "I know nothing about that. I couldn't begin to calculate the odds and choose a winner."

"Since you hold the stronger hand in this matter, I'll choose one college to win. You get the remaining three. If my choice wins, I win. Otherwise, you win. Three to one odds."

"What if there's a tie?"

"Ties are against the rules. However, should one occur, you still win. I only win if my choice wins hands down."

Asmodeus and Junior spent another hour hashing out what each would do should the other win. A loss for Asmodeus promised a decade of demeaning and painful servitude. But at least he had a chance to hold on to everything he'd built.

He met Junior's gaze. "I want a binding handshake."

"Don't you trust me?" Junior asked silkily.

"Not for a nanosecond."

Junior spat into his palm. Asmodeus spat into his own palm and gripped Junior's outstretched hand. Their skin sizzled and a flash of hellfire engulfed them, binding them to their words.

Junior wiped his palm on his jacket. "Which college do you choose?"

A knock on the office door saved Asmodeus from answering. Poindexter peeked inside, then froze, staring at Junior.

"Come in," Asmodeus said, grateful for the interruption. He needed time to determine which college to pick. "Don't be shy."

Dex sidled toward the desk, keeping as wide a berth as possible between himself and Junior.

Lucifer, Jr. looked Dex up and down. "The sight of fresh meat makes me hungry. I'm going for a snack. Asmodeus, we can conclude our...agreement later."

"Until then." Asmodeus waited until the sound-proof door closed behind Junior. "Poindexter, to what do I owe this visit?"

"Sir, I know what's going on—the Nexus, Lucifer, Jr.'s plans, the threat to the university and its students. Um, I also know who drank the superheroes' milk, if that's worth anything. I'm afraid I broke into your office—"

"I know you and *Mandrake* broke into my office." At Dex's surprised stare, Asmodeus added, "I know everything that goes on at this university."

Dex shifted. "Yes, well, I'm only a junior, but I want to help save the university from Lucifer Jr.'s plot. And I really don't want to be a drodent or an indentured slave...sir."

Asmodeus smiled indulgently. "Just keep up the good work. And remember, *everything* depends on the outcome of the Spring Games and Project Fair."

Dex's eyes widened. "Even defeating Lucifer, Jr.?"

"Everything.

"I won't let you down, sir." Dex slunk out the door.

Two minutes later, another knock rattled the door.

"Come in, Mandrake," Asmodeus called.

Drake shuffled in, discomfort showing on his face. "Sir, I know what's going on—the power of the Nexus, Lucifer, Jr.'s foul plot, the threat to the university and its students. I'm afraid I broke into your office and—"

"It's charming how you and Poindexter protect each other," Asmodeus said. "Being friends *and* rivals must be difficult."

Drake paled. "How did you know?"

"I know everything that goes on at this university."

Drake gulped and nodded. "I'm only a junior, but if I can help in any way, I offer you my service."

Asmodeus gave Drake the same indulgent smile he had given Dex. "Just keep up the good work. And remember, *everything* depends on the outcome of the Spring Games and Project Fair."

Drake cocked his head. "Even defeating Lucifer, Jr.?"

"Everything."

Drake nodded. "You may rely on me, sir."

Those lads were a special pair, talented, astute and innovative. Their willingness to confess to the break-in disturbed Asmodeus, but he could always assign them additional course work in Moral Corruption.

But back to the matter at hand. If Asmodeus didn't back the right horse, he would be trampled under Junior's cloven hooves.

CHAPTER TWENTY-THREE

Dex met Isaac and Lexington in the skyscraper frat lobby. Gilbert was upstairs helping Alfred vacuum and dust. Isaac and Lexington had also given their assigned underclassmen the slip.

Since the scientists' clothes had vanished with their frat house, Dean Corleone had supplied new clothing and basic class supplies—notebooks and leaky black pens.

Isaac pulled a slim toolkit from under his new lab coat. "Ol' Gizmo will never miss it. These probes are much finer than any I possess. With them, I can recalibrate Rosie's pelv—"

"Forget your danged robot." Dex winced. Armadilloman's accent had a way of rubbing off.

Isaac drew up indignantly. "What have *you* stolen?"

"Nothing worth noting," Dex said. "I'm trying to appear cooperative. Besides, I've got me a better idea."

"Mind you, old man," Lexington said, "I don't have another project you can use."

"It ain't *y'all's* project I was thinking of." Affecting Dr. Arcanum's cultured tones in an attempt to fight off Armadilloman's infectious twang, Dex said, "No, gentlemen, I have a much greater theft in mind. We'll steal their best project."

Dex led them to the basement, which he'd discovered while searching for the rumored Tahitian underground pool. Instead, he'd found a wondrous place filled with cast-off equipment and storage boxes. They disguised themselves with old superhero costumes set aside for charity. Isaac fashioned a robot costume from an empty cardboard box and small pipes taken from the pumps and furnaces.

"Rosie ought to think you look hot now," Dex said.

"Jealous? At least I have a girlfriend."

Dex snorted. "Yeah, next time I want a girlfriend who can rip my arms off, I'll write up an order."

The few students they passed in the Super Quad paid them little notice. One, however, complimented Isaac's superhero identity.

"Come on, Robodweeb. Y'all can sign autographs later," Dex said.

"I'll thank you to call me Roboman," Isaac snapped. "Who are you? Supernerd?"

"Go give yourself an oil lube."

"Quiet," Lexington said. "You'll draw attention. Now, Dex, show us this project you discovered."

"I can't *show* it to y'all. But I can show you where it is—or thereabouts."

Adjusting his cardboard box, Isaac said, "You still haven't told us what we're looking for."

"An invisible helicopter."

Isaac and Lexington stopped in their tracks.

"Yesterday, I heard the rotors," Dex said. "I looked up and saw a superhero wannabee hovering in midair. So I followed him. I saw that pantywaist coming down while dirt was kicked up. Ergo, invisible helicopter. Come on. It's over yonder."

"That accent is *really* annoying, old man," Lexington said.

"What about your affected accent?" Dex retorted. "I happen to know you're from New Jersey."

"At least *I* made a change for the better."

"How do we find an *invisible* helicopter?" Isaac asked.

"Oh, we'll know it when—" Dex crashed into something metal and fell sprawling. "See?"

"No, but I can feel it." Isaac ran his hands across the air, feeling the helicopter's shape, doing a better job than one of those annoying mimes.

Lexington crept up, his hands before him. "How do we get in?"

Dex snatched a shiny object dangling in midair and held up the key. "They left it in the door."

"Unbelievable," Lexington said.

Dex pressed a button on the key fob. The helicopter beeped. "It has a locator device."

"Splendid, Dex, old man, but can you *fly* a helicopter?"

"Err, I was hoping you could," Dex said.

Lexington shrugged. "I come from money; I've always had a chauffeur or pilot."

"There must be another way," Dex said. "We only have to move it enough they won't find it in time for the Project Fair."

"What about that truck?" Isaac pointed toward a flatbed semi-truck parked alongside a fuel truck.

Dex glowered. "The superboobs said trucks produced too much danged pollution to have them on campus."

According to the windshield stickers, *these* trucks had passed stringent emissions tests in five dimensions. Of course, they had less horsepower than a riding lawnmower. But it proved enough for their purpose.

The two-week truce passed quickly. Holding the six-pack of Lone Stars Armadilloman had given him, Dex rode with Gilbert in the elevator, which played the same piece of Muzak drivel. At each floor, the elevator picked up two more of their clanking entourage. In bulging lab coats, glass tubes tinkled amid the many goodies tucked inside pockets. At last, their lab coats were proving useful as something besides napkins.

In the lobby, a dozen superheroes had gathered. Mr. Gizmo handed out brown paper bags. "A snack for the road."

Gilbert's eyes grew big. "Can I have two? I'm a growing boy."

"You can have mine," Dex said. "*I* don't intend to eat anything they've prepared as a 'last meal.'"

"I say," Lexington said, nodding toward the exit. "That's new."

A metal frame and conveyor belt leading to an X-ray machine stood before the double doors. "They installed a metal detector!" Dex said indignantly.

Isaac huffed. "You'd think they didn't trust us."

"As if the security cameras weren't insulting enough." Lexington leaned in close and whispered, "How will you get through with the you-know-what?"

"I've got it covered." Dex strode to the metal detector. He dug out the keys in his pocket, including the one to the invisible helicopter.

The Avenging Ninja held out a plastic basket. Dex dropped the keys in the basket and strolled through. The alarm blared, as it had for each scientist who passed through. Using the wand, Cat-Man-Do found every bit of contraband. No matter. After the superheroes reclaimed their precious wire cutters and pliers, the Avenging Ninja held the basket out, offering the keys. As far as Dex was concerned, the dunderheaded dolts couldn't even scream that their project had been stolen.

Dex scooped up the keys and strolled off, whistling "Anything You Can Do I Can Do Better."

"That, my man, was smooth," Lexington said as they headed toward Arcane Sciences.

Gilbert lagged behind, digging through the lunch sack. "All right! Egg salad!"

After an exhausting five minute walk, Dex and his peers gathered around the plot of dirt where their fraternity had been. They waited an hour before black-robed Dark Arts masters with long beards and stooped shoulders hobbled into the Arcane Sciences' Quad.

The sorcerer professors raised their hands and chanted. One foul-smelling sorcerer trod onto the bare ground. Using a stick, he scratched runes in the dirt then retreated. The stench traveled with him like a portable miasma.

The Gamma Ray Delta house materialized about two feet off the ground, then landed with a resounding thud. Except that the walls, porch, and roof were coated in ice, it looked the same.

Dean Evil studied the frat house, his finger touching his lip. "Why is it an icicle, Dean Malodorous? Or is it a fratcicle?" He snickered as if he'd made a joke.

"The students who perpetrated this *prank* sent the building to somewhere called Antarctica."

"If *students* are guilty, why not force them to undo their own handiwork, hmm?" Dean Evil's pasty lips stretched taut.

"It's much harder to undo an evil deed. That requires an act of"—Dean Malodorous made a disgusted face—"goodness."

"I trust we've established a permanent truce?" Evil said.

Dean Malodorous snorted. "Why not?"

Once the sorcerers left, Dean Evil pronounced the frat house ready to inhabit—assuming they could open the frozen door. Even the windows were iced shut.

Using a flame thrower was suggested and discarded. Gilbert suggested thermite. But thermite would blow up the fraternity and take the entire Arcane Sciences Quad with it. Only a farm boy would go ice fishing with dynamite.

"We could wrap the house in blankets," someone said.

"Maybe the witches would loan us their hair dryers," another underclassman said.

His upperclassman mentor rolled his eyes. "Do you realize how long the extension cords would have to be?"

They debated until the doors and windows defrosted on their own. It felt good to be home, even if the chambers were frigid.

CHAPTER TWENTY-FOUR

Drake dipped a quill in the inkwell, then scribbled a few lines on his essay, "Using Magic to Subjugate." Lying sprawled on his bed, Jeffrey gave a ponderous sigh. Drake darted him a glare, then returned to his theme. Things were going well. Otherwise, Drake might have turned his roommate into a toad again. The lad took moodiness to new depths.

Drake missed Dex's company. Yet Dex had changed. The last time Drake had seen him, Dex was carrying a long-neck beer and spoke with a twangy accent.

Jeffrey sighed again.

Drake rolled his eyes and scribbled another line.

Jeffrey gave a frustrated growl.

Drake slammed his journal closed. "What?"

"Nothing."

"Spit it out or cease the heavy breathing."

"It's just that I'm having a bit of trouble," Jeffrey said. "I missed some classes last week and there's a test coming up."

"Why did you miss class?" Anger surged through Drake. Jeffrey's laziness would lower Drake's mentoring grade.

Jeffrey shrugged. "Scardos and Garius dragged me into one of those endless Dungeons & Demons games."

"I warned you about them." The D & D club was the biggest on the Dark Arts campus. The dueling club used to be, but it died out, along with its members. Sometimes the D & D diehards played nonstop for days. They drank highly caffeinated tea and sent out for meat-lovers pizza, a concoction of blackened lizard, goat entrails, fish eyes and octopus sausage. Between the rancid pizza and the lack of bathing, any room hosting a marathon campaign grew pretty rank. Despite himself, Drake asked, "So, how did you do?"

"Fairly well. I found a staff of experience points and instantly became a fifteenth level white wizard."

"Fifteenth level, not bad—wait, did you say *white* wizard?"

"We wanted to see how the other half lived."

"I *suppose* that could be beneficial." For an instant—an instant for which Drake chastised himself—he considered joining the game. He had an old seventeenth level barbarian fighter of flexible alignment from his freshman year—

"It wasn't all that beneficial," Jeffrey said. "Torrence was playing a paladin and kept sacrificing himself and getting us all killed. I was resurrected nine times. Personally, I've had enough of dying and coming back."

Drake shuddered. Drowning as a cat, then recovering from the poison in his own body had been the most grueling experience of his life—an experience he vowed Dex would one day suffer.

"Avoid the D & D crowd like the proverbial plague," Drake said. "You'll never become an evil sorcerer with a horde of minions unless you study hard and get good grades."

"How does one acquire a horde of minions, anyway?"

"The usual method. Start by giving privileges to a few select men." Drake's term paper on the subject had received perfect marks. Then again, he had his father's experiences—good and bad—to draw upon. "Once you win their devotion, you give them well-crafted weapons and fitted armor. The rest is easy. Your loyal core of men go to villages and farms and conscript young, healthy men into your service."

"Don't they refuse?" Jeffrey asked.

Drake snickered. "Most people obey if you're pointing a weapon at them. When you force them to serve in your evil horde, they won't risk death by speaking out for a mere principle or moral belief. In fact, most people will do mental contortions to convince themselves *their* side is in the right. If they don't, you can sway them with a few well-phrased arguments."

Jeffrey raised a skeptical eyebrow. "Such as?"

"You'll learn that next year in the Making It Sound Reasonable seminar."

Jeffrey gave Drake an imploring look.

"Very well," Drake said. "Say you've had a popular governor murdered. Even loyal minions *might* wonder whether your cause is just. So, you 'spin' the murder."

"How will turning the body around and around help?"

"'Spin' is a term Dex uses. It means to cast a different light on the matter, one favorable to your position."

"So you shine a light on the body?"

"You're baiting me, aren't you, Jeffrey?"

Jeffrey grinned. "Maybe a little."

Drake sighed. "Back to the murdered governor. Suddenly, books turn up showing the governor has been collecting more taxes than the law allowed, and keeping the excess. If that doesn't work, you hire a few maidens or, in urban areas, young boys, to swear the governor molested them."

"So what should I do about my test?" Jeffrey asked. "Murder the professor, then spread rumors?"

"While a properly evil thought, the old masters know how to

deal with assassination attempts. It's safer to cheat. The Black Sash has files full of class notes and old exams."

"I rather hoped *you* would help me," Jeffrey said, a hint of pathos in his green eyes.

What are you up to, you little sneak?

"I missed Spell Casting Basics when Professor Malfeasant described the elements of staff magic," Jeffrey said. "Since you just made a staff, I thought you could explain—"

Suspicion clenched Drake's gut.

"I only want to learn from the best," Jeffrey said.

"Oh, very well." Drake's weather animation staff was his finest work and he hadn't risked showing it off to anyone but the project selection panel—and Professor Hook, the wood shop instructor, and Myrtle, the fraternity house mother. Still, Drake was dying to reap more admiration. And Jeffrey knew he would end up as worse than a toad if he crossed Drake.

He disabled the wards around the trunk holding his staff. Using the key on a chain around his neck, Drake unlocked the chest. The staff's gems glittered as he laid it on the work table. Jeffrey rolled off his bed. His eager expression looked odd on his usually surly visage. Yet Drake understood Jeffrey's excitement. If evil sorcerers were capable of loving anything, it was their craft. Any doubts Drake harbored regarding Jeffrey's suitability to wield magic vanished.

"A staff begins as an ordinary a hunk of wood," Drake said, reciting from one of Professor Hook's lessons.

"That much I know," Jeffrey said impatiently.

"You asked for help."

"Sorry. Go on."

"Staves should be made of hard wood, such as oak."

"Do hard woods hold magic better?" Jeffrey leaned forward to examine the staff.

Drake chuckled. "No, but they can double as a club. Trust me, anyone struck with an oak staff knows they've been hit."

Jeffrey traced a carving. "You spelled your name wrong."

"Those are *runes*, idiot."

"What do they do?"

"They weave detailed instructions for each spell the staff can perform, allowing a single incantation to enable a complicated spell," Drake said. "The less space for runes, the fewer spells the staff can perform."

"So size *does* matter."

Drake grinned. Sometimes Jeffrey's company was almost tolerable. "While the runes determine what spells the staff is *capable* of, the gems provide the necessary power. The wrong stones will render a staff useless—or worse, dangerous."

"So the gems and runes work in tandem. Which stones did you use?"

Drake whacked the back of Jeffrey's head. "Have you been skipping Crystology too?" He fingered a thumbnail-sized diamond. "Diamonds bind and strengthen. Agates are for control and change. Rubies intensify spells and amethysts protect the user from the staff's effects."

Jeffrey's stare hardened. "A mood stone? What in the name of darkness is that for?"

"It adds my own viciousness to the storm."

"What if you're in a good mood?" Jeffrey snorted. "Never mind. What's the amber stone do?"

"Protection from witchcraft. I wouldn't put it past the Hex Omega Tau's to try to ruin my presentation."

"It's great that your staff will represent Dark Arts at the Project Fair," Jeffrey said. "It's sure to win."

"I see you didn't skip Practical Fawning," Drake said, though he felt a stir of craftsman's pride. Dean Malodorous had proclaimed the staff "adequate"—high praise from him. Professor Licentious had been so impressed, he helped Drake obtain a summer apprenticeship with the one-eyed Dark Lord.

The Dark Lord was hard on his troll and goblin flunkies, but treated his summer apprentices well—good food and wine, corporate junkets into the Lands of Men to steal their magic trinkets. It was rumored he had a bevy of elf maidens in his employ who would do *anything* for the Dark Lord's apprentices. For once, Drake looked forward to summer.

"Is there anything else I should know?" Jeffrey asked.

"Volumes, but I think you know enough about *staves* to pass your exam." Drake dug through his desk, then tossed a well-worn pamphlet on Jeffrey's bed. "I suggest you read this again."

"'Graduate or Else'? You really *are* a prick, Drake."

"Don't get all mushy on me, Jeffrey."

After securing his staff, Drake left their room in search of Scardos. As he walked down the hall, he nodded to Cardimon the Craven, still stuck in his familiar's body. Since Cardimon had the only neutered familiar, no one was surprised that the cat had run off with his human body. The odds favored finding Cardimon's body in a village brothel.

Drake located the Dungeons & Demons game—by the stench of pizza—in Garius the Gross's room. Five other Black Sash members huddled around the table, tossing dice and animating figurines.

Torrence rolled the dice. "Muahahaha! My third-level hero plunges into the Pit of Doom and takes five hundred points of damage." With a shrill scream, an animated, silver-clad figurine jumped into a tiny fire pit burning on the game board.

"Idiot, you're out of the game—again," Scardos said.

"Jeez, this is hard," Torrence said. "It's so natural to kill the good guys."

"At least you're not taking us with you." Scardos glared at Garius, who shrugged sheepishly. Apparently they had solved his paladin-sacrifice problem by making Garius the dungeon master.

"Scardos," Drake said in his best menacing voice.

"Come to join in, Barbarian Bob?" Scardos jeered.

Drake cringed at the reminder of his troubled freshman year. "No, it's a bit...scented in here. Could I have a word?"

Scardos twitched. "We're in the middle of a game."

"That could last for days, and I have better things to do with my time." Drake gave his most formidable glare. To his delight, Scardos paled and followed Drake into the hall.

Quick as a cobra, Drake grabbed Scardos by the collar then twisted until he choked off Scardos's breath. Scardos had always been weak in Escaping From Angry Mobs class.

"I know you're trying to sabotage my mentoring grade," Drake growled. "You will not involve Jeffrey in anything distracting for the remainder of the year. Do I make myself clear?"

Scardos wheezed but remained defiant. Drake gave the fabric another twist. Scardos's eyes bulged.

"You always were a slow learner," Drake said. "Leave Jeffrey alone. Understand?"

Scardos managed a nod.

"Good." Drake held on for emphasis. "Because should you forget your promise, I'll rip out your spine and use it as a croquet mallet."

He released Scardos, who dropped to the ground rubbing his red throat. "Has anyone ever told you that you're a prick?"

"With surprising regularity."

The Spring Games and Project Fair was less than a month away. Dex paced in his private workroom. Why hadn't Dr. Arcanum decided which projects passed the first cut? Surely he recognized Dex's genius. The bomb's cold fusion ignition system was a masterpiece. Dex had drawn inspiration for its design from an episode of *The Dukes of Hazzard* when they souped up the *General Lee* for a dirt-road race.

A red circle on the bomb plans showed the one missing piece to Dex's project: a rare and unstable gas that would change the bomb from inert to active. The gas, known as Gas X, was harmless under most conditions. Under the right circumstances, it's effects bordered on magic. Not quite—as this was science.

The cold fusion ignition would charge the miraculous mixture, then disperse nanobots in a cobalt-blue mushroom cloud. Dex's illustration was sheer artistry. He'd drawn exploding and crashing aircraft above a sea of panicked civilians running to their doom. How could the dean not appreciate that?

Nanobots were another stroke of inspiration. Dex had kept them as pets in a petri dish. By accident, he spilled a gaseous and powdered metal mix into the dish. Fearing he had harmed his pets (and because gas fumes were choking off his airways), Dex had an asthma attack. While grabbing his inhaler, he spritzed medicine into the dish. The gases, powdered metals, and the key ingredient in Dex's inhaler combined. Amid a small blue cloud, his nanobots mutated into a viable life form. A voracious life form.

Albuterol was nothing to wheeze at.

If Dr. Arcanum recommended the project, Dex had to demonstrate it for the selection committee. A test required a working bomb. Fortunately, Dex had completed a small-scale version of his bomb. It required only a minuscule quantity of Gas X, which Dex had siphoned out of the chem lab during a mutant rampage drill. If the committee chose his project, perhaps Dean Evil could obtain the necessary quantity of Gas X for the full-scale bomb. After all, the future of everyone in Arcane Sciences depended on the success of Dex's project. Not that the deans knew it.

Dex plopped onto the rickety stool with one leg worn down from him tilting back, then tapped the bomb's casing with a screwdriver. The metallic tinkling against a weapon of mass destruction soothed his nerves. The little version of his bomb—Tater-Tot—would make an impressive demonstration. Dex had named it that because it resembled a large, golden-fried tater-tot—and because he'd been hungry.

He'd dubbed the larger bomb the Fully Loaded Baked Potato. It only seemed right to keep the spud theme. Once these babies went off, it'd be mashed taters all around.

Gilbert poked his head inside the lab. Though Dex would never admit it, he appreciated the distraction. Maybe Gilbert would want to head to the Student Union for a snack. Maybe they'd run into Drake and Jeffrey there. No, wait, Dex didn't want to see Drake until the project selection committee chose his project for the Fair.

The Fair. Dex groaned and threw up his hands. "Argh!"

Gilbert scooted in uninvited. "What's wrong? Has your project been sabotaged? Who do you think did it?"

"Shut up, Gilbert. Although my project should win the Project Fair by a substantial margin, *I*, unlike many foolish scientists before me, like to hedge my bets." The judges rarely awarded any project the maximum three hundred points. If the superjocks won all three Spring Games, they'd receive three hundred points, and the project portion would potentially lose its value. Dex smacked his fist into his palm, then winced. "We must prepare as a team!"

No one was more disadvantaged at sports than mad scientists. Dex hated sports. Every ball that had ever been thrown at him homed in on his crotch.

Gilbert stood on tree-trunk legs, scratching his head with his big hand, his arm muscles bulging.

Dex grinned. "I see a light at the end of the tunnel."

"Are you dying?"

"Not that sort of light." Poor Gilbert had brawn but no brains. This semester, however, that would be a plus. Dex jumped off his stool. "Come, Gilbert, we have work to do."

"Not more studying. My head feels like it'll explode."

"Whose fault is that? You might have tried *passing* a class last semester. Now you have a double load."

"Hey, I *almost* passed Maniacal Laughter. I would have too, if the professor hadn't insisted on a perfect bell curve."

"Yeah, that's the bane of us all. Forget that now. It's time to begin your training. You, Gilbert, may save the College of Arcane Sciences." *And the university.*

"You think I'd pass then?"

"You'd have it made. You'd be our only real jock." Until Gilbert's arrival, Lexington was the closest thing to a jock at the College of Arcane Sciences, due to his 125 bowling average— though Lexington cheated, using a radio-controlled ball.

"I don't understand," Gilbert said.

"Of course not. You're Gilbert." Dex wrapped an arm across Gilbert's shoulder, but made it just halfway around. "How'd it look if the *only* athlete failed? That would mean one hundred percent of our athletes failed. That sort of statistic draws unfavorable attention. It'd be easier to pass you. You might even score a car." Dex led Gilbert into the hall, then locked his lab.

"Dex, Dr. Arcanum wants to see you. Said it was important."

"Why didn't you tell me?"

"You sounded so excited about the games, I hated to interrupt." Gilbert grinned. "Besides, you mentioned a car. You think they'd let me have a truck? A tornado wiped out my parents' last one."

"Forget I said anything about a ride, Dorothy. Meet me under the astrolabe in an hour. Bring anything you can toss, aim, or fire."

"What are the events?" Gilbert asked.

"Dean Corleone changes some of the games every year. Something to do with the rules and their numerous corollaries. The postings won't be out until Wednesday, but there's no reason not to start whipping you into shape." Dex hurried toward the administrative building.

"See you in an hour," Gilbert called after him.

In the event of catastrophe, the administration building became a self-sustaining biosphere, capable of replenishing oxygen, water and food for three decades. Of course, the bio-dome only had enough space to preserve the instructors and boasted a lock-down security system second-to-none.

Dr. Arcanum's office door stood ajar. Inside, a gigantic Venus flytrap munched on a boa constrictor. Genetic mutation was the doctor's specialty. It was rumored his knowledge came from the old ways—druidic practices, voodoo, and an ancient Chinese secret gleaned from his dry cleaner.

"Ah, Poindexter, come in." From behind his mahogany desk, Dr. Arcanum gestured for Dex to sit.

Lush carpet muffled Dex's footsteps. It was like walking on a cloud. Money was definitely a good thing. So how could loving it be wrong?

The leather cushion, as supple as butter, sank soundlessly under Dex.

"I've finished reviewing the project proposals." Dr. Arcanum waved a hand over stacked notebooks. "I find yours exceedingly superior." He turned Dex's proposal around and pointed at a phrase. "However, I'm unfamiliar with this term."

Dex grinned sheepishly. "It's just a buzzword. I thought it sounded impressive."

"Ah. Then it's a good use of subatomic psychic vortex." Dr. Arcanum closed Dex's neatly typed proposal. "Are you ready to test your design?"

"Tater-Tot, er, I mean the smaller version, is ready to test. All I need is a delivery system."

"Not a problem. We always have spare rockets around. I'll arrange a demonstration for tomorrow."

"Yes, sir." Dex rose.

"If your test proves as impressive as your claims, Poindexter, your project will represent the College of Arcane Sciences."

Dex's heart pounded. His blood burned through his veins. This was better than sex! Okay, he *assumed* it was better than sex.

Nah, he was probably wrong.

Then he remembered he lacked the necessary Gas X for his big bomb. Dex felt suddenly...deflated. Hanging his head, he said, "There's a problem, Dr. Arcanum. I don't have enough—"

"I'll obtain the necessary Gas X."

"Sir, may I ask why you're helping me?"

Arcanum smiled. On his bony, pasty features, it was like a skull laughing because it knew everyone would end up the same. "I've watched your progress and see a bit of myself in you."

That was a scary—yet complimentary—answer.

"Having no son of my own, I've decided to foster your career." He raised a finger. "Assuming you don't disappoint me. I'm counting on you, Poindexter. I've even spoken to the dean and he agrees that you're a promising talent."

"You've spoken to Dean Evil about *me*?" Dex pointed at his bony chest.

"I never said I'd spoken to Dean Evil." Dr. Arcanum winked then flicked both hands. "Until tomorrow, Poindexter."

Dex retreated, bowing as he slipped out. He strolled across the grounds, his elation returning. Under the astrolabe, Gilbert waited with the most complete assortment of sporting gear Dex had ever seen. Somewhere, the farm boy had found a football, soccer ball, basketball, baseball, volleyball, tennis ball, hand ball and even a tether ball—just to name those Dex recognized. Beside them lay a tennis racket, squash racket, racquetball racket, and a *jai alai* cesta.

Gilbert had also ripped up a telephone pole, presumably for caber tossing, and brought a glow-in-the-dark Frisbee.

"Did I get enough stuff?" Gilbert asked.

"I'd say so." Staring at the Frisbee, Dex asked, "Shall we start with fetch?"

Gilbert snorted in laughter. "Good one, Dex. Really, what games do you expect? I hope it's football or basketball. I was on my high school teams."

"Let's start with your throwing arm, okay?" There was usually a throwing game.

Gilbert picked up the football and cocked it back over his shoulder. "Go long, Dex."

Instinctively, Dex covered his crotch. "Just throw it."

"Aren't you going to run and catch it?"

"Run? Catch?" Dex pronounced the words as though they were a foreign language. "No."

Gilbert let the ball fly.

Dex nodded appreciatively as it sailed out of sight. Between Gilbert's unnatural strength—for a mad scientist—and Dex's Fully Loaded Baked Potato, the College of Arcane Sciences couldn't lose.

Dex and Gilbert hauled Tater-Tot to the Administrative Bio-dome, where Dr. Arcanum and the project selection committee waited. The tip of a rocket protruded from an underground silo. Once the rocket had its payload, it lifted off.

Only then did Dex wonder about the target.

Giving a nonchalant wave, Dr. Arcanum said, "I chose Gatorwaters. Once that insignificant swamp town is gone, the university can buy the land at distressed prices then develop it. I'll be building factories there. I hope you'll apply for a summer internship."

Dex could hardly believe his good fortune. Ergo, something had to go wrong. Inside the back cover of Dex's used first-year chemistry book, a previous owner had scrawled the words which had plagued Dex throughout his college career: *Never Doubt— Something Will Go Wrong.*

Yet the rocket flew true, creating a beautiful smoke streak. The rocket peaked, then plummeted toward Gatorwaters.

The bomb exploded. A blue-tinged mushroom cloud rose.

"Impressive, Poindexter," Dr. Arcanum said. "The blue smoke adds an elegant touch."

Sadly, the phosphoric powders failed to spell out D-E-X, but that had been a long shot.

Gilbert stared slack-jawed.

"What do you think of your mentor's achievement?" Dr. Arcanum asked Gilbert.

When Gilbert could work his jaw properly, he said, "I don't think mankind is ready for that kind of power."

Dr. Arcanum laughed. "When is it ever?"

"I tried to explain—but he's"—Dex lowered his voice—"a bit slow. He has a great arm, though."

Dean Evil strolled over. "How long before it's safe to occupy the wasteland?"

Dex beamed. "It isn't a wasteland, Dean Evil. That was a genuinely smart bomb." Dex had stolen part of the bomb's brain from Isaac's robot brain design, but saw no reason to share credit. "My bomb's nano technology mimics spore dispersion. These 'spores' reproduce at an incredible rate. That was the cloud you saw. The explosion provided the spark to bring the nanobots to life. Once the nanobots infiltrate a living creature, they seek out the neural cortex. If the brain functions above a preset intellectual level, the nanospores devour the cortex, killing the host. Plants and most animals are unharmed—except for white mice. I don't know why."

Dean Evil chortled. "Too bad we can't use it on those annoying superturds, eh? Unfortunately, their corsets would fail the intelligence test." No one corrected him.

Dex basked in the adoration. "I suppose we could set the intelligence quota to that of a slug."

Dean Evil touched his lip. "An intriguing thought." He spun around. "Gentlemen, if there's no disagreement, I declare Poindexter's project shall represent our fine institution."

Dr. Arcanum clapped Dex's shoulder. "Congratulations, Poindexter. Come to my office tomorrow and we'll discuss your project's remaining needs." Quietly, he added, "Among other things." Louder he said, "Good lad. Don't forget—my office, bright and early."

Bright and early usually meant more on the bright side than early. Ergo, any time before noon would be "early" enough.

Not that Dex would sleep tonight. He couldn't wait to gloat about his triumph to Drake.

CHAPTER TWENTY-FIVE

The Spring Games and Project Fair was the one occasion where everyone wore T-shirts, jeans or cutoffs, and sneakers. Drake's fitted tee sported the Black Sash logo—a bloody heart skewered by a sword and draped with a black sash. The shirt's back bore one of Drake's favorite sayings, "The wages of sin are pretty good." Jeffrey's shirt read, "Evil Sorcerers Are Well-Staffed." Drake felt flattered at this complement to his Staff of Living Weather, though he didn't understand why so many people snickered and grinned. Well, soon they would all envy his staff!

In a pinstriped suit and ascot, Dean Corleone stood in human form before a microphone. Beside him, on a marble stand, rested a gigantic tome. Rumor listed several possible sources of the unusual leather binding, including a troublesome student, Dean Corleone's ex-wife or perhaps an incontinent demon who lost bladder control on the dean's Persian rug.

Lucifer, Jr. paced below the stage, then settled onto a chair beside Dean Selena and stared at her with moony eyes.

Dean Corleone tapped the microphone. "Can everyone hear me?" His booming voice shook the leaves off nearby trees.

Drake covered his ears.

Giving an evil smile, Dean Corleone lowered the volume. "Before we begin, let me review a few basic rules. One, only human students may participate. Two, murder will result in forfeit and a stern scolding. Three...."

"Same old, same old." Dex slipped up beside Drake. He sported a white T-shirt, complete with pocket protector, leaky black pens and slide rule. The loose-hanging shirt proclaimed, "I'm Not Angry, I'm Mad!"

Seeing Dex made Drake's stomach knot as it brought home how much rode on the games and projects. The College of Dark Arts *had* to win—to save the university, to defeat Lucifer, Jr. Dean Corleone had said as much. Poor Dex. Drake would miss him when he was turned into a drodent. Sadly, after the auditors' negative reports, Drake could think of no way to convince the Board of Trustees to reverse their decision to close one college. The best he could hope for was to prevent his fellow sorcerers—and especially himself—from becoming Lucifer, Jr.'s indentured slaves.

"What game are you participating in?" Dex asked.

"Obstacle course," Drake said.

"Gilbert's also running the obstacle course," Dex said. "For once, Gamma Ray Delta stands a chance of winning."

Drake snorted. *A snowball's chance in the dean's office.*

"I drew the catapult keg toss," Dex said.

Drake nodded. "Jeffrey is doing that one as well."

"Now," Dean Corleone boomed, regaining everyone's attention. Blood trickled from tenderer ears. "The three-legged race."

"*That's* original," Dex said. "Take your places, kiddies."

As though the dean had heard, he glared at Dex. "From the College of Olde Wyrd Charms, Phoebe and Prudence."

Witches jumped up and down, their unfettered breasts bouncing under skimpy crop tops.

The brunette twins jogged to the Hex Omega Tau bench in the witches' pavilion. Each poured a bucket of water over her head. Water sluiced down their thin cotton tops, soaking the fabric so it clung, semi-sheer, to their curves. They shook their long hair, sending a spray of droplets flying in remarkably slow motion. Cheering erupted in the stands.

"Wow." Dex's knees buckled and he staggered into Drake.

"Indeed," Drake gasped, leaning back against Dex.

With T-shirts plastered to their pert breasts and shorts molded to their shapely rears, the twins stepped past the starting line, their heels barely touching the chalk. The slogan "You Can't Touch This!" rippled across Prudence's chest. Phoebe's shirt bore the warning, "And You Better Not Try!"

Another curvaceous witch tied the twins' center legs with a leather strap. The thought of soaking wet, bound twins made Drake quiver. He shoved aside a brewing fantasy. Two witches would be twice the trouble—though it might be worth the risk.

"Representing the College of Valor, Honor and"—Dean Corleone gagged"—Justice for All are Cricket and Armadilloman."

Mikey, in his Cricket outfit, hopped to the starting line. Chirping springs in his boots let him jump five feet forward. Armadilloman scuttled to catch up. Unlike the witches, the do-gooders waited a full step behind the starting line.

Phoebe and Prudence tottered in their haste to lodge a protest. "No fair!" they chorused. "His boots have springs!"

Dean Corleone shrugged. "The rules don't prohibit the use of springs. I'll add a rule for next year."

The dean tapped the huge tome. Pages flipped of their own accord and he scribbled a line. An undeclared superhero bound Armadilloman and Mikey.

"For the College of Dark Arts, Scardos the Scary and Torrence the Terrible."

Torrence and Scardos rushed to the line, their faces set in concentration as a sorcerer bound their legs. Scardos's shirt read, "I'm Evil. Get Over It!" while Torrence's proclaimed, "Evil...It's A Right Good Thing!"

"Lastly, for the College of Arcane Sciences, Isaac." The dean glanced at the page, then squinted at the mad scientists' pavilion. He leaned toward them and said, "You lads understand the concept of the *three*-legged race, don't you?"

"It's elementary, sir." Isaac produced a metal rod with a caster on the end. It looked suspiciously like one of Rosie the Robot's legs. Perhaps it *was* Rosie's leg, for Isaac's T-shirt read, "Love Hurts." He hooked the device, like an obscene codpiece, to a chastity belt-like contraption. "I call it Insta-Leg. With this, I can perform the three-legged race solo."

The other contestants shouted, "No fair!"

Dean Corleone sighed. "The rules specify three legs and human students. However, I can add a rule for next year."

The book ruffled to a new page and Dean Corleone scratched down a few lines, saying, "No mechanical limbs...."

Scardos pulled out his wand and said, "The two shall be as one." His and Torrence's bodies merged into a two-headed, three-legged creature that crossed the starting line.

The other contestants opened their mouths, but Dean Corleone said, "Next year. For now, it's legal. So if the contestants will please line up *behind* the starting line."

Grumbling, the contestants backed up, except for the superheroes, who were already at the proper starting point.

"On your marks. Get set—" The dean whipped up a Tommy gun and shot a rat-a-tat-tat into the air. A flight of geese honked and plummeted from the sky in V formation. One smacked onto Dean Mediaman, another on Prince Raymond. The rest landed in quick succession on Lucifer, Jr.'s head. Still ogling Selena, he didn't seem to notice the avian assault. However, Deans Mediaman and Prince Raymond shouted in outrage.

Failing miserably at an innocent expression, Dean Corleone shouted, "Go!"

Isaac sped to the lead, Phoebe and Prudence close behind. Scardos and Torrence ran third.

Cricket and Armadilloman counted, "One, two, three, *hop*." They hopped—Mikey forward and Armadilloman straight up. Their bound bodies snapped taut under the force, then slammed back together. They thudded to the dirt track.

Drake grinned. It felt strange not having to cheat to defeat them.

"They should have taken force and trajectory into account," Dex observed.

Isaac's Insta-Leg veered right, turning him into the path of the merged Scardos and Torrence. At the last second, the leg did a 180-degree rotation at the knee. Scardos and Torrence stumbled. Breasts bouncing in perfect unison, Phoebe and Prudence took the lead. Prudence, Scardos's ex-girlfriend, looked back and snickered. Scardos pulled out his wand and zapped the dirt ahead. A mud puddle appeared in time for Prudence's foot to land with an oozing splash.

Mud splattered the witches' legs—protection spells during the games had been banned decades ago. "Yuck!" Phoebe shrieked.

Prudence slipped and fell against her twin. The two tumbled to the ground in a tangle of long, delectable limbs. Soon mud coated them from head to toe. Dex gave a soft moan. Whirs rippled from the stands as telephoto lenses zoomed into focus.

"You clumsy cow!" Phoebe batted her sister's head. "You've taken us out of the race."

"Me? This is *your* fault, Miss Two-Left-Feet."

Mikey and Armadilloman doubled their efforts, trying to hop to the witches' aid. After two spectacular splats, they ended farther away than when they began.

Isaac's third leg swung up between his thighs and kicked his butt. He howled and ran in circles while wrestling with the belt catch, but couldn't detach the thrashing leg.

"Wow," Dex said. "If that *is* Rosie's leg, her meanness is hardwired into her machine parts."

The three-legged race was at a standstill. Witches rolled in the mud and pulled each other's hair. Isaac was receiving the butt-kicking of a lifetime. The superheroes floundered, then lay as still as road kill. Scardos/Torrence, the one team still on their feet, gawked at the muddy girls like adolescents with their first nudie magazine.

"Move, you idiots!" Drake shouted. He threw a rock and struck Torrence's hard head. Had it hit anyone else, it might have knocked him unconscious.

Torrence looked up. "Huh?"

"Run, you morons!" Drake shouted.

Torrence and Scardos awoke from the hypnotic effect of mud-wrestling females. The merged pair turned and hobbled, unchallenged, to the finish line.

"The College of Dark Arts wins the three-legged race," Dean Corleone declared, then muttered, "Took long enough." Realizing he still held the microphone, he flushed a faint demon green. His gaze traced the field where Isaac's Insta-Leg had him pinned in a hammerlock. Cricket and Armadilloman lay unconscious, and Phoebe and Prudence each had a handful of muddy chestnut hair.

"Given the unlikelihood that any other contestant even finishes," the dean said, "I award the full hundred points to the College of Dark Arts."

The rule book gave a loud "Ahem," then ruffled its pages to a different spot. Dean Corleone pulled out reading glasses, then peered at the page. "Oh, yes. I'd forgotten that last year the faculty decided losing is for chumps and no points would be awarded in the games other than for first place."

Lucifer, Jr. looked away from Selena's ample endowments. "An interesting rule, Asmodeus."

"We have many interesting rules," Dean Corleone said. "Next up, the catapult keg toss."

Dex slapped Drake on the back so hard, Drake almost felt it.

"Gotta go beat your roommate into dust," Dex said.

"Not literally, I hope."

"Relax, Drake," Dex said. "We'd never kill your roommate."

"I know," Drake said wryly. "You can't afford a forfeit."

"Bring forth the catapults for inspection," Dean Corleone ordered.

The keg toss was the one holdover game from last year. Several heroes pushed their catapult toward the launching line. The catapult appeared ordinary, except the scoop had been modified to hold a beer keg. Prince Valorous and Sir Eloquence marched to the controls. Valorous's T-shirt had ruffles on the neck and sleeves. His prancing minstrel plucked a lute.

The minstrel burst into song. "Prince Valorous with his dainty hands, hands so free of calluses, did build this mighty catapult while drinking wine from chalices. Once he hit his little thumb. Oh, what a sad tragedy—"

Dean Corleone glared at the minstrel, who fell silent, his shaking fingers dropping away from his lute strings.

Several sorcerers, including Scardos/Torrence—who were having trouble with the separation spell—pushed the Dark Arts entry. The sleek black catapult had iron spikes and a demon's head on its main axle. Jeffrey and Garius the Gross took their place beside the siege engine.

Last year, the witches and scientists had used draft animals to haul their catapults. After the horses trampled Dean Corleone's prized petunia garden, he added a rule that only human students could move the catapults.

Gilbert pushed the mad scientists' catapult to the line. It wasn't possible to assemble enough of the other mad scientists around the catapult to accumulate sufficient muscle mass to move it. So much the better. If they wore out their farm boy, Drake had one less competitor to worry about in the obstacle course.

Two imps in black and white vertically striped shirts capered around the catapult. One imp used a gadget that detected illegal electronic gadgetry, the other a gadget that detected illegal magical modifications.

Last year the scientists had supercharged their firing mechanism, resulting in a win and a rule against electronic enhancements. Dex and Lexington gave the imps innocent smiles. Suspicion gnawed at Drake's gut. No mad scientist could resist using *some* sort of gadgetry. Yet they weren't foolish enough to disqualify themselves.

The crowd's murmuring escalated as two witches sashayed to the launch line. Two hulking heroes pushed the girls' catapult, which technically complied with the new rule. The Hex Omega Taus' catapult was metallic pink and decorated with opalescent bows. Last year the witches had used a pony keg, resulting in the "standardized keg" rule. Though the witches claimed the rule unfairly disadvantaged them, since they were women and kegs were heavy, the dean reminded them that each college bore different disadvantages in each game. The ladies would have to be more ingenious—within the rules, of course. Although they had conned the muscle-headed heroes into doing the hard work, by rule, the witches had to move their own keg.

Tabitha and Samantha sidled up to their catapult. Samantha smiled and blew a kiss at Jeffrey, who grinned back. The lad had much to learn. If it would help her college win, Samantha would smile just as sweetly as she gutted Jeffrey.

The imps tested the other catapults, then loped back and pronounced them legal.

"The—ahem—heroes will go first," Dean Corleone announced.

Witches heaved sighs as Valorous and Eloquence, arm muscles bulging, hefted their keg. Valorous's minstrel struck up a jaunty rendition of "Go Team, Go."

Dean Corleone turned a smoking glare the minstrel's way. Caught up in his groove, the minstrel added a riff on his lute. The dean grunted a spell. The ground split under the minstrel's feet. He tumbled, instruments and all, into the chasm. Strains of "Nearer My God To Thee" drifted farther and farther away.

Drake snorted. *If he thinks he's getting nearer to God, he's in for a shock.*

The chasm healed; only a jagged crack in the dirt showed it had ever existed. Heroes and superheroes stared, horror-struck, at where the minstrel had stood. Their shocked gazes shifted to Dean Corleone. Despite the heroes' scandalized expressions, Drake couldn't help but believe most of those from the Order of

Virtue Hall were glad to see the annoyance go.

"Gentlemen," Dean Corleone said to Valorous and Eloquence, "load that keg before I declare a forfeit for your college."

Glowering, Valorous and Eloquence cranked the keg into firing position. Valorous gave the lever a vicious yank. The keg sailed across a field striped with chalk yard lines. The keg splatted down, spraying a fountain of beer and wood shards, near the 1200 yard line.

The referee imps grabbed sticks attached by a measuring length of giant's intestines and raced onto the field. They scampered to the point of impact, then measured back to the closest yard marker.

"Twelve hundred eight yards, four inches," one barked.

The audience clapped politely.

"Now, the College of Dark Arts," Dean Corleone said.

Jeffrey and Garius hoisted the evil sorcerers' keg. Grunting and huffing, they staggered with its weight between them, pausing every few steps to rest. With a mighty heave—and an even mightier grunt—they pushed the keg into the scoop.

Jeffrey drew out his wand, then Garius pulled the lever. The keg launched into the air. Jeffrey spoke an incantation, and fixed wooden wings sprouted from the keg's sides. It glided impressively to the end of the 1350-yard field.

"That's my lad." Drake looked for Dex to rub it in, but Dex was manning the scientists' catapult.

The imps raced to the keg's landing site. "Thirteen hundred sixty-five yards, two feet, four inches."

The evil and mad alumni muttered appreciatively, while the witches and heroes groused. Dex and Lexington looked unworried, which concerned Drake.

"Simmer down," Dean Corleone said. "It isn't illegal to juice the keg once it's in flight—*this* year anyway." With a long-suffering air, he tapped the book. "The page is full."

The book tensed and shuddered. A fresh page sprouted from its spine. The dean added another rule, then said, "Now the College of Olde Wyrd Charms."

Tabatha and Samantha walked, hips swaying, to their keg. It bore a pentagram but otherwise looked normal. They each took an end and lifted, making great huffing noises.

"Wow, that circuit training paid off," Tabitha said. As they carried the keg, however, Drake noticed their muscles weren't straining, nor were the witches sweating—a sight he had been anticipating. The scientists, too, noticed; Dex and Lexington wildly signaled the dean. As Dean Corleone ambled toward the witches, Tabatha and Samantha exaggerated their grunts to absurd levels.

The dean slipped a hand under the keg and lifted it as easily as balancing a tray. "What is in this keg?"

Tabatha turned wide blue-grey eyes to the dean. "What do you mean?"

"By rule, the keg must contain beer."

"Um...it's light beer?" Samantha said.

The dean shook the keg. "Why don't I hear any sloshing?"

"It's a bit frothy?" Tabitha said hopefully.

He dashed the keg on the ground. Gas hissed from the cracked keg. "Helium?" Dean Corleone's voice squeaked several octaves higher than usual.

"Oh, piffle," Samantha said, in a mouse-like squeal.

Dean Corleone gave them a baleful glare, then returned to the podium. "The College of Olde Wyrd Charms is disqualified," he squeaked, his back straight and dignified. No one dared to laugh. Lucifer, Jr. raised his eyebrows, but said nothing. The dean continued, "Lastly, the College of Arcane Sciences."

Gilbert moved to Drake's side. "Don't we have a neat catapult? I pushed it over all by myself."

Drake would have suspected that Gilbert was trying to intimidate him, but...it was Gilbert.

Drake wondered how Dex and Lexington would move the keg without Gilbert the Strong. The two laid out several hollow wooden cylinders, then set a board on top. They rolled the keg onto the platform, then pushed the platform forward. As one cylinder rolled out the back, Lexington or Dex wrestled it to the front. Their faces were so red from even this minor exertion, Drake thought they might be having strokes. They used a pulley system to haul the keg into the scoop. In all, they did a good job of minimizing their literal weakness. Damn them.

"Ooh," Gilbert said. "This should be good."

Drake fervently hoped it would *not* be good. If the sorcerers won here, his performance in the obstacle course mattered a whole lot less—though he wouldn't mind gloating if Dark Arts swept the games.

Dex and Lexington both gripped the lever. "One, two, three!" They threw their puny weight into pulling the lever. Miraculously, the keg launched.

Panels opened in the keg's rear; two exhaust tubes emerged. On the sides, jet engines slid out. With a piercing whine, they fired and the keg rocketed forward, soaring out of sight.

Drake growled in his throat. What chance did he stand running an obstacle course against the behemoth standing beside him? Well, there was always sabotage. As long as Drake didn't kill Gilbert (or render him unconscious via spell or potion, or paralyze him via same, or teleport him to a Hell dimension, or set a plague of locusts on him, or physically attack his person or newt him) sabotage was legal.

The imps ran after the keg.

"You disqualified us for putting helium in our keg," Samantha complained, her scantily clad bosom heaving. "What about rocket fuel?"

"Actually," Dex drawled, a smug grin on his face, "we created a rocket that runs on beer. We didn't alter the keg's contents, merely its outer housing, which is legal."

Dean Corleone glanced at the rule book, which shrugged its pages. "Very well," the dean said. "Subject to confirmation the keg contained only beer, I declare the College of Arcane Sciences the winner and award them one hundred points."

Gilbert nudged Drake, sending him stumbling. "Looks like it's up to us to break the tie."

Drake rubbed his throbbing ribs. "So it seems."

Drake and Gilbert headed for the hedge wall surrounding the obstacle course. Dean Corleone spoke into the microphone. "The obstacle course is divided into four sectors, the faculty of each college having designed one. All contestants may bring such potions, gadgets, etc. which he or she believes will be of aid, but *these items may not be used directly on another contestant's person.* The first contestant to emerge, in any three-dimensional state, will be declared the winner."

Drake, Gilbert, Hexaba and The Buzz stood at separate entrances. Hexaba concerned Drake most. That girl could cheat. At least the rules required traversing the course without flying, so neither she nor The Buzz could fly above the hedge wall. Still, the superhero's utility belt held an odd assortment of gadgets. Gilbert carried a bulky backpack, while several pink-flowered pouches floated behind Hexaba. Drake's satchel contained the water pistol filled with animation fluid, his wand, water, salve and bandages. One should always carry salve and bandages. College life had taught Drake that much.

"I caution you not to violate the rules," Dean Corleone said. "At the least, you will be disqualified. At the worst, you may find *yourselves* being violated."

You can count on me, Dean Corleone. Drake's gaze swept across the student sorcerers. *You can all count on me.* Was this what do-gooders felt when they tried to foil the plots of hard-working evil folk—weighty responsibility and desperation to succeed? At least Drake's motives weren't selfless. His own life was at stake. He *wasn't*—gak—a hero.

"Get ready!" The dean waved his hands, and the door before Drake dissolved into an open archway. "Go!"

Wand in hand, Drake leapt through, then froze to survey his

surroundings. Tall hedges formed the expected maze, which if properly traversed would lead to the next quadrant. The passage behind Drake sealed.

Man-sized mutant plants lurked in the shadows. Clearly, the mad scientists had created this quadrant. A vine latched onto Drake's ankle and spiraled up his leg.

Drake poked it with his wand. "Frost most deadly."

An icy curse spread down the vine, freezing it in its tracks. The ice flowed along the tendril to a giant plant with bell-shaped flowers that skulked in the hedge wall.

Drake snapped off the frozen vine and crept along the path, which ended in a T. *Left or right?* In any maze, following the right-hand wall eventually led to the exit. But Drake had no time for "play it safe" methods.

A large red blossom shot a stream of spores. Drake ducked. The spores struck a plant across the way; it toppled into a heap. Feeling lucky, Drake took the left path.

Hexaba's shriek cut through the hedge walls. Drake smiled. Whatever it was would slow her down—

Something as solid as a charging horse knocked Drake into the hedge. Thorns sliced into his arm, shoulder and cheek. A waxy flower clamped onto Drake's bare forearm.

"Sorry!" Gilbert cried. "My glasses fogged while I was running." He grabbed the flower's stem and squeezed until it released Drake. Acid bubbled and burned on Drake's forearm. Gilbert pulled out a canteen and rinsed away the acid.

"I was running to help—" Gilbert began, but Hexaba's scream interrupted. "Come on!" Gilbert tugged on Drake's arm, sending a shock of pain through him. "She's this way."

"I'll catch up," Drake said drily.

As Gilbert pounded off to aid the maiden in distress, Drake resumed his course. With luck, The Buzz would also waste time playing the hero.

Drake's arm throbbed. He glanced at the bleeding punctures and bubbly skin. He'd suffered worse, and Gilbert's first aid had stopped the acid from eating a hole in Drake's flesh. *Fool.* Gilbert was engineering his own defeat.

As Drake ran, he applied salve and bandaged his arm. He rounded a turn. A swaying swamp monster blocked his path. This must be the right way. Nothing that ugly would be guarding a dead end.

The monster shambled forward. Drake pulled out his water pistol and sprayed animation potion on the hedge. "*Virat!*"

Spiky tendrils whipped around the swamp monster. The monster gave a surprised grunt as the vines dragged it toward the hedge row. Dodging another groping vine, Drake raced past the roaring swamp monster and found the exit door.

A metal plate of cheese lay before the door. Drake kicked the plate aside with the rubber sole of his sneaker, then reached toward the door handle. He froze. Mad scientists always had one last trick up their lab coat sleeves. While the swamp monster thrashed against attacking vines, Drake inspected the metal door and frame. Sure enough, a red-coated wire ran along the top. Drake grabbed the wire and pulled it free.

Swamp gas enveloped Drake from behind. A slimy, leaf-covered hand clamped onto his shoulder. He thrust the live end of the wire into the swamp monster. Nothing happened.

The wire was a decoy! As the swamp monster's sinewy hands slid around Drake's throat, he strained forward. There had to be another wire, more subtle, better hidden.

The cheese plate! Sure enough, Drake spotted a clear-coated wire attached to it. He lunged forward, breaking free of the swamp monster's slimy grasp. As Drake grabbed the wire, avoiding the metal plate, the swamp monster's hands again closed around his throat. Drake yanked the wire free, then jabbed it into the monster's gut. The creature shrieked and shot backward.

The swamp monster lurched up. Drake grabbed the handle and tugged open the door. The creature charged. Abandoning caution, Drake jumped through and slammed the door behind him. Something heavy thudded against it. A lock clicked, preventing Drake's return—not that he would have considered it for a moment.

Drake stood in another hedge maze. He took a shuffling step forward. *Crack!* Gooseflesh rose on his arms as he heard the unmistakable sound of a delayed-reaction spell being tripped.

Dean Malodorous's disembodied voice boomed, "Answer this riddle or face the basilisk's stare."

Dean Malodorous had "leaked" the setup to Drake. He had thirty seconds to answer correctly, or the spell shielding him from the basilisk's stony gaze would drop.

Drake braced himself. The Dark Arts faculty members were some of the best riddlers around.

"What is black and white and red all over?"

Drake snorted. A trick question. Most people would answer "a newspaper," but the voice clearly said "red" and *not* "read."

"A zebra with a sunburn." Drake *knew* the answer, having heard the lame riddle many times in both forms, though he had no idea what a zebra was.

Evil laughter rolled from the sky. "Correct. Move along."

Drake ran down the path. He couldn't avoid the spell traps, so he might as well make good time between them. Drake rounded a bend and heard a *crack!*

"Answer this riddle or face the answer," the voice boomed.

It was probably some other monster. A bit unoriginal. Could be a griffin, a wyvern or—Drake shuddered—Blackie.

"I have wings but do not fly."

That let out the griffin, the wyvern *and* Blackie.

"I have eyes but do not see, a mouth but do not speak."

That let out Dean Corleone. Drake had never seen the dean fly, but Dean Corleone certainly used his mouth to speak.

"What am I?" the voice asked, starting the thirty-second timer.

Hmm. Wings, but can't fly, eyes but can't see. As precious seconds slipped away, Drake stroked his beard and looked heavenward, as though the answer would be there.

And it was.

"A house!" Drake shouted in his haste to get the answer out before the stone structure hovering overhead squashed him.

The evil laughter rolled again. "Correct."

Crack. From over the hedge, Drake heard another contestant trip a spell.

"Answer this riddle or face the wyvern's fury!"

So that's where they put the wyvern. Drake turned to move on, but the riddle stopped him cold.

"What is the meaning of life?"

"Hey," Gilbert shouted. "That's not a fair riddle."

The voice didn't answer. Drake knew he should go, but what if the farm boy managed a correct answer?

"Uh, uh." Gilbert's voice rose in pitch with each passing second. Finally, he blurted, "42!"

"Is that your final answer?" the voice boomed.

"Yes."

"I suppose I must accept it. Move along."

42? Brow furrowed, Drake ran. From the other side of the hedge, he heard Gilbert's footfalls. Then Drake rounded another bend and faced a T-junction. He turned left and—.

Crack.

"Answer this riddle or face the ogre's wrath."

An ogre. Splendid. Drake didn't relish the thought of having his arms ripped off.

"I am big, green, dumb and disgusting. What am I?"

"Uh, an ogre?"

"Very good. Move on."

Drake had a niggling suspicion his professors had made his riddles easier than those of the other contestants.

He reached a dead end, raced back past the T-junction, then wound through several turns until the exit portal was in sight.

Crack. His professors had set one last trap by the exit. Apparently, that was a common trait for evildoers.

"Answer this riddle or else."

"Or else what?" Drake demanded.

"Or else remain trapped here for eternity."

Drake couldn't muster enough spit to wet his tongue.

"What is in my pocket?" the voice asked, sounding bemused.

How in the nine hells should I know—

Unless I put it there.

Drake drew his wand. Using the transference spell he had used to switch the superheroes' costumes and the tutus, Drake tapped a copper ring on his finger and sent it to Dean Malodorous. An intriguing amulet with an emerald center appeared in Drake's palm.

"A ring," Drake said. "You have a ring in your pocket."

"Hmph. So I do," the dean's disembodied voice said. "I expect my amulet back, Mandrake. Now move on."

Drake passed into the College of Valor, Etc.'s quadrant. His lips curled. Their obstacle course was...an obstacle course. Two rows of tires stretched before Drake, then a wooden beam crossed a pit. Beyond that, four net ladders waited.

"No flair, no imagination." Drake raced for the tires. Sensor pads registered whether he stepped inside. *It's almost as if they don't trust us.*

Had any other college set up this course, Drake would expect a pad to be trapped, but here, he felt safe from trickery. He picked up speed as he grew comfortable with the space between tires. When Drake reached the beam, a door slammed open behind him. Hexaba emerged, alive, but not unscathed. She must have answered a riddle incorrectly, for her skin was indigo blue. Her blue skin proved she had removed her protection spell, as the rules required. Drake found the contrast with her flaming red hair strangely erotic. He shook off the effect and stepped onto the narrow beam.

"You sorcerers are *creeps!*" Hexaba shrieked.

Ignoring her, Drake walked easily along the beam, having performed this exercise many times in Escaping From Angry Mobs class. As Drake neared the beam's end, something whistled past his ear. A clump of his hair fell into the mud pit below. Drake wobbled, arms flailing, then regained his balance.

A flash of metal caught his eye. An enchanted dagger curved around and landed grip-end in Hexaba's hand.

"Cheater!" Drake taunted as he stepped to the ground.

"*You* should talk." Hexaba picked her way through the tires.

"Don't fall, Hexaba," Drake shouted. "You wouldn't want to get mud on your gorgeous blue skin."

"Prick!" she shouted back.

Next, a net ladder of knotted rope hung suspended by a

single wire from an overhead beam. The design assured the ladder would rock while Drake climbed.

As Hexaba finished the tires, The Buzz and Gilbert entered the quadrant. One of The Buzz's wings drooped. Gilbert's shirt was shredded, though there wasn't a mark on his flesh.

Drake slid a foot into a mesh hole and hauled himself up the rope netting. He tipped to the left. Drake positioned his right foot to shift his weight to neutral.

He glanced back. All three competitors were walking the balance beams. Gritting his teeth, Drake resumed his careful climb. Near the top, he glimpsed Gilbert, halfway up the ladder and climbing like a monkey.

"Gilbert, your fly is unzipped," Drake called.

Gilbert looked down. His ladder swung and he lost his grip. He hit the dirt with a surprised yelp. Dex was right. The lad would fall for anything.

"Hey, my fly isn't unzipped!"

"My mistake." Drake hauled himself over the top and dropped to the thick mat below.

A split second later, The Buzz dropped onto his mat. Blue Hexaba was halfway up her wildly swinging ladder. She muttered an incantation and the woven rope turned into a wooden lattice. Drake snarled. He should have thought of that.

Next came the classically uninventive rope swing. The water below didn't even hold spikes or monstrous creatures. Drake and The Buzz each grabbed a rope, then ran and launched themselves. A whistling sound passed overhead. Drake glimpsed Hexaba's enchanted dagger just before his rope went slack. He splashed into the crystalline water. Drake spat out a mouthful. Wait, it was sparkling spring water, with a twist of lemon.

"Why are you picking on me?" Drake demanded. "I've left you to your frilly prince.

"I hate your entrails!" Hexaba shouted from atop the ladder. "Nobody breaks up with me until *I'm* ready."

"*You* broke up with *me*!" Drake shouted as he pushed to his feet.

"You were supposed to pursue me!" Hexaba said in outrage. "It's just like last summer—you never wrote, never sent a gift."

"But we agreed—"

Her face turned purple with fury. "You *knew* I didn't mean it."

"I'm a sorcerer, not a mind reader."

Gilbert dropped to his mat, then Hexaba followed. "If you really loved me," she said, rushing toward the rope, "you would have known."

Drake blinked hard. "Who in the Transdimensional Hells ever

said anything about love? You and I are *evil*. Love is for sappy do-gooders." He slogged through waist-deep water. Hexaba and Gilbert landed, safe and dry, as Drake dragged his sodden body from the pool. "You never loved *me*, Hexaba."

Her T-shirt clad bosom heaved. "Of course not. But you were supposed to be hopelessly in love with *me!*"

"If you want a mutually beneficial alliance to pursue conquest and victory, I'm your man," Drake said. "If you want a fawning man-slave, find some hero to twist around your finger. I'm done."

"Y-you're not done," Hexaba sputtered. "I'm not through with you."

"Too bad." Drake hated letting go of his dream of Hexaba as a powerful wife and partner, but he would be damned if she would turn him into a spineless milksop.

The Buzz jumped onto the first of several widely spaced boulders in another pool. When his foot touched the fourth one, it sank. The Buzz pitched forward. His helmet cracked against another stone. He whimpered, "Mother," then tumbled into the water.

"I didn't think the goody-two-boots had it in them," Drake said. "You'd think his professors would have warned him."

"That's cheating," Gilbert said, eyes wide with shock.

Hexaba and Drake turned scornful looks on the mad scientist.

"Didn't your professors warn you about the pitfalls of *your* quadrant?" Hexaba asked.

Gilbert's face reddened. "They tried, but I plugged my ears with my fingers and went 'la, la, la' so I couldn't hear."

"Figures." Drake turned toward the treacherous stepping stones. Moving quickly was the trick. His soaked jeans made that impossible. With a quick wand wave, Drake zapped the water onto Hexaba, who shrieked. Grinning, Drake took a running start and leapt. The first stone was solid. Using his momentum, he jumped to a stone ahead and to the right. As it sank, he managed to push off. He landed on a stone to his left. It stayed solid. Drake jumped to the next. Solid. A splash behind him betrayed that Hexaba or Gilbert had taken a spill.

Drake kept moving. Solid. Sinker. His foot slid backward, painfully stretching his thigh muscle, but he launched himself. The next stone was slick, and Drake almost slipped off the edge. Two more leaps brought him to the muddy shore. His foot slid from under him and Drake landed on his knees in the muck. The Buzz, his wits recovered, was passing through the portal.

Drake slogged to his feet and raced through the portal. A turnstile smacked his gut. Gasping, Drake stepped back. The device spat out a hand-sized ticket marked with three rectangular boxes. Printed below were the words, "To exit the course, you must complete three out of four carnival events."

Gilbert whooped from beside Drake. "I wonder if they'll have a tilt-a-whirl. I love those. They make me feel like I'm flying. Ooh, and maybe corn dogs and cotton candy!"

A man with a greased mustache and a gold jacket waved them to a curtained booth. "Step right up. This way to the kissing booth." The man gave a lewd wink as the four contestants straggled up, all of them wet and muddy, one still blue. "You may choose to kiss either of our volunteers for a stamp on your ticket, or you may forfeit and move on. Remember, my little chickadees, you only get one forfeit.

"Behind curtain number one, we have Biff." The barker drew back the right-hand curtain, revealing a sun-bronzed young man with enormous muscles. Biff was thoughtfully applying lip balm.

"Behind curtain number two, we have Hildagard."

"Damn!" The Buzz said, jumping back in surprise.

Hildagard leered with bloodshot eyes. Her nose resembled a crooked carrot. Warts covered her green skin. She parted cracked lips to reveal brown teeth and an ulcerated tongue.

"That has to be the ugliest woman in creation," The Buzz said, cradling his broken helmet.

"Buzz!" Gilbert reproved. "It's not nice to judge a person by her looks. She probably has a great personality."

"*You* gonna kiss her?" The Buzz asked.

"Heck, no! I'm using my forfeit," Gilbert admitted. "Besides, I never kiss on the first date."

"You could always kiss Biff." Drake gave an evil laugh. His merriment faded as Hexaba sauntered to Biff and planted her lips against his recently oiled ones.

Drake turned his gaze to Hildagard, that being a more pleasant sight. Obviously, the witches had rigged the first booth to induce the men to waste their forfeits. No doubt later events would present difficult or impossible challenges for men.

Looking at Hildagard, Drake shuddered and fleetingly considered kissing Biff. As Hexaba broke off her prolonged lip lock, Drake stomped up to Hildagard. She smelled like frog piss. *The things I do for this university.*

Tossing Hexaba a meaningful look, Drake said, "I've kissed worse." He pressed his lips against Hildagard's cracked ones. She pushed her putrid tongue into Drake's mouth. He jerked away, but not quick enough to avoid the taste of decaying flesh.

While The Buzz and Gilbert stared, horrified, Drake thrust his ticket at the barker. "You owe me a stamp."

Staying at arm's length, the barker stamped Drake's ticket.

"This way, contestants," the barker said.

As Drake followed, he pulled out his waterskin and shot a stream into his mouth. He swished it around and spat it out, wishing his tongue would shoot out as well.

The next booth consisted of a tall pole with a round bell on top. "Choose a mallet, any mallet!" the barker said. "Then hit the pad and ring the bell!"

Drake was glad he had saved his forfeit. He doubted he could hit the pad hard enough. That the witches had included a game Hexaba couldn't hope to win surprised him. Yet Hexaba wasn't using her forfeit.

A row of mallets—some iron, others wood, some trimmed in gold, others inlaid with precious gems—rested against the rail. Gilbert selected a plain iron mallet. The one at the row's end drew Drake's eye. This mallet was pink, with the word "Princess" inlaid in rhinestones.

How obvious. The mallet must be bespelled so that the user would ring the bell. The ploy complied with the rules, since any contestant could use it. But the witches had decorated it so that no self-respecting man would choose it—with the exception of Tutu Tornado. And Drake, who was clever enough to—

Ding! Crack!

"Duck!" Gilbert cried.

Something heavy clanged against Drake's skull. Black spots danced before his eyes as the bell clunked to the ground.

"Oh, gosh, I'm sorry." Gilbert helplessly held the mallet out as though that would undo the damage. "I guess I hit it too hard—knocked the bell clean off."

Drake rubbed his aching head and found a goose-egg sized lump. At least it wasn't bleeding.

"What do we do now, man?" The Buzz asked. "It's not fair to make us forfeit when we didn't get a try."

"You will all receive a stamp." The barker waved them over. One more stamp and Drake could run for the exit. Hexaba hadn't forfeited yet, either. Drake wasn't sure he could outrun her. In that one respect, she was a fast woman.

"The next event is the pie-eating contest," the barker said.

Gilbert's face lit up.

The Buzz nodded. "I can do that."

I wouldn't be so sure. The "pies" were probably filled with worms, or offal, or something worse.

The barker led them to a table laden with sugared, golden-crusted pies. "Eat three pies in one minute to earn the stamp."

Hexaba shook her head in disgust. "I forfeit. My figure would never recover."

Witches never had to watch their weight. The pies were definitely suspect.

"I forfeit too," Drake said, praying the final task was something he could handle.

Hexaba and the others looked at Drake in surprise.

Drake shrugged. "I don't care for sweets." *Or worms.*

Gilbert and The Buzz sat at the table. The barker pulled out a stop watch. "Ready, set, go!"

The Buzz and Gilbert began shoveling pie. To Drake's surprise, the pies looked and smelled like cherry. Neither contestant looked repulsed by the taste.

Yet it *was* a trick, Drake felt certain. Or was the trick to make him *think* it was a trick? Gilbert's hands became almost a blur as he shoveled down pie. That lad really liked his food.

"Time!" the barker called.

Gilbert and The Buzz stopped. The Buzz had barely finished his third pie. Beside Gilbert lay six empty tins.

"That was great!" Gilbert said, sticky cherry filling smeared around his mouth. "May I have another?"

"No time, sonny, we have to move along," the barker said as he stamped the two participants' tickets. The final booth had four stalls, each containing two dozen floating balloons. Darts lay on the counter.

"Your darts must burst six balloons in your area," the barker announced.

Drake scowled. He *had* been tricked. Had he kept his forfeit, he could have run for the exit and easily won. He grabbed a dart, as did the others. Fortunately, a good part of his ill-spent youth had included hanging about in taverns, drinking and playing darts—although a dart board didn't drift around, unless he drank too much.

Drake's first toss grazed a balloon, but left its skin intact. A *pop* and a girlish squeal told Drake that Hexaba had one. She stopped to file a jagged nail. Drake aimed and threw. The rubbery skin burst. A numeral one lit up on the back wall.

Two, three. Other pops from Drake's right showed The Buzz and Gilbert were getting the hang of the game. Drake tossed, missed, tossed, hit. The number four appeared on his scoreboard.

Drake threw and hit. *Five.* After three frustrating failures, Drake popped the last balloon. Hexaba's score showed four. The Buzz had five.

Gilbert popped his sixth. "Yippee!"

Drake raced ahead of Gilbert and thrust out his ticket. The barker stamped it and Drake ran toward the door marked EXIT in glowing pink. In a sugar-hyped blur, Gilbert passed Drake.

No, I have to win! I can't fail. I won't!

Gilbert pulled on the door...and held it open instead of

passing through.

Drake grinned in disbelief. Manners were such a liability.

Yet as Drake started toward the doorway, Gilbert pushed against Drake's chest, stopping him cold.

"*Ladies* first." Gilbert's blue eyes were glassy.

"There's no lady here—oh, you mean Hexaba." Drake rolled his eyes. "Hold the door if you want. *I'm* going through."

"*That* would not be polite!" Gilbert roared. He grabbed Drake's upper arm, then gripped his ankle. The world tilted as Gilbert lifted Drake overhead.

"You're not allowed to physically attack me," Drake grunted out. "You'll be disqualif—"

Gilbert heaved. Drake flew through the air, then slammed into a tree trunk. He collapsed in a breathless, throbbing heap. The Buzz raced by, not giving Drake a glance. *How unheroic.*

Gilbert reopened the exit door and held it like a valet. Instead of trying to pass through, The Buzz pushed Gilbert, who didn't so much as dent under the pressure.

"*I'll* hold the door for the lovely lady," The Buzz said.

"*I* will." Gilbert shoved The Buzz, who flew backward. His damaged wings fluttered enough to stall his flight.

The Buzz charged back toward the door. "Out of the way, *boy*. This is man's work."

"I was here first!" Gilbert lifted The Buzz, giving him a spandex wedgie, then tossed him aside.

Drake tried to sit, but pain stabbed through his side. He had a cracked rib, he was certain of it.

Why were Gullible Gilbert and Captain Annoying acting so strangely? While it wasn't unthinkable for The Buzz or Gilbert to be so stupidly polite as to lose by holding the door for Hexaba, fighting each other for the dubious honor seemed out of character. Was there some spell in the air around the exit? Then why wasn't Drake affected?

The pies. By rule, all spells had to affect any who didn't forfeit.

At the booth, Hexaba hit her sixth balloon.

Drake crawled toward the exit. He *wouldn't* be a drodent. No devil would steal Drake's dreams of conquest.

Pain knocked away his breath, but he drew another and kept on. He would *not* lose. Maybe Gilbert and The Buzz would distract each other long enough that Drake could crawl past.

The Buzz darted around, taunting and jabbing at Gilbert, whose refusal to release the door handle hampered his ability to retaliate. Hexaba ambled up the path while Drake continued his agonizing crawl. The more he gasped, the more the swelling pain pushed the air from his lungs. Drake was within a yard of the portal when Hexaba stooped beside him.

"How appropriate, crawling like the worm you are. I'd kick you while you're down, but that would disqualify me." She patted his head and strolled through the portal.

Drake collapsed in a miserable heap. He had lost. Luckily, when his project won, it would break the three-way tie. But that didn't compensate for being beaten to a pulp and thrown face down in the dirt.

The magic hedges surrounding the obstacle course dissolved. Drake lay sprawled on a field before the guests, faculty and students. How humiliating. Thank the darkness his parents were embroiled in a siege and couldn't attend.

"The Colleges of Valor and Arcane Sciences are disqualified for physically attacking other contestants," Dean Corleone said.

Gilbert and The Buzz charged to the demon dean, who rolled his eyes and began scribbling rules for next year's games.

Dex knelt beside Drake. "You came pretty close. Of course, I *won* my event."

"Your roommate...was almost...the death of me."

Wearing a smug expression, Dex pushed up his patched glasses. "I guess it comes down to the projects."

A malevolent grin tug at Drake's lips. His weather staff was exceptional. Yet confidence shone in Dex's magnified eyes.

Drake considered telling Dex that Dean Corleone was counting on the College of Dark Arts to win. But that would be pointless. A mad scientist saw his plans through, even if it meant destroying the world beneath him.

Dex helped Drake to his feet. As they trudged across the field, Valorous ran to Hexaba.

He held out a waterskin. "You must be thirsty after your exertions, my love. Won't you drink?"

Smiling sweetly, Hexaba squeezed the bag's contents onto the grass. Valorous gaped in horror. Hexaba laughed. "Honestly, Val. Do you think I didn't know you've been trying to slip me the Good Witch potion? That waterskin—and the punch at the Winterball—glowed like a hundred candles."

Unlike witches, who saw magical auras all the time, Drake had to focus his magic senses. A potion powerful enough to make an elephant fall in love with Valorous was seeping into the ground. Realizing how much that spilled punch at the Winterball had cost Valorous, Drake gasped out a chuckle.

"I'm shocked you *paid* for lewd sex acts," Hexaba added. "As if I need a potion for that."

Valorous's eyes lit with a lust Drake had thought impossible for a hero. "So, you'd still consider—"

Hexaba smacked Valorous's face. "Come near me again and be prepared for a major transformation."

Valorous gulped. "Into a newt?"

Hexaba brandished her enchanted dagger. "Into a eunuch."

Valorous hastily retreated to the hero's pavilion.

As drodents pushed catering carts across the grass, Dean Corleone announced, "It's been an exciting event so far, with all three colleges tied at one hundred points each."

Dean Mediaman coughed.

Smirking, Dean Corleone said, "Sorry. I forgot your boys were...competing. I'm sure they'll do better on their project." He muttered, "They could hardly do worse." Louder, he said, "The Project Fair will begin after lunch."

CHAPTER TWENTY-SIX

Dex paced along the sidelines, a rant swelling inside. Gilbert's failure left the games in a three-way tie. Obviously, he buckled under the stress.

As the rant's pressure built, Dex flapped his arms to emphasize his thoughts. Who did Lucifer, Jr. think he was? Okay, so he was Lucifer's son. That devil-boy could rot in Hell. Okay—maybe he would anyway.

"I *will* foil his plan!" Dex's bomb was a sure-fire winner. A mad cackle burst from Dex's gut.

Lunch finished, Deans Corleone, Evil, Malodorous and Mediaman, along with Prince Raymond, took their seats on the judges' platform. Lucifer, Jr. escorted Dean Selena back from a gourmet picnic.

Selena sat down and stretched out a stockinged foot for Lucifer, Jr. to massage. For a devil bent on universal domination, he was pretty whipped.

Selena clapped her hands. "This nonsense has gone on long enough, Asmodeus. Let's see these damned projects."

Dean Corleone rose. During the obstacle course finale, he had transformed into full demon state. The dean bared his fangs. "Each project is worth, potentially, three hundred points," Dean Corleone said. "Each college may award up to seventy five points, seventy for devastating capabilities—"

Prince Raymond cleared his throat. "We prefer the term 'usefulness.'"

"Fine, seventy for its *usefulness*, and another five points for presentation. The two deans from the Collage of Valor, Honor and Justice for All will have their votes averaged." Corleone glared at the five deans. "I remind our esteemed judges they must award points solely on merit. Overt favoritism will result in having your school's entry disqualified." His eyes glowed a fiery yellow and he mouthed something more. The deans paled and nodded. Even Lucifer, Jr. nodded appreciatively.

Smiling—not that it made him look in any way pleasant—Dean Corleone said, "As the superheroes and heroes represent our newest college, they have the honor of presenting first."

Mediaman and Prince Raymond bowed their heads. While Raymond made the gesture appear cordial, Mediaman's brief sneer betrayed his true feelings. The inability to hide their feelings explained why many superheroes wore masks. That, and to protect their pretty faces from scars.

Dex smirked. Going first was no honor. Judges usually scored first projects low in case a better one came along.

The Buzz and Armadilloman trotted onto the demonstration area, a square of grass marked by chalk lines. They carried an artist's easel and an oversized sketch pad.

"We've had a hiccup," The Buzz said. "Our helicopter has been *misplaced.*"

"How does one misplace a helicopter?" Dean Corleone asked.

"It's easy when the helicopter is invisible," The Buzz said.

That earned a few chortles from the crowd.

"If I were the sort to cast blame"—The Buzz glared at a bench crowded with student scientists—"I'd say it was stolen."

"Are you accusing someone?" Steam rose from Dean Corleone's horns. His eyes bulged, and his stench swelled.

"Without actual proof—" The Buzz started.

"Then no," the dean finished. "So you wish to forfeit."

"No, no, no," The Buzz said, while Armadilloman hurried to set up the easel and pad. "Although we don't have the helicopter in our possession, it *does* exist. If it pleases the judges, I'd like to present the specifications in lieu of a project."

"It does *not* please the judges," Dean Corleone snapped.

"Give him a chance," Dean Mediaman said.

As expected, Prince Raymond backed him up.

While the deans argued, Drake sidled beside Dex.

"Crossing to enemy lines?" Dex asked.

Drake's arm sported a fresh bandage and he moved with great care, protecting his cracked ribs. "Just wondering if you had something to do with 'misplacing' their helicopter."

Dex reached into his jeans pocket and pulled out a key ring with a locator button. "They *might* have better luck finding their chopper if I returned this."

Drake grinned. "Aren't you the clever tinker? But I wouldn't worry about returning that gadget. I'm certain they'll run into their project eventually."

"A compliment. I'm suspicious."

"You wound me, Dex. However, I want to thank you for ensuring the College of Dark Arts wins the Project Fair."

Dex snorted. "You haven't seen *my* project."

"I don't have to. It's *yours.*"

Dex glowered. *That was a good burn.* A fact which made him even madder. "Wait and see."

"Disqualified," Dean Corleone said, ending the argument.

"No fair," Armadilloman whined.

"The details contained within our blueprints verify the

possibility of such a helicopter." The Buzz tapped the apparently blank page on the easel.

"Exactly," Corleone said. "The *possibility*. However, there are no points awarded for *potential*. You must produce results."

As Dr. Frankenstein often said, *Potential is nothing! Kinetic is everything!*

Dex thrust his hand toward Mandrake. Drake took it between his thumb and forefinger and shook.

"Sorry I have to beat you," Dex said. "It's been good knowing you. Maybe life as a drodent won't be so bad. I'll sneak you some snacks now and then."

"Don't count me out yet," Drake snarled.

The superheroes still whined in front of the judges table. Only now even whinier princes and knights had joined them.

"Surely some clause or provision in the rules covers such contingencies," Mediaman said.

"The rules say they lose," Dean Corleone said.

"I suggest a bit of charity might be considered," Prince Raymond said, "since this is our first year to participate."

"Life's lessons are hard learned, Raymond," Corleone said.

Prince Raymond gave an amiable smile. "I only meant, dean, that you should let our lads enter their second-best project. Should it lose, then whoever wins has won by gracious means. After all, it's only their *second*-best project."

Dex and Drake broke out laughing. Trust a do-gooder to think anyone here cared about appearing gracious. Next thing, they'd try the "gentlemanly thing" approach.

Sure enough, Mediaman said, "It's the gentlemanly thing to do."

Dean Selena folded her arms across her ample bosom. "Then I can feel free to vote no."

As a unified force, the do-gooders whipped out clinking sacks and slim checkbooks.

"All right, dean-o," a masked superhero said, "what'll cost to let them enter another project?"

Dean Corleone's eyes misted. A lusty grin split his demonic features. "How much have you brought?"

A small mountain of gold spilled across the table top. As checks drifted onto the cash, the dean addressed the crowd. "Perhaps it would be...*fair*."

Drake leaned close. "I didn't think he knew that word."

"I thought he'd choke trying to get it out," Dex added.

The visiting superheroes and princes trooped back to the bleachers. Prince de la Realm ran forward carrying a sheathed sword. A rainbow pattern of amethysts, emeralds, sapphires, rubies, and topazes encrusted the sheath. Like most student princes, Prince de la Realm wore a white T-shirt with a large red cross on the chest. Below it read: "Campus Crusaders." The back stated: "We're looking for a few virtuous women." The prince had drawn a line through "virtuous" and written "reasonably good" in its place. Who knew a hero could have a sense of humor?

The prince drew the blade. "Zee sword is special, yes? It glows in zee dark, letting zee wielder see without having to carry a torch. We call it zee Sword of Light."

"That's it? A pointed flashlight?" Dean Corleone rolled his bloodshot eyes.

Prince de la Realm waved the sword. "This sword is an improvement over zee original, which only glowed blue in zee presence of goblins."

Dean Evil raised his hand. "I don't see it glowing."

"There is no reason for it to glow when it is not dark."

Dean Corleone rubbed his temples. "Judges tally your scores. Remember—base scores on performance and presentation *alone*." He raised a clawed finger. "You've been warned." He glanced at the do-gooder spectators. "And no refunds."

While Corleone raked in gold and pocketed the checks, the judges determined the scores. Mediaman and Prince Raymond whispered furiously. Prince Raymond's face turned red, as though he were asphyxiating. He glared at his fellow "good guy," who shrugged and shook his head. At last, they scrawled something on cards, then flipped them for everyone to see.

Prince Raymond, with his feathered plume, had penned an elegant sixty; Mediaman offered a meager black-marker ten. The other deans had written a one, the minimal allowed score.

Prince Raymond scowled. "I was trying to be fair. Can I change my score to seventy-five?"

"No," Dean Corleone said flatly.

"You should have done a few lunges or something," Prince Raymond told the disconsolate Prince de la Realm.

For the benefit of those who couldn't see the cards or do simple arithmetic, Corleone announced, "For the *ever useful*"—his voice reeked of sarcasm—"Torch Sword, the School of Valor, Honor, and Justice for All is awarded thirty-eight points."

Dex and Drake burst out laughing. Thirty-eight points was insulting!

Dean Corleone called the witches to present next, as they were the second-newest college on campus.

A lithe and sexy number strutted her leather-clad derriere toward the now-vacated patch of ground. Dex would have crawled forty miles through broken test tubes just to smell the tire tracks left by the truck that carried her dry-cleaning.

"Isn't that Sabrina?" Drake asked.

Dex drooled in answer.

"Still suffering from love's sting?"

"I have a crush on her, if that's what you mean." Sabrina was even hotter than Hexaba—in a depraved sex-kitten way.

Sabrina curtsied to the judges, then stood with her hands clasped. "If I may draw your attention to my right." Like a game-show hostess, she swept an arm outward.

A stream of gorgeous babes sauntered toward the field. As they passed, a few scientists swooned. Several sorcerers fell to their knees, bowing and scraping.

Dex's lungs labored. He fumbled for his inhaler. After Dex squeezed off a couple of puffs, Drake reached across.

"Mind if I borrow it?" Drake rasped. At Dex's quizzical stare, he added, "Hey—it's been a while. And they *are* enticing. Enchanting, actually."

Dex handed over his inhaler. "I'll say."

Drake spritzed a puff then drew a deep breath. "Not bad. It makes my chest tingle—" Drake rubbed his trim beard. Then he narrowed his gaze and stared so hard his eyes watered. "They're *not* enchanting. They're *enchanted.*"

The line of beauties paraded before the judges.

Dean Selena smirked at her peers. Even Dean Corleone wasn't unaffected; his horns doubled in length and his tail did a charmed-snake dance. Only Lucifer, Jr. appeared unmoved, his gaze locked on Dean Selena.

The babes cooed, winked and blew kisses. They shook their slender shoulders, then kicked up their heels and giggled in delight. They were totally hot. And a little familiar.

"I think I've seen these girls before," Dex said.

"In your dreams," Drake said. "And in mine as well."

Holding a freshly plucked rose, a knight rushed to one of the babes. He dropped to a knee, then swore fealty to her. A prince vowed to slay a dozen dragons using a spatula, if she would smile at him.

Sabrina smiled wickedly. It made her even more desirable. Dex sucked another dose from his inhaler.

"May I introduce," Sabrina said, slowly circling the babes, "the village girls from Bramblethorp. I believe many of you here"— she swept her arms toward the kowtowing evil sorcerers—"saw them last when you 'invited' them to the Winterball."

They were *those* girls? Impossible. Yet the stunning babes held studio head shots alongside their improved features. This was the first time Dex noticed they were carrying anything.

If one studied the photo long and hard, one might see a resemblance—insofar as the face in the photo and the girl's face both had two eyes, a nose, and a mouth.

"We call it 'The Swan Spell,'" Sabrina said.

Dean Corleone clomped down the steps, Lucifer, Jr. hard on his heels. Dean Corleone took the first girl's framed photograph and pressed his nose to the glass, then Lucifer, Jr. did likewise. They sniffed the girl, touched her cheek and even stroked her hair. After inspecting three others, they nodded to the judges and declared the project valid.

Huddled over score cards, covering them as if their neighbors might cheat, the deans scribbled their scores.

"Hot chicks are far more dangerous than a magic nightlight blade," Dean Selena said, showing a seventy five written in silvery ink. "Nicely presented, Sabrina. I especially liked the slow turn."

Prince Raymond nodded and flashed another seventy five, written in rolling calligraphy.

Mediaman flashed a black marker sixty five. He winked at the now-beautiful girls. "Minus ten for no cleavage."

Dean Malodorous flashed a card bearing a dripping, blood-red thirty-five. "Fetching, but they reek of innocence."

Dean Evil flashed the last card—a shakily scrawled thirty-five, splattered by drool.

"Clearly, hot chicks *are* more valuable than a glowing sword," Dean Corleone said. "We award the School of Olde Wyrd Charms two hundred fifteen points."

Not shabby. Still, Dex expected more for his bomb. "Best of luck," he said to Drake, not meaning it, but it seemed the sort of thing a friend might say.

"And to you." Drake's words completely lacked sincerity.

As the babes strutted away, Dex and Drake perked to attention. Either of them might be called next. Dex scanned the crowd. Where were Lexington, Isaac and Gilbert? He'd sent them to the student union to "borrow" a big screen TV so the audience could enjoy the spectacle. If those cretins cost him even one presentation point, he'd shave their pointy heads and paint them green.

"Shall it be a coin toss?" Dean Evil asked.

"I prefer to arm-wrestle," Malodorous answered, setting his elbow on the table with a thud.

Dean Evil fished out a quarter. "I call heads."

"I say by strength, not chance!" Malodorous roared.

Dean Evil flipped the coin. It landed on the back of his hand which he immediately covered with the other. He peeked at the coin. "Heads. *Your* college presents next."

"I didn't call it," Malodorous snapped.

"There's only heads and tails, and I called heads."

"I demand a do-over."

Dean Corleone pounded the judges' table. "Enough. The College of Dark Arts will present next."

"I demand the place of highest honor," Dean Malodorous said. "I'll not see it handed to"—he flicked his hand toward Dean Evil—"those loathsome pranksters."

"You're just mad that our pranks were better." Dean Evil stuck his thumbs against his temples and wiggled his fingers.

Dean Corleone's voice boomed across the field. "The sorcerers are first because their college comes first in the university name." As he sat, he added, "Besides, Dr. Arcanum bought the right to present last."

Smirking, Dex said, "It always comes down to money."

"You scientists think you can buy anything," Drake growled.

Dex blinked innocently. "Can't we?"

Drake huffed. "Perhaps it's as well. Once my project earns a perfect three hundred, we can end this farce."

Dex grunted at Drake's retreating back.

Lucifer, Jr. crept from behind the judges' table and watched Drake approach the field. Drake bowed, then raised a finger. Jeffrey rushed to hand him a jeweled staff.

That Drake hadn't conjured the staff in a puff of smoke boded ill. Could his staff be so impressive that a flashy entrance would only cheapen it?

"The College of Dark Arts wishes to demonstrate the latest in weather control—the Staff of Living Weather."

Keeping eye contact with the judges, Drake thrust the staff forward. "Note the embedded stones. They empower and focus the spells and protect the sorcerer and the surrounding area. Thus, a sorcerer could summon a monsoon without ruffling his hair."

Dean Corleone narrowed his gaze. "How large is the protective area?"

Drake swept out his arm in an arc, illustrating the space around him. "Give or take a hand span."

"So *we* are not in the protective range," Dean Corleone said.

Drake blanched. Clearly, he hadn't considered the dangers of demonstrating his project. Drake, though an admirably evil schemer, lacked scientific vision.

No, wait. Dex had neglected to include safety devices on his bomb. No matter. Nothing could go wrong with *his* project.

"Fear not, Asmodeus." Dean Malodorous leaned forward. The carved face on his chair back drew a gulp of air, then held it as the smelly sorcerer leaned back. "I'll cast a spell to shield our platform."

Just great. The dean promised to protect only the judges. Then Dex imagined braless witches, soaking wet. He hoped for cold rain, though that was sure to earn Drake the full ten presentation points—curse him.

Dean Malodorous waved his hands and intoned some sorcerous drivel. A shimmer like a giant soap bubble enveloped the judges' platform. Dex longed to puncture the bubble—not so the judges would have to suffer the same messy weather consequences, but because he was dying to gauge the pop factor of the bubble's surface tension.

Drake flipped up his staff and caught the lower end in his other hand. Holding it parallel to the ground, he said, "Each glowing rune holds a complex weather spell that I can activate with a simple incantation." He swept his hand along the staff's length.

"What spells have you stored?" Corleone asked.

Prince Raymond rested his chin against his fist. "And how damaging are they?"

Dean Malodorous failed terribly at looking innocent. "Why, Raymond, didn't we agree that the projects were to be called *useful*? What makes you think the spells would be harmful?"

"Two reasons, my foul-odored friend. First, your student gave as his example a monsoon. Second, he's an *evil* sorcerer."

This time Malodorous's confused expression looked genuine. "What spells would you consider useful?"

"Gentle rain to end drought. Stopping flooding rains and redirecting hurricanes that lash against the shore."

Malodorous rolled his eyes. "For a moment, I thought you were serious. Please, Mandrake, continue your demonstration."

Drake raised the staff. "Now, I will conjure a living tornado subject to my commands." He drove the staff's tip into the ground and spoke an alliteration-filled incantation.

The embedded stones twinkled and the runes glowed brighter. Drake repeated his blather—at least it sounded the same to Dex, like bad poetry. The only worthwhile incantation for launching a project was, *Please work. Please, please, please work.*

A breeze gusted. The grass at Drake's feet stirred. Its greenness deepened. Then daisies popped up. Honeysuckle vines snaked up the poles of the scientists' pavilion, adding shade. Similar vines quickly covered all the "athlete" pavilions, making them look like garden gazebos. It was sort of nice.

Not a tornado appeared. Dex smirked.

The witches plucked flowers and tucked them behind their ears, while the superheroes and scientists guffawed. Poor Cricket laughed so hard he peed. Mortified, he hopped away. Smirking princes pointed at Drake; his peers looked disgusted. Jeffrey laughed in delight. Well, *that* was gratitude, Dex thought, as a snort escaped his own mouth.

Lexington, Isaac and Gilbert arrived pushing a big screen TV on a cart. "Did we miss anything?" Isaac asked, wrangling extension cords.

"We aren't too late, are we?" Gilbert asked.

"No." Dex swept his arm toward the flowering field. "This is Mandrake's project."

"Wow," Gilbert said. "The field looks much nicer. You'll have a hard time beating that, Dex."

"What took you guys so long?" Dex snapped.

"Managing the cables and extension cords," Lexington said.

From the College of Virtue's pavilion, Armadilloman called out, "Hey, Mandrake, could you manage a few bluebonnets? They're my stepmother's favorite."

"You're a thoughtful boy, Tex," shouted a woman from the guest pavilion.

Drake aimed his staff at Armadilloman. In angry tones, he uttered another incantation. The staff glowed.

Bunnies, chicks, kittens, and puppies rained from the sky. The fuzzy animals scampered and played, tumbling and wrestling. Witches gathered them up, cuddling and cooing over them.

"Wow," Gilbert said. "That's even better! I think you should concede and save yourself the embarrassment, Dex."

Dumb farm boy. But Gilbert was right, in that Drake's failure was good for Dex and ultimately for the College of Arcane Sciences.

Drake stared in horror at the staff. "It was supposed to rain frogs and locusts!" He threw his staff to the ground. "I don't understand. It worked last night." Drake's eyes bulged. "This isn't my staff." He turned on his roommate. "Jeffrey! What did you...how could you bring the wrong...?"

Jeffrey swallowed a guffaw, then sobered under the furious glares of Deans Malodorous and Corleone. "I don't know what you're talking about, Drake," Jeffrey said. "I watched you make this. It's your staff."

"It isn't," Drake insisted. "Dean Corleone, my project has been sabo—"

Dean Corleone's eyes glowed like molten lava. "Unless you have hard evidence, you would be unwise to make accusations."

Drake gaped like a big-mouth bass. Not a word came out. He stomped off the field, not even waiting to see his scores.

The "good guys" each awarded a generous score of fifty, praising Drake for his use of onomatopoeia in the second spell. Dean Selena offered Drake's staff sixty points—because her witches were taken with their new pets. Whether the frolicking kittens, puppies, bunnies and chicks became familiars or spell ingredients remained to be seen. The other judges gave Drake a one. For a presenter to receive a one from his own college dean was unprecedented. Leave it to Drake to set *that* record.

Rising, Corleone said, "For the"—he gritted and bared yellow fangs—"Staff of Joy and Good Tidings—"

"That name was my suggestion." Prince Raymond beamed.

"It certainly isn't mine," Corleone growled. "For the staff—I refuse to say it a second time—the judges award a score of one hundred and twelve points."

Drake stormed back toward Dex—it was the only storm his friend had managed. Dex tried to look consoling. "Tough break, Drake. But hey, you earned more points than the princes. Actually, you earned more than *twice* the points."

"Keep it up, and I'll see if I can't turn you into a bunny with that useless staff." Drake rubbed his temples. "I can't believe Jeffrey brought the wrong one. Someone must have switched it on him. I'll kill the idiot." He took a few steps toward Jeffrey, then turned back. "Good luck, Dex—and this time I mean it. If only one of us can win, I'd want it to be—well, me—but since it won't, I'd rather it was you. I suppose."

Drake's heartfelt words, so kind and unlike him, choked Dex up. "It won't be the same without you here. Though I'll see you around campus when you're a drodent."

"Thanks, Dex," Drake said, head bowed. "Did you mean it about sneaking me treats?"

"What are friends for?" Dex didn't know the answer to that question and doubted Drake did either.

"Who represents Arcane Sciences?" Dean Corleone called.

Dex raised his hand. "Me, sir."

Dean Evil added, "Poindexter shows great promise. I do not misspeak when I say his project will 'blow you all away.'" He giggled, then clapped a hand over his mouth.

Dex swaggered onto the flower-covered field. From his pocket, he pulled the universal TV remote he had converted to a rocket controller. The up and down buttons were still for up and down. The numbers set the launch timer. The red power button turned on the rocket engines.

Dex squelched the mad laughter bubbling inside. *After* the successful launch and deployment, followed by glorious and magnificent carnage, he could, would, and should gloat.

"My project, esteemed faculty, needs no elaborate explanation." Dex flashed a grin at Drake, then raised the remote. "Without further ado, I give you"—he paused, not for dramatic reasons, but because Fully Loaded Baked Potato suddenly didn't sound impressive—"the Nanobomb."

Dex pressed the power button. A rumble came from beyond the Arcane Sciences' administration bio-dome. Even here, a faint tremor shook the ground. The rocket rose, steam and smoke rolling off its metal casing. The sight stole Dex's breath away.

He snagged another puff from his inhaler, then said, "In a moment, you'll note a trajectory change. I've selected Hilldale for my demonstration." Dex waved for Lexington, Isaac, and Gilbert to approach.

While Gilbert pushed the big screen TV on a cart, Lexington and Isaac managed the wires, cables and orange extension cord.

"In order to witness the bomb's devastating power," Dex said, "I—actually Dr. Arcanum—had cameras set up throughout the town. Via satellite, we can watch the townspeople's demise."

Mediaman and Prince Raymond lurched to their feet. Dean Corleone's glare made them flinch, but they stood their ground.

"Asmodeus!" Prince Raymond said. "We cannot allow this boy to kill people as part of a university-sanctioned project!"

"Order him to land that thing somewhere remote—and without detonation," Mediaman said.

"Sit down," Dean Corleone said, baring his fangs. "Or did you fail to read the fine print of your professorship contracts?"

Heads ducked, their faces ashen, Mediaman and Prince Raymond stumbled back to their seats.

Dex checked his watch. "Time for the trajectory change."

He aimed the remote at the climbing rocket and pressed the button to switch from launch to rocket. The light for DVD lit up.

The rocket soared, a glint of silver against the sky. Dex pressed numbers representing degrees, and arrow buttons to indicate the directional plane of the angular sequence.

The rocket's course altered. The glorious feeling of victory at his fingertips—or more accurately, in the palm of his hand—coursed through Dex's veins.

As the rocket passed overhead, it screeched like a great metal beast wailing its death rattle. Its trajectory fell off mark.

The bomb exploded. A fiery glow filled the sky. Then sound waves rocked the pavilions and judges' platform. The noise rattled Dex so hard he swore his joints had shaken loose.

Heat blasted them. Twisted bits of metal, smoke trailing, rained onto the nearby hills. Dex's project had failed. How was that possible?

A cobalt blue cloud burst above the assembly, releasing Dex's psychopathic nanobots of death. His precious pets drifted downward, eager to feed on brain stems—*their* brain stems. Ah, well. He preferred death to serving in Lucifer, Jr.'s army. In that respect, the bomb wasn't a total failure.

Prince Raymond smacked his palms against the judge's table.

"Tell us, boy, what death rains upon us?"

"What will happen over the next few moments?" Mediaman asked. "And how can we stop it?"

"I'll save us," The Buzz shouted.

"You can't, moron." Dex pointed at the spreading blue cloud. "Fly into that cloud and nanobots will devour your cortex." Why he warned The Buzz, he wasn't sure, as he would have enjoyed watching The Buzz fall from the sky—even if it preceded his own death by moments.

Dean Corleone turned to Malodorous. "Can you stop this with a spell?"

Malodorous shook his head. "I don't understand nannybots. Therefore, I have no spell against them."

"In that case," Corleone said, "I suggest you tally the score quickly."

"I'd appreciate that." Dex still expected to win and wanted to die knowing he had.

"Wait." Dean Selena pointed upward. "The cloud isn't coming down."

The cloud spread in stratiform, growing thinner and thinner. Could it have been caught in the jet stream? Would it spread destruction across the entire university dimension, wiping out all intelligent life? Fleetingly, Dex wondered if he might not get extra points for that.

"Perhaps the Nanobomb doesn't work high in the atmosphere," Dean Corleone suggested.

"I believe it does," Prince Raymond said. "Look."

Had the cloud descended, bringing Dex's death, it wouldn't have been less horrifying. The cobalt cloud devoured all hints of pollution. Gone were the sooty clouds from nearby Nuevo Pittsburgh's factories and Bramblethorp's fireplaces and forges, leaving the sky clean and pale blue.

"Impossible," Dex muttered. Suddenly empathizing with Drake, he said louder, "I don't understand what happened."

Prince Raymond raised a fist in salute. "Your bomb has cleaned away centuries of pollution. Bravo, lad!"

Unfortunately, Dex's nose agreed with Prince Raymond. Dex greedily drew in the fresh, sweet air. His lungs had never felt better, not even after a triple overdose of Albuterol.

Prince Raymond flashed a score of fifty. Mediaman followed with a matching score. When Dean Selena raised a scorecard marked sixty, Dex felt a sense of *déjà vu*.

Selena shrugged at the "heroic" judges. "I'm torn. There's a lot of money in cleaning up pollution."

Deans Malodorous and Evil awarded the obligatory one. Dex had tied with Drake for second place.

"One hundred twelve," Dean Corleone announced, his expression impassive, considering what had just been lost. "Tallying all scores, I declare the College of Olde Wyrd Charms the winner—and reigning champions." Corleone bowed to Dean Selena. "Three years running. I congratulate you and your ladies on a fine job."

Lucifer, Jr. screamed, "You cheated! You knew!"

Corleone cast a wicked grin at the devil. Then he glared at the other deans with a look that clearly labeled them losers. He did everything but place his thumb and forefinger in an L on his horned forehead.

Why was Lucifer, Jr. upset? He'd *won*. Dex threw down the remote in disgust and stormed off the field.

Drake hurried alongside. "Don't feel so bad. After all, your score was more than *double* that of the heroes."

"Oh, that's really funny," Dex grumbled. Then he snickered. "Did I sound that condescending?"

"Are you saying *I* sounded condescending?"

"A bit," Dex admitted.

"Thank you. And yes, you were annoyingly condescending."

It felt like old times—except it was their last time. Soon the Board of Trustees would close both their colleges and turn them into drodents. "You realize this means there won't be any treats," Dex said.

Drake nodded. "For either of us. Our careers have bombed as badly as...well, your bomb."

Dex's anger flared. "I destroyed Gatorwaters with"—again, the name Tater-Tot lacked fierceness—"Nanobomb, Jr. Nanobomb should have worked! Gilbert can verify it. He witnessed my project demonstration. He even helped me install the full-scale bomb onto the rocket."

"You think I was any less prepared? I fully tested my staff. Jeffrey was a witness. He—"

Dex and Drake looked at one another. "Gilbert," Dex said, "Jeffrey," Drake said, "sabotaged my project!" they exclaimed.

"I'll kill him," they both said. "No," they agreed, "we'll torture them first, then kill them, then resurrect them and kill them again!"

"Remember the university motto," Drake said.

"'No body, no crime,'" Dex said.

"It loses something in translation," Drake noted.

"Who cares? First, let's kill Jeffrey—he's small—he should be easy. Then we go after Gilbert."

"I demand to speak with you!" Junior paced before the judges' table waving a clawed finger toward Asmodeus.

Sighing, though celebrating inside, Asmodeus strolled over. "Do you blame a bookmaker for knowing the odds?"

Junior sputtered.

"Perhaps for you, gambling makes life interesting," Asmodeus said. "For me, it's controlling the outcomes. I won. Now keep your part of the agreement. Convince the board to abandon the plan to close the Colleges of Dark Arts and Arcane Sciences and to force graduates into indentured service. *And* you'll fund a generous endowment sufficient to make up for those that were withdrawn."

Junior glared for a moment, then shook his head and chuckled. "To the victor goes the spoils."

Suspicion gnawed at Asmodeus's gut. Something must have changed since they made the bet. "Spit it out, Junior, before you choke on your smugness."

"I know something you don't know." He practically sang the words. "During the last ten days, there's been a change of heart, you might say, on the Board of Trustees."

A change of heart usually referred to grave robbery, followed by a mad scientist's operation. "What are you saying?" Asmodeus asked.

"Oh, you're still in charge. I don't want the university anymore. I'll wager you won't want it either when you find out."

"Find out what?" Asmodeus roared.

"Ever since you and I started buying votes, several board members decided selling votes made a lucrative side business. So, they put their votes up for sale in public domain auctions—with a minimum starting bid."

"Of course."

"Guess who bought the lot of them?" Junior snickered so hard he nearly fell over. "White wizards."

"White wizards! You can't mean—"

"Oh, but I do." Junior handed Asmodeus a sealed document. "Read it for yourself." He walked off, cackling and swishing his forked tail. Pausing, he looked back. "You know, Asmodeus, I'm not so sure you won."

Dex and Drake tracked down Jeffrey and Gilbert. The freshmen dolts waved.

"Have the witches really won three years in a row?" Jeffrey asked.

"Yes," Dex said. "And you two are dead meat."

"Women always win," Gilbert said. "You want to know why?"

Dex expected he would regret asking. "Okay, tell me why, *then* we'll kill you."

"It's *because* they're women," Gilbert said. "'Women' stands for 'weakness of men.'"

"Are those really what you want for your last words?" Dex asked.

Drake cast the freshmen a scorching glare. "Prepare to suffer before you gasp your last breath."

"We'd love to stick around," Jeffrey said, "but we can't."

Gilbert nodded. "We came to say goodbye."

"It's not goodbye," Dex said. "With your grades, you'll be a drodent next year." That fact might have consoled him if the same fate didn't await *every* sorcerer and mad scientist.

"And," Jeffrey added, "since you two have been such nice guys, we wanted to confess." He looked sidelong at Gilbert. "Isn't that right, *Clark*?"

"That's right, *Harry*," Gilbert said.

"You've been using assumed names?" Drake asked. "Why, how *evil* of you, Harry."

"Hey!" Dex exclaimed. "The use of aliases is an advanced class. Have you been playing dumb?"

Gilbert, or whoever he was, winked. "They catch on fast."

"Maybe we'll see you around campus next year," said Jeffrey, who was now apparently Harry.

"Although we won't be at your colleges anymore. We're changing majors."

"You can't escape becoming a drodent that easily," Dex said.

Clark ripped off his shirt, revealing shiny, red and blue jammies.

"Is that...spandex?" Dex gasped in horror.

"Yeah. I'm one of"—he nodded toward The Buzz and several other members of the spandex brigade—"them. So my Arcane Sciences GPA doesn't count."

"That does it!" Dex wound up a fist. Though he'd never struck a soul, he was going to flatten Gilbert, or rather Clark. It was Dex's one chance before his mind got wiped. He let his punch fly at Clark's solar plexus.

Dex's fist felt like it struck steel. His knuckles throbbed. Clark didn't so much as flinch. That farm boy's gut was as hard as his head.

Clark rolled his eyes. "You can't hurt me, Dex. Come on, Harry. I think they need time to digest all this."

"Wait. Jeffr—Harry, tell me that you aren't a"—Drake swallowed, looking a touch queasy—"hero."

"No." Harry shook his head then wiggled his eyebrows. "And I'm not a superhero either."

Drake exhaled in relief, then grabbed Harry's shirt. "Then why, by all that is dark and evil, did you sabotage my staff?"

"That staff was too dangerous. But thanks for showing me

how to make one. I thought *my* staff did rather well. I'm planning another for my project next year—with improvements."

"You won't live to see next year!" Drake flexed his fingers. A stream of what sounded like profanity spewed from Drake's mouth. Jagged orange light burst from his fingers and snaked through the air toward Harry's throat.

Harry flicked his wand and deflected the jagged light into the ground.

Drake reeled as though struck. "A white wizard?"

Harry inclined his head, then added, "Although not yet, really. I'm still learning."

Drake made a strangling noise. "So I wasted my valuable time and wisdom on you?"

"Actually, I learned a lot," Harry said. "You've both been really nice. I mean it."

"Really, *really* nice," Clark said.

Drake sputtered, wringing his hands as though he had Harry's neck between them. "What did you hope to accomplish—besides sabotaging our projects?"

Harry's expression turned serious. "Know your enemy."

Clark nodded. "The Affiliated Council of Heroes and Superheroes knew your colleges would cause trouble for the College of Valor, Honor and Justice for All during its first year on campus. So they planted moles—us—with the top students in Arcane Sciences and Dark Arts to counter your efforts."

Despite himself, Dex felt a swell of pride that the Nosy Do-Gooder Council considered *him* a top student and thus a threat.

"We were supposed to warn of any dangerous plans." Harry chuckled. "But you made our job easier when you turned on each other."

"I hope our credits will transfer," Clark said.

"With your GPA, you'd better hope *not*," Dex muttered, seething.

"Not *those* credits," Clark said. "I did some freshman studies at the Intergalactic Cross-Curricular Institute—the ICCI."

"Wait, what did he mean *our* credits," Drake asked Harry. "You aren't a hero."

Harry gave a nasty grin worthy of an evil sorcerer. "The Board of Trustees has ordered the university to open a College of White Wizardry next year—a *co-ed* college. I already tested out of my freshman year—thanks to your mentoring."

Dex and Drake exchanged horrified glances. That couldn't be true!

Harry and Clark strolled away. After a few steps, Harry turned back and called out, "See you guys next year."

Drake and Dex stared at each other in stunned silence. Harry and Clark's earlier comments sank in and stung deeply.

Dex grumbled, "What did they mean by we've been nice? *Nice!*" That was a low blow. Dex wouldn't have said it of his worst enemy—well, maybe of his enemy. But he had labored all year mentoring Gilbert, or Clark. Dex deserved kinder treatment.

Groaning, Dex said, "What'll Dean Evil say—or worse, do—when he finds out I've been mentoring a *spy!*"

"It won't matter," Drake said, scowling. "Not after the board has us turned into drodents."

Dex snickered. "We may have revenge yet, when Harry learns his diploma comes with strings. The white wizards' college won't have a court order protecting it from the drodent clause—or indentured servitude."

"Too bad we won't be able to enjoy it," Drake said.

Dean Corleone headed for Drake and Dex. Dex tensed. Thanks to his failure, both Dark Arts and Arcane Sciences would be closed, their students turned to drodents, and Dean Corleone would lose his job to Lucifer, Jr. To Dex's surprise, however, Dean Corleone put an arm around Dex and Drake's shoulders.

"Well done, lads."

"But you were counting on me and I failed you," Drake said.

"Counting on you?" Dex sneered. "He was counting on me!"

"I was counting on you both," the dean said. "And you both performed admirably."

"Admirably?" Drake said. "We lost."

"You mean we were sabotaged," Dex grumbled.

"I told you I know *everything* that goes on at the university," Dean Corleone said.

"So you knew our roommates were spies?" Drake asked, his gaze narrowing. "Why didn't you warn us?"

Dean Corleone shrugged. "I didn't want the Affiliated Council of Heroes and Superheroes to realize I was on to them. I knew my two best students would keep their moles in check."

"Yeah, we did a great job of that," Dex said.

"No need to look so glum, lads." Dean Corleone's fangs glinted. "Junior and I made a bet on the games, and I won."

Dex and Drake exclaimed, "You bet on the witches?"

"Based on information gleaned from the Nexus, and the fact the witches won the past two years—a bit of trivia Junior should have checked on. Compulsive gamblers are so cocky."

"So you weren't counting on us?" Drake asked.

"Nonsense, my boy. I needed you to be absolutely convincing. You created splendid projects which your faculty wholeheartedly endorsed. Your surprise and distress at the sabotage was genuine and convincing. Lucifer, Jr. never knew the odds were stacked in my favor. Under the terms of our bet, he must convince the Board of Trustees to rescind its decision to close your colleges and fund an endowment to replace the ones we lost."

"What about the indentured servitude?" Dex asked.

"Off the table. Permanently." Dean Corleone patted their backs. "Because you performed so well, I'll see that your grades and summer jobs suffer no negative ramifications."

"Excuse me, dean, but why didn't you prevent the white wizards from buying their way into the university?" Drake asked.

The dean's jaw tightened. "That happened on my bowling night. No one can watch everywhere all the time—not even a demon."

Dex's heart lightened. The Colleges of Dark Arts and Arcane Sciences would remain open. He and Drake would not become mind-wiped drones. Best of all, Dex still had his summer internship with Dr. Arcanum. World domination lay within his grasp. A mad cackle escaped his throat and he rubbed his hands. When he and Drake graduated, the universe better watch out.

THE END

ABOUT THE AUTHORS

Linda L. Donahue (www.lindaldonahue.com) was born in Burns, Oregon. As an Air Force brat, she traveled extensively while growing up. Now she lives in Garland, Texas. She has a BA in Russian Studies and a BS in Computer Science with a minor in Electrical Engineering from Southern Methodist University and a MAT in Earth Sciences from the University of Texas at Dallas. While she taught high school for 18 years, currently, when not writing, she teaches tai chi and belly dance. She also spends a lot of time taking care of animals, including cats, a rabbit and a sugar glider.

Julia S. Mandala (www.juliasmandala.com) was born in Kansas City, MO and lives in Plano, TX. She holds a B.A. in history from Kansas State University and a J.D. in law from Tulane University Law School. In addition to writing and being editor of The Fantasy Writers Asylum, she enjoys scuba diving, belly dancing and traveling with her husband, Larry.

ABOUT THE COVER ARTIST

Brad W. Foster is an award-winning artist who has had work published in over a thousand books, magazines, comics, and indefinable small press publications—the man needs a hobby! Brad has created seven covers for Yard Dog Press publications— Illusions of Sanity, Wolf's Trap, Hammer Town, Dadgum Martians Invade the Lucky Nickel Saloon, Fairy BrewHaHa at the Lucky Nickel Saloon, Jaguar Moon, and now Bride of Tranquility.

Brad draws to live and finds it interesting that he also lives to draw. You can find out even more about Brad and his work at: http://www.jabberwockygraphix.com.

Yard Dog Press Titles As Of This Print Date

A Bubba in Time Saves None, Edited by Selina Rosen

A Man, A Plan, (yet lacking) A Canal, Panama, Linda Donahue

Adventures of the Irish Ninja, Selina Rosen

The Alamo and Zombies, Jean Stuntz

All the Marbles, Dusty Rainbolt

Almost Human, Gary Moreau

Ancient Enemy, Lee Killouth

The Anthology From Hell: Humorous Tales From WAY Down Under, Edited by Julia S. Mandala

Ard Magister, Laura J. Underwood

Assassins Inc., Phillip Drayer Duncan

Bad City, Selina Rosen & Laura J. Underwood

Bad Lands, Selina Rosen & Laura J. Underwood

Black Rage, Selina Rosen

Blackrose Avenue, Mark Shepherd

The Boat Man, Selina Rosen

Bobby's Troll, John Lance

Bride of Tranquility, Tracy S. Morris

Bruce and Roxanne from Start to Finnish, Rie Sheridan Rose

Bubba Fables, Sue P. Sinor

The Bubba Chronicles, Selina Rosen

Bubbas Of the Apocalypse, Edited by Selina Rosen

The Burden of the Crown, Selina Rosen

Chains of Redemption, Selina Rosen

Checking On Culture, Lee Killough

Chronicles of the Last War, Laura J. Underwood

Dadgum Martians Invade the Lucky Nickel Saloon, Ken Rand

Dark and Stormy Nights, Bradley H. Sinor

Deja Doo, Edited by Selina Rosen

Dracula's Lawyer, Julia S. Mandala

Dragon's Tongue, Laura J. Underwood

Duckrt, Zeb Rosenzweig

The Essence of Stone, Beverly A. Hale

Fairy BrewHaHa at the Lucky Nickel Saloon, Ken Rand

The Fantastikon: Tales of Wonder, Robin Wayne Bailey

Fire & Ice, Selina Rosen

Flush Fiction, Volume I: Stories To Be Read In One Sitting, Edited by Selina Rosen

The Four Bubbas of the Apocalypse: Flatulence, Halitosis, Incest, and... Ned, Edited by Selina Rosen

The Four Redheads: Apocalypse Now!, Linda L. Donahue, Rhonda Eudaly, Julia S. Mandala, & Dusty Rainbolt

The Four Redheads of the Apocalypse, Linda L. Donahue, Rhonda Eudaly, Julia S. Mandala, & Dusty Rainbolt

The Garden In Bloom, Jeffrey Turner

The Geometries of Love: Poetry by Robin Wayne Bailey

The Golems Of Laramie County, Ken Rand
The Green Women, Laura J. Underwood
The Guardians, Lynn Abbey
Hammer Town, Selina Rosen
The Happiness Box, Beverly A. Hale
The Host Series: The Host, Fright Eater, Gang Approval, Selina Rosen
Houston, We've Got Bubbas!, Edited by Selina Rosen
How I Spent the Apocolypse, Selina Rosen
I Didn't Quite Make It To Oz, Edited by Selina Rosen
I Should Have Stayed In Oz, Edited by Selina Rosen
In the Shadows, Bradley H. Sinor
International House of Bubbas, Edited by Selina Rosen
It's the Great Bumpkin, Cletus Brown!, Katherine A. Turski
The Killswitch Review, Steven-Elliot Altman & Diane DeKelb-Rittenhouse
The Leopard's Daughter, Lee Killough
The Lightning Horse, John Moore
The Logic of Departure, Mark W. Tiedemann
The Long, Cold Walk To Mars, Jeffrey Turner
Marking the Signs and Other Tales Of Mischief, Laura J. Underwood
Material Things, Selina Rosen
Medieval Misfits: Renaissance Rejects, Tracy S. Morris
Mirror Images, Susan Satterfield
Mirror, Mirror and Other Reflections, James K. Burk
More Stories That Won't Make Your Parents Hurl, Edited by Selina Rosen
Music for Four Hands, Louis Antonelli & Edward Morris
My Life with Geeks and Freaks, Claudia Christian
The Necronomicrap: A Guide To Your Horooooscope, Tim Frayser
Playing With Secrets, Bradley H & Sue P. Sinor
Redheads In Love, Linda L. Donahue, Rhonda Eudaly, Julia S. Mandala, & Dusty Rainbolt
Reruns, Selina Rosen
Rock 'n' Roll Universe, Ken Rand
Shadows In Green, Richard Dansky
Stories That Won't Make Your Parents Hurl, Edited by Selina Rosen
Strange Robby, Selina Rosen
Tales from Keltora, Laura J. Underwood
Tales Of the Lucky Nickel Saloon, Second Ave., Laramie, Wyoming, U S of A, Ken Rand
Tarbox Station, Rhonda Eudaly
Texistani: Indo-Pak Food From A Texas Kitchen, Beverly A. Hale
That's All Folks, J. F. Gonzalez

Through Wyoming Eyes, Ken Rand
Turn Left to Tomorrow, Robin Wayne Bailey
The Twins, Selina Rosen
Villains In Training, Julia Mandala & Linda Donahue
Wandering Lark, Laura J. Underwood
Wings of Morning, Katharine Eliska Kimbriel
Zombies In Oz and Other Undead Musings, Robin Wayne Bailey

Double Dog
(A YDP Imprint):

#1:
Of Stars & Shadows, Mark W. Tiedemann
This Instance Of Me, Jeffrey Turner

#2:
Gods and Other Children, Bill D. Allen
Tranquility, Tracy Morris

#3:
Home Is the Hunter, James K. Burk
Farstep Station, Lazette Gifford

#4:
Sabre Dance, Melanie Fletcher
The Lunari Mask, Laura J. Underwood

#5:
House of Doors, Julia Mandala
Jaguar Moon, Linda A. Donahue

Just Cause
(A YDP Imprint):

The Bitter End
Selina Rosen

Death Under the Crescent Moon
Dusty Rainbolt

The Ghost Writer
Selina Rosen

It's Not Rocket Science: Spirituality for the Working-Class Soul
Selina Rosen

Meditations of a Hoarder
Melinda LaFevers

Not My Life
Selina Rosen

The Pit
Selina Rosen

Plots and Protagonists: A Reference Guide for Writers
Mel. White

Vanishing Fame
Selina Rosen

Non-YDP titles we distribute:

Chains of Freedom
Chains of Destruction
Jabone's Sword
Queen of Denial
Recycled
Sword Masters
Selina Rosen

Three Ways to Order:

1. Write us a letter telling us what you want, then send it along with your check or money order (made payable to Yard Dog Press) to: Yard Dog Press, 710 W. Redbud Lane, Alma, AR 72921-7247

2. Use selinarosen@cox.net or lynnstran@cox.net to contact us and place your order. Then send your check or money order to the address above. *This has the advantage of allowing you to check on the availability of short-stock items such as T-shirts and back-issues of Yard Dog Comics.*

3. Contact us as in #1 or #2 above and pay with a credit card or by debit from your checking account. Either give us the credit card information in your letter/Email/phone call, or go to our website and use our shopping carts. If you send us your information, please include your name as it appears on the card, your credit card number, the expiration date, and the 3 or 4-digit security code after your signature on the back (CVV). Please remember that we will include media rate (minimum $3.00) S/H for mailing in the lower 48 states.

Watch our website at
www.yarddogpress.com
for news of upcoming projects
and new titles!!

A Note to Our Readers

We at Yard Dog Press understand that many people buy used books because they simply can't afford new ones. That said, and understanding that not everyone is made of money, we'd like you to know something that you may not have realized. Writers only make money on new books that sell. At the big houses a writer's entire future can hinge on the number of books they sell. While this isn't the case at Yard Dog Press, the honest truth is that when you sell or trade your book or let many people read it, the writer and the publishing house aren't making any money.

As much as we'd all like to believe that we can exist on love and sweet potato pie, the truth is we all need money to buy the things essential to our daily lives. Writers and publishers are no different.

We realize that these "freebies" and cheap books often turn people on to new writers and books that they wouldn't otherwise read. However we hope that you will reconsider selling your copy, and that if you trade it or let your friends borrow it, you also pass on the information that if they really like the author's work they should consider buying one of their books at full price sometime so that the writer can afford to continue to write work that entertains you.

We appreciate all our readers and *depend* upon their support.

Thanks,
The Editorial Staff
Yard Dog Press

PS – Please note that "used" books without covers have, in most cases, been stolen. Neither the author nor the publisher has made any money on these books because they were supposed to be pulped for lack of sales.

Please do not purchase books without covers.